ALDERNEY

A Fantasy Adventure

-THE COMPLETE TRILOGY-

-SECRETS & LIES-

-VISITORS-

-GHOSTS-

RICHARD BOWEN

ISBN: 978-1-916820-99-9
Paperback edition

NOTE : CONTAINS ADULT CONTENT (18+)

Dedicated to my grandchildren

CONTENTS

Preface

The island of Alderney is the most northerly of the Channel Islands sitting just eleven kilometres off the coast of North West France. Approximately five kilometres long and with a population of barely 2000, the magical island of Alderney holds many secrets. Victorian forts, German World War II fortifications, a Roman fort, tunnels, caves, and many other mysteries and wonders.

A crime-free paradise that gives children and families a safe haven to explore and enjoy life to the full. Where children are able to grow up safely and, more importantly, explore and play to their heart's content without adults interfering!

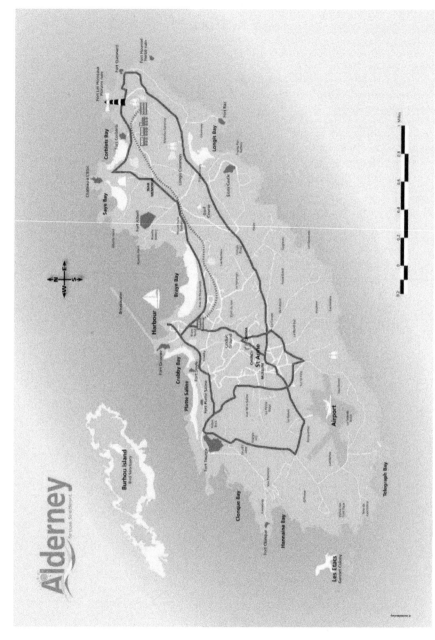

CHAPTER 1

BREAKING

"HURRY UP," Alex bellowed as he took aim and threw a pebble up to Ben's bedroom window. "WE'LL BE LATE."

He glanced to look at his watch on his wrist to see it was five thirty in the morning. Alex was beginning to get impatient. They were supposed to be meeting up with their good friends, Luis and Chloe that morning down at the harbour.

As the sun slowly came into view over Fort Albert to the east, the reflection from his watch dazzled Alex. *I've been stood here ten minutes already,* he thought. *It's always the same 'cos Ben's such a lazy sod ... One last try to wake him.*

He sauntered over to where he'd parked his Vespa 50cc scooter and opened his backpack that was balanced on the seat. Alex had packed the backpack the night before. He'd always been a stickler for punctuality and being prepared for any eventuality. The backpack was packed with his usual assortment of odds and ends. Torch, mobile phone, a reel of fishing line he'd borrowed from his Dad, a tin box with lead weights and hooks inside and a length of rope. A pack of sandwiches were screwed up in the corner of the bag with a can of juice and a couple of apples. He sighed just as he was about to give up looking, but then he spotted his woollen hat and concealed inside was a golf ball. *This'll do the trick.*

Alex grinned to himself as he walked back to beneath Ben's bedroom window and steadied himself as he took aim. With one swing of his arm the golf ball flew upwards and unerringly towards the bedroom window. He watched as the ball hit the glass, shattering into a thousand pieces. *Oops. That wasn't meant to happen.* He raised his hand to his mouth in an attempt to stop himself laughing.

Jeez, he must be as deaf as a door post! Alex shrugged his shoulders and turned away when he felt a thump on the back of his head. "OUCH!" He screamed as he realised he'd been hit with the very same golf ball he'd thrown up to Ben's window. Looking back up to what was left of the window pane he could see Ben leaning out with a big grin on his face.

"SERVES YOU RIGHT YER BUGGER!" Ben shouted. "You've made a right mess up here."

Alex sighed as he picked up the golf ball and placed it back in the backpack on his scooter. *Ouch, that really hurt.* Alex grimaced with the pain as he rubbed the back of his head.

"I'LL BE DOWN IN A MO'."

Alex hadn't heard Ben, as in that moment he was deep in his own thoughts. *That was stupid. I've now got a pane of glass to pay for and I've only got my money that I've saved from selling golf balls.*

Alex lived near the challenging island nine hole golf course and he would spend most evenings on the course looking for golf balls that had been lost with wayward shots from the local players … And there were plenty of 'em! Each morning he would place a box full of golf balls at the end of the drive to the house with a sign, 'GOLF BALLS FOR SALE £1 EACH'. Passers by would always buy them …

"Alex! ALEX!!"

Alex's thoughts were interrupted by the shouts from Ben who by now had crept up behind Alex to surprise him.

Alex turned round to realise his friend was stood right next to him. "Sorry about the window, I'll pay for it." Alex gave an apologetic smile as he looked down to Ben who was considerably shorter than him.

"To right you will," replied Ben as he grinned broadly. "Nah, forget it, I'll tell my Mum it was a bad shot by a golfer!"

They both laughed as they heard the recognisable sound of a 50cc Honda scooter in the distance which was drawing closer. They both knew it was a Honda as a four stroke engine had a deeper, richer sound than the two stroke engine of Alex's Vespa. Most teenagers who lived on Alderney could ride a scooter. Something that wasn't possible in most countries.

The boys knew who it would be this early in the morning. The noise from the Honda grew louder until a screech of brakes signalled the approaching scooter was negotiating the nearby

2

bend close to Ben's house. "That'll be the girls then!" said the boys in unison. They laughed hysterically.

"Yeah, Lilly's steering doesn't get any better," Ben joked. *In fact her driving is bloody awful. She'll kill herself one of these days,* he thought.

Alex was still nodding in agreement as the Honda screeched to a halt as it mounted the pavement in front of the two boys.

The engine spluttered to a halt and as the two girls jumped off, both boys shouted "HI LILLY. Who's this you've got with you?"

They knew it was Usha, Lilly's sister. They loved to wind her up because she had a very short fuse and lost her temper very quickly, but in a funny sort of way. Usha pulled off her crash helmet revealing her shoulder length curly blonde hair that glinted in the early morning sunlight. Even though she was only fifteen years old Usha was independent and her confidence far outweighed her young age. Usha stood about four foot six inches high in flat shoes but she could still intimidate. She strode defiantly over to Ben and pushed him over. *I'll teach you,* she thought.

"YOU KNOW WHO I AM!" Usha stood over Ben, hands on hips with a stern look in her eyes as he lay on the ground.

"USHA!" Lilly shouted in a certain dominating tone. "That's enough."

"OR WHAT?"

"Just cut it out. Say sorry to Ben and forget about it."

At that, Usha grinned widely, bent down, grabbed hold of Ben's hand and pulled him to his feet. "Sorry Ben." *In your dreams mate.*

"Good to see you both," said Alex and he smiled. "Got everything you need?" he asked Lilly.

"Of course we have." Lilly was a confident sixteen year old. Clever, attractive, quite slim with long straight blonde hair who always caught the boy's eyes at the local school. She was the tallest of this group of friends and so it seemed on most occasions she was the natural leader. "Come on you lot, let's get going." Lilly scanned the small group with her piercing blue eyes. "The other two will be wondering where we are."

The four teenagers scooped up their backpacks and scrambled up and onto their scooters.

Luis and Chloe were sat on one of the bench style wooden tables outside the local chip shop come restaurant which looked out over the small but busy inner harbour. The two friends had arrived on Luis` scooter ten minutes earlier.

"I wonder where the others have got too?" Chloe playfully punched Luis in the side of his ribs and then continued to brush her long brown hair.

"Dunno," Luis grunted, as he winced from Chloe's playful punch. "I suppose they've had to wait for Ben as usual. He's such a lazy sod don't you think?" Luis continued to peer through his binoculars at the horizon looking to see how many container ships were passing by in the distance on their way up through the English Channel.

Chloe gazed at Luis' torso in admiration. He was the new kid on the island and was a bit of a hunk. Thick black shaggy hair that fell to his well muscled shoulders. *His semi bronzed skin is just crying out to be caressed. I could certainly do a number on you matey!* He was a good athlete. She'd watched him at school running on the track and playing football. In the few weeks he had been on Alderney, Luis had made quite an impression with the girls. *If only I could make him see ......* And in that moment, the sound of familiar scooters approaching interrupted Chloe's thoughts.

Luis jumped down from the table. "About time." He passed his binoculars to Chloe as the scooters roared into view.

Lilly and Alex gave each other a sideways glance and yelled "HANG ON" as they pulled the handlebars of their scooters towards them, causing the front wheels to lift from the ground. Ben and Usha clung on with all their strength as the scooters wheelied across the road and came to a shuddering halt a few metres in front of Luis and Chloe.

"I SUPPOSE YOU TWO THINK YOU'RE CLEVER" Chloe shouted. *They're bloody crackers.*

Luis just stood his ground, opened mouthed. He felt a playful punch to his stomach, not for the first time that morning, as Chloe shouted at him. "WHAT ARE YOU

GAWPING AT?" Luis was lost for words for once in his life. His warm dark brown eyes were transfixed as he gazed unashamedly at Lilly. "HELLOOOO." Chloe yelled right in front of Luis' face. "GET A GRIP BOY." Chloe punched him again.

Ben, Alex and Lilly jumped off the two scooters and ran over to Chloe and Luis where they were stood hands on hips. A look of panic appeared on their faces.

"What's up Chloe?" Alex asked.

She didn't say anything but just pointed towards the two scooters. They all turned to see Usha lying motionless on the ground pinned down by one of the scooters that had tipped over on it's side. They all immediately started to move forwards, towards where Usha was lying motionless.

"STAY BACK" Lilly shouted as they got closer.

"But ..." And before Ben could finish, Lilly jumped in front of the group with her arms outstretched.

"No, stay away. Please, I know what I'm doing," Lilly insisted. "Just keep away."

Lilly turned and knelt down beside her sister, hiding Usha from the full view of her friends. Lilly turned her head towards the group. "Usha's fine, just give us a minute." She gestured to the others to stay back. *Just keep cool gal.*

Turning back to her sister, Lilly held Usha's head with her left hand. She could see that her left leg was broken in two places and blood was pouring out of a dip gash on her left arm onto the road. "Usha," Lilly whispered. "Grab my amulet." Usha reached out to touch the amulet around Lilly's right wrist and as she did so the amulet released an intense yellow halo and in an instant the yellow light was gone. All signs of the injuries had disappeared. Usha was healed. *Phew!*

"Usha, you can get up now," Lilly whispered. "If the others say anything, just tell them you was pretending to be hurt to give them a scare. And give them that grin of yours, it always works."

The two girls jumped up from the ground and quickly joined the others.

"What?" The group of friends surrounded Usha.

"That got you all going eh?" Usha's face contorted with a huge impish grin. Ben and Alex playfully pushed her as they all burst into laughter.

"Typical Usha," Chloe said. "Always the joker."

Luis stood there silently, quite dumbfounded at what he'd just witnessed. *I've come to the conclusion this island is weird!*

"COME ON" Lilly shouted. "Enough mucking about, let's get going."

This Saturday had been planned a couple of days before. To meet up at the chippy before heading off to the north west of the island to explore Fort Tourgis before hopefully spending the night there in tents.

The group climbed up onto their scooters. Chloe upfront with Luis sat behind, Alex with Ben and Lilly with Usha.

"YOU TAKE THE LEAD CHLOE," Lilly shouted. "Go on Alex, you follow them. I'll catch you all up in a mo'." The two scooters roared off.

"You okay?" Lilly turned to look at Usha.

"Yeah I'm fine. Just hurry up and send Grandad a message to let him know what's happened. We need to catch the guys up before they start to wonder what's going on or have any suspicions."

"Okay, done." Lilly put her phone in her pocket. "Hold on sis', don't want you falling off, ha!" The scooter started first time and away they went in hot pursuit of the others.

Message …
Hi Grandad. Need to get
to Chippy. Burn mark.
Thanks. Lilly x

CHAPTER 2

WHAT GOES ROUND

"So understand don't waste your time, Always searching for those wasted years ...." Richard's ring tone, Wasted Years by Iron Maiden broke the silence of the early morning. His hand hit his mobile phone to stop the music as he rolled over in bed trying not to disturb his wife, Bea, who was luckily still sound asleep. He peered through half opened eyes. "Jeez, who's this at half past six in the morning?" he mumbled.

Richard pressed a button to open the text on his phone. *Here we go again. It's Lilly.* He read the message as he clambered out of bed, still half asleep. "Right, better get cracking and go and clean up any potential trouble," he grumbled quietly to himself.

Twenty minutes later and Richard had left the house and was climbing into his old shop van. He'd owned and run a convenience store on the island for over twelve years and he'd not long retired. After a couple of attempts with the ignition key, the engine spluttered into life. *Must get this van serviced, sooner rather than later.* After a couple of revs, it was into gear and on his way.

It was a five minute drive down to the chippy. That's about the average drive time in Alderney, nothing is very far away. *The van seems a bit sluggish this morning. Just as well I s'pose on this little lane down the hill with all these loose chickens strutting around looking for scraps of food.* A nearby friend kept about sixty chickens in the field running parallel to the lane. The trouble was, the chickens didn't always stay in the fields. Unsurprising really, considering there are no fences!

As Richard glanced over to the field on the left there was the usual commotion of chickens running around aimlessly chased by the odd cockerel. He could see a couple of chickens entering one of the assorted sized hen houses dotted around the field. *Egg laying time,* he thought.

To the back of the field stood an old stable which was the overnight shelter for the two horses which also occupied the field. They were slowly munching on the vegetation underneath one of the three wind scorched hawthorn trees. Over the years, the trees had grown at an angle from west to east due to the strong westerly winter winds giving the appearance of lopsided umbrellas.

Richard's gaze turned back to the lane in front of him. "WHOOAA!" he shouted as he swerved to avoid hitting the last remaining chicken in the road. "STUPID BIRD!" He tried to compose himself. Richard slowed down as he reached the junction with the road from the right at Ladysmith. The bend in the road formed a sort of bridge over a stream that came from a spring further up the hill. The stream ran into a water trough below the bridge before overflowing through the lush vegetation into the valley below. Walkers and the like would often follow the footpath around Ladysmith.

Strange name. He'd often wondered about it.

Richard pushed down on the accelerator and the van travelled further down the hill passing a footpath to Fort Tourgis on his left. The sea and the horizon was now in view directly ahead. The smell of seaweed was in the air and the crashing of waves onto the vast shingle beach could be heard easily in the stillness of the morning.

The van slowed down as Richard approached the junction with the main coastal road. To his left was the old water mill which was currently being restored to it's former fully working glory. Further over to the left on Tourgis Hill was the huge, mainly derelict Victorian structure, Fort Tourgis, which dominated the skyline.

Richard turned right onto the main coastal road, Platte Saline. A couple of digger drivers were already working on the beach to his left. Platte Saline beach is a long stretch of predominately gravel chippings which the local builders use during their working day.

The sun is really bright today. Richard adjusted the visor to stem the glare away from his eyes. To his right was an assortment of bungalows which were set back from the road with long drives giving the impression of self importance for the occupiers.

One particular property always stood out for Richard. The building was nothing special but the significance of it's history was important. The two huge pillars either side of the entrance to one of the concrete driveways on his right marked what remained of part of Alderney's dark past harking back to the Second World War of which there are many other examples across the island. These pillars are poignant in the fact that they indicate the entrance to what was a prisoner of war camp during that dark episode of history. *Really sad.*

Richard sped on and up onto the road travelling around Crabby bay. Another stony beach with Fort Doyle, which was built in 1793, on the left and the local state of the art hospital halfway up the hill to the right.

The chippy was in sight and Richard slowed the van as he looked around to make sure his destination ahead was clear. He didn't need any awkward questions this morning.

Richard pulled up outside the chippy and he immediately spotted the position where Lilly had used her amulet. It always left a scorched mark about the size and shape of a rugby ball. He manoeuvred the van into position so that the front wheel was next to the mark.

Right, let's get this sorted. Richard jumped out of the van. He slid open the side door and pulled out a spare wheel and propped it up against the front wheel of the van to convince any passer-by that he was replacing a wheel. He pulled the left sleeve of his shirt up his arm to reveal an amulet identical to Lilly's which consisted of twelve different coloured crystals. Richard placed his hand on the scorched mark and in that moment the amulet released an intense red halo and the scorched mark had gone.

"HELLO." A shout in the distance.

"HELLO." The same voice again, but this time the shout was closer. Richard turned to see a fisherman coming towards him from the harbour. He recognised him immediately. It was Alex's father, Frank Bean.

"Oh hi Frank, how are you doing?" Richard tried to stay calm. He could feel his hands shaking as he pulled his shirt sleeve back down to hide the amulet.

"You alright Richard?"

"Yeah, I'm good thanks." *Try to keep my voice steady.*

"It's just that I thought …."

"Thought what Frank?" Richard interrupted.

Frank had that enquiring look on his face "It's probably nothing, but I thought I saw a strong flash of red light up here."

"Oh really? Probably the sun reflecting off something Frank. Maybe a piece of glass. Nothing to worry about I wouldn't think eh Frank?" *Hmm.*

"Nah, suppose you could be right Richard. Anyway, what are you doing here this early in the morning?"

"Changing this wheel." Richard grabbed the spare wheel. "I'd just finished when I heard you shout." Richard stood up and threw the wheel in the van and slid the door shut with a thud.

"So Frank, have you been out in the bay putting your lobster pots out?" Richard asked, trying to change the subject.

"Yeah, that's right …. Actually I meant to say. I spotted your Granddaughter Lilly and some friends including my lad Alex early this morning on their scooters. Looked like they were on their way up to Fort Tourgis."

"Oh right." Richard smiled. *Nosey sod.*

"Those scooters are death traps Richard. You need to have a word with Lilly and her friends."

"Yeah, I will do Frank …. Thanks for the concern. I'll see you around. Got to go now." *Don't need any more awkward questions.* Richard jumped in the van and turned the ignition. The engine spluttered into life and with a full turn of the steering wheel the van spun round. Richard heaved a sigh of relief. *I must text Lilly and then get myself some breakfast.*

"COME ON VAN, NEED TO GET HOME." Richard drove away as he watched Frank disappear into the distance in his rear view mirror.

10

CHAPTER 3

GIVE US A LIGHT

Lilly and Usha skidded to a halt on the gravelled parking area just before the turn off at the bottom of Tourgis Hill.

Across the road at the base of the hill they could see another reminder of the Second World War fortifications that are found on Alderney. A huge concrete bunker which would have been built around 1942. It would have housed anti tank guns to defend the beach and bay that stretched out behind the girls from invaders.

The engine of the scooter chugged steadily in neutral as Lilly fiddled with her phone. "I'm just checking my phone Usha before we catch up with the others."

"Okay, hurry up."

"Right, Grandad's cleaned up down at the chippy. Let's go … Hang on sis'." Lilly put the scooter in gear and with a twist of her wrist the scooter shot forward throwing gravel everywhere. Lilly steered the scooter across the road and turned onto the narrow coastal lane which led to Fort Clonque about half a mile away on the other side of the bay.

As Lilly steered the scooter along the lane, Usha gazed up to her left admiring the vast scale of the Victorian stonework of Fort Tourgis. The lane veered around to the left and took them to the small car park where their friends scooters were parked.

"Where are they?" Usha asked as the two sisters climbed off the scooter.

"Not sure …. They can't be far away. ALEX …. BEN."

"HELLO" Usha yelled. "IS ANYONE AROUND?"

"OVER HERE." A voice boomed from behind where the girls stood.

"In here." Another voice in the distance from behind them could be heard.

"That's Chloe's voice," Lilly said.

The two girls turned to see an old wooden door, open just to the right of a wooden bench at the rear of the parking area. The door was partly hidden by a tangled mess of brambles and ivy which cascaded down the western stone walls and banks of Fort Tourgis.

"Come on Lilly, let's see what the others are up to," Usha said.

The girls picked up their backpacks and walked over to the partly opened wooden door. The door creaked and groaned as Lilly grabbed hold of it. Usha stepped inside with Lilly's hand on her shoulder.

"Careful Usha, watch your step, it's quite dark in here."

The girls stood still, letting their eyes adjust to the semi darkness.

"WE'RE OVER HERE," Ben shouted.

Lilly could just make out the silhouetted shape of Ben towards the back of the space in front of her. A bright beam of light suddenly shone into their eyes temporarily blinding them.

"SORRY GIRLS," Ben shouted as he lowered his torch to illuminate the floor in front of Lilly and Usha. "Walk towards the main light."

The girls could now see that the floor was covered in thick dust that had obviously built up over many years. All manner of tools and rubbish were scattered across the floor.

"Be careful where you walk girls." Ben pointed to the floor. "All sorts of stuff scattered all over the place."

The girls gingerly walked across the floor brushing away cobwebs that were in front of them with their hands until they reached Ben.

"We need a light in here," Usha grumbled.

"Yeah I know." Ben replied. "This place hasn't been used in years and there doesn't appear to be any power. There's a light bulb hanging down from the roof above your heads but it doesn't work. The others are further back in here looking to see if they can find a light bulb that works or some sort of power switch." Ben turned to point his torch to highlight the others.

In an instant, Lilly reached up to the light fitting. The amulet spontaneously emitted a white halo and disappeared in a flash, leaving the hanging light bulb above them shining brightly.

Ben spun round. "What the ..."

"I just touched it." Lilly smiled at Usha. "Must have been a bad connection." *I do have my uses.*

The three other teenagers stopped looking amongst the assorted items in front of them and joined Lilly, Usha and Ben.

"Good work Lilly," Chloe said. "Certainly better now with some light in this place."

"So Ben, what is this place?" Alex had an enquiring look on his face.

"Yeah, come on Ben, what is it?" Luis asked.

13

"It's an old German Second World War ammunition store," Ben explained. "My Dad was given the use of it by a local carpenter a couple of years ago just before the guy died. He also used to renovate old furniture and he was really interested with antiques, especially jewellery and the like."

Lilly gave Usha a knowing glance. They'd heard the story before.

Ben continued. "The trouble is, this place is too far out of the way for my Dad to use it as a workshop so he hasn't done anything with it. Shame really, but he won't give it to anyone else 'cos this carpenter guy was a big friend of his. So there you go. I think my Dad's been in here once to store some tents away."

"Yeah, I know the guy you're on about. He was a big friend of my Grandad." *He's talking about Dave.* "A really good guy, a sad day when he died." At that point Lilly could feel tears welling up in her eyes and she turned away momentarily to compose herself.

Usha held Lilly's hand reassuringly. She knew how Lilly felt.

"So what are we doing here?" Lilly asked.

"Well," said Ben. "Somewhere, amongst all this paraphernalia, there are a couple of tents that my Dad put in here about two years ago. I thought we could use them up in the grounds of Fort Tourgis. The weather's looking good overnight so I thought it would be cool to camp out tonight. What do you think?"

"Yeah, come on Lilly. It should be good," Luis said enthusiastically, with the others nodding in agreement.

"Right then, sounds like a good idea," Lilly said. "We'd better crack on and find these tents. We'll need some sleeping bags as well."

"No probs`," Ben replied. "My Dad reckons there should be about ten in here."

Chloe and Usha looked at Ben quizzically.

"When the lease at the camp site over at Saye Bay changed hands, I think about six years ago, they sold everything off cheap and bought a load of new stuff to kit the camp site out with more modern gear," Ben explained.

"So there could be other bits and pieces in here we could use if we're camping tonight?" Alex asked.

"Yeah, sure."

"Right, let's get looking," said Usha.

"FOUND THE TENTS," Luis shouted.

As the others continued to rummage around the chaotic mess, Lilly took the opportunity to carefully scan the area looking for anything that could possibly explain why she felt connected in some way to this place. She was sure it had something to do with her Grandad and his friend that had died. Lilly just couldn't put her finger on it. *Gonna have to chat to Grandad about this place.*

"HERE." A shout from Chloe cut through Lilly's thoughts. "Found the sleeping bags guys and luckily I've just found a mallet. Be handy for knocking in the tent pegs."

"Cool," Ben said. "Let's get this gear outside and then we can park the scooters in here for the night. They'll be safe in here."

The group picked up the tents and sleeping bags and dumped them on the gravel in the car park.

"Right, let's get the scooters inside," Ben ordered.

Alex grabbed hold of his scooter and wheeled it through the door, followed by Chloe and then Lilly.

They turned and reached the door to head back outside. "I'll turn the light off." Lilly stood behind the door out of sight as she placed her left hand on her forehead and raised her right hand to reveal the amulet. In an instant, a white halo emitted from the light bulb and seemed to be absorbed by the amulet. Darkness once more.

As Lilly stepped outside into the bright sunlight, Ben grabbed hold of the creaking wooden door and pulled it shut. He then locked it and put the old key in his jacket pocket. "Did you manage to find a light switch Lilly?" Ben asked.

"Yeah …. Sure." *Wouldn't you like to know!*

CHAPTER 4

A HEAD FOR HEIGHTS

It had been a long haul and a bit of a struggle up the hill with their backpacks, tents and sleeping bags. As they approached the huge stone built arch, which formed the main entrance to Fort Tourgis at the end of the grass track the group had been following, they all stopped to read the rusting metal sign high up on the wall to the left.

Luis read the sign out loud. "Danger, this building is unsafe. Enter at your own risk."

"Take no notice Luis," Chloe said. "Loads of visitors come up here to look around. You've just got to be sensible and very careful."

"Yeah Luis," Ben added. "And that goes for all of us." As he gave all of them a look. "Some parts of the fort are really unsafe, so yeah, we have to be careful. Got it?"

The group all nodded in agreement as they walked through the arch. In front of them was a flattish grassed area the size of half a football pitch and to the left were stone walls with ramparts probably fifteen metres in height. On the right stood the main structure about twenty metres high with a low stone wall running the entire length in front. And so it went on. Everywhere the group looked, they were surrounded by Victorian history.

"Awesome," exclaimed Usha.

"Right," said Lilly. "We need to find somewhere suitable for these tents."

"What's wrong with this flat area here?" Luis asked.

"It's all stonework underneath this grass." Lilly scuffed the grass with her shoes to reveal the stones. "It was probably some sort of parade ground for the soldiers back in the day, or maybe a communal courtyard when a lot of Italian families were housed here in the 1950's and 60's. They came to Alderney to help with a lot of construction work that was happening on the island and of course, the market gardening. Alderney once had a thriving daffodil industry. That's why at the right time of the year you can see huge clumps of daffodils growing in the fields."

"Oh I see," replied Luis.

"I know just the spot." Ben strode away from his friends. "Walk this way."

The group followed Ben across the courtyard and through a gap in the stonework to the left.

"Up here." Ben clambered up the grass bank followed by the teenagers. The ground then levelled out to reveal a vast grassed area, sloping upwards to the left following the gradient of the hill and completely flat straight ahead.

"This grass looks as if it's been mowed recently," Chloe said.

"Yeah, the local Wildlife Trust try to keep places like this looking reasonably tidy for the visitors," replied Lilly.

"LOOK AT THESE." Alex by now had wandered further on ahead.

The group caught up with Alex who was studying two semi circular areas marked by stone set in the ground. Running parallel with the stones were, what looked like, railway lines.

Lilly studiously walked around the area. "These were batteries built in the Second World War by the Germans. They had two big guns situated up here which were rail mounted so that they could point them in different directions across Platte Saline beach and beyond, out into the channel." She pointed towards the bay in the distance.

The group stood there momentarily in their own thoughts as they gazed out over to Platte Saline and beyond to the horizon, an occasional gust of wind from the North disturbing their hair.

"This is perfect," Luis said. "Let's get these tents put up." The teenagers set about their task.

The two tents were up and they were quite big, easily able to accommodate the group's bags leaving enough space to sleep three in each tent comfortably.

"So us girls will have this tent then." Chloe pointed to the one on the left. "And you boys can have the other."

"Fine." Alex rubbed his hands together. "Are we going to do a bit of exploring now?.... We need to keep an eye out for any wood so we can have a bit of a fire later on. It'll help keep us warm tonight."

"That's a great idea, but we must be extra careful in there." Ben pointed over to the main building. "Some of the flooring is really dodgy."

"We'll split up shall we?" Lilly turned to Luis. "Do you want to come with me?"

"Too right I do Lilly." Luis' face wasn't able to conceal his delight at the thought of being with Lilly by himself.

"Of course he does," Chloe grumbled. She was totally peeved off as she'd fancied her chances with Luis. *Damn it.*

"COME ON BEN .... Let's go down here." Usha pointed to the flight of stone steps that led down to the basement. It was like an external corridor that ran from one end of the building to the other, about one hundred metres in length.

Alex and Chloe had found another gap in the low wall in which another flight of stone steps took them down to the basement. "Be careful Chloe," Alex said, "there's a loose stone in this step."

"SO WHAT!.... I don't care."

"Don't be like that." Alex had a reassuring tone in his voice. *C'mon gal, you're better than that.*

"It's always the same Alex .... Lilly somehow always manages to attract all the good looking guys."

"Well thanks for that .... I'm obviously not good enough for you then?" *Typical.*

Chloe could see that she'd upset Alex. "Sorry Alex, I didn't mean it like that. I like you a lot, I really do. It's just that ...."

Alex put his arm around Chloe. "I know, but don't let it get to you."

Chloe kissed him on the cheek. "You're the best Alex, thanks."

"Let's go across here." Luis stepped out onto a stone bridge that crossed over to the main building. He half turned and held out his hand towards Lilly who instinctively grabbed hold with her right hand. *He has a gentle but strong grip.* They slowly sidestepped across the bridge.

"That's gotta be a ten metre drop to the basement so don't let go of my hand Lilly." She smiled and nodded her head in agreement.

Luis stopped on reaching the other side and pulled Lilly towards him. They stood there close together, first looking down at the drop below and then .... For a few moments they were lost in each others eyes.

God, she smells so good.

Lilly's blonde hair danced in the breeze as they stood there lost in the moment. The sun gave the illusion of making Lilly's steely blue eyes sparkle out of control. *This is just heaven. What a guy, his hair, those muscles, his ...*

"Lilly." Luis interrupted her thoughts. "We need to move from this spot, it's quite dangerous standing here."

You got that right .... God he's gorgeous. "Err, oh, yes we should," she stuttered.

They both stepped into what was the stone framework of a doorway long gone. Lilly pulled her hand away from Luis' grip realising that her amulet was in full view.

"That looks expensive?" Luis had spotted the amulet glistening in the sunlight.

"It probably was. My Grandad gave it to me when I was born."

"Nice." *That looks REALLY valuable.*

"You two alright up there?" Usha called out from down below.

"We're fine Usha." Luis had spotted Ben and Usha down below in the basement. He could see them through the broken floor boards that was once a floor. "You found anything down there?"

"We've managed to collect a few bits of wood," Usha yelled.

"That's good .... We'll catch up with you in a bit."

Luis turned his head to see that Lilly was stood over the other side of this huge room. She was peering out of one of the many windows that were set at regular intervals along the exterior stone wall that overlooked the road below and Platte Saline Bay in the distance. *Doesn't she look just gorgeous and what a figure. Just got to play my cards right.* "LILLY .... How did you get over there?"

"Ha! Very carefully .... You need to keep to the sides. It's the strongest part of what's left of the floor."

"Okay, I'm coming round to you. Give me a couple of minutes. Stay put Lilly." *Jeez, this looks rather dodgy.*

Luis slowly and carefully side stepped around the edge of the room keeping his back to the stone walls. Every floorboard creaked with every movement of his feet. He was within a metre of Lilly when she offered him her right hand.

"Take my hand Luis .... Need to be careful 'cos that last floorboard is loose."

As Luis took her hand, the floorboard underneath his feet broke away and fell into the basement below. Luis instantly felt himself falling .... *Whoa*

"I'VE GOT YOU." Lilly instinctively grabbed Luis' hand as she held onto the window frame with her left hand. The amulet on her right wrist began to emit a blinding green pulse and the power of the light was growing stronger. Lilly held onto Luis who was dangling below her with her right hand.

"LUIS .... USE BOTH HANDS."

Luis swung his other arm round to grab Lilly's hand. He could feel the extraordinary strength that Lilly was exerting. Her grip was almost crushing his hands. He looked up to see Lilly's eyes that were now glowing dark green, nearly black. *I'm a gonna!*

Lilly pulled Luis up in a micro second to stand next to her. She loosened her grip from Luis as she instantly collapsed in his arms.

"LILLY, LILLY .... Oh jeez, what's going on? Lilly..... Lilly, please be okay."

He knelt down and carefully placed Lilly on the only remaining safe bit of flooring, cradling her head in his hands.

"HELP .... HELP ..... ANYONE!"

Lilly wasn't moving and Luis was beginning to panic. *Shit!*

A voice from below bellowed out. "WHAT'S GOING ON?" It was Alex.

"IT'S LILLY, SOMETHING'S WRONG WITH HER."
"HANG ON, WE'LL BE THERE IN A MO'" Alex shouted.
"Come on Chloe, sounds like Lilly's in some sort of trouble ....
We'll get the others on the way. Okay?"
"Coming Alex". They both clambered up the stone steps and
immediately bumped into Usha and Ben.
"What's going on?" Ben asked.
"I think Lilly might have had an accident or something.
We're not sure yet." Chloe turned to Usha. "Don't worry girl,
I'm sure your sis' will be fine."
The four of them ran to the stone bridge.
"WHAT HAPPENED LUIS?" Ben shouted.
"I ..... I'm not sure." Luis was clearly in shock. "Lilly's out
cold and we're now stuck over here with no way out."
Ben turned to the other three. "I'm not sure what's going on
but we need to get them back to this side and onto this bridge."
They nodded in agreement.
"I saw four strong looking planks back down there," Alex
said.
"And I've got some rope in my bag," said Ben. "Will the
planks be long enough Alex?"
"I reckon."
"Right, you stay here Usha to keep an eye, whilst we all get
the stuff." Ben was being assertive as the three ran off.
Usha sat down and looked nervously over at Luis and her
sister. "You alright Luis?"
"Yeah, but Lilly .... I'm really worried."
"Don't be. She'll be fine. I've seen this happen before so try
not to worry." She hadn't, but it was a case of reassuring herself
as well as Luis.
The others were back. Alex took charge and they carefully
slid the four planks in place over the precipice below. Luckily,
the planks were just long enough. Alex then tied one length of
rope around the planks to form a more stable platform.
"Right guys," Alex said. " You just need to try and keep
these planks steady whilst I crawl across with this rope to
secure the other end." He glanced across at Luis. "I'm coming
over now."
"Be careful," Chloe said with a quiet, concerned voice.

A bit of a wobble and Alex reached the other side and tied the rope to secure the planks. *Thank Christ for that!*

"Jeez, am I glad you're here," Luis sighed.

Lilly was still out cold which made it easier for the two lads to gently carry her to safety across the planks, over the stone bridge and then placed her gently down on the grass. The friends sat around her pondering what to do next with worried frowns on their faces.

Usha discreetly pulled a small teddy bear out of her pocket which she always had with her and poured water onto it. She leant over Lilly, one hand with the teddy over Lilly's mouth whilst a few drops of water trickled from the teddy into Lilly's mouth. She whispered in Lilly's ear. "Teddy's here." A gasp of air erupted from Lilly's mouth and she sat up. "Oh sis', you had us all worried." She threw her arms around Lilly.

"Why are we all sat here?" Lilly asked.

The friends looked at one another in bewilderment.

"Don't you remember anything Lilly?" Ben asked. "Anything at all?"

"Just standing next to Luis … And ... That's it, sorry. Why?"

"Hmm, sounds about right," Chloe mumbled. *Anything for attention eh?*

Ben turned to Chloe. "Stop it Chloe, can't you see she's confused."

"Makes two of us then," Luis said. *Weird.*

"Whoa, come on guys. Just be thankful we're all okay." Usha tried to calm the situation as she hugged Lilly once more.

"You was so brave Alex." Chloe embraced and kissed him. "My hero." *Hmm that's rather nice.*

Alex could sense his face blushing up and he could feel his heart pounding. *Wow, this is sort of cool.*

The group cheered and clapped.

22

CHAPTER 5

ADRENALIN DRUNKIES

It was early evening and the sun was low in the clear blue sky to the west. The group had spent the afternoon exploring around the grounds of Fort Tourgis. They'd found the little sentry outposts that were dotted around connected by trenches that had obviously been dug out during the Second World War. It was fascinating to see and feel history around them. They'd also been busy with their phones taking photos and making little videos.

The occasional visitor had passed through. Dressed in their all weather gear, hiking boots, binoculars and backpacks. Interesting conversations had been struck up.

The sound of the wildlife and the noise of the sea had occasionally been broken by the unmistakable drone of a Dornier aircraft landing and taking off at the airport in the south of the island about a kilometre away.

The teenagers were now back where they'd erected their tents earlier and the boys were busy building a small fire. Luckily Luis had some matches with him.

As the girls were putting together something to eat for everyone, Usha noticed the key that Ben had used earlier that very morning to open his Dad's store was on the ground in front of her, lying in the grass. It had obviously fallen out of Ben's jacket pocket when they'd been erecting the tents. *There's a stroke of luck. It's the key to the store that Ben used.* Usha quickly picked the key up and immediately took Lilly to one side. "Look what I've found." Usha carefully showed her sister the key, out of sight of their friends.

"The store key. That's brilliant Usha `cos we need to take another look in Ben's store when we're by ourselves."

The girls bent down.

"Pick up that piece of granite Usha," Lilly whispered and pointed to a small black stone in the grass. Lilly held the key in her right hand. "Now hold my hand with your hand with the stone in it."

Lilly closed her eyes as they held hands and in an instant, Lilly's amulet emitted an orange glow to their hands and as fast as it appeared, it was gone.

Lilly opened her eyes and the girls hands parted, revealing an exact duplicate of Ben's key.

"Hide the new key Usha and make sure you get this original one back to Ben." Usha nodded and they both continued to help Chloe with the preparation of the food.

It was fairly dark by the time they all gathered round the fire to eat and chat about the day.

"Who fancies a toasted marshmallow?" Luis asked.

"OH YES!" They all shouted.

"HEY." A shout from about five metres away behind the group interrupted their jovial high spirits. "What's going on here?" The voice was closer and a beam of light from a torch scanned across their faces.

"Oh hi Sergeant." Alex stood up. It was Peter, one of the three local policemen stationed on the island.

"Oh it's you lot …. I should have known …. Ha! No worries. Just doing my rounds in the police van and I knew you were all up here somewhere 'cos I bumped into Lilly's Grandad earlier. He said you were perhaps staying up here overnight."

"Right Sergeant. Do you fancy a toasted marshmallow?" Luis asked, and they all laughed.

"Okay, I'm off then, behave yourselves and keep the noise down." Peter turned to go …. "Oh by the way, there's been reports of flashes of bright lights up here. Anyone seen anything?"

"No, we've not seen anything eh guys," Luis replied as the friends shook their heads.

"Right then, enjoy yourselves. I'll see you around." Peter strode off into the darkness.

Peter was no sooner out of earshot and Ben opened a crate of beer. "Anyone fancy a bottle?" *Stupid question.*

"Too right," Chloe called out and they all grabbed one.

An hour later and Chloe was out for the count. She'd downed three or four beers and had dragged herself into the tent and managed somehow to get inside her sleeping bag.

Alex, Ben and Usha were in the other tent telling jokes and generally messing about whilst looking at each others phones, admiring the pictures and videos they had taken earlier that day.

"Hey you two," Alex muttered. "Take a look at this video I recorded today."

The three of them huddled round Alex's phone. The video played and Usha gulped in disbelief at what she was watching.

Alex had obviously recorded Lilly and Luis earlier that day. As the events played out in front of them, seeing Lilly catch Luis and pull him to safety and the dark green pulsing lights, Usha's mind filled with dread.

Lilly's secret is out and there for all to see. Usha's thoughts were racing with wild trepidation as she tried to keep herself together.

"That's way cool don't you think guys?" Alex said.

There was no reply from Ben, he'd fallen asleep. The after effects of the beer had taken its toll.

That's lucky, thought Usha.

"What do you reckon Usha?" Alex was drunk. "Be cool to upload it to the internet on one of the social media channels." He had a drunken slur to his voice.

25

"Err … Yeah … Good idea Alex …. I'd leave it though until tomorrow when you're a bit more sober. Don't want to make any mistakes with it eh?"

"Hic … Good thinking Usha, I'll do that." Alex turned the video off and pressed lock on his phone. "I'm gonna hit the sack anyway, my head's spinning."

"Okay Alex, I'll see you in the morning. Night Ben." *He's sound asleep, that's lucky.*

Usha dropped the original store key in Ben's jacket pocket as she stepped out of the tent.

Jeez, what are we going to do? Where's Lilly?

Usha spotted Lilly sat down by the fire with Luis. "Sorry to interrupt you two …. Can I just have a quick word Lilly before I turn in?"

"Yeah …. Sure," Lilly replied, as the two girls took four or five steps away from Luis.

Usha whispered "We're in trouble sis`. Alex recorded a video of you saving Luis and he's going to upload it onto the internet. He's asleep now and I did manage to convince him to wait until tomorrow morning."

Lilly gasped, raising her hands to her mouth. "Grandad's going to have to sort this out. Send a text to him on your phone. He'll know what to do. Okay?"

Usha nodded. "I'll do this text and then go to bed, night Lilly."

"Night Usha, try not to worry. Fingers crossed and all that." *Bloody hell!*

TEXT …..
Hi Grandad. There's a
Video of Lilly on
Alex's phone. Needs
deleting. Love Usha x

The last embers of the fire danced and crackled in the darkness. The air was still and the sound of gently lapping waves breaking on the beach nearby could be heard in the stillness of the night. Luis and Lilly were laid on their backs, next to each other as they soaked in the atmosphere.

"Isn't the night sky just beautiful," Lilly whispered. "You can see every star in the sky. Look, there's the constellation of Orion and over here is the north star. You can see Ursa Major, there's loads of stars in ....."

"Lilly." Luis interrupted "What happened earlier today? You saved me from falling to my death. What's going on?"

"That's very melodramatic Luis."

"But ...." Luis tried to continue.

"Must have been adrenaline that kicked in." Lilly rolled over to place herself on top of Luis. "Forget about it Luis." She placed her index finger onto Luis' lips. *This is rather nice.*

Luis held Lilly as she kissed him full on the lips. *This is getting out of hand.... Here I am lying on the grass kissing and caressing a girl I barely know.*

Luis gave Lilly a gentle push to stop her advances. "Sorry Lilly, it's been a long day and I think maybe you've had a bit too much to drink."

"You could be right." Lilly giggled. "Good innit?" Lilly continued to kiss Luis. *What a hunk.*

"Okay, enough Lilly. Sorry. We need to get to our beds before this all gets out of hand."

"Spoilsport .... But I suppose you're right." *Unfortunately.*

CHAPTER 6

SEEING IS BELIEVING

"Woman you can change my world, Woman you can change my world ..." Richard's ring tone, Woman by the Scorpions alerted him to his phone. He picked it up to take a look who'd text him this late at night. *Hmm .... It's Usha, what does she want?*

He read the text. *Christ .... Another mess to sort out.*

Richard made his way upstairs to his computer room. He'd been a computer buff ever since the early eight bit days and knew his stuff. Through the 1980`s he'd been a member of a computer software hacking group that involved people from all over the world.

The hackers would have their suppliers and swappers that got hold of original copies of new releases. Richard would hack into the code to include, what they termed as, trainers, into the games to make them easier to play. Then it was a case of distributing copies freely into the public domain. The practice ruined a lot of the software houses but in those days it was classed as harmless fun.

Over the years as technology improved and progressed, Richard had thrown himself into keeping up with all the techniques to enable him pretty much free access into any security system in the world. Phone technology in particular was simple fare for Richard. He viewed it as cyber hacking for the good of all.

Richard sat down and fired up the systems. Twelve screens in total connected to seven or eight computers and consoles.

Right, concentrate. He hadn't hacked into the phone networks for a considerable period of time, so this was going to be far from easy.

Fifteen minutes later and he was in. *Just got to figure out Alex's password now.* He turned to another keyboard to bring

28

up an automated program. *This should do the trick.* "I'll just port this program over into this other computer and it should give me what I want."

"Gotcha!.... Now then, let's see what you've got Alex."

Richard scrolled through the files and .... *There it is.* He ran the video.

"What the ...." Richard watched what had happened earlier that day at Fort Tourgis. *Lilly's powers are increasing. We need to talk before it all gets out of hand.*

Richard downloaded the video onto a spare usb memory stick he had kicking around and then deleted the video on Alex's phone. *Just need to check his trash can and history files.* Richard deleted all the connected files and then ran a scanning program through Alex's phone to delete any other possible connections to the video.

Richard locked Alex's phone and then powered down his computers. *I'll text Usha to let her know it's sorted and then off to bed.*

"You light the skies up above me, A star so bright you blind me, Don't close your eyes, Don't fade away .... " Rule The World by Take That played as Usha's hand grabbed her phone to see that her Grandad had sent her a text ...

TEXT ....
Hi Usha. Video
sorted. Need to
talk later. Love
Grandad xx

The three girls pulled themselves out of their sleeping bags. It was just coming up to seven o'clock in the morning and the sun was already midway up in the sky, it's rays heating up the tent.

"Ohhhh my head hurts," Lilly groaned.

"Mine's a bit like that this morning," Chloe replied.

"Serves you both right," Usha growled as she continued to brush her hair. "You shouldn't have drunk so much."

Usha gave Lilly a thumbs up and Lilly nodded approvingly with a smile.

"You three getting up?" A voice from outside.

The three girls crawled out of their tent into the blinding rays from the sun to see the three lads were already up, and by the looks of things they'd been up for some time as their tent had already been taken down.

"Morning sleepy heads," Luis jokingly called out. "Come and look at this. Alex wants to show all of us something on his phone before he uploads it onto the internet."

They all grouped around Alex.

"This will blow your mind." Alex excitedly scrolled through his files on the phone. He began to get more frantic. "WHERE IS IT?... IT'S GONE. I DON'T BELIEVE THIS." His voice increasing in volume as he searched in vain for the missing video file.

"What's up Alex?" Usha asked with a very calm and controlled voice.

"I had a vid' .... But .... You saw it Usha last night."

"Don't know what you're on about." *Sorry Alex.* "Does anyone here know what he's on about?"

The friends were shaking their heads.

"I think we all had a bit too much to drink last night Alex, including you," Luis said. "Don't you think Lilly?" He turned to look at Lilly who had a sheepish look on her face.

"You're probably right Luis." Lilly sighed. But her heart was pounding. She'd never felt like this before. Her thoughts were elsewhere. *He's a dreamboat.*

Alex put his phone in his pocket. "You maybe right, I dunno, it's just that .... Oh, forget it."

Chloe grabbed hold of Alex's hand. "I don't care what the others think, you're still my hero." She gave him a gentle peck on his cheek.

"Come on guys, we need to go. I've got to go to work today," Ben muttered. "Grab your things. We'll get the scooters from the store and we'll catch up later."

CHAPTER 7

ONCE UPON A TIME

Lilly and Usha pulled up on the drive outside their house and jumped off their scooter. Usha pulled her crash helmet off. "We had a good time eh Lilly?"

"Um, yeah …. I'm just a bit worried what Grandad's going to say. I'm also concerned about Alex, what if he blabs his mouth off what he saw?"

"And what's Alex going to say Lilly?… Nothing. And if he does, who's gonna believe him? Don't worry about him. To be honest I think you're going to have more problems with Luis don't you think?"

Lilly sighed …. "He's a dreamboat." Her face had lit up at the mention of his name and the sparkle was back in her blue eyes. "I've never felt like this before Usha. There's a connection."

"Okay, okay, I get it thanks …. Stop all the drooling will you. Oh jeez, what are we going to do with you?" *My God sis', you've only known the guy for a day or so and you're already a lost cause!*

"Oy! You two. Are you coming inside or what?" The girl's Mum, Susan, was standing in the open doorway, hands firmly on her hips. "WELL?"

"Sorry Mum, we're coming," Usha replied. "Come on sis'."

The girls dumped the backpacks in their bedrooms and were busy getting themselves ready to go to work. Like most teenagers on Alderney, they had part time jobs when the school was closed and it was a good way of topping up their pocket money. Lilly and Usha were waitresses at one of the local cafes in town. They also helped out in the kitchen preparing food and washing the assorted pots. It was good experience, good fun and a great way of catching up with all the local gossip.

Today they had a split shift. A couple of hours in the morning and then another two in the afternoon.

"Come on you two otherwise you'll be late." Susan called from downstairs.

"Okay, we're coming," Lilly yelled, as the two girls skipped and jumped down the stairs. They headed for the front door.

"Oh girls .... Your Grandad phoned earlier and would like to see you, so I told him you'd both give him a visit for lunch. Alright?"

"Yeah that's great Mum, we'll do that," Usha replied. "It'll be nice to see Grandad. See you later."

The girls waved to their Mum and closed the door behind them.

"We'd better go on the scooter," Lilly said. "Especially as we're visiting Grandad later."

"That's alright with me. Saves all that walking."

The girls sat astride the scooter and sped away.

The café is quiet this morning. Just a couple of visitors sat at the table over in the corner. *Just as well it's quiet 'cos my sis' is not on the same planet this morning.* Usha gave Lilly a scowled look of disdain.

Lilly was leaning on the counter and appeared to be lost in her own thoughts.

A group of twelve visitors entered the café and scattered themselves around the empty tables and chairs.

There was no reaction from Lilly as her thoughts overcame every other instinct. *I know nothing about Luis and that's the thing. It's exciting, it's thrilling. If this is love, wow! All the other girls fancy him, so why me? Why the attraction? Is it just luck? Or could it possibly be my destiny?* Her mind was racing ....

"Excuse me!" Usha growled at Lilly. "HELLOOOO." She yelled directly into Lilly's face. "Any chance of some help here?"

"Dur ... Oh ... What did you say sis'?"

"I seriously need some help Lilly .... Look." Usha pointed to the crowd of visitors staring at the girls with demanding looks.

32

"Yeah, sorry sis'. My fault. I'll crack on."

Usha huffed and puffed as she started to take the orders. *Come on Lilly. Get your arse in gear.*

Lilly and Usha were still arguing about events at the café earlier, when they arrived at their Grandad's house on the scooter.

"Okay Usha, I get it," Lilly snapped. "Let's forget it for now. We'll see what Grandad has to say."

"We certainly will. He must be in the back garden 'cos this front door is locked." Usha gave up swinging on the door handle.

The two girls wandered round to the back of the house.

"Hi Grandad," Lilly said.

"Oh hello girls. Didn't realise it was lunchtime. I've been so busy trying to build this greenhouse I lost track of time."

"You seem to be winning the battle," Usha said.

Richard put his screwdriver down and got up off his knees. "Right girls, let's get off inside up to my computer room and we'll have a chat. We don't want to be too long as your Grandma will be back from the shops later and you'll both be wanting lunch. No rest for the wicked."

The three of them entered the computer room and Richard powered up one of the consoles.

"Lilly, could you pass me that vase from over there." Richard pointed to the window sill on the far side of the room. Lilly gave him the vase and Richard tipped it up on end. The usb memory stick dropped into Richard's hand. "Can't be too careful eh?"

The girls nodded in agreement.

Richard inserted the usb memory stick into the console and found the file he'd downloaded from Alex's phone the night before.

"Sit down girls and watch this." The video played and there was a stunned silence as the events with Luis and Lilly played out. "I've not seen that happen before," Richard said. "Not even using my amulet, so we've a few issues to deal with."

"Just recently, I've been feeling more 'connected' with the amulet," Lilly mused. "I can't explain it but every time I use it I feel more powerful. The thing is, is it dangerous Grandad?"

"I don't know the answer to that Lilly but there has to be an explanation. We need to find out what's going on before you lose control."

"So what DO we know?" Usha asked.

"Well I've never told either of you the story that goes with the amulets or your little teddy Usha so I think now would be a good time. Just remember, a lot of this is based on legends and myths. Some of this story was related to me some years ago by my friend Dave who's no longer with us sadly." *God bless you mate.*

"That's who used to have that store down at Fort Tourgis," Lilly interrupted.

"Yeah that's right." Richard nodded and smiled.

The girls were transfixed as their Grandad continued to explain how two or three hundred years ago, privateers plundered and shipwrecked many ships around the Channel Islands, including Alderney. They were, in essence, pirates that had permission from various governments to raid ships of their valuable cargoes.

Many of the ships used by the privateers were financed by local island families such as Le Mesurier and Carteret. That is why many outsiders consider the Channel Islands to be wealthy countries.

In the year 1820 the Treasure of Lima which they think could now be worth about two hundred million pounds was taken from Lima in Peru to Cocos Island just off Costa Rica to be buried for safe keeping.

In 1832, the ship Jupiter sailed from Peru to Hamburg in Germany and on it's return trip to Lima the following year it was shipwrecked on the rocks north west of Alderney. Apparently the soldiers aboard were thrown into jail and the Jupiter was looted by local privateers. Many believe that the Treasure of Lima which included gold statues and jewelled stones went down with the ship whilst some locals in Alderney think that some of it, if not all of it, was brought to shore and hidden.

34

The jewelled stones of the Treasure of Lima were reputed to possess mystical powers especially when strung together with gold braid to form amulets and were part of the Inca treasure that was stolen by Spanish soldiers during the wars in South America in the early nineteenth century.

Richard went on to explain.

"Dave had some good contacts in the antique trade in the islands and he gave me these two amulets that he'd been given a good thirty or so years ago. He reckoned there had to be more but he never said where."

Richard continued. "I've worked out that the different colours of the jewelled stones or crystals obviously have different powers. The white crystals give off a white halo and possess some sort of healing powers."

"Yeah, but I've found out," Lilly interrupted, "that it must give off some sort of electrical current 'cos I got a dead light bulb to power up."

"Interesting," Richard said. "The red crystal, as we know, gives off a red halo and seems to make things disappear. And now we know the green crystal emits a dark green halo and seemingly super human strength. Mind you, the dark green eyes are not a good look Lilly!

The one thing I do know about the crystals is they are precious stones. I'll have to do some research online and get back to you. In the meantime, you need to be careful, especially when you're with your friends." Richard gave the girls a knowing look.

"Your teddy is an interesting story Usha," Richard said. "I've just got time to explain before we have lunch."

The girls listened intently as their Grandad told them the story.

"As you know, I was born in Wales and in 1977 there was an exhibition that included the wooden Nanteos Cup which was rumoured to have been made out of the cross that Jesus was crucified on. Anyway, it went missing for a while and when it was returned it was slightly damaged. They didn't make too much fuss at the time as they were so relieved to get it back.

The teddy was given to me by my Great Grand Father with the strict instructions to never get it wet because it was stuffed with wooden shavings. Years later, my Mother told me that apparently the riddle of the missing bits of wood from the Nanteos Cup was explained by the fact my Great Grand Father repaired the cup and used the shavings to stuff the teddy. The legend goes that the Nanteos Cup had supernatural healing powers when drunk from it."

"That's what happened with Lilly," Usha interrupted.

"What?"

"Up at the Fort. Lilly was out for the count. She was barely breathing after she collapsed. I soaked the teddy with some water and wet her lips with it. Lilly immediately recovered."

"Amazing .... It seems like the legend is true then. You need to take great care of that teddy Usha."

Usha nodded in agreement. "So the cup behaves a little bit like the fabled Holy Grail?"

"I suppose it does," Richard replied. "But don't go thinking that makes you both invincible, in fact, you need to be more careful than ever until we can figure out what we're really dealing with. I'll get online as soon as I can to see if I can find any more information."

"HELLO .... HELLO UP THERE." A shout echoed through the house.

"That sounds like your Grandma girls. Time for lunch eh? Better look sharp or you'll be late back to work."

CHAPTER 8

PAGE TURNERS

Annie Dodds, the librarian, was busy sorting out the returned library books which had built up over recent days. Not for the first time in the last few days she was in a world of her own daydreaming .... *It was so lovely the other night having Richard all to myself at home, in bed with me* .... Annie's husband owned a business in the UK which he controlled remotely on the internet in Alderney and occasionally he would have to attend business meetings in the UK and around the world. This had been one of those occasions and Richard had been her secret lover for years ... *Richard always gives me what I desire. Exciting, passionate sex. Oh how I wish* ... Annie caught sight of Chloe sat down on the floor in front of one of the sets of book shelves in the corner of the library.

Anne summoned Chloe over with a wave. "Miss Chloe Mollins," she growled. "I know you only work here on a part time basis but a little more effort would be appreciated."

"Sorry Mrs Dodds." *Blah blah blah. Who cares.*

"Well quite. Here. I've sorted these returned books out alphabetically, so if you wouldn't mind putting them back on their correct shelves, it would help. Okay?"

"I'll get on with it now." Chloe picked up a stack of the books and she turned to go with a soulful look on her face. *Miserable cow.* Her heart wasn't really in it. She hated the job and only did it to help her Mum out financially. Her Dad had died a couple of years ago in a car accident and she missed him dreadfully. Chloe's heart was broken but she'd stayed tough not only because of stuff that had been said to her at school, but for her Mum as well.

Annie beckoned Chloe back and put her arm round her to try and reassure her. "Chloe, I'm sorry, I didn't mean to upset you.

I know what you've been through and you know that you only have to ask if you need any help or advice."

"Thanks Mrs Dodds, that means a lot." Chloe smiled briefly as she carried the books over to the shelving.

"Hi Annie. How are you?" *She looks as gorgeous as ever. Stunning. My God, she really went for it the other night ... She was really turned on that's for sure ...*

Annie turned to see Richard standing at her counter. "Oh hello Richard. Haven't seen you in here for some time." *Jeez, I'm already feeling damp between my thighs. Just seeing Richard and the thought of what we did the other night ...* Annie had a slight tremble in her voice as she tried to control her lustful passion. She'd always had a bit of a thing for him even though he was married. *Oh Richard. If only.*

"Well, you know how it is. Busy, busy, busy."

Annie nodded in agreement.

"You still giving Chloe a hard time then?" Richard playfully winked at Annie.

"No ... No, not at all.... It's just, you know how these youngsters are. But Chloe's a good girl who just needs a bit more support than some of the others, you know."

Richard smiled and nodded reassuringly. "Absolutely. You're right of course. Anyway, I'm here 'cos I'm after some sort of reference book. Anything to do with shipwrecks and that sort of thing around the seas of the Channel Islands, in particular Alderney. Lilly's doing a project for school and I said I'd help her out." *Ha, if only. Another white lie.* "Do you think you might have something?"

"I'm sure we will. In fact, Chloe's tidying that section right now."

"Thanks Annie, I'm sure Chloe will be a big help." Richard sauntered off towards the girl.

"Hi Chloe, how are you doing? Did you enjoy yourself with Lilly and her friends yesterday?"

"Oh hello Mr Morgan. Yeah it was good thanks and I think your Lilly has found herself a new admirer." There was a glint of mischief in Chloe's eyes.

"Who's that then?"

"Oh his name's Luis Garcia. He's fairly new to the island. His dad's a plumber you know and Luis works full time with him."

"Does he now. So I guess he's older than Lilly then?"

"I think he's seventeen."

Richard paused for a moment. "Hmm … Right then. Err, I'm looking for some sort of reference book about shipwrecks. Perhaps you know where to look?"

"You need to be looking over there in the corner Mr Morgan." Chloe pointed to the top shelf of the shelving unit.

"Thanks Chloe, I'll take a look …. Oh, and say hi to your Mum for me will you."

Chloe smiled and nodded to Richard. She picked up the books and carried on organising the shelves in front of her.

This row of reference books are covered in dust. Richard spotted what looked like the very one he needed … Shipwrecks in the Channel Islands 12th-19th Century. *Perfect.*

Richard sat down at one of the five available tables. The book was quite old with some water damaged pages but all the text and maps were still legible. *This is strange, this book isn't dusty unlike the others on the same shelf.*

Inside the front cover there was only one date stamp. *This book has only ever been taken out of the library once and that was over twenty years ago. This is weird.*

Richard quickly flicked through the pages from back to front stopping at one in which the corner had been creased over as a marker. "That's interesting," Richard whispered to himself. The page was information about the ship Jupiter which had sunk near Alderney in 1833. It also went on to list what cargo it was shipping and there it was …. Lima Gold. *Bingo! I have to admit I'm feeling pleased with myself.*

Richard ran his fingers across the page and he caught the corner marker, turning it to it's normal position revealing a hand written number. "Number 77," Richard whispered to himself. *It has to be a page number.* He quickly turned to the page to reveal what looked like an extract of the ship's log. It listed names of sailors that were on board that fateful day in the year 1833 and one name and his nationality was circled in pen.

"Garcia .... Peruvian." Richard gasped. "It surely can't be." He slammed the book shut.

"Everything alright Mr Morgan?" Chloe was stood immediately behind Richard.

"Oh, yes thanks." *How long has Chloe been stood there? Did she see what I was looking at?* "Could you put this book back for me Chloe? And could you do me a favour?.... Would it be possible for you to find out who took this book out previously for me please? It's about twenty years ago, a bit before your time I know, but there should be some sort of record. Thanks."

"Yeah sure Mr Morgan." *That's a strange request.*

"Great. There's no rush. If you don't see me around just send me a text 'cos you've got my number. Alright young lady?"

Chloe nodded and smiled as Richard left the library saying goodbye to Annie as he did so, deftly leaving a note in Annie's hand. ***I'll pick you up outside the church at 9pm Friday xx Richard.*** Annie kissed the note and then crumpled it up before placing it in her pocket. She felt increasingly hot and flustered as Chloe approached her ...

"You okay Mrs Dodds? You look a bit ..."

"No. No I'm fine Chloe. You get back to what you was doing. I'm just going to the bathroom to freshen up. Keep an eye on things for a mo' please." *Jeez Richard. I need you now. I'm feeling so randy just thinking about Friday.*

CHAPTER 9

HORMONES

The two girls were coming to the end of their afternoon shift at the café and were busy cleaning out the fridges and washing the pots and pans. It had been very quiet and they'd only served a handful of customers, so they had taken the opportunity to discuss the implications of the amulets and Usha's teddy. They were both excited and fearful at the same time, wondering where the situation would lead them.

Usha continued wiping down the tables and clearing away the few remaining pots and cutlery whilst keeping an eye out for potential customers.

Lilly was in the back kitchen preparing vegetables and the like, to put in the fridges ready for the following days menu and was in a world of her own. She was listening to music on her iPhone using her headphones and as she worked, Lilly was moving and singing along to the music.

Usha's concentration was interrupted by the sight of two scooters pulling up outside the café. It was the three boys. The engines became silent as Alex hopped off his scooter and was first to enter, quickly followed by Luis and Ben who looked decidedly bedraggled.

"Hope you lot have got clean boots," Usha growled. "I've not long mopped the floor."

"And hello to you too," Alex snapped. *Stroppy mare!*

"Sorry Usha," Luis and Ben said in unison. "We've both been working at the same house" Ben explained, "and we've just finished. Thought we'd drop in and grab ourselves some pasties and a bottle of coke."

Luis nodded in agreement as he scanned the café for any sight of Lilly.

"You looking for Lilly?" Usha enquired.

"Err … Yeah," Luis stuttered with an embarrassed voice.

"She's through the back in the kitchen." Usha pointed over her shoulder.

Luis leapt over the counter and entered the kitchen. *What the ... Here was the girl he thought he knew, singing and dancing with all her heart oblivious to his presence.*

He recognised the song. It was Eternal Flame by The Bangles. *Lilly's voice is great.* She continued to sing ....

"Close your eyes, give me your hand, Do you feel my heart beating, Do you understand, Do you feel the same, Am I only dreaming, Or is this burning an eternal flame ..."

Without thinking, Luis placed his hands on Lilly's hips and she spun round to face Luis with a startled look, which quickly changed into a huge smile. She pulled the headphones from her ears as Luis held her closer and they melted together. *I can feel the hairs on the back of my neck standing up,* thought Lilly. She started to sing again with Luis joining in as they danced together. *This is just heaven.*

As the song finished, the two of them held each other tighter and kissed each other passionately. Lilly could feel herself becoming aroused. *My knickers are getting damp. I've never experienced this feeling before.*

Ben, Usha and Alex stood in the doorway of the kitchen, clapping, whistling and shouting encouragement, when a voice from the front of the café boomed. "HEY YOU LOT! WHAT'S GOING ON?" It was Richard.

The three teenagers stood aside with sheepish looks as Richard strode over to the entrance of the kitchen.

Lilly and Luis were still kissing. "What do the two of you think you're doing?" Richard tapped Luis on the shoulder.

They separated and turned towards Richard. "Grandad" Lilly stuttered. "We ...."

"We what?"

"Nothing." Lilly felt embarrassed and was feeling hot and flustered in more ways than one as her face turned red.

"Sorry Mr Morgan," Luis mumbled. "It was just a bit of fun, you know." His face was bright red as he turned to Lilly. "Sorry gal, I'd better go." Luis squeezed Lilly's hand before marching out of the kitchen turning to Ben as he did. "You coming Ben?"

The two lads left the café followed by Richard who was definitely in a huff!

"I'd better get going as well," Alex said. "I promised Chloe I'd pick her up from the library."

He clambered onto his scooter and he was gone leaving the two girls standing despondently in the cafe.

Usha placed her arm reassuringly around Lilly. "Come on sis', forget about all the crap. We need to finish up and get off home."

"Okay," Lilly replied, "but I know a quicker way. Stand back." Lilly touched the orange crystal on her amulet. She closed her eyes and in an instant an orange halo materialised and then disappeared to reveal a spotless kitchen.

"That's a bonus," Usha joked. They both grinned.

Meanwhile, Chloe was just leaving the library after her shift had finished when Alex pulled up on his scooter.

She ran over to him and threw her arms around him. "Oh Alex, I'm so pleased to see you." She kissed him on the cheek.

Alex could see that her eyes were teary. *She's having one of her bad days.* "Come on girl, hop on the scooter behind me. You can have tea at my place if you like. My Mum's got the day off from the hospital so she won't mind cooking for an extra mouth."

Chloe nodded and smiled. She'd always been fairly close with Alex and since her father had died he'd been a great shoulder to cry on with all her problems. She jumped on the scooter behind Alex and put her arms around his waist as they pulled away.

Alex and Chloe arrived at his house which was an imposing building with great far reaching views. His Dad had built it a few years earlier and it was in a prime situation at the top of the road that cut straight through the middle of the local golf course.

Alex parked the scooter on the drive and immediately went over to his `For Sale` box to see how many golf balls he'd sold that day. The box was empty and his money box was full with

43

money. *Cool, the money will come in handy.* "Fancy helping me look for some more golf balls Chloe?"

"Yeah, why not."

"Okay, give us a minute. I'll just let Mum know what we're doing and I'll grab the dog. We can give her a walk at the same time." Alex was in and out of the house in a flash with the dog bounding along behind him.

"Right come on," Alex said. "Let's get going 'cos it'll take a couple of hours to look round the golf course. Oh and my Mum says you can stop the night if you want. She's already phoned your Mum to let her know."

Chloe gazed and smiled at Alex. "You're the best." She kissed him tenderly on the cheek.

It was a long walk, but the teenagers didn't care as they chatted about life and general stuff. Chloe felt more at ease in those precious moments than she had done for a few weeks. They stopped for a rest and sat down on one of the benches that were dotted around the golf course.

"Do you think there's something weird going on with Luis?" Chloe asked.

"Not sure I know what you mean girl. I reckon something is going on, but I can't put my finger on it. It's like this afternoon .... Lilly's Grandad came in the café and sort of lost his cool with Lilly and Luis. Not really what you expect from Mr Morgan 'cos he's always been pretty cool with all the kids."

"That's strange. Mr Morgan was at the library earlier today. He was nice, as he always is, but he was acting rather strangely. He was studying a reference book about shipwrecks. It just seemed odd because he very rarely comes in and when he does it's usually just for a chat with me or Mrs Dodds."

Chloe continued. "And the really weird thing about it was that he asked me to find out who had taken that book out 'cos it only had one date stamp on it. Something's definitely going on."

"Did you find out?"

"I didn't have time today, but I need to look in the records when Mrs Dodds isn't there."

"Well if you need me to help just ask. We need to get to the bottom of this I reckon. It could be important .... I do think Lilly is involved with all this. Why else would her Grandad lose his temper this afternoon? And you know, I still remember filming Lilly and Luis up at Fort Tourgis."

"You still going on about your lost video? Come on Alex, you was drunk."

"Yeah but ..."

"You was drunk Alex. You need to forget it," Chloe snapped. "Sorry mate, I didn't mean to shout at you." She kissed Alex on the lips.

Alex wrapped his arms around her as they caressed and kissed before rising from the bench.

"Come on, let's go and see what my Mum's cooked for tea." Alex called out for the dog and they strolled home across the golf course hand in hand.

CHAPTER 10

DISCOVERIES

Lilly rolled over in her bed and through half closed bleary eyes she caught sight of her clock. Nine in the morning .... *Jeez, I need to get up.* Luckily she didn't have to go to work that day. She quickly got dressed. She brushed her hair as she made her way down stairs and into the kitchen.

"Oh hi sis`." Usha was in the process of finishing her bowl of cereals. "Mum and Dad have gone to work. Mum said they'd be out all day so we'd have to sort ourselves out for lunch."

"Right .... I'll get something to eat then. What are we doing today?"

"Well I know that Ben's working with his Dad over on the other side of the island, so how about we go and take a look around his Dad's workshop. We've got the key." Usha held up the copy of the key Lilly had made the other day.

"Good idea gal .... I'll get myself sorted and you pack some stuff together. Don't forget a torch, just in case, and we'll get going."

The girls straddled themselves over onto their scooter. Just then, their Grandad's van pulled up.

"Here we go," Lilly muttered. *Bloody hell!* "More trouble and strife."

Usha sighed.

"Here's my two princesses." Richard climbed out of his van and made his way over to them. He kissed them both on their cheeks.

In unison, the two girls replied. "Hi Grandad."

"I'm glad I've seen you both this morning `cos I've got something to say. I just wanted to say sorry to the pair of you about having a go at you yesterday at the café. I was bang out of order. I don't want to spoil your fun and you're both old enough to be responsible for yourselves, if you know what I mean." *Fingers crossed.*

The girls nodded.

"The one thing I would say Lilly is just to be careful when you're with Luis. Okay?"

Lilly smiled.

"Right, on that note, I'm going. Love you both." Richard gave them a hug. "Catch up with you later." Richard waved to the two girls as he drove off in the van. *Well that went better than expected.*

"Right sis' let's get going," Usha muttered in Lilly's ear and the scooter sped off spluttering as it disappeared down the road.

Five minutes later and the girls arrived at the parking area at Platte Saline.

"We'll leave the scooter here," Lilly said. "And we'll walk round the corner of Fort Tourgis to Ben's workshop."

Usha nodded in agreement. "Probably for the best, then we won't draw attention to ourselves."

The sisters picked up their bags and headed off down the lane. Their hair danced from side to side as the wind hit them in their faces as they turned the corner before reaching the wooden door of the workshop.

The girls glanced around to make sure no-one was looking and Usha put the duplicate key in the door and turned it. "Clunk." It worked and the door creaked, as if it was relieved to be released from it's bonds.

Lilly pushed the door open and the girls stepped inside. "Close the door Usha and I'll sort the light out." Lilly closed her eyes and concentrated momentarily, visualising the light bulb. This was the first time she'd tried using her powers without touching her amulet.

"That's enough Lilly, the light's dazzling me. Turn it down before it explodes!"

Lilly's eyes opened to see the room bathed in a dazzling white light. Usha was knelt down with her hands shading her eyes. *Jeez, turn it down gal.*

"Ha, that's pretty good." Lilly laughed.

"I'm impressed Lilly, but next time, try it with your eyes open so you've got more control …. But at least now, you seem to be getting more of a handle of what you're capable of."

"Yeah, it's going to take practice I suppose …. Lock the door Usha. Just in case, y`know."

The greater distribution of light than their previous visit revealed a much larger area in the workshop than before. The floor was thick with countless years of dust and the girls could tell it was a combination of gravel, concrete and floorboards depending on the sound beneath their feet.

The surrounding walls and roof were solid granite rock slowly narrowing further back in the workshop. The various shapes of the rock indicated that this place had been tunnelled out by hand probably by a few poor souls in the Second World War.

Rubbish and antique style tools along with ancient machinery were scattered around the workshop, some barely distinguishable as the cobwebs had virtually hidden them.

"What exactly are we looking for Lilly?"

"I don't know …. It's just that I felt some sort of connection with this place when we were here the other day with the guys. And then when Grandad mentioned about his friend who'd died and the fact that he'd given him the amulets, plus Ben had said his Dad had been given this place by Grandad's friend. So there must be something here sis'. But what?"

Usha shrugged her shoulders.

"Just keep looking Usha." Both girls moved slowly towards the far end.

"How about you try 'connecting' with your mind and the amulet?" Usha asked. "I know you've never done anything like this but surely it's worth a try?"

Lilly sighed … "Okay, I'll give it a go. Stand back just in case something goes wrong." Lilly stood in the middle of the floor and raised both hands to waist height, her palms away from her. She closed her eyes and cleared her thoughts. Lilly concentrated on an image of her amulet in her head and suddenly she was no longer in control of her thoughts.

Usha watched intently as the amulet on Lilly's wrist started to glow all the colours of the rainbow and then vibrate. *Has Lilly lost control?*

Lilly opened her eyes which were now glowing jet black in a scarily sort of way and she slightly turned to face Usha.

Usha panicked momentarily and froze as she suddenly lost all control of her movements and watched helplessly as Lilly's amulet glowed with increasing intensity.

Usha started to walk in a zombie type of way. She had no control of her own movements and could do nothing as Lilly seemingly was controlling her. *This is really weird.*

In front of her, Usha could see something glowing rhythmically in time with Lilly's amulet. Usha's arm rose up, still under Lilly's control, and her hand grabbed the object in the wall. She pulled it towards her and in that moment the two girls were released from whatever force they had both experienced.

"LILLY .... are you okay?"

"Yeah, I think so. You?"

"Pretty much .... Come and take a look at this." Usha pointed to the object in the stone wall. "It looks like some sort of statue that's been made into a lever. Awesome."

"Wow, it looks like an Inca figurine .... And look what's happened over there in the floorboards. It's a trapdoor. The lever must have opened it."

The two girls studied their discovery and lifted the trapdoor to reveal a rope attached to the underside and hand hewn steps leading down to ...

There was a noise at the wooden door.

"Usha, grab the bags and the torch and get down there," Lilly whispered as she pointed to the trapdoor. "I'll get the light." Lilly instinctively powered the light off. *Getting good at this.*

The girls hurriedly clambered down the steps below the floorboards and pulled the rope to close the trapdoor behind them.

"Stay perfectly still Usha. Don't say a word and keep the torch switched off," Lilly whispered.

The wooden door to the workshop swung open, creaking and grinding as it did. The store space was engulfed in sunlight. "RIGHT BEN, DON'T HANG ABOUT," a voice shouted. The girls squirmed and cringed as they hid below. It was Ben and his Dad, Mr Allens.

"Okay Dad, but where are they?"

"There should be a couple of toolboxes near the back wall. Here, I'll help you."

The two of them walked across the floorboards, sending dust through the holes and cracks onto the girls below. It seemed like forever as the girls looked at each other through the gloom trying to stay calm.

"GOT THEM," called Ben.

"Good lad. Let's get going then 'cos we don't want to be wasting any more time on that job."

The big wooden door closed as the sisters breathed a sigh of relief.

"Phew, that was close Lilly." Usha switched her torch on.

"Wow, look around Usha."

Usha waved the torch around to reveal a small room with a low tunnel running off in the direction of Fort Tourgis.

"We need the proper gear on Usha to go any further ….
Look, there's water further down the tunnel."

"You're right gal. Another day then." Usha turned to head back up the steps to the trapdoor when the light from her torch caught a glimmer of something below the steps. "What's that?" She held the beam of light still, to let Lilly see the object.

Lilly bent down and moved her hand across the floor. "Got it." She dusted the object off. "It's a pendant on a chain Usha. I wonder." She passed it to Usha.

"Let's get out of here." Usha pushed upwards on the trapdoor and the sisters clambered out.

Lilly quickly powered the light back on. "That was so close …. I thought they were supposed to be working at the other end of the island today."

"So did I." Usha took another look at the pendant they'd found. "This crystal looks the same type as those on your amulet Lilly. It's a dark reddish colour. I wonder if the chain is gold?" Usha hung it round her neck. "Should look nice when it's been cleaned up."

Lilly nodded in agreement. "So what exactly happened to me sis'?"

The girls sat there for a few minutes describing to each other what they saw and felt.

"It's amazing Usha. I seem to be getting more powers and gradually achieving some sort of control over them just by using my mind, or sub conscious, or something like that."

They both laughed.

"You don't really know do you?" Usha joked. *You have no idea sis'.*

"Come on. Let's go 'cos I'm hungry." Lilly beckoned to her sister. "We've got everything haven't we? …. I'll sort the light, you get the door."

The two girls stepped out into the daylight and locked the wooden door behind them.

They slowly walked hand in hand back down the lane towards Platte Saline. The sun was at it's hottest time of the day, high in the sky and looking to their left the girls could see two fishing boats bobbing up and down out in the bay. The colour of the sea was a mix of blue, indigo and almost black as they turned the last corner into the parking area where they'd left the scooter.

"Is that Grandad sat there?" Usha pointed over to the small grassy bank which formed the boundary between the parking area and the beach in Platte Saline Bay.

"It sure is." Lilly had already spotted Richard's van parked up.

As the sisters drew closer they could detect the smell of fish and chips.

"Gawd, I feel really hungry," Usha muttered.

Lilly nodded in agreement.

Richard's head turned as he heard the girls footsteps and he smiled. "Good to see you both." He gave them both a bag of fish and chips.

"Thought you'd be hungry. Your Mum told me you were looking after yourselves today and I spotted the scooter so I called in at the chippy at the harbour. I took a chance that you wouldn't be too long before you appeared. So tuck in girls."

Lilly and Usha sat down either side of Richard to devour their lunch. They were so hungry and it was rather nice to be sat there eating with the lapping of the sea and the expanse of sand in front of them.

"So where have you two been this morning?" Richard asked. "Because I've tried phoning you a couple of times and getting no answer."

The sisters jumped at the opportunity to tell their Grandad of the morning's adventure.

"An exiting development then and that would explain why you're both covered in dust. Tell you what, come up to my place this afternoon and I'll show you what I've found out. We'll take a look at the pendant as well eh, Usha? Your Grandma will be out so we'll be okay."

CHAPTER 11

AWESOME

It was early afternoon when Lilly and Usha arrived at their Grandad's house. Richard was busy in the back garden topping up the bird feeders. He'd normally do it first thing every morning but he had immersed himself on the internet trying to find any other information that tied in with the Lima Treasure and any possible connections with local families. As always, Richard had lost track of time when he was on his computers and what with meeting up with the girls earlier, his time had flown by.

"Hi Grandad." The two girls called as they walked into view.

"Hi girls, what's new?"

The girls shrugged their shoulders.

"Help yourselves to a drink out of the fridge, I'll be with you in a mo' .... Just got to finish dealing with these bird feeders."

The sisters disappeared into the kitchen to grab the cold drinks.

"Here you are Grandad." The girls stepped back into the garden. "We've got you a drink as well."

"Oh thanks girls, let's sit down on the bench shall we and I'll tell you what I found out at the library."

The three of them sat on the bench under the weeping willow tree. The tree gave a welcome dappled shade in the hot afternoon sun. It was a favourite place for Richard. He would often sit and watch the variety of birds as they helped themselves to the bird food he'd provided.

Richard explained to the girls how he'd found a book in the library which gave details of the shipwreck in the early eighteen hundreds and that it had, as part of it's cargo, the Treasure of Lima. It was listed in the Captain's Log as Lima Gold. Richard then continued to tell the girls how one of the sailors involved in the shipwreck was Peruvian. His surname being Garcia.

"That's Luis' surname," Lilly interrupted.

"Yeah I know …. It could be just a coincidence, but to be honest girls, I just don't know. We might have a bit more of a clue if young Chloe can find out who took that book out of the library twenty years ago."

"Hang on! What? How is that Chloe's involved?" Usha snapped. "She's a bit of a loose cannon."

"Hold it right there young lady," Richard replied. "Yes, she's had her problems over the last couple of years or so, but she's a good girl at heart. I'm disappointed in you Usha, you should be trying to help her instead of throwing accusations around."

Usha sighed.

Richard continued. "Anyway Lilly, this is why I told you to be careful when you're with Luis. It could be nothing but we don't know for certain."

"I do believe there's some connection. I can really feel something when I'm with him."

I bet you'd like to feel something! Usha raised her eyebrows and gave Lilly a stare.

"What's that look for?"

Usha sat there giggling.

"Right you two, let's take a look at this pendant you found."

Usha handed the pendant to her Grandad. "It's a bit grubby."

"Don't worry, we'll soon have it sparkling like new. Let's go in the old shop store and I'll sort it out." The two girls followed Richard into his store.

Richard had built the store years ago, across the length of the back garden to enable him to store goods for the convenience shop he used to run before he retired. These days it was full of tools and machinery which he used when he repaired other peoples lawn mowers and pretty much anything that was motorized.

"Get the lights please Lilly," Richard asked.

Without thinking, Lilly obliged in an instant as the store lit up.

"I'm impressed. You're going to have to show me how to do that 'cos my amulet is identical to yours Lilly." Richard walked over to one of the benches and switched on a buffing machine. It was actually a grinding wheel that he'd changed to use as a polishing wheel.

Richard carefully handled the pendant and chain as it was buffeted by the wheel, stopping occasionally to judge which part to polish next. It didn't take long and he switched the machine off.

"There you go Usha." Richard passed her the pendant. "As good as new I reckon. The chain is definitely gold, the same as the amulets, and the crystal ... What a beauty. What do you think Usha?"

"Wow Grandad, that's excellent and the colour is stunning. Such a deep red. That's brill, thanks." Usha's face lit up and she was smiling from ear to ear.

"I take it you're happy then?" Lilly asked.

"It's really cool eh .... The thing is, what does it do?"

The three of them laughed.

"I'm sure you'll find out at some point gal," Richard said. "And that's the point, none of us really know what each crystal does."

"Well, that's not strictly true Grandad," Lilly said. "I mean, they obviously work together like when I was able to control Usha's movements in Mr Allens' store."

"Yeah, I get what you're saying Lilly but each crystal must have, or transmits, different powers and it's going to take time to find out as and when you use these powers."

The girls nodded in agreement.

"One thing I do know for sure is that each time I use my amulet, the strength and power exerted appears to feel stronger. It's going to take practice to be able to control these powers so I don't hurt anyone," Lilly said.

"Exactly." Richard nodded in agreement.

"So, let's see what you can do Lilly," Richard said. "But just be careful."

"Okay." Lilly took two or three steps back from Richard and her sister. She closed her eyes and cleared her head of any thoughts. Lilly visualised the amulet and immediately sensed she was in control. She opened her eyes that were now glowing white. Lilly turned slowly and as she felt the surges of energy flowing through her body, she lifted her hands, pointing them at the various electrical tools on Richard's work bench. The tools burst into life creating a cacophony of noise and the lights in the store were flashing on and off.

Richard stood open mouthed and in awe at what he was witnessing whilst Usha jumped up and down clapping and laughing.

The noise subsided as Lilly lowered her hands and the machinery spluttered to a halt.

"AWESOME," Usha shouted.

Lilly's eyes returned to normal. "How was that?"

"Yeah ... Err ... Well, what can I say," Richard stuttered. "So is that what you intended to do Lilly?"

"Pretty much .... Each time, I seem to get better control."

"How about trying something else," Richard suggested. "Let's go back into the garden. This is going to sound a bit naff .... Usha, get some empty tin cans out of the recycling bin and line them up on that table in front of the wall."

"You've been watching too many cowboy films." Usha placed the cans on the table.

"You're kidding me, right?" Lilly asked.

"No, not at all," Richard replied. "Just stand about five metres away and see what you can do to each can."

Lilly shrugged her shoulders and faced the cans. "READY?" *Clint Eastwood eat your heart out!*

"IN YOUR OWN TIME," Richard shouted.

Lilly closed her eyes and concentrated on the image of her amulet in her mind and as she felt the energy building up, she raised her hands and opened her eyes to reveal the usual glowing and ..... Nothing. *What the hell?*

Richard and Usha watched with interest.

I'll try something slightly different. Lilly repeated her usual technique, but this time she raised just one hand and as the energy built she threw her arm forward in a thrusting motion .... "Clang!" The first can went flying. With another thrust the second can flew away.

Usha by now couldn't control herself as she laughed, shouted and jumped up and down. "YEAH, GO LILLY." Usha lost control of her next jump and she faltered towards and in front of the tin cans and at that moment, Lilly sent a power pulse hitting Usha, sending her flying across the lawn three metres away.

"LILLY, STOP." Richard ran to Usha. "You alright gal?"

Usha rolled over giggling with a big grin. "Awesome."

They all started laughing.

"Are you sure you're alright sis`?" Lilly asked.

"Yeah, course I am .... Why?"

"`Cos your new pendant you're wearing is pulsing." Lilly had a concerned look on her face. "Can't you feel it?"

Usha glanced down at the pendant around her neck to see it throbbing red pulses of light.

Richard and Lilly looked at each other and then glanced at Usha who was about to touch the pendant. "DON'T!" They both instinctively shouted ....

In that moment, Usha had grabbed the pendant. She stood there fully surrounded by, what looked like, some sort of energy field. It was the height of Usha and glowed red.

"AWESOME." Usha had a huge grin on her face.

Richard picked up one of the empty tin cans and threw it directly towards Usha. The can hit the energy field and flew off over the wall into the neighbour's garden. *Wow!*

"Try moving an arm Usha," Lilly said.

Usha stretched one arm out and turned around on the spot. The energy field immediately covered a larger area surrounding Usha.

That's incredible. Richard stepped a little closer to Usha. "You'd better let go of the pendant now Usha."

Usha loosened her grip on the pendant and it stopped pulsing, dispersing the energy field at the same time.

The three of them stood there momentarily stunned and then burst into cheers and laughter.

"Hmm, right," Richard said. "It looks like the power pulse from Lilly must have hit your pendant Usha, bringing it back to life so to speak."

Usha nodded in agreement. *Brill.*

"Could you see both of us through the shield sis`?" Lilly asked inquisitively.

"Yeah, sure, why?"

"Well, I don't know about you Grandad, but all I could see was the shield," Lilly said.

"You're right Lilly." Richard nodded in agreement. "It was as if you wasn't there Usha."

"AWESOME!…. Like being invisible."

"I wish," Richard joked. "Right then. You two need to go 'cos it's school tomorrow and your Grandma is due home about now. Just remember what I said, be careful, at least until we know more."

The two girls nodded and waved their goodbyes as they left their Grandad's house in an excited mood.

CHAPTER 12

FINGERS ON THE PULSE

Alex and Chloe had been having a fairly lazy morning watching a couple of films on DVDs and listening to their favourite music from a huge collection of CD's that Alex had accumulated over the years. It had been great for Chloe, after staying the night, not to have to deal with her family issues. She hadn't felt this much at ease since before her father died a couple of years ago and life certainly had picked up over the last two days as she and Alex had become closer.

"I really ought to be going Alex," Chloe whispered in his ear as she snuggled up a bit closer on the sofa they were sharing. She kissed him on the cheek. "My Mum probably needs a hand with some of the chores before she goes to work. She's on the afternoon shifts this week 'cos the hospital are short of staff .... Sorry Alex." Chloe lifted herself up from the sofa. "I really must go."

"Yeah I know .... Give me a couple of minutes to sort out and I'll give you a lift home." Alex left the room.

"MUM," Alex shouted. "I'm going out for a while. I'm going to give Chloe a lift home."

Alex popped his head round the door. "You ready gal?"

Chloe nodded and followed him out of the house as she smiled and waved to Alex's Mum.

The teenagers clambered onto the scooter. "Can you thank your Mum for me when you get back Alex?"

"Yeah of course .... She likes having you here anyway. Girly talk and all that." *And so do I.*

A few minutes later and the scooter pulled up outside Chloe's house. Most people knew where she lived because the garden had been left to do it's own thing since her father died. It was very overgrown and definitely needed a bit of muscle.

Alex and Chloe approached the front door which was slightly open.

This looks a bit odd. "Let me get the door Chloe." Alex grabbed the door and pushed. The door stuck halfway. Alex peered around the door and to his horror saw Chloe's Mum sprawled out on the floor. *Oh shit!*

Alex glanced back at Chloe. "It's your Mum Chloe .... She's out for the count".

Alex and Chloe squeezed though the gap of the partly open doorway. Alex closed the door behind them to give the pair of them more room to move.

"Oh Mum, what have you done?" Chloe sobbed as she knelt down by Carol, her Mum.

"Chloe ... Chloe.... I think she's just passed out 'cos she's drunk. Can't you smell the drink on her?"

Chloe nodded and continued to sob uncontrollably.

"We need to move her so we can try and help her. Chloe ... Are you listening?" *Jeez what a mess.*

Chloe stood up wiping away the tears from her face. "Nearest room is the lounge .... We'll have to see if we can move Mum onto the sofa."

"Okay. I'll get hold of your Mum under her arms and you get her legs. Just take it nice and easy Chloe."

Luckily, Carol was quite slim and not too tall and the two teenagers eventually managed to manoeuvre her onto the sofa, propping her up slightly between the armrest and the back.

"I'll get some black coffee on the go." Chloe disappeared into the kitchen.

Alex knelt down and started to gently tap the cheeks of Carol. "Mrs Mollins ... Mrs Mollins ... Hello. Come on." Alex was quietly spoken as he didn't want to scare her. *She's obviously been drinking in this room.* There was empty bottles strewn about the floor. Partially filled glasses and broken glass were randomly dotted around the room. *Some serious drinking.*

Chloe stepped back into the room and placed a cup of coffee on the small side table next to the sofa. She had a blanket under her arm. "How's Mum doing?" She tenderly placed the blanket over Carol. "Oh Mum, Mum."

Chloe stroked Carol's hand as her Mum stirred and slowly opened her eyes.

Chloe threw her arms around her Mum and kissed her on the cheek. "Oh Mum .... You're gonna be alright. Don't worry."

"I ought to go," Alex said. "I think your Mum will be alright once she's sobered up."

Chloe stood up and hugged Alex. "Thanks Alex. I don't know how I would have managed without you." She kissed him gently on the cheek.

"No worries .... I tell you what, I promised Ben that I'd pick him up from work, so I'll call back round later to see if everything's okay."

"That'd be nice." Chloe kissed him again.

Alex disappeared from view out of the front door.

Chloe glanced at her watch. *Jeez, Mum was due at work half an hour ago. I'd better phone them to let 'em know she won't be in.*

Chloe found the hospital number on her phone and dialled it. After a couple of rings someone answered at the other end. *"Alderney Mignot Hospital. How can I help?"*

"Oh hello .... My name's Chloe Mollins and I'm ringing on behalf of my Mum, Carol. Unfortunately she isn't very well and she won't be able to come in to work today, sorry."

"Right, thanks for letting us know Chloe. Hope your Mum's better soon," replied the voice on the other end of the phone.

Chloe hung up.

"WHAT THE HELL DO YOU THINK YOU'RE DOING?" Carol shouted in a drunken slur. She'd been stood behind Chloe for the duration of the phone call.

Chloe turned to face her Mum, whose eyes were full of hatred.

"HOW DARE YOU TELL THEM I'M NOT GOING TO WORK," Carol shrieked with venom.

"But Mum ..."

Carol staggered, managing to stay upright with the aid of the wall. "AND WHO WAS THAT WITH YOU?"

"Mum, you know who ..."

"DON'T YOU GIVE ME ANY LIES," Carol interrupted with a menacing voice. "IT WAS SOME BOY WASN'T IT? YOU LITTLE TRAMP!" Carol's voice was raging. "I BET HE'S

ONLY AFTER ONE THING …. TO GET INSIDE YOUR KNICKERS!"

Chloe tried to say something. Anything. But her Mum was out of control. The alcohol was in control.

"YOU'RE A TRAMP," Carol raged, "A TART." She ranted out of control as her legs, arms and hands were swinging at Chloe.

"Mum. Don't. You're hurting me," Chloe cried out, but still the blows to her head kept landing. Chloe finally lashed out to defend herself and Carol slumped to the floor.

Chloe turned, blood running down her face as she staggered out of the front door in floods of tears.

Alex pulled his scooter over on to the gravel parking space by the side of the lighthouse. He'd drove round to the north eastern side of the island to pick up Ben who'd been helping his Dad on a carpentry job, fitting a new kitchen.

Alex sat there admiring the lighthouse. He'd never really studied it before. The lighthouse was also known as the Mannez Lighthouse and was constructed in 1912 using local granite stone. It had a height of thirty seven metres. *Impressive.*

"Hi Alex." A voice interrupted his thoughts.

"Oh hi Ben…. You been busy?"

"Just completed the job, it looks good …. Do you know, we had to go to my Dad's store today for a couple of toolboxes. Haven't been there in months and now twice in two days … Ha! It was strange though. I could have sworn that someone else was there. Obviously not, but it just seemed weird at the time".

"Oh right. That does sound a bit strange …. Hop on. I've just got to call in on Chloe on the way 'cos I promised."

"That's fine."

By the time the two lads reached Chloe's house, Alex had told Ben about how he'd found Chloe's Mum. They screeched to a halt on the driveway to see Chloe lying face down and motionless.

"CHLOE," Alex shouted as he jumped off the scooter and ran to her. *Oh shit!* "Ben, check in the house for Mrs Mollins."

Ben dashed past Alex and Chloe into the house, his heart thumping heavily in his chest. He reappeared almost instantly. "We need an ambulance Alex. I'll phone now." *What a bloody mess.*

Alex gently turned Chloe over, cradling her head in his hands. *There's so much blood. How long has she been lying here? Why did I leave her?* Thoughts were racing through his mind.

Ben knelt down beside Alex and put his arm around his shoulders. "Keep thinking positive thoughts mate …. She'll be alright. She's a survivor." *This looks seriously bad.*

Alex nodded to his friend as tears rolled down his face. "If anything happens to Chloe …" Alex sobbed.

"It won't mate. The ambulance is on its way. I can hear the sirens in the distance."

Alex tenderly kissed Chloe on the cheek. He ran his hand across her forehead to try and move some of the blood matted hair that was stuck to her face. "Oh Chloe." He sobbed as he rocked her back and forth like a baby.

"Excuse me, we need to get through." A voice from behind interrupted Alex's cries of anguish. Ben pulled his friend away from Chloe to let the paramedics work on the girl.

"Mrs Mollins is inside." Ben pointed to the house. "She needs help as well."

By now, two or three people had assembled on the driveway to see what all the commotion was all about.

"Come on now, give these people some room to work in." A voice boomed through the crowd. It was the local Sergeant, Peter Cordy. He approached the two lads. "Come with me boys, there's nothing more you can do here."

"But Sergeant."

"No buts. I'll take you up to the hospital for a quick check up and then we'll see how Chloe and her Mum are getting on when the ambulance gets them up there, okay?"

The boys nodded and followed Peter.

An hour had passed. The boys had been checked over and had given statements to the Sergeant with Alex also giving details of the events at Chloe's house earlier that day.

Ben was pacing back and forth across the waiting area in the hospital whilst Alex was sat silently in his own thoughts .... *I should have stayed. I could have stopped this happening.*

They'd been told that Mrs Mollins was sobering up in a private room. She had no injuries but had been sectioned, which meant that they would be flying her out to the larger island of Guernsey to receive treatment and counselling at the major hospital. Alderney is one of a group of islands that fall under the legal jurisdiction of Guernsey.

Chloe was in the intensive care unit and was being monitored constantly.

The main entrance doors opened. Luis, Lilly and Usha walked in accompanied by Richard. The three teenagers gathered round Ben and Alex whilst Richard went off to find someone to see how Chloe was.

Richard eventually found a nurse. It was Alex's Mum, Mrs Bean. Coincidentally she was covering the shift that Chloe's Mum should have been working.

"Hi Beth, How's young Chloe doing?"

"Not too good I'm afraid .... Such a shame 'cos she's a really nice girl when you get to know her. She stayed last night at my place and this morning you know, 'cos she's taken a shine to my Alex. It's hit him hard I think."

"I'm sure it has." *Poor Chloe is always the one to suffer.*

Beth continued. "Lots of scratches and bruises, but ...."

"But what?"

64

"She must have received a heavy blow to the head. There's been internal bleeding and a blood clot has formed in her brain."

"Meaning what?" Richard had a concerned look on his face.

"It means that if the clot doesn't disperse in the next couple of hours, it could leave her paralysed."

Richard gasped. *Bloody hell!* He thanked Beth and returned to join the teenagers who were trying to cheer Alex up. Richard whispered in Lilly's ear. "I'm going outside, follow me in a couple of minutes." Lilly smiled in acknowledgement.

Richard walked out of the main doors.

"I'm just going outside to see where Grandad is." Lilly walked out through the doors.

"What's this all about Grandad?"

Richard told Lilly exactly what Beth had told him a few minutes earlier. "We have to try and help."

"But how? Neither of us know if I'm able to do that sort of thing."

"I know Lilly. If it is possible, it means that you've literally got to get inside her head. It's dangerous but I feel that we have to try."

"You do know Grandad, that if it works, Chloe might remember something." Lilly held her Grandad's hand for reassurance.

"It's a risk we're going to have to take Lilly. Do it. I'll go and find nurse Bean to see if she'll let a couple of you sit in with Chloe."

Lilly and Richard walked back inside the hospital. Lilly went back to her friends in the waiting area whilst Richard disappeared down one of the corridors to look for the nurse. Five minutes later he returned with Beth.

"Alex. Lilly. Come with me please," Beth said in a softly spoken voice and she led them down the corridor to the intensive care unit. "Right then you two, don't worry about all the equipment attached to Chloe. Just sit quietly either side of her. You can talk to her but she won't respond physically because she's heavily sedated. The experts always say that the patient can hear you, so it does give them some comfort and assurance that a friend is there with them."

Beth pushed the door open. "There you go guys. I'll be back in a little while."

"Thank you Mum," Alex said and the teenagers walked to Chloe's bed.

Lilly gasped and put her hand to her mouth as the enormity of the situation dawned on her. Chloe lay there motionless with various different tubes and sensors attached to her. She was covered in bruises notably around her eyes and her head was bandaged where she had obviously suffered a bad head wound.

Alex sat down to the left of the bed and tenderly held Chloe's hand and started whispering to his girlfriend. Tears were rolling down his face.

Lilly handed Alex a tissue. "Here Alex, take this." She sat down close to Chloe to the right of the bed and held Chloe's other hand gently.

Lilly reached out and tenderly placed her right hand on Chloe's forehead. She breathed deeply and cleared her mind of any thoughts. Again, she took a deep breath as she lowered her head to hide her eyes from Alex. She concentrated on the image of her amulet in her mind and then instantly she could see what Chloe was thinking. For a moment, Lilly thought she was imagining the images and thoughts, but no, what she was seeing was events that had happened between Chloe and her Mum earlier that day. *This feels like I'm in Chloe's dreams.*

Lilly could feel her eyes pulsing and her power was increasing. She delved deeper into Chloe's brain and suddenly she 'felt' the arteries and veins flowing around her friend's brain. *There it is, the blood clot.* Lilly's thoughts were massaging the arteries around the blood clot …. And then it released itself as the blood flowed through into the blood starved brain. Lilly could see the nerves instantly starting to heal and the electrical impulses kick starting the brain back into life.

Lilly slowly moved her hand away from Chloe's forehead and she gasped as the amulet relinquished it's power.

"You alright Lilly?" Alex asked.

"Err … Yeah I'm fine." Lilly lifted her head. "Must be tired, I keep nodding off. I tell you what, I'll leave you two alone for a while." Lilly stood up to leave.

"Alex. Lilly," Chloe murmured.

"Oh Chloe," Alex whispered. "I thought I'd lost you."

Lilly smiled. "I'll see you guys later." She left the room feeling euphoric. *Brilliant .... Amazing.*

Lilly entered the waiting area and beamed a big smile towards her Grandad. He nodded approvingly.

"I think Chloe's going to be alright." Lilly was unable to control her voice.

The four friends couldn't conceal their delight as Luis wrapped his arms round Lilly and kissed her passionately. Usha's smile on her face couldn't hide her delight that Ben had put his arm around her shoulders.

Richard stood there silently. *My Granddaughters are growing up.*

"Come on guys," Richard said. "Fish and chips are on me. Let's go down to Braye Chippy."

"What about Alex?" Ben asked.

"His Mum is going to take him home when she's finished her shift here at the hospital. Besides, he wants to stay with Chloe."

"Here you go guys." Richard passed the generous portions of fish and chips around.

It was a glorious evening, sat at the diners tables outside the chippy. Richard sat there quietly thinking about the day's events, whilst the four youngsters were discussing Chloe and her predicament.

"I'm off then," Richard announced. "Who wants a lift home?"

Ben and Usha shouted, "YES PLEASE."

"Is it alright if Luis gives me a lift Grandad?" Lilly asked.

"I'll make sure she's not late," Luis added.

"That's fine ..... Just remember it's school tomorrow."

Richard clambered into his van and beckoned Usha and Ben. The three waved as the van pulled away.

"Your Grandad's alright you know." Luis put his arm round Lilly.

"Yeah, he's the best." She kissed Luis full on the lips and they were both lost in the moment.

"Come on gal .... I'll take you home. It's been a long eventful day."

CHAPTER 13

DO YOUR SUMS

"TIME FOR SCHOOL GIRLS," Susan shouted upstairs.

"We're coming Mum." Usha picked up her school bag and peeked round Lilly's bedroom door. "You ready sis'?"

"Yeah, sure." *Have I got everything I need for the exam?* Lilly was in her final year at school and today was her last day and her last exam.

The two girls bounded down the stairs, jumping off the final two steps into the hallway.

"How many times do I have to tell you?" Susan said. "Don't jump off the stairs like that, you'll hurt yourselves."

The sisters looked at each other and started giggling. "Sorry Mum," Lilly said. "We'd better get going, you coming sis'?"

"Okay girls, I'll see you later. Good luck with the exam Lilly."

"By the way Lilly, are you working at the café after school?" Susan asked.

"Yes Mum, but I'll finish my shift in time to pick up Usha. Okay?"

Susan hugged both girls before waving to them as they left on their scooter.

It was a two minute journey down Braye Hill to St Annes School, the only school on Alderney. The girls waved to friends they passed, who were walking to school.

What a lovely morning, Lilly thought. The air was crisp and clear with blue skies all around. The sea, which was visible across Braye Bay directly in front of them glistened in the sun with three or four various shades of blue.

"It's like a mill pond out there today," Usha said. "Too nice for school," she joked.

The girls parked up outside the school and made their way inside, casually chatting to friends they passed.

"Right Usha, you have a good day. I'll pick you up this afternoon after school."

"You too sis' and do your best in the exam." The girls hugged and headed off in opposite directions to find their lockers.

Lilly had her head in her locker. *Where's that ruler? And I need a spare pen.* "What the ..." Lilly squealed.

Two hands had gently grabbed her waist from behind. She spun round to face Luis who instantly kissed her. *Wow!*

Lilly eased Luis away slightly. "Luis, you shouldn't be here. If any of the teachers see you, they'll kick you out. You need to go now or they'll be trouble."

"Well there's gratitude for you." It was Alex who was stood slightly behind Luis. "I did tell him Lilly, but he wouldn't listen."

Lilly threw her arms around Alex and kissed him on the cheek. "Alex, I didn't think I'd see you today."

"Exam!.... Last one, same as you." Lilly nodded. "Luis picked me up on his scooter 'cos mine's broke down and he was passing my place on his way to work."

"How's Chloe?" Lilly asked.

Alex's face lit up. "She's gonna be alright. Just needs rest now."

"Err, I think we need to make a move," Luis interrupted. "We seem to have attracted a crowd."

The three friends glanced around to see that they were surrounded by at least twenty other students.

Lilly spotted two teachers approaching from further down the corridor. She grabbed hold of Luis and kissed him passionately on the lips. Luis could feel his face reddening up with embarrassment as the crowd cheered and clapped.

"Gotta go .... Good luck both of you in the exam." Luis squeezed through the crowd of pupils and ran off down the corridor to the exit.

Alex and Lilly sat down. They were in the school hall with about twenty other students for their final exam of the year before leaving school for the last time.

The two friends were both sixteen and both in their final year at school. These exams would determine their future in terms of employment, or further education which a lot of the kids preferred. To carry on their education it meant studying for A level qualifications in Guernsey. This would mean leaving Alderney which Lilly was far from happy about. Alex on the other hand eventually wanted to go to university which meant he would have to achieve his A levels first.

"Right everybody." A voice from the front of the hall. "Good morning. You have two hours for this maths exam. Good luck. You may start now."

"What a relief." Alex sighed as he sauntered out of the school hall with Lilly. "I'm glad that's over with."

"Yeah, bit on the tough side." Lilly glanced down the corridor to see it was completely blocked with students.

"What's going on down there?" Alex asked. "Come on, let's take a look."

The two friends walked towards the crowd of students who by now were shouting and muttering between themselves.

"That's your Mum there Alex." Lilly pointed towards the middle of the crowd.

"What's she doing here?"

Lilly shrugged her shoulders.

The other students stepped away from each other allowing Lilly and Alex to walk through to see Chloe and her Mum stood in the middle of the melee looking totally perplexed.

"Mum. Chloe. What's going on?" Alex stuttered.

Chloe stepped forward shakily and threw her arms around Lilly.

Lilly was frozen to the spot momentarily. "Chloe."

"Lilly," Chloe whispered in Lilly's ear, "Lilly, you saved me …. You really did save me."

Lilly tried to compose herself. She could see tears were running down Chloe's swollen and bruised face.

"Chloe, you're confused."

"Mum, what are you doing here?" Alex asked.

"The hospital discharged Chloe this morning," Mrs Bean explained, "providing she stays with us, being as I'm a nurse. I

70

was taking her home but she was insistent on coming here first to see Lilly. I've no idea why. Do you know why Lilly?"

"No. Sorry Mrs Bean. I really don't know." *Another white lie.*

"Right then. Come on Chloe," Mrs Bean said. "There's been far too much excitement this morning young lady. You coming Alex? 'cos I can give you a lift seeing as your scooter has broken down."

"Yeah, okay Mum."

Alex turned to Lilly and kissed her on the cheek. "You at the café later?"

"I'm on my way up there now. Just got to collect all my books, get the scooter and I'm away. I'll see you later maybe."

CHAPTER 14

SOCIAL MEDIA

It was lunchtime and the café was busy with local workers and tourists. The place was heaving and Lilly had been left by herself. *By myself again. Not for the first time. Bloody typical.*

"Any chance of some service over here?" boomed a voice from over in the corner.

"YEAH, I NEED ANOTHER CUPPA OVER HERE DARLIN'." Another voice shouted.

There was muttering and moaning about the service to be heard in every direction as Lilly struggled to keep her composure. She was flustered and could feel her anger at being left in this situation building up when the door flew open.

It was Luis. He stood there, glanced around and immediately realised his girlfriend was being hassled. He was only seventeen, but he was a strapping young lad with a physical presence. The murmurings subsided as he walked over to the counter and kissed Lilly on the cheek.

"YOU GOT PROBLEMS GAL?" He made sure everyone in the café heard.

"Oh Luis. Am I glad to see you. Any chance you can help?"

"Yeah sure. But I'm not exactly dressed for it," Luis joked, as he looked himself up and down in his scruffy boiler suit.

"No probs'." Lilly threw him an apron and grinned at him lovingly.

"You gotta be kidding me." Luis gasped as he tied the apron around his waist.

Lilly giggled and blew him a kiss.

"What do you need me to do?" Luis placed his hands on his hips in disgust.

"You clear the empties from the tables and take them to the kitchen. Then take the orders whilst I serve here at the counter and prepare any food for orders."

"Is that all madam." Luis had a huge grin.

"It won't be for long. The café will go quiet after lunch ….
About an hour." *Or two!*

"Hmmm." Luis picked up an empty tray and went over to
the tables.

Lilly busied herself with the job in hand, occasionally giving
Luis a big admiring smile. *He's all mine.*

Lilly sighed with relief. It had been hectic for the last couple
of hours.

"My hero." Lilly purred as she threw her arms around Luis
and kissed him on the lips.

The two remaining customers at the tables smiled and
looked away.

The pair sat down at one of the empty tables for a well
deserved drink. They had no sooner settled when Celia Perez,
the reporter from the local weekly paper entered the café
accompanied by a cameraman. She walked up to their table,
microphone in hand.

"It's Lilly isn't it?" Celia pushed the microphone purposely
forward into Lilly's face. "Lilly Gat. That's right isn't it?"

"Who's asking?" Luis interrupted.

"It's alright Luis," Lilly said. She held his hand to reassure
him and herself. "Yeah, that's me … And?"

"Perhaps you could comment on the incident at Mrs
Mollins' house yesterday involving her daughter Chloe?" Celia
asked.

"Not really," Lilly replied. "I wasn't there was I … And you
know that surely from the Police report if you're doing you're
job right eh?" Lilly looked Celia directly into her eyes.

"You was there at the hospital though …." Celia pressed on.

"And? Chloe's my friend. I went to see her." *I can see
where this is going.* Lilly held Luis' hand a little tighter.

"Apparently Lilly, I have it on good authority that you was
present in Chloe's room when she made a miraculous
recovery." Celia pressured Lilly further.

Lilly squeezed Luis' hand a little more and she could feel
her heart pounding faster in her chest.

Celia pounced on Lilly's hesitation. "This isn't the first time is it Lilly?"

Lilly's eyes glanced at Luis. He had the look of someone who also wanted an answer.

"I have no idea what you're talking about." Lilly had a faltering voice. She took a deep breath. "It's just a coincidence that I was there. If you have information on so called good authority, then show me what proof you've got."

"But ..."

"Thought so .... You're following up on an Alderney rumour. You're clutching at straws for a story that doesn't exist." Lilly's voice was getting more confident. "As for your comment of 'you have it on good authority', well I'm sorry, you haven't, 'cos everyone at the hospital has to sign a confidentiality agreement. I have nothing further to say on the subject."

"Lilly. I'm just doing my job."

"Yeah. Not very well it seems." Luis intervened.

"You're digging for something that isn't there." Lilly released Luis' hand and stood up. "I need to close now .... Luis, do you mind getting the door for these two cretins?"

Celia turned to Lilly as she stepped out of the café. "I'll be keeping an eye on you."

Luis closed the door. "Do you mind telling me what that was all about?"

Lilly placed her hands around Luis' waist. "It's nothing Luis, absolutely nothing." She kissed him on the cheek and noticed there was a look of doubt in his eyes.

"Look Luis, if it makes you feel any better, think about it. You was at the hospital as well. I went to see Chloe and sat with Alex. He never left the room. Ask him yourself if you don't believe me. I left the room before Alex. End of."

"It's not that I don't believe you gal, it just sounds a bit odd if you know what I mean and all of a sudden you've now got a reporter on the case."

"Luis please, I don't want us falling out over this. It's just silly nonsense. Come on, hold me tight and give me a kiss."

The pair stood there for a moment lost in their passionate embrace when Lilly suddenly remembered about having to pick

Usha up from school. Lilly glanced at her watch over Luis' shoulder.

"Sorry Luis, I need to go right now. Got to pick Usha up from school."

Lilly was sat on her scooter outside the school. She was lost in her own thoughts as she waited for Usha. She was worried about Chloe. She was worried about Luis. She was also concerned about Celia. *What if? What if? What if?* Her head was swimming with different scenarios.

"LILLY. LILLY." A shout interrupted her thoughts. It was Usha. School was out and crowds of students were heading home. Lilly spotted Usha mingling in and out of the crowds and waved to her.

"OVER HERE USHA."

Usha hugged her sister.

"Had a good day sis'?"

"Yeah. Sure. Can we just go?" Usha demanded.

The sisters drove off on the scooter.

As soon as the school was out of sight, Lilly felt a nudge in her back. "PULL OVER."

The scooter slowed to a stop and Lilly turned to Usha. "Come on, what's up?"

"School, that's what …. And so called friends," Usha muttered. "There's been all sorts of stuff going round the school about you Lilly. Some of my friends have even called you a witch. It's all over the local social media. What are we going to do sis'?"

Lilly placed her arm around her sister's shoulders to reassure her. "Not sure sis'. Let's go and drop off your stuff at home. Then we'll go and see Grandad to see if he can help sort this mess out."

The two girls arrived at Richard's home.

"I bet he's working round here." Usha turned the corner of the house.

"GRANDAD," Lilly shouted.

"Over here." Richard was bent over in the corner of the garden pruning a few of his rose bushes. He stood up to see

75

where the girls were and as he did, he caught himself on one of the rose thorns, gouging a deep scratch in his arm. "Ouch. You bugger ..."

"LANGUAGE GRANDAD," Usha shouted.

Blood was pouring down Richard's arm. "Let's take a look Grandad." Lilly held his arm.

Richard held his arm out and before he could do or say anything, Lilly passed her hand over his arm and it was healed.

"Hmmm, thanks Lilly."

"How did you do that Lilly?" Usha asked.

"Don't know .... It just seemed instinctive."

"I'm not being funny Lilly, but you've got to stop doing this sort of stuff," Richard said. "You just don't know who's going to be around. You've got to be more objective as to how you use these powers. Do you understand what I'm saying?"

"You're right Grandad, but at the time, it seems the right thing to do."

Richard smiled. "I know .... Anyway, why the visit?"

Usha started to tell Richard what was going on at school.

Richard interrupted. "Tell you what, let's go for a walk and you can tell me all about it."

As the three of them sauntered off down the road, Usha picked up where she'd left off and explained to Richard what had been happening at the school.

"Okay, as I see it, the first thing to do is sort out the social media stuff," Richard said. "It's a big ask, but I'll try and fix all that tonight when I get on my computers."

Usha smiled and put her arm around Richard's waist as they walked further down the road.

"Chloe knows I helped her," Lilly stuttered.

"What?" Usha asked.

"What?" Richard exclaimed. "Mind you, we knew we were taking a chance."

"Well, at least, I think she knows," Lilly explained. "She visited the school earlier today with Alex's Mum and she told me that I'd healed her. The thing is, when I sat with Chloe at the hospital, I saw images and her thoughts of what had happened earlier that day. I couldn't help it. It just happened."

Usha looked at Lilly in a knowing sort of way.

"So I'm guessing now," Lilly continued. "But do you think it's possible that at that moment, Chloe knew it was me in her thoughts?"

"I suppose so, but we're not going to know for sure are we," Richard replied.

"There's something else as well," Lilly said. "That reporter woman, Celia Perez, was at the café this afternoon and she was digging. She reckons she's got inside information from the hospital."

Richard sighed. "Right okay girls, for the moment you're going to have to bluff 'em out. Be careful what you say if anyone asks. In the meantime I'll try and catch up with Alex's Mum, the nurse, to see if I can find anything out. And just give Celia a wide berth for now 'cos believe me, she's an interfering busy body."

"CHICKENS!!" Usha shouted.

"What the ..." exclaimed Richard.

Richard and the girls had been so preoccupied in conversation, they'd walked into the field where the chickens were kept. They all laughed as the birds surrounded them demanding food.

"Okay girls, it's time for you to go. Your Mum and Dad will be wondering where you are and it looks like I've got a busy night ahead on my computers."

The two sisters gave Richard a big hug and ran off.

It was the following morning and Beth was trying to wake Alex up. "ALEX. ALEX."

Alex stirred as he turned over on the sofa he'd slept on overnight, to see his Mum stood over him. He glanced at his watch and could just make out the time through his sleepy eyes. He stretched out his arms and yawned.

"Mum, it's half past five in the morning."

"I know what time it is my lad. You need to be up and about 'cos I'm due in work at six. You've got to be up to look after Chloe. She's still in bed getting some much needed rest, but she's still very shaky on her feet."

"Okay Mum." Alex pulled himself up onto his feet. "Don't worry, you get off to work."

77

Beth smiled and kissed Alex on his forehead. "You're a good lad." Beth stepped out of the house.

Richard was on a mission this morning. He'd been busy throughout the night on his computers, sorting out his Grandchildren's concerns on social media. It had been complicated. Now he needed to find out what problems there were at the hospital, if any. *Need to do it without drawing any suspicion.*

Richard pulled the van into the hospital car park. *Pretty quiet.* He climbed out and sat down on one of the garden benches that surrounded the car park and glanced at his watch. *Nearly break time for the nurses.*

The main door of the hospital entrance opened and two nurses walked out, cups of tea in hand. Richard spotted Beth.

"Hi Beth, fancy a chat?"

"Yeah, why not. What brings you here?"

"Just came to ask how Chloe was doing."

Beth smiled. "She'll be okay. Still very shaken up though …. Did you know that she had a severe head wound Richard?"

"No I didn't Beth. All I knew was what you told me the other day when I brought her friends up to the hospital." *Not strictly true!*

"It's just that …. I shouldn't be telling you any of this Richard."

There was an uncomfortable pause.

Richard gently held Beth's hand.

"Beth, I've known you since you was knee high to a grasshopper. I've watched as you've grown into a young mother with a family to be proud of. And you have a very important job." Richard tried to sound caring as he spoke.

"The thing is, after you and Chloe's friends left, the consultant in charge that day called in to monitor Chloe's progress. After removing her head bandage to inspect the wound, it was if nothing had been there. Unbelievable. He also checked the monitoring machines that were attached to Chloe to look at the read outs. Apparently there was some sort of an anomaly at about the time her blood clot dispersed when young Lilly was sat alongside Chloe with my Alex."

"And that proves what?"

"Well, nothing really …. It just seemed very odd at the time."

"Who was the consultant?"

"You're really pushing your luck Richard. It was Dr Perez." Beth stuttered.

"I had a feeling it would be him."

"Why?"

"Have you looked at social media from yesterday?"

Beth gave Richard a quizzical look.

"Obviously not. Typical Alderney scenario that takes only one comment to spark a debate off and generally coming up with the wrong answers. And you know who's stirring it up? Dr Perez's daughter, Celia."

"The reporter?… The doctor should know better. He shouldn't be telling his daughter anything, especially with the job she has."

Richard nodded in agreement. "Look, I need to go Beth."

"Yeah, and I need to get back to work." Beth glanced at her watch.

"Beth. Thanks for the info." Richard turned to go. "Hand on heart Beth, what you've told me, stays with me and if I was you I'd watch yourself with Dr Perez."

"I know." Beth walked back into the hospital.

Richard breathed a sigh of relief and he returned to his van.

Better call in at Lilly's place.

CHAPTER 15

MIND OVER MATTER

Usha was at school. She'd left her sister in bed earlier that morning, zedding! It was break time and Usha had her head in her locker looking for books for her next lesson when she felt someone standing close behind her. She glanced round to see Ben who had a smile as big as the proverbial Cheshire Cat.

Ben placed his hands around her waist and kissed Usha on the cheek.

"Hi," Ben said.

"Oh hello Ben." *Awesome.*

Usha closed her locker and held Ben's hand. "Let's go and sit down over there for a minute." Usha pointed over towards a bench.

The two youngsters pushed themselves through the students, who were seemingly walking back and forth aimlessly.

They sat there holding hands in a slightly embarrassed way.

"What lesson have you got next?" Usha asked.

"History ... I hate History. What have you got?"

"English .... I hate English."

And the two friends burst into laughter and spoke in unison. "I hate school."

Usha began to feel faint.

"Usha, are you alright? All of a sudden you look dreadful." Ben was concerned.

Usha could barely hear Ben's voice. Everything was becoming a blur. But what she could feel was her pendant pulsing underneath her school blouse. She could feel herself falling, or so she thought.

Ben could barely contain himself. "USHA .... What's happening?"

Usha was now prostrate on the corridor floor. A crowd was gathering around the two friends and she could feel herself slipping from consciousness. Then, blackness. Somehow, Usha was connecting with Lilly's thoughts. *How can this be, Lilly's in trouble.* She knew it, she could feel it, and now .... Usha could see what Lilly was seeing.

Lilly was still in bed at home. She was in a dreamlike state. Her amulet was pulsing and taking her to an unknown place and Lilly seemed to be not in control. She was able to think, and her visions were almost in black and white, blurred around the edges. *Lilly was with Chloe, or so she thought.* And then she realised what she was seeing. *Chloe's dreaming.*

Lilly could see Chloe and her Mum fighting again, as she had done when Lilly had saved Chloe at the hospital. But this time she spotted something in the hand of Chloe's Mum. *A bottle of pills. So that's why Mrs Mollins had been so violent. She was high on drugs as well as being drunk.*

What happened to the pills? A thought popped into Lilly's head. It was Usha. **Find the bottle Lilly.** Another thought from Usha. Lilly realised that somehow, Usha was communicating with her.

I can see Chloe struggling with her Mum. Bloody hell she's knocking the shit out of Chloe, the bitch! Now Chloe's fighting back, go on girl! Christ her Mum must be high as a kite, she's not holding back. Chloe's just lashed out at her Mum in self defence and knocked the bottle out of her Mum's hand. Chloe's picked it up and stuffed it in her pocket and now she's staggering out of the front door and has collapsed on the drive.

Where are the pills now? *I can't see them Usha and Chloe's dream is becoming fainter.*

What's happening to Chloe? Another thought from Usha.

Lilly concentrated on her power and then ..... *I can see the bottle next to Chloe.* Lilly looked closer, *There's a name on it .... P E R ... Perez, and it's empty. Oh jeez, Chloe's took all the pills. She's taken an overdose and she's .... She's dying. Help her Usha.*

Lilly woke up in a cold sweat as the amulet relinquished it's control.

In the same moment, Usha's pendant stopped pulsing and she was conscious. She sat up surrounded by a crowd of students and Ben was knelt beside her holding her hand.

81

"Jeez gal, what was all that about?" Ben had a concerned tone of voice.

"How long have I been out Ben?"

"A few seconds, you must have fainted."

The young lad helped Usha to her feet as the crowd dispersed.

Awesome.

"Ben, phone Alex and get him to check on Chloe."

Ben gave Usha a stern look.

"JUST DO IT BEN."

"Okay, Okay ….. Anything to keep the peace."

Usha kissed Ben on the cheek. "Trust me."

Usha got her phone out and quickly phoned for an ambulance to attend Mrs Bean's house where Chloe was staying. Within two minutes, the sound of a siren could be heard as the ambulance sped up the hill.

"We'd better get off to our lessons Ben."

"S'pose. I'll catch up with you later."

Richard drove his van onto the drive at Lilly's house. His Granddaughter was sat outside on one of the benches.

"Hi Grandad."

"Hi princess." Richard kissed her on the cheek. "How's things?"

"Well …." Lilly hesitated and then she told him how herself and Usha had communicated and been in Chloe's dream. And hopefully, how they'd saved Chloe's life.

"Wow! And I thought I was having a bad day. Someone at the hospital isn't doing their job right and I think I know who it is. There should have been a toxicology report done on Chloe's Mum. If there had have been, Chloe might not be where she is now….. How do you feel now Lilly?"

"Yeah, I'm okay. I'm just so worried about Chloe."

"I thought I saw the ambulance travelling at speed up to Mrs Bean's house. Hopefully, they got to Chloe in time."

"It's not just that though Grandad. Chloe knows. She definitely knows about us." Lilly was feeling anxious. "I don't know how she knows, but I saw it in her sub conscious today. Chloe knows about the amulet and the Treasure Of Lima. I also saw a vague memory of a map, a really old map. There was just so much going on in her head, it was difficult to unravel all the information."

"We knew there was a chance that something like this could happen when we made the decision to clear the blood clot in her brain at the hospital Lilly. The point is, how do we get round the problem?"

Lilly shrugged her shoulders. "I don't have any ideas at the moment. This particular power of mind control is obviously a two way thing, don't you think?"

Lilly continued. "The other thing to consider is the fact that Chloe sub consciously must have got into my head whilst I was asleep. She contacted me. Probably a cry for help."

"Hmmm ... Well at least we've got a couple of days to think it through, but the priority for now is Chloe's well being eh?"

"You're right of course."

Lilly glanced at her watch. "Sorry Grandad, I need to go. I'm looking after the café this afternoon." Lilly gave Richard a kiss on the cheek and a hug. "I'll see you later perhaps." And with a wave, she disappeared on her scooter.

What the hell are we going to do? Richard climbed back in his van. *What if ....* **"And the wild, the willing and the innocent, Are down, down in the jungle tonight ...."** by UFO was playing on his phone. It was his ring tone. *Who's this?* He picked his phone up.

"Is that Richard?" a voice in his ear. It was Beth, the nurse at the hospital.

"Hi Beth, what's up?"

"We've a problem with Chloe .... And my lad Alex seems to think you can help."

"Ask away."

Beth explained. "We think Chloe's taken an overdose. Obviously we're pumping her stomach out, but there's a problem. We don't know what she's taken and we can't treat her in case there's a reaction."

"You must have the bottle."

"What bottle Richard?"

There was a moments pause as Richard fought with his conscience.

"You're going to have to trust me on this Beth. She had a bottle of tablets that were her Mums. They were given to Mrs Mollins by Dr Perez."

"That explains a lot Richard. The same doctor was on the ambulance that attended to Chloe earlier. He must have removed the bottle to cover his tracks."

"That sounds about right." *The crafty bastard!* "But he's not stupid. He'll have got rid of the bottle by now. Beth, you need to ring the Medical Centre and urgently request Mrs Mollins' medical records. They'll give you the answer you're looking for."

"Thanks Richard, I'll get on it."

"No probs` Beth …. And please, no questions asked."

"Richard, I trust you, believe me. You take care."

School was finished for the day. Ben and Usha were sat on one of the benches outside, waiting for Luis and Lilly to pick them up on their scooters. Ben and his girlfriend were discussing the day at school and how it had seemed rather boring, apart from that is, Usha's 'episode'.

Luis turned up first to Usha's disgust. *Typical!*

The three friends were laughing and joking when the distinctive sound of Lilly's four stroke scooter could be heard approaching.

"THAT'S LILLY!" The three teenagers shouted in unison, and they started to laugh.

Luis watched intently as Lilly drove up the school drive, her blonde hair blowing in the wind. He could immediately smell her perfume in the air as she stopped the scooter's engine in front of them. She gave a big smile as she dismounted the vehicle.

"Hi guys. How we all doing?"

"You're late," Usha muttered.

"Sorry sis'. Couldn't be helped. Been busy at the café this afternoon." Lilly turned and kissed Luis on the lips. *That's rather nice.*

"How's Chloe?" Usha asked "Does anyone know?"

"I caught up with Alex earlier," Luis said. "He was a bit shook up actually. Apparently he'd been fixing his scooter outside his house and he thought Chloe was asleep in bed. He got a phone call from young Ben here, telling him to check on Chloe. When he did, he found Chloe unconscious, apparently from an overdose of drugs and then the ambulance turned up just in time. Alex is up at the hospital now with Chloe. So Ben's the hero of the day."

Lilly and Usha gave each other a knowing look and smiled.

CHAPTER 16

IT`S ALL A BLUR

It was the weekend and the island had seemingly become extremely busy overnight due to a Dark Skies Festival. The hotels, along with various self catering and bed and breakfast establishments were bursting at the seams. Even the camp site at Saye Bay had seen an increase in numbers. The last time Alderney had seen visitor numbers like this was back in August 1999 when the island experienced a total solar eclipse.

Alderney is unique in that there is little or no artificial light pollution at night. Astronomy has seen a boom over the years and star gazers will travel anywhere to gain access to dark clear skies to record and photograph phenomenon of great interest.

There was an added bonus this particular weekend for the younger generation. Bunker Parties!

The Alderney Bunker Parties are legendary for anyone that visits on a regular basis. These parties take place in any one of the old Second World War German Bunkers underground and are all night affairs until five or six in the morning. Some of these fortifications are huge complexes and have been wired up with lighting and sound systems ready for all night raves and discos for all ages. And there's always plenty of booze flowing.

This weekend is going to be awesome. Usha thought.

Lilly and Luis were meeting up with Usha and their friends in about an hour outside the Braye Chippy. In the meantime they had a bit of catching up to do. They were at Lilly's.

Her Mum and Dad were out joining in on a night time walk with some of their friends up to the Butes Cricket Ground where a barbecue was being held.

Luis walked up the stairs and reached the landing, glancing around for Lilly's bedroom.

"Where are you Lilly?"

"Second room on your left." She smiled to herself as she looked at herself in the full length mirror. She could feel the hairs on the back of her neck bristling with anticipation.

Luis stood in the open doorway. He glanced in and he felt his heart racing as he looked adoringly at the girl he'd fallen in love with. Lilly stood perfectly still, wearing just the smallest of panties to cover her modesty. As she watched in the mirror, Luis' eyes were wandering. *He's probably lusting over my body.*

Lilly was slim with an hour glass figure. She turned to face Luis and as she raised her arms, her hands clasped her long blonde hair to reveal soft pert breasts with nipples straining to be caressed.

Lilly's body is so perfect in every way. Luis could feel his emotions almost jumping for joy uncontrollably ….

"LUIS… LUIS!" Lilly's voice reverberated down the stairs.

Luis shook himself. He'd been day dreaming whilst he'd been looking at a framed photo of Lilly on the kitchen table. *Jeez.*

"LUIS. Are you there?"

"Err … Yeah, coming."

As he climbed the stairs, Lilly shouted again. "SECOND ROOM ON THE LEFT."

"I know." *No, surely not.*

He stood in the open doorway to see Lilly stood in front of her full length mirror with her back to Luis. *This is really feeling weird.*

"Don't just stand there gawping …. Zip the back of my dress up please."

Luis walked into her bedroom. He gently pulled the zip up and then kissed the back of Lilly's neck.

Lilly spun round and took a step back from Luis.

"Well?…. What d'you think?" Lilly asked.

"Perfect …. Absolutely stunning."

Lilly spun round again. She was wearing a slightly tarty number. A red mini dress with a Chinese style pattern that sat tightly around her thighs. A low cut plunging neckline that left little to the imagination as her pert fulsome breasts strained to contain themselves.

"Wow! I'm gonna have to keep an eye on you at the party."

Lilly leant forward and threw her arms around Luis' neck and kissed him passionately on the lips.

"Don't worry, I'm all yours," Lilly replied.

"Come on gal, let's get going."

Luis clambered onto his scooter. "What are you waiting for gal?" He had a big grin on his face. "How are you going to get on in that skirt?"

"Watch me." Lilly held the lower part of her skirt and shuffled it up over her upper thighs to reveal her panties. Lilly threw her one leg over the pillion seat and she was on.

"You sure about this gal?"

"Absolutely …. They're clean!"

"Okay … Just make sure to hang on tightly." Luis revved the engine and pulled away.

Minutes later, they arrived at Braye Chippy. *There must be over three hundred people down here,* Lilly thought.

Luis was off his scooter first and immediately was aware of the whistles and woo wooing from the lads in the huge crowd.

Lilly held Luis' hand as she slid off the machine. She waved to the crowd with unadulterated bliss and blew them kisses to an even greater cheer of approval.

"Lilly, you're embarrassing me."

"Come on, lighten up, it's just a bit of fun." Lilly encouraged her skirt down her thighs. She bowed to the crowd and laughed.

"Thought it might be you putting on a show," Usha said. "You're a hussy," she joked.

Usha and Ben had been filling their faces with snacks and bacon butties whilst they'd been waiting. "There's a barbecue just round the corner at the Moorings," Ben said. "We've been listening to one of the live bands playing. They're great."

The Moorings is a restaurant come bar with a decked area looking out over Braye Bay and regularly host live bands and artists.

As the four friends listened they could hear the thumping guitar track of Radar Love by Golden Earring resonating through the sea air. *"I've been drivin' all night, My hand's wet*

*on the wheel, There's a voice in my head, That drives my heel
…"*

"Love this track." Luis clapped his hands. "One of my faves."

A group of lads strolled by giving Lilly the once over. "HI LILLY, LOOKING GOOD GAL."

"Thanks guys." Lilly gave them a pose as Luis stood there glaring.

"Here comes another scooter guys," Usha said. "There must be at least fifty down here now."

"It's Alex, he must have fixed his scooter." Lilly pointed down the road. "He's got Chloe with him … Cool."

"HI GUYS," Alex shouted as he switched the engine off. "Look at all these people."

Chloe got off the scooter. Ben, Usha and Luis each hugged and kissed her in turn.

"Look at you girl." Lilly put her arms around Chloe and held her tight. "Good to see you out and about. And you look so much better."

"I'm good thanks and I do feel much better …. Just look at you gal, quite the glamour girl this evening …. And look at the lads round here, they're all giving you the come on." The two girls laughed and kissed each other.

Uprising by the band Muse drifted through the air and it seemed as if the hundreds of teenagers present were singing in unison as they jumped and danced around … *"They will not force us, And they will stop degrading us, We will be victorious, so come on …."*

"THIS IS JUST BRILL," Alex shouted. "Just what Chloe needs, a bit of girl bonding."

"And a drop of booze," Chloe added with a smile.

"OH YES … AWESOME," shouted Usha.

"I'll get the drinks in then." Luis turned to the group of friends. "Anyone want to help me?"

"Come on Luis, I'll help." Ben grabbed Luis by the arm. "Won't be long guys." And the two lads disappeared into the crowd to find the bar.

"Well that leaves me with three pretty girls," Alex joked as he stood with his arm around Chloe's waist. She kissed him on the cheek.

"So, how are we getting to the bunker party?" Usha asked. "'Cos it's a long walk, which sucks."

"Grandad's going to pick us up and take us all." Lilly glanced at her watch. "In about ten minutes .... Hmmm, the boys will have to be quick with the drinks."

"Did you behave yourself earlier when you was by yourself with Luis?" Usha had that impish grin on her face.

"Of course I did." Lilly had a really naughty look. "But I did tease him!"

The four friends laughed, with Usha and Chloe waving a single finger side to side in Lilly's face.

Ben and Luis had struggled to get to the bar and decided on six bottles of beer. *No spillage on the way back,* Ben thought.

As they pushed and shoved their way back through the crowd they came to a stop. Luis turned to Ben. "Do you think Lilly's a tease?"

"No I wouldn't say that mate, but she's very mature for her age and she knows what she wants ... Why?"

"It's probably nothing, but there's been the odd occasion like earlier today where I didn't feel in control of the situation. It was if she was giving me the come on, and not for the first time."

"Ha ... Lucky for you then. Come on, we need to get back to the others before Lilly pulls some other guy." Ben gave Luis a wink.

The hard rock pounding of The Scorpions grew louder as the two lads pushed their way through the crowd.

"Someone's got a good taste in music," Luis said. "Another one of my faves, it's called The Zoo."

"I meet my girl, She's dressed to kill, And all we gonna do, Is walk around to catch the thrill ...." Brilliant.

Finally the two lads reached their friends who were dancing and singing to the music. They all gathered round for their beers.

"CHEERS." Lilly thrust her arm upwards to the evening sky. The friends cheered and clinked their bottles.

"ANYONE FOR ANOTHER?" Ben shouted over the thumping music.

Lilly bent her head towards Ben's ear. "My Grandad will be here in a minute to pick us up and take all of us up to the Bunker Party."

"What about our scooters?"

"When my Grandad's dropped us off he's going to come back here and pick them up and he'll take the scooters to our houses."

"Cool."

Richard carefully drove his van through the crowds that were encroaching onto the road as he approached the Braye Chippy. *Jeez, haven't seen this number of people down here in years.* "COME ON GUYS ….. Get out of the way." He could see Lilly and her friends about fifty metres away and he started to honk the horn on the van to attract their attention. *Looks like they're already having a good time.* The van pulled up and Richard climbed out. The sound of music was deafening and Richard waved to a few familiar faces in the crowd. He was well known on the island.

The young friends ambled over to Richard.

"Hi guys." Richard struggled to make his voice heard.

"HI MR MORGAN," the friends shouted.

"Hi Grandad." Lilly kissed him on the cheek.

"Look at you young lady …. All grown up. A bit tarty don't you think?" Richard had an evil glint in his eyes and grinned.

"COME ON GUYS, LET'S GET GOING," Usha shouted.

They all clambered into the van accompanied by cheers and shouts from the crowd as Lilly struggled to contain her body in the tight dress.

Jeez, we're gonna have to keep an eye on you girl. Richard smiled to himself.

As Richard drove along the coast road he glanced in his rear view mirror. The teenagers were all preoccupied kissing each other, laughing and joking. *Ha! The good old days.* "HOLD ON." The van hit the tight bend at the bottom of Tourgis Hill and he laughed to himself as the teenagers rolled across the floor of the van in fits of giggles.

Richard drove past Fort Tourgis on his right, and onwards to the junction near the airport. He steered the van onto the grass track which would take them to the Bunker Party. It was a bumpy ride as the teenagers shouted or cheered at every bump. The track continued through overgrown vegetation until a large flat open space opened up in front of them and Richard pulled the van over to a stop.

This was the Giffaine in the south west of the island. It was aptly named The Guns by the local population because this vast expanse of land was littered with German Second World War fortifications, some above ground and many below. Huge concrete structures with walls two metres thick in places. Many of the gun emplacements and bunkers had been hidden for decades by brambles and wild vegetation, whilst others had been cleared for tourism and in this case, a Bunker Party.

For the uninitiated, the whole area feels surreal and creepy. At night, it's in total darkness, you have to be brave, or mad, or both!

Tonight, lights were shining at strategic points powered by a diesel generator. Crowds were milling around, drinking and waiting for friends. Rave music could be heard emanating from below ground. All rather surreal ... But exciting.

"Okay guys, everyone out." Richard slid the side door open.

"AWESOME," Usha shouted.

"Thanks for the lift Mr Morgan." Chloe climbed out of the van.

"Right guys, you got everything?" Richard asked. "Phones, torches, money?"

Lilly and Usha hugged Richard. "Don't worry Grandad, we'll be fine."

"Hmmm, we'll see. Take care of each other." Richard turned to the others. "Enjoy yourselves guys."

Richard climbed back in his van and drove out into the darkness. *Gotta pick up the scooters.*

"Right guys, this is my treat." Alex pulled out six coloured wrist bands, one for each of them. "You need to wear these to gain access to the Bunker Party."

Chloe flung her arms around Alex and kissed him. "They must have cost you a fair bit of money."

Alex shrugged his shoulders. "You'll just have to help me find more golf balls!"

"THANKS ALEX," his friends shouted.

"RIGHT, LET'S DO IT." Lilly grabbed Luis' hand.

The entrance to the bunker complex was three metres below ground level accessed by a grassy sloping path.

"Careful as you walk down here," Luis said. "It's a bit slippy."

"You got that right." Usha carefully negotiated the slope holding Ben's hand as they walked behind Lilly and Luis. Chloe and Alex were close behind.

At the bottom of the slope the friends turned to their left and entered the gloomy, dimly lit corridor and as they walked further, the beating sound of techno music became louder with every step.

They turned another corner and were met by a couple of familiar faces, two local lads that organised the Bunker Parties every year. Tim and Adam were checking all entrants for their wrist bands and any concealed drugs.

"Hi guys, long time no see," Adam said. "If you don't mind guys, we just need to check you over. You know how it is these days with drugs and so forth."

"Yeah sure …. There you go." Lilly stretched her arms out to each side at shoulder height, forcing her skirt to ride up high on her thighs and her bosom to heave to bursting point.

"Err yeah, thanks Lilly." Adam could feel his face glowing.

"Don't think you'll find anything in there mate," Tim joked.

"Sorry Adam," Lilly said. "Couldn't resist it." They all burst out laughing.

"Go on in guys, get out of here!" Adam joked with a knowing look to Lilly.

The friends walked further down the corridor in high spirits. A huge concrete room opened before them filled with old friends and visitors. The place was heaving shoulder to shoulder and the music was pounding out it's rhythm from the next room. Some bunkers had up to twenty rooms depending on the size of the concrete structure.

"Where's the bar?" Chloe asked.

"Over there." Ben pointed to one of the rooms over to the left.

"Right, let's start as we mean to go on," Alex said. The friends eased themselves through the dancers into the next room and grabbed a few bottles of beer.

"THE MUSIC'S GREAT," Usha shouted.

"Come on, let's go to that room over there where the main action is." Lilly grabbed Luis by the arm and led him into the main room followed by their friends.

The DJ's were busy with playing the various tracks of music. The lighting system was working a treat as different coloured pulsing rays of light were dancing around the room.

Throbbing lights were everywhere creating strange patterns on the concrete walls. The music continued endlessly into the early hours of the morning. Lilly and her friends danced and sang as the night passed by. Empty bottles of beer were stacking up as the teenagers became more uninhibited as the booze took hold.

As the hours went by the number of party revellers had dwindled and somehow the friends had become separated. The music pounded on ….

I need some air, thought Lilly as she gradually pushed her way through the dancers until she was outside at the bottom of the slope. The cold air hit her like a sledgehammer and her head was spinning, but she managed to stagger up the slope.

She sat down briefly on one of the many plastic chairs dotted around and noticed other teenagers sitting and lying around as they chatted amongst themselves. Lilly glanced up at the stars in the clear sky. *That's the Orion Constellation there.*

"Hi Lilly." A voice from behind made her jump. It was Usha. "Have you seen the others?"

"Not for some time sis'."

"Lilly …. My pendant has started pulsing and look, your amulet is as well."

Lilly jumped up with a look of trepidation on her face.

"Lilly, what's going on?"

"Usha, what's up?…. Talk to me."

Usha was transfixed. Her pendant was pulsing steadily and then her eyes turned red.

"Usha …. What the hell!"

Usha started to walk slowly away as if controlled by some external force.

Lilly quickly pulled a torch out of Usha's pocket and turned it on so she could follow her sister. Usha continued to walk until another underground bunker complex came into view. Lilly watched intently as Usha made her way down some steps to the entrance which was blocked by a large rusty wrought iron gate. It was padlocked.

Lilly stood next to Usha and shone the torch down the corridor. It looked very much like the Party Bunker they'd left. Usha suddenly heaved a big sigh.

"Sis', you okay?" Lilly asked.

"Why are we here?"

Lilly shrugged her shoulders. "Don't know. But there's obviously a reason. Your pendant and my amulet are still pulsing as well. I think we need to get in here. Your pendant brought us here so we need to take a look."

"Agreed, but how?" Usha pointed to the padlock.

"No probs'." Lilly threw her hand forward and the padlock dropped to the ground. "Give us a hand to open this gate 'cos it's rusted up and heavy." The two girls pulled the gate open as it creaked and groaned.

"Come on Usha," Lilly said. "Let's take a look. Just be careful where you walk. We need to stay close."

The girls gingerly walked down the corridor. The torch light was creating all manner of weird looking shapes as Lilly shone the light back and forth until they reached the main room. Other corridors and rooms were visible, all seemed identical to the Party Bunker until they reached the centre of a circular room.

"Lilly, look up there." Usha pointed upwards. "You can see the stars."

There was a three metre diameter circular hole in the roof.

"Probably where the gun mounting used to be," Lilly said.

Lilly stood directly beneath the hole and realised it framed the Orion Constellation in the sky above. Her amulet started to pulse stronger and brighter but she felt in control. Lilly stepped aside and beckoned Usha to stand exactly where she had just stood.

"Tell me what you see sis'," Lilly said.

"The Orion Constellation .... And?"

"Look at your pendant."

Usha's pendant was pulsing brighter and stronger.

"Don't touch it until we know what's happening."

"Do as Lilly says Usha." A voice from behind the girls. It was Chloe and stood with her was Richard who had his hand on Chloe's shoulder.

"Chloe, Grandad, what are you doing here?" Lilly had an astonished look on her face.

Usha stood open mouthed in disbelief.

Chloe reached around her neck and revealed a dark red pendant on a gold chain.

"That's exactly the same as mine," Usha exclaimed. "And it's pulsing in exactly the same rhythm as mine."

"Not only that." Richard pulled his sleeve up. "My amulet is doing exactly the same thing."

"AWESOME," Usha cried out.

"Chloe .... How?.... Why didn't you tell us?" Lilly asked with a distinct frustrated voice.

"Sorry Lilly .... Long story for later."

"We were all 'summoned' here for some reason," Richard said.

Chloe had stepped to the centre of the room and stood under the gaping hole in the concrete above. She looked up to gaze at the Orion Constellation and immediately grabbed hold of her pulsing pendant hanging around her neck.

"NO DON'T," Richard shouted.

Too late. Chloe stood there in a trance like state, her eyes glowing dark red. "I AM A CHILD OF THE STARS."

"STAY BACK GIRLS," Richard shouted. "This is really weird stuff."

Chloe held out her arms to the side and instantly a beam of light concentrated on her pendant.

96

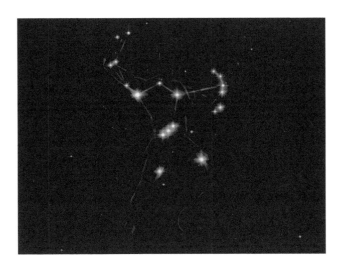

Richard looked up to see the beam was coming from the middle star, Alnitak, that forms part of Orion's Belt. "Girls, grab my hands and hold Chloe's hands to form a circle. I've an idea."

The foursome stood in a circle holding hands and suddenly three further beams of light passed through the hole above their heads and concentrated on Usha's pendant and the two amulets of Richard and Lilly. Two beams were emanating from the other stars in Orion's Belt, Alnilam, and Mintaka. The third beam was from the star in Orion's Sword and was concentrating on Richard's amulet. The four of them were completely helpless until suddenly the beams of light disappeared and they all collapsed in a heap ....

Moments later, the three girls and Richard stirred. "Everyone okay?" Richard asked with a concerned look on his face as the girls slowly got themselves to their feet. They glanced at each other in bemusement.

Usha pointed at Chloe. "Your hair Chloe, look at your hair. It's .... It's."

"We know Usha .... It's awesome," Lilly interrupted.

Usha giggled.

Chloe pulled her long brown hair around her shoulders. "I've got a blonde streak. What the ..."

"Very becoming young lady." Richard smiled at her.

"So, I'm very confused here," Lilly said. "What just happened here and what is Chloe doing here?"

"Yeah, come on Grandad, what IS Chloe doing here?" Usha had an impatient tone.

Richard gave Chloe a knowing glance. "First things first," Richard said. "Has anyone got any recollection of what just happened?… 'Cos strangely I have an image in my head."

"So have I," Chloe said.

"And we have too," Lilly and Usha added.

"Hmmm, okay then. It's far too late to do anything now." Richard glanced at his watch showing four thirty in the morning. "We need to get out of here and back to the boys."

"But what about Chloe?" Usha asked.

"Look …." Richard said. "We'll get together this afternoon. Me and Chloe will explain everything …. Now then, we need to go guys …. Sort the padlock out Lilly on the way out."

Richard and the girls climbed the steps back onto the grass track. It was just before dawn and there was a fresh westerly wind blowing in off the sea.

"Let's find the lads." Richard led the way back to the Party Bunker. "It looks like a battlefield here!"

Empty bottles, crates and left over food was scattered over a large area. A good forty or so party goers were either sitting around suffering with hangovers or sleeping the booze off.

"There they are," Chloe said. "Talk about sleeping like a baby!"

"I'll leave you to it then." Richard climbed in his van. "I take it you lot are walking?"

The girls nodded and smiled.

"We'll meet this afternoon yeah, I'll text you later." Richard waved and drove off.

CHAPTER 17

LAS TRES MARIAS

It's a lovely afternoon. Richard was planting up his last tomato plant that he'd grown from seed, in the greenhouse. The sun was beating down and the many birds in the garden were singing. *This is bliss. A bit of me time before the girls arrive.* He hadn't really given the recent developments much thought since he left them earlier that day, but now it was dawning on him that today would be important in so many ways. Possibly life changing.

"Light up, Light up, As if you have a choice, Even if you cannot hear my voice, I'll be right beside you dear ...." Richard's ring tone, Run by Snow Patrol interrupted his thoughts.

"Hi Richard, it's Beth. Sorry to bother you today. You okay?"

"Oh hi Beth, yeah I'm fine thanks. What's up?"

"I thought you might like to know that Dr Perez has left the island."

"Why does that not surprise me. So does anyone know where he's gone?"

"Not yet. All they do know is that he left the island last night on a chartered boat heading for France. He took advantage of all the celebrations around the island hoping that no-one would notice."

"So I take it the Police were on to him?"

"Oh yeah, for sure. Since the incident with Chloe they've been digging around."

"I'm sure they'll realise what's been going on and they'll be more revelations to shock everyone. I'm sure of that Beth."

"Well, the Police did tell me that Interpol had been notified so it sounds like it's seriously heavy stuff."

" Karma springs to mind. Does young Chloe know about this?"

"I believe so ... Why?"

"Nothing really. It's just that Chloe and my girls are coming up to see me and they're due any minute." Richard glanced at his watch.

"Well Richard, I'd better let you go. I just thought you would like to know and by the way, thanks for the info the other day."

"No probs' Beth. You take care."

"HI GRANDAD." Usha walked into the back garden followed by Lilly and Chloe. The three girls took it in turn to kiss Richard on the cheek.

"This is all very nice," Richard joked. "We should do this more often. Let's sit down shall we."

They all sat under the willow tree to take advantage of the dappled shade it provided from the hot afternoon sun. The three girls all looked at Richard in anticipation of what was to come.

"Where shall I start?" Richard asked himself. He looked towards Chloe and she nodded reassuringly.

"I've spoken to your Grandma about this and she is of the same opinion that the three of you need to know something that's really important." Richard had a serious tone in his voice. "You see .... The three of you are related." There was a long silence, then .....

"What! What do you mean Grandad?" Usha stuttered. "How CAN we be related?"

"Let me explain please and then you can ask as many questions as you like. Okay?"

The three girls nodded.

Richard went on to explain that he once had a son called Philip that Lilly and Usha had never met. Many years ago, Philip had a big fall out with the family and he never spoke to them again. In fact, he went so far as changing his surname by deed poll from Morgan to Mollins.

Lilly glanced at Chloe. Her eyes were welling up with tears.

"He was my Dad," Chloe blurted out and sobbed.

"Oh Chloe," Lilly said in a caring voice.

Usha placed her arm around Chloe's shoulders to try and comfort her friend .... Her cousin .... "You're our cousin. How long have you known about this?"

"I've always known, but my Dad wouldn't let me talk about it. He'd even threaten me sometimes. It was the same with my Mum."

"And I couldn't tell anyone 'cos it would have caused more trouble with Philip," Richard added.

"Did you ever make up with Uncle Philip, Grandad?" Lilly asked.

"Yeah sure, about a year before he died. But by then, Chloe's family life was set in stone, so to speak."

Richard went on to explain further that his best friend Dave Haynes who used to own the workshop below Fort Tourgis, also rented the bunker up on the Guns where they'd all experienced the Orion phenomenon. The bunkers in disrepair on Alderney are rented out for private use and Dave used to grow mushrooms in that bunker because the conditions were ideal. "Dave found the pendant that Chloe now has, in that very bunker and that's why I think it drew us all there. I used to go up to the bunker with Dave to help him with his mushrooms and he showed me the pendant he'd found. For whatever reason, Dave was adamant that he would give it to Philip when the time was right."

Richard continued to explain that Dave gave Philip the pendant just before he died. And about six weeks later, Philip died in a car accident and Chloe was in the car as well.

"I was in the back seat and suddenly the steering failed on the car, but Dad had no chance to stop the car," Chloe blurted out. She was sobbing uncontrollably. "The car ran into the back of a bus. The last thing I remember was, as my Dad was taking his last breaths he gave me the pendant and told me not to wear it unless my life was in danger."

Richard held Chloe's hand to try and comfort her. He then went on to explain that Chloe's Mum, Carol, had been having an affair with Dr Perez unbeknown to Philip. "I thought at the time and still do that Dr Perez was responsible for both Dave and Philip's deaths. They both knew along with me, that Dr Perez's Grandparents had lived in Peru. The doctor was born there and it's likely that he had corrupt connections in South America. We all thought that Dr Perez knew about the existence of the Lima Treasure and therefore he would use any devious means to get his hands on it."

Richard went on to explain that his son Philip was investigating Dr Perez at the time of his death. Philip had told Richard that Dave had died of an overdose and his doctor was Perez. "The next thing I heard was that Philip had died in a car crash whilst in the UK and that the Police were treating it as suspicious. They knew that the steering had been tampered with but had no clues as to when and where. I later found out from Carol, that Dr Perez had borrowed the car for a couple of days before it was transported to the UK."

"So you think that Dr Perez was after Chloe's pendant and the Lima Treasure?" Lilly asked.

"Oh for sure." Richard then told the girls about his earlier conversation on the phone with Beth, the nurse.

"So he's done a runner then," Usha added.

"Dr Perez has also left other casualties behind eh Chloe?" Richard glanced at his recently revealed Granddaughter.

Chloe nodded in agreement.

"As I said, Dr Perez was having an affair with Chloe's Mum, Carol, with the ulterior motive of finding Philip's pendant. Carol had a growing drink problem since the death of Philip and she didn't realise that Dr Perez was spiking her drinks with a cocktail of drugs, which explained her mood swings. The doctor would prescribe her all manner of pills in an attempt to coerce her into revealing the location of the pendant."

"WHAT A JERK," Usha shouted.

"It's terrible how desperate people get," Lilly added.

Richard went on. "Dr Perez then saw his chance with Chloe after the incident at home with her Mum. He was there at the hospital and again, he was there at Alex's house when Chloe was staying over. He knew that Chloe had her Mum's tablets and he was going to take advantage of the situation."

"Yeah, he knew alright," Chloe interrupted. "But this time, I was one step ahead of him. I knew it was going to be dangerous but I had to trust my instincts, that between them, Lilly and Usha would save my life."

"WOW!" exclaimed Usha.

Chloe explained, "After I'd spent the night at Alex's, the following morning I stayed in bed whilst Alex was outside fixing his scooter. His Mum had already gone to work. At some point I had to go to the bathroom and through a side window I saw Dr Perez's car outside. I shouted out for Alex but I think he must have given himself a break and wandered off."

"So what did you do?" Lilly asked.

"Well I realised that this was the moment. I rushed back to the bedroom and grabbed the pendant out of my bag and shoved it down the side of my ankle sock. I heard the sound of footsteps coming up the stairs and then … Dr Perez entered the bedroom. He was cussing in some sort of foreign language and I could see the fury in his eyes as he grabbed my wrists." Chloe held her wrists out to show them the scars. "He then forced me down onto the bed. I kicked out but he was too heavy and strong for me. I thought he was going to rape me, but then …."

"What?" Usha asked impatiently.

"He stuck a needle in my arm, a hypo. Some sort of sedative I think. All I remember then is him forcing a bottle of tablets down my throat and …"

"And that's when you connected with me," Usha interrupted.

"Wow," Lilly said. "That's some serious grief."

The group were interrupted by steps from behind and a voice. "Who wants a drink?" It was Bea, Richard's wife. She placed the tray of drinks on the table.

"Thanks hun'." Richard smiled approvingly.

"So I gather you've told the girls then Richard?" Bea asked.

"Of course."

"So girls, what d'ya think?"

"It's …." Usha hesitated ….

"AWESOME." The three girls shouted as they ran to their Grandma and gave her a hug.

Bea placed her hands on Lilly's head, then Usha's and finally Chloe. "Love the blonde streak gal."

Chloe hugged Bea once more. "I love you Grandma."

"It's lovely to hear you say that ... Finally after all this time we're a proper family again." Bea could feel tears welling up in her eyes.

"We all love you Grandma," Lilly said as they each gave Bea another hug and kiss.

"The Three Marys back together again," Bea said.

"What did you say Grandma?" Lilly asked.

"The Three Marys .... The three of you all have a second name. It's Mary .... You were all given that name after your Great Grandmother's name, Mary Morgan."

Richard nodded in agreement.

"Of course, that's it." Lilly gave Usha and Chloe a knowing look. "The Latin Americans call the three stars in Orion's Belt, Las Tres Marias or The Three Marys."

Bea smiled at her Granddaughters. "I haven't a clue what you're on about young lady. But it sounds interesting anyway."

CHAPTER 18

COMINGS AND GOINGS

Today is going to be a good day, Chloe tried to convince herself as her thoughts wandered …. *My boyfriend Alex is leaving the island later today.*

Now that he was sixteen, Alex had decided to attend college in Guernsey to study for his A levels, something that he was unable to do on Alderney. He was flying out later that morning, the very thing that Chloe had been dreading for weeks as the two teenagers had grown very close and now considered themselves to be an 'item'.

To make matters worse, her Mum, Carol Mollins, was still undergoing treatment in Guernsey for alcohol and drug addiction. Although she was making steady progress, it was difficult to see when she would be able to return to Alderney.

There's been a plus side though, Chloe thought. *I've been staying with Alex and his lovely parents, Beth and Frank.*

Chloe considered herself to be one of the family and had grown fond of Beth in particular. A sort of cosy Mum daughter type of relationship.

Chloe smiled to herself as she thought about some of the conversations they'd had. The perils of men and boyfriends. Falling in and out of love. And all that sort of stuff.

Alex sat nervously next to Chloe in the terminal building at the airport waiting for his flight to be called. He wasn't a good passenger when it came to flying, especially when it came to flying in the small Dornier 228 twin turboprop aircraft that the local airline used. It would only be a fifteen minute flight to Guernsey, but it was fifteen minutes too long for Alex. He much preferred to travel by boat and he had been expecting his Dad, Frank, to take him to the larger island of Guernsey aboard his fishing boat, but it wasn't to be unfortunately. Frank had

105

sailed to France that very morning as he could get a better price for his catch.

Alex squeezed Chloe's hand a little tighter. She smiled and kissed him on the cheek to try and reassure her boyfriend.

"It'll be okay hun'," Chloe whispered in his ear.

"Yeah I know.... It's just .... You know."

Chloe nodded and placed her arm round his shoulders. She looked around impatiently. *Where are the others? They promised they'd be here to see Alex off. Where are they?*

Chloe glanced at her watch. There was a big clock hanging up on the wall directly in front of the teenagers. *It's the same time .... Why do I do that?*

Her thoughts wandered again to the previous evening she'd spent with Alex. His Mum and Dad had gone out for the evening to let the teenagers have a bit of private time. *How many bottles did we drink? Don't remember, but we enjoyed ourselves as we kissed and cuddled. The way Alex carried me to the sofa. He was so gentle as he slowly undressed me, caressing every inch of my body making me shiver with excitement. His kisses were long, wet and passionate as he explored every detail of me.*

Chloe smiled to herself as she remembered how she'd literally torn Alex's clothes off. His physique was mind blowing for a lad of his age. Rippling muscles in all the right places just aching to be caressed. *I ran my fingers across his chest and slowly manoeuvred them lower down until I reached his groin. Alex moaned as I held him gently, feeling him pulsing with excitement.*

I remember arching my back as Alex's hand ran up between my thighs and through my delicate curls. I could feel the anticipation building up inside me as I writhed in ecstasy ....

"HI CHLOE." Usha shouted enthusiastically as she burst into the terminal building through the entrance followed by Ben, Lilly and her boyfriend Luis.

"Oh … Hi guys," Chloe stuttered as her thoughts were interrupted. She stood up and hugged her three friends in turn whilst Alex remained seated.

"So how's the main man?" Lilly bent over to kiss Alex on the cheek. "All ready and raring to go?"

106

"Yeah ... Sure," Alex replied with some hesitation.

"He's nervous," Chloe said. "He doesn't like flying."

"Yeah okay .... Don't need to remind me."

"Bing bong .... Would all passengers holding boarding cards for flight GR147 to Guernsey make their way through security ready for boarding. Thank you."

"That's you Alex," Chloe said. "Come on."

Alex reluctantly stood up. "Time to go then guys."

The friends took their turn to hug Alex and wish him luck. He turned lastly to Lilly and as he hugged and kissed her on the cheek, he whispered in her ear, "Look after Chloe for me."

Lilly nodded and smiled. "Don't worry, I will. You take care of yourself."

"Come on guys, give Chloe and Alex a chance to say their goodbyes," Ben said. "Let's get outside so we can watch Alex's plane take off." The four friends followed each other out of the terminal building.

Chloe and Alex waited in the queue at security, arms wrapped tightly around each other.

"Promise me you'll phone every day." Chloe gazed lovingly into Alex's eyes.

"You know I will." He kissed Chloe passionately on the lips as other passengers in the waiting queue looked on with slight embarrassment. "And if I get time I'll call at the hospital to see how your Mum's getting on."

Chloe smiled as she tried to disguise the fact that her eyes were welling up with tears. "You need to go Alex, they're calling you."

"Don't forget, I'll be back for a week in five weeks time just in time for your birthday." Alex turned to go. "I love you hun'."

"I love you too." Chloe waved as he wandered into the distance with the other passengers.

Five minutes later and Chloe had joined her friends stood by the security fencing outside, waiting for Alex's plane to take off.

The twin turboprop engines fired up on the Dornier 228 and turned slowly onto the runway. It was a westerly wind blowing today so the aircraft had to taxi to the eastern end of the main tarmac runway which is eight hundred and eighty metres long.

The friends watched as the Dornier 228 increased the engine revs and then …. The pilot unleashed the full power of the engines as it powered down the runway, passing the teenagers as they frantically waved and cheered to the nineteen passengers on board. The aircraft lurched upwards into the air, swinging from side to side in the gusting upward surge of wind as it flew over the cliffs and turned towards Guernsey.

"Well, that's that then," Ben said as he walked towards their scooters. "Ouch!… What's that for?" He felt a nudge in his ribs.

"Serves you right," Usha snapped. "Can't you see Chloe's upset?" Usha grabbed Ben's hand tightly. "Come on, let's grab your scooter and go."

Lilly kissed Luis on the cheek. "You go Luis, I'll cadge a lift with Chloe. I think she needs some company for a while."

"Okay love. I'll catch up with you later." Luis clambered onto his scooter. A couple of twists with his wrist encouraged his machine into life and he sped off.

"Fancy an ice cream Chloe?" Lilly asked. "We can get one from inside the terminal."

"Yeah sure …. Why not."

The two girls sat on the bench outside the terminal building enjoying their ice cream cornets.

"Alex will be alright."

"Yeah I know and his Mum and Dad have been great over the past few weeks. They're lovely …. Changing the subject, can I ask you something Lilly?"

"Course you can. Anything."

"Have you and Luis …" Chloe hesitated and she could feel herself blushing. "Have you had sex with Luis yet?"

Lilly smiled and looked into Chloe's eyes. "No, not yet. When I feel the time's right I suppose, but it will be my decision, not his. Been close one or two times, but to answer your next question, I'm still a virgin. How about you?"

"We was close last night. I mean, really close. Alex managed a bit of self control … Just. I really wanted him but he knows I'm not sixteen until he returns for a weeks break from college. It worked out okay for us though. His Mum and Dad turned up earlier than we expected and we only just managed to get our clothes back on before they came in the room … I didn't have time for my bra so I stuffed it down the sofa and retrieved it this morning."

"Ha, turned out like your ice cream then!"

"What?" Chloe glanced at her cone in her hand. It was all floppy and the ice cream was running down her hand. "Oh yeah, see what you mean." Chloe giggled.

"It needs your tongue round it."

"Stop it Lilly. Stop encouraging me."

The two girls were laughing hysterically as they were suddenly interrupted by the sound of a police car, siren blaring as it sped towards them and screeched to a halt outside the terminal building.

"What's this all about I wonder?" Chloe asked.

Lilly shrugged her shoulders.

The two front doors opened and Sergeant Peter Cordy and another local policeman stepped out. They immediately opened the rear doors to reveal Celia Perez, the local journalist, sat between two official looking guys.

"Do you think they're detectives?" Lilly whispered.

"Could be I suppose." Chloe shrugged her shoulders. "Plain clothes and all that …. Maybe?"

The two officials pulled Celia from the car. She spotted the two girls sat on the bench and immediately scowled at them. "YOU BITCHES .... I won't forget what you've done."

Celia continued to hurl abuse towards Lilly and Chloe as she was escorted into the terminal building by the two burly officials followed closely by the two policemen.

"Someone's not very happy with us," Chloe said. "Serves her right."

Lilly nodded in agreement. *Well deserved.*

The terminal building doors opened and the two policemen reappeared. Peter turned to the girls. "Sorry about that you two."

"So what's going on then?" Lilly asked.

"The FBI have requested that Celia needs to give evidence at a hearing in Washington DC in the absence of her father, Dr Perez," Peter explained.

"Hang on. You're telling us that they caught up with the doctor and then they've lost him?" Chloe grumbled.

The Sergeant continued to explain that after the doctor escaped to France, he doubled back to the UK before catching a flight to America using false documents. Interpol had issued an all ports alert out for him and the FBI apprehended him when the doctor landed in Washington DC.

"So how have they lost him?" Lilly asked.

"A county judge allowed him bail. A lot of money apparently and the FBI seem to think that the Mafia somewhere in South America are behind it," Peter explained. "And of course he's disappeared."

"Of course he has," Chloe muttered. *Bloody hell!*

Lilly held Chloe's hand to reassure her cousin.

"Well girls, we need to go. We've got some road works to sort out. Put some signs up, that sort of thing. You two have a good day."

The two policemen slid into their patrol car and slowly drove away.

"Well that's just bloody typical isn't it," Chloe grumbled.

"Look on the bright side gal, at least the Perez family are out of our hair for the time being."

"S'pose."

"You going down to the café?" Lilly asked. "You could start training today, ready to cover for me when I start my apprenticeship."

"Oh yeah, I forgot all about that. It won't be long before you start your cooking and preparation apprenticeship at that new hotel in town, The Blonde Hedgehog. Your Dad's the head chef there isn't he?"

"Yeah. He's been there since they opened last year. It just seemed the sensible thing for me to do and it meant that I didn't have to go to Guernsey college full time like your Alex. It's something I've always wanted to do and the hotel are paying for me to go to college one day a week. I love cooking anyway. That's why I took the part time job at the café when I was still at school. Good experience you know."

"Should be cool gal. You could maybe catch up with Alex as well when you go to Guernsey for the day."

"Good idea … And if you need to send him anything, I could take it."

Chloe smiled and nodded in agreement. "Come on then, let's get on my scooter and shoot down to the café."

It was a five minute trip down to the café in town. As the two girls pulled up outside the establishment they spotted Usha inside, through the window. She was busy serving tea and scones to a couple of visitors.

"There's a stroke of luck Chloe."

"What do you mean?"

"The café looks quiet, thankfully…. If it had been busy we'd have felt the wrath of my sister, ha."

The two girls grinned and high-fived each other as they entered the café.

"HI SIS', HI CUZ'," Usha shouted. "How we doin'?"

"Hi Usha," Chloe replied. "Yeah, we're good thanks, you been busy?"

"Nah, not really."

"So here we are then …. Las Tres Marias," Lilly said.

"What?" Usha and Chloe asked in unison.

"Las Tres Marias … You know …. The Three Marys."

"Oh yeah," Chloe said. "I'd forgotten about that".

111

The three girls laughed.

"On that subject, we need to try and figure it all out don't you think," Lilly said. "You know, the Lima Treasure, the maps or images in our heads and all the rest of it. Especially while the Perez family are off island."

The three girls nodded in agreement.

"I tell you what." Usha glanced at her watch. "Ben's picking me up on his scooter in a couple of minutes. I'll get him to drop me at Grandad's place and I'll have a word with him about arranging a time for all of us to meet up. Ben won't mind 'cos I think he's helping Luis out on a job this afternoon."

"Sounds like a plan," Chloe said. "That'll give Lilly a bit of time to show me the ropes here at the café."

"THAT'S A HIGH-FIVE THEN GIRLS," Usha shouted as the sound of Ben's scooter arriving outside broke into the conversation.

Ben stayed seated on his scooter as he spotted the girls through the window of the café. *Oh Jeez,* he thought. *I'm outnumbered!*

The three girls bounded out of the café, shouting, woo wooing, waving and blowing kisses at Ben much to his embarrassment.

"Hi Ben." Usha whispered in his ear and kissed him on the lips as she lifted herself up onto the scooter behind her boyfriend. "Thanks for picking me up. Any chance you could drop me at my Grandad's place?"

"Yeah sure. No probs' hun'."

"SEE YOU TWO LATER." Usha waved as Ben drove the scooter up the road.

"Come on gal." Lilly turned to Chloe. "Let's get on with some café type work."

CHAPTER 19

POWER OF THE PEN

Another glorious afternoon, Richard thought to himself as he struggled to move another piece of timber into place. It was a perfect day for starting his latest project, a sun room situated to the rear of the back garden. He'd been meaning to tackle the work over the previous weeks but recent events with his Granddaughters and their friends, with the added complication of corrupt actions by Dr Perez, who'd apparently been struck off by the Medical Council, had interfered with all his plans.

Right, let's grab a handful of screws and .... His thought process was interrupted by the sound of two scooters arriving on the front of the property. *I'm not going to get much done now then.* His three Granddaughters appeared in the back garden.

"HI GRANDAD," Chloe called out. "Everything okay?"

"Hi girls. You all come to give me a hand?" *In my dreams.*

The three girls smiled at each other.

"That's a no then I take it." Richard gave them all a hug. "So, how are we going to tackle this? Any ideas?.... No?... Well firstly I think we need to figure out what maps or images we have in our heads so we're going to need some paper and a pen."

"I'll get some." Usha dashed into the kitchen immediately followed by the others and rummaged through the drawers looking for a pen and a drawing pad.

They all sat down around the kitchen table.

"The images we have aren't exactly maps are they?" Lilly asked.

"No you're right," Richard replied. "More like clues, sites or places. So what do you have Lilly?"

Lilly took the pen and paper from Usha. She scribbled as she spoke. "I've got this image of an arch pointing to the north with, what looks like, a lot of sand on the other side .... And strangely, two or three different coloured triangles."

Chloe and Usha turned the paper round to study what Lilly had drawn.

"Hmm, I wonder," Richard muttered. "How about the stone arch that leads you to the beach at Arch Beach? You know, the arch runs underneath the road that takes you down to the beach at Saye Bay."

"But what about the triangles?" Lilly asked.

"Got it," Usha exclaimed. "Tents."

"That's right," Chloe said. "You'd pretty much draw a tent in the shape of a triangle and ..."

"And the arch takes you from the campsite to Arch Beach," Richard interrupted. "That would make sense."

"I've got a bit of a bad feeling about this image Grandad," Lilly said.

"Why?"

"It's just ... Well you know. During the Second World War the campsite was used as a labour camp for prisoners of war. I mean ... We all know that they were treated badly, but there's one story that's never been verified. Some of the inmates told of the story of one prisoner being badly beaten up in the tunnel and was bricked up alive in the arch and left to die."

"We're all doomed, doomed," Usha groaned jokingly. "Sorry guys. I know they were bad times back then. I was just trying to lighten the mood."

"Okay. Back to the job in hand," Richard said. "Who's next?"

Usha grabbed the pen and paper. "This is what I've got." Usha scribbled frantically.

"What's that?" Chloe squirmed her face in puzzlement.

"It's a cow .... Can't you tell?" Usha grumbled. "I know, my drawing's not up to much."

They all laughed.

"Sorry Usha. Carry on."

"The other part of the picture is supposed to be a tall standing stone. And I could just make out an island in the distance out to sea."

"We don't have any standing stones on Alderney do we?" Lilly asked.

"Not Neolithic, no," Richard replied. "There is one possibility that would fit the image. There's, what locals call, the Madonna Stone on the southerly coastal path to the west of Val du Saou. It was moved to that position in the sixties after being found in a nearby field. Someone once told me it used to be a stone lintel that would have been used over a door or window. It was like a scratching post for the grazing cattle out there. That would explain the image of a cow. The other thing that fits, is that on a clear day on the south coast path you can see the other Channel Islands including Jersey."

"So how about you Grandad?" Usha asked.

"Well mine's easy." Richard picked up the pen and paper and proceeded to draw a cone with what looked like the ramparts of a fort to the side. "Come on, you should all get this as it's close to one of your favourite places."

"GOT IT," Chloe shouted excitedly. "That's the white cone just above Fort Tourgis."

"Yeah, it's that simple. The white cone is actually a navigation marker for passing ships."

"Want to see mine?" Chloe scribbled away on a sheet of paper.

Richard audibly gasped at Chloe's drawing.

"What's up Grandad?" Lilly asked. "What is it?"

"You sure that's right Chloe?" Chloe nodded. "Well those two stone pillars are pretty much what's left of Lager Sylt behind the airport. It was a Nazi Concentration Camp, the only one in the UK during the Second World War." Richard visibly sighed heavily.

"What are these?" Lilly pointed to what looked like matchstick men.

"That's what I saw Lilly ….. Hundreds of people and they were all wearing the same clothes," Chloe replied.

"Most likely prisoners of war Lilly. Most of them were Jews and a lot of them died here building the bunkers for the Germans," Richard explained. "A terrible and shameful part of history."

115

"So okay then, we've got these clues, but what do they mean?" Usha asked. "Are we missing something here? What? I don't get it".

"You're right Usha," Richard replied. "We have to figure out what the connection is, if any, between the Treasure of Lima, which is basically what we're looking for, these clues we've just got and also the powers we seem to have acquired. Not only that, what's the connection between the Orion Constellation and the treasure? We also have to assume that Perez is in with the Peruvian based Mafia so it's a safe bet they'll stop at nothing to get the Lima Treasure."

"I still need to check out the library book," Chloe said. "It has to be important doesn't it?"

"Yeah, you're right," Richard replied. "It may give us this connection we're looking for."

"Well, we're either gonna have to break in, or somehow distract Annie Dodds the librarian, whilst I'm there on one of the afternoons I work."

"Hmm, I'll get back to you on that," Richard replied. *Gonna have to be a bit careful. I don't want to upset Annie.* "In the meantime, we need to check out these clues. But ... And this is a BIG but .... No-one is to visit any of these sites by themselves, 'cos we have no idea what we're dealing with. GOT IT?"

The three girls nodded and smiled. "Got it Grandad."

"Is there anything else we need to cover today?" Richard asked.

"We need to take a look at that tunnel we found," Lilly replied. "The tunnel that me and Usha discovered under the floor of Mr Allens' workshop come store, down below Fort Tourgis."

"Yeah, that's where we found this pendant." Usha held up her pendant.

"Right, okay girls. Just be careful when you go down there."

"Before we go Grandad, we want to show you something," Chloe said. "We've been practising haven't we girls."

"Oh yes?" *Hmm.*

"Come on girls, let's all go out into the garden and show Grandad what we can do."

116

The three girls followed Richard into the garden and stood about two metres apart in a circle. "Just stand over there Grandad." Lilly pointed to the tree which was about ten metres away. "Stand still and you'll be fine."

"Don't like the sound of this." Richard grumbled as he walked over to the tree.

"READY GIRLS?" Lilly shouted.

Richard watched intently as the three girls raised their hands toward the blue sky above. They closed their eyes and as they did, their faces changed from their normal cheerful expressions to ones of deadly intentions. The girls eyes opened to reveal piercing white lights.

This is really weird, Richard thought to himself.

Suddenly, the three girls drew their left arms down to their side. They all chanted three or four words in some sort of language which Richard didn't recognise. The girls in unison clenched a fist with their raised right hands and in an instant lightening type regular pulses emitted from them into the sky. Their arms moved to an angle above their heads to make the pulses of lightening fuse together, at which point the pulses were increasing in strength until ..... "CRASH! BANG!..." The sound of thunder pounded overhead. The ground shook beneath Richard's feet. *Wow!*

The lightening pulses decreased until the girls started to wave their right arms from side to side. As they did so, rainbows danced across the sky in a spectacular display of colours.

The three teenagers then brought their arms down and positioned all of their hands waist high pointing towards each other. Their eyes were now dark green, almost black in colour.

Again, they chanted in some indistinguishable language and then ... A green pulse of light emitted from Lilly's hand and it hit Chloe's hand before passing onto Usha. And so it went on, round and round from hand to hand. *It's like watching footballers heading the ball to each other for practice,* thought Richard.

Their green eyes instantly changed to a blood red colour and ..... The girls were gone.

"WHAT!….. That can't be …. How?" Richard briefly panicked, his heart was thumping. "This can't be happening? LILLY ….. CHLOE ….. USHA …. WHERE ARE YOU?"

A huge gust of wind seemed to spiral around the garden and in an instant, the girls were back, laughing and giggling.

"THAT WAS …. AWESOME," Usha shouted. The three girls high-fived. "What d'ya think Grandad?"

"You could have warned me you was going to disappear …. Where the bloody hell did you go?"

"We don't know is the honest answer," Lilly replied. "It's like being in another world, but we haven't figured out how to control the time that we're there yet."

"Did you all have control of what you was doing?"

"Oh yes," Chloe replied as the others nodded.

"And you could see each other all the time?"

"All the time," Usha replied. "Clear as day."

"And what's with the chanting?" Richard asked.

"What chanting?" Chloe replied.

"You don't know what I'm on about do you? Any of you?" Richard asked.

The three girls shook their heads.

"Let me show you." Richard held his smart phone up for them all to watch. "I filmed pretty much everything."

The group stood around Richard's phone and watched as the events unfolded in front of their eyes.

"WOW! LOOK AT THE LIGHTENING BOLTS" Usha shouted.

"Yeah. Cool eh," Chloe said.

"Had no idea we were chanting," Lilly said. "I've got an app on my phone that will tell us what language it is. It also translates to English."

Richard attached a connecting cable to Lilly's phone from his own and played the video again. The chanting started, "Hanan Pacha, Ukhu Pacha, Kay Pacha."

"Wow. What's that supposed to mean?" Usha asked.

Lilly looked at her phone. "Apparently The translation is World Above, World Below, This World. And the language is known as Quechuan which is used in South American countries, predominantly in …" Lilly paused.

118

"What's up Lilly?" Chloe asked.

"Quechuan is spoken in Peru .... In Peru."

"Let me have a look." Richard took the phone from Lilly. "It also says that it was the language used by the Incas."

"Could this be the link we're looking for Grandad?" Usha asked.

"It could be gal. Tell you what. I'll spend a bit of time on the internet tonight. See what I can find out." Richard glanced at his watch. "I need to go girls. I've got to pick your Grandma up from the allotment. She'll be expecting me .... So what are you girls doing now?"

"We're going to watch the footie," Lilly replied. "Luis and Ben have been in training for the last few weeks since they joined the local team, the Alderney Nomads. Should be good."

"Yeah, they're playing a team from Guernsey," Usha said. "And then there's a bit of a do on afterwards."

"Ha, thought there'd be some beer involved," Richard replied. "Well you three enjoy yourselves, I'm off or I'll be in trouble with your Grandma." He walked to his van and climbed in ..... "COME ON GIRLS," he shouted. "Get these scooters on the move 'cos they're in the way."

The three girls ran to their machines and climbed on. A couple of twists and the engines sparked into life. Richard waved to them as they drove away into the distance.

CHAPTER 20

MATCH DAY

"AL DER NEY, AL DER NEY, COME ON NOMADS, COME ON NOMADS, COME ON NOMADS ..." The small crowd of locals were making their presence felt as the two teams warmed up out on the pitch. The weather had turned for the worst over the last couple of hours and the strong westerly wind was howling down the pitch. To make matters worse, it had started to rain.

"GOOD JOB WE'RE WRAPPED UP," Lilly shouted. "Wouldn't fancy playing footie in this."

Usha and Chloe nodded as they stamped their feet in an attempt to keep them warm.

The football pitch is situated below and behind Fort Albert which was heavily refortified by SS prisoners of war during the Second World War. It sits above the Victorian Mount Hale Battery complex which includes the Arsenal building. It always has visitors perplexed to see a football ground surrounded by hundreds of years of history which also includes a sea view.

The players trotted back into the club house to change into their playing strips.

"How about a drink to keep us all warm?" Chloe pulled a hip flask out from under her coat.

"Thought you'd never offer," Lilly joked as she nudged Usha with her elbow.

The girls took it in turn to take a swig from the flask.

"Mmm that's good," Lilly said and she licked her lips. Chloe nodded approvingly. "Do I detect a drop of whisky in this coffee?"

"Only the best." Chloe's face was beaming. "Mind you, looks like someone's struggling."

Lilly turned to see Usha huffing and puffing. "You okay sis'?"

"You could have told me it had whisky in it." Usha tried to stop herself from coughing and spluttering. "Give us another shot." She grabbed the flask and had another swig as Lilly and Chloe laughed hysterically.

The crowd cheered and waved their blue and white scarves as the two teams trotted out onto the pitch. Luis and Ben stopped momentarily to kiss Lilly and Usha on their cheeks as the girls wished them luck.

"Pheee!" The ref's whistle sounded as the game kicked off. Every touch by an Alderney player was greeted by cheers and clapping as the local team appeared to gain the upper hand initially.

"COME ON REF' …. THAT'S A FOUL." Usha yelled as Ben was up-ended with a strong tackle by the Guernsey player. Ben picked himself up gingerly and immediately squared up to the opposing player giving him an intimidating stare. Four or five players rushed in to intervene, pushing and shoving. The referee parted the players, dishing out yellow cards and warning Ben to control himself.

"It's a free kick," Chloe said. "Could do with a goal here after all the chances we've had."

The players jostled with each other in the Guernsey penalty area as the cross from the free kick swung in at pace at chest height.

"GO ON LUIS," Lilly shouted. "HEAD IT."

Luis dived in and headed the ball towards the goal as a Guernsey defender caught Luis flush in the face with his boot. "GOAL!" The crowd erupted jumping up and down. "YES!" Usha yelled. "Get in there ... Great goal Luis ... Hang on, what's up with him?"

Luis was prostrate on the grass motionless and the players were calling to the trainers to attend to Luis who was obviously injured.

"I need to help him." Lilly had an anguished look about her as she started to walk onto the pitch.

"Lilly, you can't." Chloe pulled Lilly back. "There are too many people around .... He'll be alright. I promise."

The crowd applauded as Luis was stretchered off the pitch. The trainers were trying to stem the blood gushing from a bad head wound as they passed the girls into the club house.

A substitute ran on to cheers from the crowd.

"I need another drink," Lilly said. "Can't cope with all of this."

"He'll be fine." Chloe handed Lilly her hip flask. "It's nearly half time. We'll find out how he is then. Okay?"

Lilly nodded.

"COME ON GUYS," Usha yelled. "GET STUCK IN."

The rain had eased off now but the visitors still had the wind behind them as they attacked the Alderney goal. A shot ... It hit the bar .... "OH NO," Chloe shouted as it hit the back of the goalkeeper and bobbled into the net.

"What a soft goal to give away. That's one one now," Lilly said.

"Pheee!" The ref's whistle blew.

"AND THAT'S HALF TIME," Usha shouted as the players trudged off the pitch to applause and cheers from the crowd.

"Grab a beer for me. I'm just going to see how Luis is." Lilly walked off into the club house and then spotted the coach. "How's Luis, Mr Fish?"

"Oh hi Lilly. Yeah, he'll be fine. A bit concussed and a bad gash on his forehead that looks worse than what it is. I'll tell him you've asked after him."

"Thanks Mr Fish."

Lilly rejoined the girls who were jumping around to keep themselves warm in the biting wind.

"Where's that beer?" Lilly asked.

The three girls high-fived and clinked their bottles as they joked with some of the crowd.

The two teams ran out onto the pitch for the second half to cheers from the crowd.

"Pheee!" The ref' blew his whistle to start the second half of the game and the team from Guernsey immediately started to press hard.

"Looks like the Guernsey lads have been given a rocket at half time," Chloe said.

"Yeah, they look a different team to earlier in the match," Usha replied.

The Guernsey team were clearly on top as wave after wave of attacking moves were frustrated by the local team's defence. Tackles were flying in from every direction as the dominance continued.

"Ooo! That was a seriously bad tackle by our central defender," Lilly said. "Oh sugar! We're down to ten men …. The ref's just sent him off."

"Yeah, and now we've got to defend a free kick," said Chloe.

"GOAL! What a great strike by the Guernsey forward ….. He's been threatening to do that for the last half hour." Usha grumbled.

Lilly glanced at her watch. "There's only two minutes left girls."

The Alderney goalkeeper thumped the ball up field in one last desperate attempt to give his strikers a chance at goal. As Ben ran between two defenders the ball bounced over his head.

"HE'S CLEAR!" Usha yelled. "GO ON BEN."

The crowd roared their disapproval as the last defender scythed Ben down to the ground in the penalty area with an open goal in front of him.

"OFF! OFF! OFF!…." The crowd chanted and then cheered as the defender was shown a red card. He left the pitch to jeers and boos.

"IT'S A PENALTY," Chloe shouted. "And Ben's going to take it himself."

The crowd hushed as Ben waited for the ref' to indicate he could take the penalty.

"I can't look." Lilly turned her head.

"GOAL!" The crowd went wild jumping up and down, waving their blue and white scarves, shouting and cheering.

"IT'S GONE CRAZY," Usha shouted.

"Pheee!" The ref' blew the final whistle.

The crowd cheered and applauded the players as they trooped off the pitch. The three girls were woo wooing as Ben walked by with a huge grin on his face. Usha threw her arms around him and kissed him full on the lips, much to the delight of the crowd.

"MY HERO," Usha shouted as Ben walked into the club house waving to the crowd.

"A draw ... Who'd have thought it," Lilly said. "Right, are we going in the club house for some drinks and something to eat?"

"You two go," Chloe replied. "I'm gonna grab my scooter and nip down to my Mum's place. Alex's Mum promised to meet me there so I could grab some of my stuff to take up to her place. Plus I'm expecting a phone call from Alex in about an hour. So you two go and enjoy yourselves with Luis and Ben."

"Okay. Catch you later." Usha kissed Chloe on the cheek.

Lilly and Usha made there way through the crowd and entered the club house. It was heaving, no doubt because the rain had started to fall again and everyone was taking shelter.

"Let's grab something to eat sis'." Lilly pointed over to the buffet laid out at the far end of the hall. "We'll get ourselves a beer as well whilst we wait for the lads getting a shower and change of clothes."

The two girls pushed and shoved their way to the buffet and bar.

"That's Luis' Dad stood behind you," Usha whispered. "You know, the plumber, Diego Garcia. Looks a bit shifty if you ask me." Usha continued to fill her plate up with sandwiches and cake. "Grab a couple of bottles Lilly."

Lilly turned to the bar to get the bottles.

"You're Lilly aren't you?" Diego asked in broken English.
"Excuse. My English no good."

"Oh, hi Mr Garcia, yes ... I'm Lilly."

"I've hear .... Heard a lot of you. I mean ... About you. My
Luis. He tells me things."

"All good I hope." Lilly smiled. "He scored a good goal
today don't you think?" Lilly tried to change tack with the
conversation. She didn't feel comfortable talking to him. There
was something strange about his demeanour. The way he
shuffled his feet, his eyes were darting around the room and he
spoke with a certain menacing tone. He was drunk as well
which wasn't helping. *Need to hold myself together.*

"Yes yes. Football okay .... But my Luis ... He need to
work more. No time for girls."

Usha nudged Lilly in the small of her back.

"Oh ... Err .... Okay Mr Garcia. I need to go now." Lilly
started to turn towards Usha, to move away. She felt a hand
grab and squeeze her shoulder from behind with some force ....

"WHERE YOU GOING? I not finished yet."

Lilly swung round, pulling his hand away from her shoulder
as she turned. Her eyes turned black as she squeezed his hand
with increasing power. "WELL, I'M FINISHED," Lilly
screamed as she twisted his arm and threw her leg out across
his ankles sending the big man crashing to the floor.

Usha beckoned Lilly away. "Come on sis', that's enough.
People are staring."

Lilly turned to walk away. "LOOK OUT." A shout from the
crowd. The teenager half turned to see Mr Garcia lunging at her
with a knife, his eyes were glowing yellow, filled with hatred.
He drunkenly swung the knife, Lilly ducked beneath it and she
punched him in the groin with all her power. The drunken man
crumpled to the floor groaning, clutching his groin. He growled
as his eyes reverted to their normal colour.

By now, three or four guys from the crowd had jumped on
top of Mr Garcia as he writhed in agony. The football players
were emerging from the changing rooms and beginning to
mingle with the crowd to watch the commotion.

Luis stepped through the crowd, his head still heavily
bandaged. "WHAT THE HELL? ... WHAT'S GOING ON

125

DAD?" He spotted the knife his Dad was still grasping. The young lad put his foot on his Dad's hand, forcing him to release the knife and he kicked it away across the floor.

"Right lads. We'll take over." It was Peter Cordy, the local police Sergeant and a couple of constables who'd just entered the club house. "Come on Mr Garcia. 'Nuf trouble for one day. You're coming with us." The three officers pulled him up from the floor and handcuffed him behind his back before frog marching him outside to the waiting patrol van. "I'll be back later to take some statements. THANKS GUYS." Peter called out as he left the building.

The club hall was silent momentarily …. "WELL DONE GAL." A shout from the crowd and suddenly everyone was shouting, cheering and clapping as the events at what they had just witnessed dawned on them.

Luis found Lilly sat quietly in the corner with a bottle of beer in her hand. "Can I join you?" Luis sat next to his girlfriend and placed his arm around her. "You alright gal?". He smiled and kissed her on the cheek.

Lilly looked at Luis with her steel blue soulful eyes. "Oh Luis …. Your Dad …. He …"

Luis put his finger to her lips. "Don't … Just don't go there. He can be a right nasty bastard at times. I should know, I have to live with him." Luis shook his head. "But a knife?…. I wouldn't have thought it unless I hadn't seen it myself today. I'm so sorry Lilly." Luis' voice had softened. "There has to be a reason …. But I can't give you one."

Lilly ran her fingers through his thick curly black hair. As she did so, she concentrated her power on the deep gash beneath his head bandage, healing it in the process. "It's fine Luis. As long as we're both okay, that's all that matters." Lilly kissed him lovingly on the lips that seemed to linger on forever. She felt safe once more in his embrace.

"Where's Usha?" Luis asked as he scanned the crowd for any sign of Lilly's sister.

"Hey you two." It was Ben approaching them. Usha was attached to his hip as she held him tightly around the waist. "Been looking for you since all the excitement finished."

126

"You okay Lilly?" Usha asked. "You look like death warmed up. I have to say though, you was awesome."

"Thanks for that sis'…. Yeah I'm okay. I thinks it's just starting to sink in what happened."

"Sounds like delayed shock," Ben said. "How's your head Luis?"

Luis raised his hands and rubbed his head. "Strangely, it feels fine. Mind you, the Doc' said to leave the bandage on until tomorrow to be on the safe side."

Lilly gave Usha a knowing look and winked playfully.

"Where'd you learn all that stuff Lilly? You know, the self defence type thingy," Ben asked.

Lilly grinned and playfully bent her arm feeling her muscle. "It's just something we've been practising with my Grandad over the past few weeks. No particular reason."

"Who's we?" Luis asked.

"Me, Chloe and Usha …. It's no big deal. It's just a bit of fun."

"Yeah, so you'll have to watch yourself now boy," Usha said as she turned to look at Ben as she bent both arms up by her side. "Have a feel of those muscles if you dare."

The four teenagers laughed uncontrollably as they helped themselves to another drink.

127

CHAPTER 21

A FEW REVEALS

Richard was busy on his computers. His wife, Bea, had flown to Guernsey earlier in the morning for a hospital appointment and then to spend the day shopping with a friend, before returning to Alderney in the early evening.

The other day, he and his three Granddaughters had stumbled across three Quechua translations which were based on Inca mythology in the South Americas. The connection with Peru, the discredited Dr Perez and Luis' family, the Garcia's, was difficult to ignore especially as the three stars in Orion's Belt had seemingly chosen the three girls on that memorable night. Their Christian names which included Mary gave even more credence to his theory of a link between The Three Marys, again an Inca belief, and the lost Inca treasure of Lima in Peru. Not forgetting the 'clues' they'd been given by the stars of Orion and then of course there was the Pacha chanting ….

Seems like the obvious place to start. He typed the word Pacha into the search engine on his computer and hit Return *….. Wow, that was quick.* Six pages rolled up onto his screen. "Hmmm." Richard quickly scanned the literature in front of him.

Well this bit we know. In Inca mythology Pacha means world which is divided into three levels, or realms, Hanan Pacha, Ukhu Pacha and Kay Pacha. "Which is what the girls were chanting." *World above, world below and this world. Apparently these Pachas, or worlds, overlap as well.*

Richard continued to read …. *So Hanan Pacha is the world above, which, according to Inca mythology includes the sky, sun, moon, stars and planets which is inhabited by the Sun God, Inti and the Moon Goddess, Mama Killa. And get this, there's a God of Thunder and Lightning, Illapa. I wonder if that's how* the girls somehow managed to conjure up their bolts of lightning and so forth the other day?

"What's this?" Richard studied the information. *Ukhu Pacha means world below or the inner world and has two realms of which, one deals with the dead which is inhabited by the ruler, Supay who is the God of Death and a group of demons in the Inca Underworld, and the other, new life, which is inhabited by the fertility goddess Pachamama known as Mother Earth, who is the mother of Inti the Sun God whose wife is Mama Killa, the Moon Goddess.* "That all sounds a bit scary and creepy."

So Kay Pacha is this world and is often affected by the world above and the world below as they battle each other. Hmm.

Jeez, this is interesting. Apparently, the world below and this world have connections in springs and caves, whilst the world above and this world are connected by lightning and rainbows.

"This looks a bit ominous." *There's one other connection. All the worlds can impact each other changing the whole order of the world as we know it. It's known as a cataclysm or Pachakutiq.* "Wow!"

Here's another interesting theory. After people die, their spirits can inhabit any of the worlds and also, some stay in this world because they have unfinished business. A few lost souls or ghosts eh?

"Run To The Hills …" Richard's ring tone by Iron Maiden interrupted his thoughts as he picked up his phone.

"Hello."

"Oh hi Dad, it's Susan. You okay?"

"Yeah Yeah, what's up?"

"It's our Lilly. She's been attacked by Mr Garcia, Luis' father."

Richard could feel his heart racing. "Is she okay?"

"I think so. She wants to come up and see you for some reason. I told her you'd be busy but she's being quite forceful about it."

"Tell her that's okay. Usha can come as well if she wants. What's happening with Mr Garcia? Do you know?"

"I've just heard they've given him bail until the next court hearing. They've stipulated a condition on his bail though."

"What's that?"

"He's not to get within one hundred metres of Lilly, try to phone her or come anywhere near the house."

"Well that's one good thing. He's a nasty piece of work you know. I feel quite sorry for his son Luis. Right, anyway, send her up Susan, I'll try and sort out what's going on."

"Thanks Dad. I'll see you soon. Byeee."

Richard had no sooner put the phone down when he heard a shout from downstairs.

"HELLO …. HELLO … ANYONE HERE?"

Richard peered over the balcony at the top of the stairs to see Chloe standing with hands on hips. She was a good looking fifteen year old girl who'd had to do a lot of growing up over the last year. Richard smiled at the state of her long brown hair. It was a mess. *She's obviously arrived on her scooter and not worn a crash helmet.* Not illegal on Alderney, but not safe either! *And just look at that blonde streak in her hair, I'm sure it's becoming more pronounced.*

"OH HI CHLOE …. COME ON UP."

Chloe made her way up the stairs. "Hi Grandad. Thought I'd call round to see how you are." She hugged Richard as he kissed her on the cheek.

"You looking good gal, 'specially the hair style. New look is it?"

Chloe ran her fingers through her unkempt hair. "Ha, see what you mean Grandad. Forgot my helmet." She shrugged her shoulders. "Oh well, not to worry."

"Have you heard from Alex at all gal?"

"Yeah sure. We phone each other every day. He's settled in fine and he's doing really well."

"That's good then. I'm pleased for you gal 'cos you deserve a bit of good fortune after all the problems with your Mum and Dad." Richard gave her a gentle hug. "Lilly and Usha are due here anytime. Apparently, Lilly wanted to see me. Something to do with some trouble with Luis' Dad. Have you heard anything about that?"

Chloe shook her head. "That's news to me."

"That could be them now …. Yep, that's definitely them. Lilly's driving skills are really good … Not!"

Chloe laughed because she knew only too well that Lilly's driving abilities left nothing to the imagination. *A bit like many of her dresses.*

"Hello … Hello … Hello." Lilly and Usha bounded up the stairs to hug Richard and high-five Chloe.

"Hi girls, good to see you've plenty of energy," Richard said as he winked at Chloe. "Come on, let's go in my computer room, then we can talk." The girls followed Richard into the room and sat down. "Right Lilly, what's all this about? Your Mum told me about Luis' Dad, so what else is there to know?"

"You should have seen Lilly, Grandad. She was …." Usha started.

"Hang on Usha," Richard interrupted. "I asked Lilly."

"Umphh," Usha grumbled and folded her arms in disgust.

Chloe leant over and gave Usha a peck on the cheek. "Don't be like that cuz', it doesn't suit you." Usha smiled.

Lilly then went on to explain what had happened in the club house after the football match had finished.

"So you gave Mr Garcia no reason to attack you?"

"No, not at all. He was drunk …. But there was something else."

"What's that?"

"Those yellow eyes of his …. They were full of hate and menace ….. He wasn't himself, if you know what I mean. Luis told me his Dad was a nasty piece of work but he would never use a knife."

"Lilly was awesome," Usha interrupted. "I mean, the guy was full on, but sis' just floored him with a couple of decent moves …. You should have been there Grandad. She was brill. You'd have been proud of her."

"Good on you gal." Chloe gave Lilly an approving hug. "It sounds like he got what he deserved."

"His eyes …. Were they yellow before and after he attacked you?" Richard asked Lilly.

"No … No I don't think so. Why?"

"It's just that I've got this terrible feeling that he may have been possessed by a demon."

"Wow!" The three girls reacted in unison as they looked at each other in disbelief.

"Hmmm, did anyone query any of your actions?"

"No, no-one." Lilly shook her head. "The police Sergeant came back later on for statements from various witnesses including Luis, Ben, me and Usha. He seemed fine about it all."

"Right, okay. Well I'm sure the police will be keeping tabs on Mr Garcia for a while now." *Gotta try to keep the girls thinking positive.*

"There's something else Grandad," Lilly continued. "I was chatting to Luis about his Dad. They don't get on. Never have done apparently, especially since they moved to Alderney last year. Luis reckons that his Dad always seems preoccupied these days with other stuff that Luis' not allowed to be involved with."

"Oh yes?"

"Luis still doesn't know why his parents moved to the island ….. Here's the interesting bit though, his Grandfather is a well practised Shaman."

"A what?" Usha asked.

"A Shaman," Lilly replied. "Apparently Luis' Grandfather is a Q'ero Indian who lives in the Central Andes in Peru near the ancient centre of the Inca Empire. He's a direct descendant of the Incas and he still undertakes Shamanic Journeying."

"That's really weird." Chloe interrupted. "Alex has been banging on about this so called Journeying to me for some time. Making out it could probably help me with some of the problems I've had over the last few years. I must admit, I just thought it was a load of nonsense."

"Maybe not Chloe," Richard replied. "Different countries and cultures all have their own variations on this practice. For many years, most people just thought of it as another odd ball cult type thing, but more recently there has been evidence to support the theories and practices of Shamanic Journeying."

"Which is what?" Usha asked in a quizzical manner.

"In pretty basic terms," Richard continued. "A Shaman is a priest who believes that everything is connected in this world and other realms. They can contact Mother Earth and can lead people into a trance like state to join the priest in a journey, hopefully to improve their life. I suppose it's a bit like dreaming in a parallel world …. Something like that I suppose."

Richard then went on to show the girls what he'd found out on the internet. The Pacha worlds in Inca mythology and how it seemed to fit in with all the connections they had. The teenagers sat in front of the computer screens absolutely spellbound as they soaked in all the information.

"So where does that leave us?" Lilly asked.

"The Shamanic Journeying is worth looking at," Richard explained. "There are too many connections to Peru, the Incas, the Pacha and the Lima Treasure for them to be just coincidences." Richard turned to Chloe. "Take the subject up with Alex next time you phone him, trying not to raise his suspicions." Chloe nodded. "The other thing we need to try and sort is that library book. When are you working there this week?"

"I'm working there in the morning actually …. I just need to figure out how to preoccupy Mrs Dodds."

"Okay, well I'll think of something Chloe," Richard replied. "I'll call in around ten o'clock."

"Well count me out tomorrow, 'cos I'm at school all day." Usha giggled. "Mind you, the bonus for me is that Ben will be there as well."

"Hmm. Not sure that's why you go to school young lady ….. Do they teach you anything there?"

The three girls laughed.

"I take it you're working tomorrow at the hotel, in the Blonde Hedgehog kitchens Lilly?" Richard asked.

"Yep!" Lilly had a big grin on her face. She loved preparing and cooking food, even more so because her Dad, Chris, was the Head Chef. "And I'm helping Chloe in the afternoon at the café."

Chloe nodded approvingly.

"Well next time you see Luis, see if you can find anything else out about his Dad and so forth. That's if you can manage to keep your paws off him." Richard winked at Chloe and Usha. The two girls giggled.

"Hello …. Anyone home?" A voice from downstairs.

"Right girls, time to go," Richard said hurriedly. "It's your Grandma. I'd lost track of time ..... Don't forget Chloe, I'll see you at the library in the morning."

The teenagers bounded down the stairs. "HI GRANDMA."

Bea hugged them each in turn as they left the house. "You really mustn't encourage the girls Richard. They spend far too much time here with you instead of doing what teenagers usually get up to."

"You'd be the first to complain if they didn't come at all .... Anyway I like having them around ..... How's your day been?"

"I'm off out now Bea .... Should only be a couple of hours or so." Richard glanced at his watch. *Just before eight. Need to get going 'cos Annie will be getting worried.*

"Yeah okay, I'll see you later. Have you remembered to pick up your bait out of the fridge?"

"Got it thanks. Gonna try round by the lighthouse this evening. Some of the guys have been saying there's loads of mackerel around so it would be nice to catch a few." Richard picked up his two fishing rods and left the house.

The van started with its usual splutter and as he pulled away he waved to Bea who was standing by the lounge window.

Five minutes later and Richard pulled the van over into a disused driveway which was in total darkness. It was just round the corner from Annie's house. He clambered out of the van and picked up the tin of fishing bait and immediately emptied the contents into a nearby bin. *Right, let's go and see Annie.*

Annie peeked through the curtain as Richard walked down her driveway and by the time he'd reached the front door Annie was opening it. "Come in luv .... Quickly." She pulled him inside and slammed the door behind him, pinning him to the wall and smothering him with kisses.

Bloody hell woman. "Annie .... Annie .... Can we ...."

"Oh Richard, I just feel so horny tonight." She kissed him again and moved his hands to caress her breasts through her blouse. "I've been thinking about you all day." *I need you .... Now!... Sex!*

Richard gently eased Annie away from his body, took her hand and led her into the lounge. "Let's get comfortable shall we?"

They both sat down on the huge sofa and chatted about the day they'd had. The pair had known each other since their early school days and were engaged to be married at one point many years ago, before they met their current partners. They'd been lovers for a number of years and Annie was a demanding woman who had an unbelievably high sex drive. The thought of Annie being a librarian always made Richard smile to himself....

Annie gasped as Richard slid his hand between her thighs and through her delicate curls to gently caress her intimately as her love juices flowed. She opened her legs wider as she succumbed to her basic desire ....

Richard glanced at his watch as Annie's naked body snuggled up to him once more and held him tight again as she felt him throb ... *Ten thirty .... Jeez, I need to go, else Bea will be wondering.*

"Annie .... Annie I have to go home."

Annie gazed adoringly into Richard's eyes and kissed him. "Can't you stay longer?"

"You know I can't luv." Richard kissed her tenderly as he dressed himself. "I really must go Annie. I'll see you tomorrow." Richard kissed her again and left the house.

CHAPTER 22

PEACE AND WAR

It was seven in the morning when Chloe stepped out of Mr and Mrs Bean's house. Alex's Dad, Frank, was also up early. As a local fisherman he knew the tides well and when to go out to sea to hopefully get a good catch.

"Morning Chloe, you're up early?" Frank called as he climbed into his van.

"Morning Mr Bean. Yeah, I'm going to take the dog for a walk over the golf course. I promised Alex I'd keep looking for golf balls whilst he was in Guernsey." She pointed to the near empty box on the drive which Alex used to sell golf balls that he'd found. "Hopefully I can find a few whilst the dog gets a bit of exercise before I get off to work at the library."

"Good for you gal. You have a good day. The fish aren't going to catch themselves, so I'll be off then." Frank started the engine of his van and waved to Chloe as he drove away.

Chloe called the dog and strolled onto the golf course. The dog was a three year old female Golden Retriever called Dapper. She was a boisterous dog with a really good temperament. Chloe called out Dapper's name again. *Where is she?*

Chloe continued to stroll across the fairway of the par 4 hole looking for golf balls stopping occasionally to glance around for any sign of Dapper. Out in the distance she could see the Alderney Breakwater in Braye Bay stretching out for about nine hundred metres. It took seventeen years to build and was finished in 1864 when, at that time it was one thousand four hundred and seventy metres long. *Magnificent sight.*

"DAPPER!.... WHERE ARE YOU?" Chloe caught sight of her in the distance. *What's she up to?* A little closer and then she realised the dog was sat next to a mole hill. There was a few scattered around.

"Good girl Dapper." Chloe patted her on the head. "There's a mole down there is there? I bet you can hear it." Chloe bent down and as she did, three blonde hedgehogs scuttled past, snuffling around in the grass. "Well, that's made my day girl. Blonde hedgehogs and half a dozen golf balls!" She chuckled to herself. "Come on girl, let's go. I've got to go to work. Let's go and find Mrs Bean."

They strolled back to the house to see Beth standing at the door. Dapper bounded up to her, tail wagging furiously. Chloe dropped the golf balls into the 'FOR SALE' box at the end of the drive and cheerfully skipped to Beth who gave her a gentle hug.

"Morning Chloe. You're chirpy this morning."

"Hi Mrs Bean. Yeah well, it's a grand morning and the air is so clear. And just look at that blue sky."

"Yeah. Picture perfect .... So are you off to the library now?"

"Sure am .... And then I'm working at the café this afternoon with Lilly."

"A busy day then." Beth smiled. She could see the increasing confidence in Chloe every day. It was satisfying to see after the years of heartache that Chloe had endured. Beth waved and blew a kiss as the young girl drove away on her scooter.

Within five minutes, Chloe pulled up outside the library. Annie Dodds, the head librarian, was in the process of unlocking the doors and switching the burglar alarm off. She then hung the bunch of keys on her belt loop.

"HI MRS DODDS," Chloe called, as she clambered off her scooter.

"Oh hello Chloe." Annie hung her coat up on one of the hooks. "Come on in and we'll see what there is to do."

Chloe followed the librarian into the main part of the building as she switched the lights on.

"So how are you doing then Chloe?"

"Yeah, good thanks. Life's on the up I think."

"I hear you've got yourself a boyfriend. Alex Bean isn't it? He's a good lad and I know his Mum well."

"Yeah, Mrs Bean's lovely …. So's Alex. Shame he's at college in Guernsey though, but we phone each other every day, so that's cool."

"Arh, that's nice. I'm pleased for you Chloe." Annie smiled approvingly. "Right gal, if you want to crack on and clean that set of shelving over there we can get these new books that's just been delivered sorted and onto the shelves."

"Okay Mrs Dodds. Will do."

An hour later and Chloe and Annie were surrounded by books. The local library committee had decided that they needed a larger section of crime novels due to the increase of interest in them since Rachel Abbott, the well known crime author had recently moved to Alderney.

"Are we going to fit all these books in? There looks to be too many here."

"You could be right Chloe. We might have to rotate a few of them …. But not this one." Annie held the book up in front of Chloe.

"Right Behind You by Rachel Abbott." Chloe read from the front cover. "That's the lady who moved here a couple of years ago isn't it?"

"That's right, she's sold a lot of books worldwide over the years …. Oh, and while I remember, I've got this other interesting new book we need to put out in the fantasy section. It's called 'Secrets & Lies' by another local author, Richard Bowen."

"Hello … Anyone here?" A voice from the front desk of the library interrupted their discussion.

Annie looked up to see Richard. *Here he is, the love of my life.* He had two cups of coffee in his hands. "Right Chloe, you carry on and I'll see what Mr Morgan wants."

Chloe nodded and as Annie turned away to walk towards Richard, Chloe noticed that the keys she would need to get into the library files were still on Mrs Dodds' belt loop.

"Hello Richard. Nice to see you. What can I do for you?" Annie asked. *I know what I'd like to do!*

"Hi Annie …. Err, nothing really." Richard held up the two cups of coffee. "I was just passing and I thought you'd like a

138

coffee seeing as it must be time for a break for you." He smiled nervously as he offered Annie one of the cups. "It's white with one sugar if I remember rightly …. That's how you've kept your figure eh?!"

Richard glanced over to Chloe. She was pulling faces at his every word and trying not to laugh.

"Oh Richard, you're not flirting with me are you? That's really very nice of you." She took the cup from Richard. "And you remembered … How do you do that?" *All this pretence is driving me nutty.*

"How could I ever forget. We've known each other for so long I could probably tell you what colour underwear you're wearing …." Annie's face coloured up. "…. But we won't go there!" *Went there last night!*

"Cheeky."

Chloe sniggered out loud.

"Come on, let's go and sit outside in the sunshine whilst this coffee is still hot." Richard motioned to Annie. "I'm sure young Chloe can manage for a few minutes." Richard gave Chloe a thumbs up as he followed Annie outside.

Chloe immediately sensed her heart was racing. The adrenalin had kicked in at the thought she had maybe five minutes, possibly six at best to find the book which would give her the serial number. She didn't have a key so she would then have to break into the filing cabinet that kept all the relevant details.

Chloe quickly scanned the reference book section … *Here we go. Shipwrecks in the Channel Islands 12th-19th Century.* Chloe noted the date stamp on the inner sleeve of the book, 20th February 2000 and the serial number was 46TK396L. She returned the book to the shelf and swiftly walked over to Annie's work station and glanced through the window to see Richard and Annie chatting and sipping coffee …. .

Richard felt Annie's hand on his inner thigh and immediately became aroused. "Stop it luv, someone will see what you're doing."

Annie leant over and kissed Richard on the cheek. "I'll always love you Richard. You know that don't you? Whatever happens."

Richard gently moved Annie's hand away, smiled and nodded approvingly. "Always Annie...."

Chloe turned to the filing cabinet. *It's still locked.* She pulled on the handle. *Oh well, desperate measures and all that.* She placed her hand over the lock. She felt the power ... And in an instant the cabinet was open. *I'm glad Lilly showed me how to do that.* The teenager soon realised that all the books had been filed by their serial numbers. "Come on .... Where's 46?" she muttered. "Come on...." Chloe's eyes were skimming the numbers as she desperately flicked through the files. *Yes ... 46 .... Come on, 46TC, no good, keep going.* Chloe was beginning to panic. Then .... "There it is ... 46TK 39 6 ... L. Got it."

"Well that was nice Annie," Richard remarked rather loudly as they opened the door to the library.

Jeez, I've got two seconds. Chloe realised she was about to be caught red-handed unless .... She grabbed her pendant to concentrate her mind on a trick her cousin Usha had shown her. Chloe was immediately surrounded by a surge of power that seemed to create a whirlwind effect. She held her breath, not daring to move.

Richard and Annie walked straight past Chloe as if she wasn't there. *It worked. It's as if I'm invisible with this power shield around me. Cool.*

"Can you hear that noise Richard? Can you hear it?"

Richard knew exactly what Annie was asking about. He realised that Chloe was using a shield. He'd heard the same noise when Usha first found out that she could produce a shield. The sound was like the wind blowing down a chimney.

"Not sure I can hear anything out of the ordinary," Richard replied. "The wind's picked up slightly outside, maybe it's effecting the extractor fans."

"Hmm, not sure .... It doesn't feel right .... That's odd, it's stopped now ..... And where's Chloe?" Annie glanced around.

"Oh hi Mrs Dodds. I thought you was still outside with Grandad." Chloe held her hand out. "Just had to get a cloth, some of these new books need a wipe." Chloe smiled at Annie and Richard as she walked back to the stack of books they'd been sorting earlier. *Phew, that was close. I just managed to close the filing cabinet and lock it.*

Richard decided to make a move before the situation got complicated. "Well it was good to catch up with you Annie. Don't forget you owe me a coffee." He turned to go, and as he did he called to Chloe, "I'll catch up with you later Chloe at the café."

Chloe nodded and winked to Richard.

"Bye then Richard. Say hello to Bea for me." Annie waved as he left the library. *Until next time my love.*

Lilly arrived at the café for her afternoon shift and as she turned the engine off, on her scooter, Chloe arrived on hers. The two teenagers clambered off their machines and kissed each other on the cheek.

"Hi Lilly, had a good morning?"

"Yeah sure. You?"

"Had a close call with Mrs Dodds at the library earlier on …. But I managed to get the info' we're all looking for. I'll show you later when Grandad arrives 'cos I haven't even looked at it myself yet."

"Well considering what you've been up to this morning makes my life look boring …. I've been working with my Dad at the Blonde Hedgehog making patisseries."

"Yummy." Chloe licked her lips.

"Yeah I know, I ate a few myself, but I don't want to start piling on the pounds."

The two girls giggled as they entered the café.

It had been a busy couple of hours at the café and the girls had just sat down at one of the tables for a breather before having a good clean down, when Richard walked in. "Any chance of a coffee you two?"

"Would that be white with one sugar then?" Chloe joked and then winked at her Grandad.

Richard gave Chloe a wry smile as he sat down at the table.

"Here you go Grandad." Lilly placed a cup of coffee on the table.

"So Chloe, what have we got from the library?" Richard asked.

Chloe walked over to her jacket which was hanging up on one of the many coat hooks behind the counter and pulled out a file and handed it to Richard. He studied the pages as the two girls sat watching, elbows on the table with their hands supporting their chins.

"Hmmm ….. Yeah ….. Well ….. Not unexpected then."

"Well?" Lilly snapped.

Richard lifted his head and looked directly at Lilly. "It's Diego Garcia …… It's Luis' Dad. Be honest, that's what we all thought. The book has only been taken out of the library once, and that was twenty years ago."

"Oh jeez," Chloe gasped. "Sorry Lilly, I didn't mean to…"

"It's okay, I did sort of have that feeling." Lilly rose from her chair. "Especially after having to deal with him the other day at the football club." Lilly picked the chair up as she felt her anger and power building up inside her. She shouted, "I'LL GET THE BASTARD." Her eyes instantly changed to black and the chair went flying across the café.

"Grandad, GET DOWN, she's out of control," Chloe shouted as she dragged him to the floor.

The café seemed to be in a whirlwind as Lilly threw her arms back and forth. The noise was deafening as furniture, pots, pans and anything that wasn't tied down flew from wall to wall.

"Chloe …. Your shield," Richard muttered as he struggled to talk. "Concentrate gal …. Power up your shield." Richard pointed to Lilly who by now was throwing pulses of power at random causing destruction all around. "Try to move your shield to enclose Lilly."

"Chloe …. NOW ….. DO IT!" Richard shouted to make Chloe focus. "NOW."

Chloe raised her hands as her eyes turned red and instantly created a shield around herself. She pushed her hands forward towards Lilly. She concentrated, and forced the shield to surround her cousin.

142

"HOLD IT THERE." Richard quickly picked up his phone. *Phone Usha.* He could hear the phone ringing. *Come on Usha .....*

"Hi Grandad, what's up?"

"Usha, listen .... No time to explain. I need you to get into Lilly's head now. Her thoughts. You need to calm her down NOW. JUST DO IT!"

"Okay."

Richard turned to Chloe. "Just hang on gal ... Just a little longer."

As Richard spoke he could see Lilly had collapsed and was now lying on the floor motionless. "Chloe .... CHLOE. It's okay. You can stop now."

Chloe released the shield and heaved a huge sigh.

"You okay Chloe? You did it, well done."

Richard looked around to survey the wreckage. *It's like a war zone.* He helped Chloe to her feet and they both stumbled over to where Lilly was lying, perfectly still. No life, nothing. *Oh Jeez, what are we .....*

The sound of a scooter broke into Richard's thoughts.

"Grandad." It was Usha. "What the ..... Lilly .... Get me some water quickly."

Chloe grabbed a water jug from the only remaining table and passed it to Usha who by now had pulled her little teddy from her pocket. Usha soaked the teddy in the water and then squeezed the water from the teddy onto Lilly's lips. "Come on Lilly."

Lilly suddenly sat up, coughing and spluttering. "Usha, you saved me." She burst into tears.

"Oh Lilly," Richard sighed as he held her tight. "I thought we'd lost you."

Chloe knelt down and hugged her cousin. "Thought you was a gonna gal."

Lilly glanced around the café. "Did I do all th....?"

"You made a pretty good job of it eh?" Richard interrupted. "Good job Usha and Chloe managed to stop you doing anything more serious."

"Awesome," Usha said. "Took a bit of serious concentration to get into your head Lilly. Your thoughts were all over the place .... And the images were bizarre. It was like watching a zombie film. Really weird."

"How do you feel?" Richard asked Lilly.

"Okay. Okay I think .... Look at all this damage."

"Don't worry about it. At least everyone's alright. Lilly, you really need to keep your feelings in check. Your emotions are driving the powers you have so you need to focus more, before you use any of your powers."

Lilly nodded.

"Don't speak, I know just what you're sayin'...." Usha's ring tone, Don't Speak by No Doubt rang out on her phone breaking the relative calm in the café.

"Hello .... Oh hi Ben ..... Whoa, slow down. You're not making any sense .... You what?... No way!..... You sure Ben?..... Okay. Stay where you are ...... Yes, yes."

Usha turned to the others. "Ben's in trouble down at the school. All hell's breaking out down there apparently with about half a dozen guys blowing stuff up and creating mayhem. Ben's locked himself in the boiler room with a couple of other kids to keep them out of harms way .... We need to get down there now."

"Come on guys, we'll go in my van." Richard helped Lilly up from the floor. "Are you up for this Lilly? You still look a bit shaky."

"Come on, let's not waste any more time 'cos Ben needs our help," Lilly replied. "Let's go."

Richard and the three teenagers stumbled through the wreckage of the café and hurriedly climbed into the van which hesitated for a moment before firing into life. *Get your foot down Richard.*

Two minutes later and Richard had parked the van up on the road just above St Annes School. Directly above the school, black storm clouds gave a sense of impending doom as lightening bolts rained down and yet, the surrounding sky was clear blue. *This all looks very surreal. Like a movie set,* thought Richard.

"RIGHT, LET'S GO," Lilly yelled.

"Whoa, hang on a mo'," Richard replied. "Let's just see what we're up against before we get involved with something that might be out of our control. Usha, pass me the binoculars out of the glove compartment please."

Richard peered through the binoculars, bringing them into focus as he scanned the school buildings and the surrounding playing fields and grounds.

"What d'ya see Grandad?" Lilly asked.

"Here, take a look." Richard passed her the binoculars.

"Well Lilly?" Chloe snapped.

"There's a couple of fires in the one building …. And I reckon there's at least four guys in the grounds so we have to assume there's others inside."

"Right. Here's the crack, listen up girls," Richard growled. "This is really dangerous stuff. Be careful. We all know where the boiler room is, so Ben is the priority."

Richard turned to Usha. "Concentrate on getting Ben and whoever else is with him out of there ….. The rest of us ….. Use whatever is absolutely necessary. We need to tackle these guys now. GOT IT?"

"Okay Grandad." The girls answered in unison as they all clambered out of the van.

Richard led the girls stealthily into the playground. He stopped, lifted the binoculars to his eyes and scanned around. He concentrated his gaze on one of the guys. *It's a demon. Yellow eyes, slightly hunched with long unkempt hair around its misshaped skull with sunken eye sockets. Bare feet and gnarled hands with six long thin like digits. Finger nails like talons …..*

"DEMONS!…. SHIT!" He turned to the girls. "Aim for the heart or sever the head, it's the only way girls …. GO …. GO!"

The three girls high-fived. "Let's do it."

Chloe and Lilly ran off to the left whilst Usha made her way towards the main entrance accompanied by Richard.

A demon lunged at Richard from the side sending him sprawling across the ground. It leapt on top of him and as it did, Richard plunged a knife deep into the creature's heart and a cloud of dust enveloped him as the demon met it's end with a blood curdling scream ….. "Go on Usha, get to the boiler

145

room." Richard pulled himself up. "I'll stay here and watch your back …. Go girl."

Usha's eyes turned black as she turned and ran down the school corridor. Smoke from the fires was becoming thicker and the visibility was deteriorating rapidly. She turned the corner. *A demon!* It lashed out and Usha grimaced as it's talons gouged three deep wounds across her chest. She kicked the creature in the groin and as it bent forward in pain, Usha threw a power pulse to it's head. The demon recoiled backwards and fell down the stairs. Usha leapt down landing directly on top of the prone creature and plunged a lightening bolt into it's heart. A cloud of dust erupted as the demon screamed it's last breath. *Awesome.*

The smoke is getting worse. Where's the boiler room door?…. Got it! Usha banged frantically on the door. "Ben … BEN …. ARE YOU THERE? BEN."

The door opened slowly …. It was Ben.

"Oh Ben, you're okay." Usha threw her arms around her boyfriend. "Come on, we need to get out of here …. NOW."

"Usha …. Look at the state of you …. Look at your eyes ….. And you're …. You're hurt …. I thought I'd never see you again gal."

"Fat chance of that boy …. Come on, we need to get going." Usha grabbed his hand.

Ben turned to look in the boiler room. "Come on, let's go with Usha." Two twelve year old girls joined Ben. Their faces filled with worry and bewilderment.

"We need to go Ben." Usha pointed up the stairs. "Get to the corridor and head for the main entrance. My Grandad should be there."

The two young girls gripped Ben's hands tightly as they stumbled up the stairs and disappeared into the smoke as they manoeuvred their way towards the main entrance doors. Usha followed slowly making sure they weren't being followed.

Richard was becoming frantic as he paced back and forth. He could here Lilly and Chloe shouting somewhere in the distance. *Where's Usha? Come on girl.* He turned to look through the main entrance door for the umpteenth time to glimpse any sight of Usha or Ben. Suddenly, three figures

146

emerged from the smoke filled building coughing and spluttering ....

"Ben. It's good to see you're alright .... You girls okay?"

The three kids nodded. Tears were rolling down from their smoke filled eyes.

"Ben. Take these girls up to my van and stay with them."

Ben nodded and turned to go. "What about Usha?"

"Don't worry mate, I'll see she's alright. Just go."

Ben took hold of the two girl's hands and ran off towards Richard's van.

Richard stepped into the smoke filled corridor. "USHA .... WHERE ARE YOU?.... HURRY UP." He suddenly heard footsteps about ten metres down the corridor. "USHA .... IS THAT YOU?" Moments later and he could make out the tell tale swagger of Usha coming towards him. *Thank God. Another few metres* .... "DEMON!... USHA, BEHIND YOU .... GET DOWN."

Usha ducked down as she heard her Grandad shout. She could feel another presence behind her ....

Richard threw his hand up and sent a power pulse hurtling down the corridor, exploding on contact with the demon's head sending it sprawling onto its back.

Usha spun round and threw herself onto the body of the demon and thrust a lightening bolt into it's heart. With a blood curdling scream and a cloud of dust, the demon was gone.

Richard ran forward and pulled Usha up off the floor. "Come on girl, let's get you out of here." They staggered outside breathing heavily from the smoke inhalation. "You did well girl .... But look at the state of you. And you're bleeding quite heavily." Richard threw his jacket round Usha's shoulders. "Come on, you've done enough, let's get you to the van. Ben will be worried sick about you."

Lilly and Chloe glanced at each other as six demons approached them. "THIS IS IT CHLOE, LET'S DO OUR STUFF." The two girls momentarily concentrated. Their eyes turned black as all hell let loose in front of them.

Two power pulses from Lilly dropped two demons to the ground and in an instant the two girls sat astride them, plunging their lightening bolts into the demon's hearts. Surrounded by the dust of their victims, two more demons threw themselves at the girls drawing blood and tearing clothes. Chloe kneed her assailant in the groin and pushed it off. She threw a power pulse at the demon attacking Lilly sending it hurtling through the air.

Lilly grabbed her amulet and instantly created a shield around herself and Chloe ….. "JAVELINS," she shouted, pointing to a rack on the playing field which held the sports equipment. The two girls held their arms out towards the rack and in an instant, two javelins flew through the air into their outstretched hands. "LET'S SHOW THEM WHAT WE CAN DO CHLOE."

The girls were now surrounded by eight demons of different sizes and weight with mean and menacing eyes. Lilly and Chloe sprung spontaneously into action, back flipping and somersaulting as they swung the javelins around at head height, slashing the demons throats causing them to combust in clouds of dust. The last two unworldly beings flung themselves forward towards the girls who, at the last possible moment, knelt down holding the javelins at an upwards angle and the demons impaled themselves in clouds of dust.

"YES!" Chloe shouted.

"They must have been the last ones," Lilly announced. "Look at the sky."

The two girls stood in awe as they watched the dark clouds slowly clear to reveal a stunning blue sky once more.

"Just look at that." Chloe pointed directly above. "Rainbows dancing across the sky …. Cool."

Richard had been watching the action unfold from his van looking through his binoculars. As he scanned the school grounds below through the fire and smoke he spotted someone making a hasty retreat from the scene. The person stopped momentarily to look back. *It's Diego Garcia, Luis' father. Thought he'd be involved with all this. Gonna have to sort him out.*

"GRANDAD …. Is everyone okay?" Chloe shouted as the two girls approached Richard and Ben.

148

"Err … Yeah …. Sure." Richard suddenly came to his senses.

"Where's Usha?" Lilly asked in a concerned tone. She then spotted her sister lying on the ground in a semi conscious state, blood still pouring out of the three deep wounds in her chest. Lilly knelt down beside her sister and cradled her head gently. "Where's your teddy?"

Usha struggled to whisper, "Lost it sis'… Not sure where."

"Here it is. I found it in the grass on the way back up here," Chloe said. "Pass that water bottle Lilly." She soaked the little teddy in the water and squeezed it out over Usha's lips.

Usha gasped and sat up as the wounds healed and the three girls hugged more in relief than joy.

The sound of sirens filled the air as the school was surrounded by the emergency services.

"We need to go." Richard climbed into the van. "This place is going to be crawling with police and so forth asking a lot of questions. In the van everyone. We'll drop the two young girls off at the hospital on the way home."

As usual, the van started with a splutter and pulled away down the hill.

CHAPTER 23

THE JOURNEY

"Have you seen this?" Bea asked.

"What's that luv?" Richard replied as he lifted his head from the pillow. *Shit, I've slept in, lazy sod. Ha!* "What are you on about?"

"Our Usha is on the front page of the local press. It says she saved her boyfriend and two young girls from that fire down at the school the other day …. Why didn't you tell me?"

"Err …. It was no big deal and anyway, I didn't think Usha wanted to make anything of it." *I can see I'm going to get grief for the next few days.*

"Typical!….. I'm going to ring Susan right now to see if she's seen this."

Oh boy ….. I'd better get up.

"I've just noticed this as well."

"What?"

"That café in town where the girls work was burgled and vandalised on the same day as that fire ….. Don't know what's happening any more on the island. Disgraceful!"

You have no idea Bea. "Yeah, terrible. Right, I'm gonna get dressed while you phone our Susan."

Richard walked into the kitchen. *Jeez, she's still on the phone!*

"She said what Susan?….. Really …… What about Chris?…. What does he think about it?….. Hmmm, yes …. I know …. But even so ….. Well so long as she's okay, that's the main thing …. What? Oh you've got to go. Alright then. You take care and I'll see you soon. Bye." Bea put the phone down.

"You've been on there for over half an hour luv," Richard remarked. "Susan and Chris alright?"

"Yeah they're fine. They're very proud of Usha. Apparently the two young girls that were with Ben at the school told their story to one of the nurses at the hospital and it got back to the local press."

"That's good then …. She's a good girl is our Usha."

"You could have told me though Richard."

"Yeah okay, don't go on about it luv." *Need to get out of here.*

The six teenagers laughed hysterically as they lounged on the grass bank at Bibette Head below the Second World War German bunkers.

"You alright Luis?" Lilly asked. "You look a bit tired." She ran her fingers through her boyfriend's black curly hair.

"Yeah …. I'm okay. Just seem to be doing a lot of work recently. My Dad's being a real slave driver at the mo' and he's just being a pain in the arse lately." Luis sighed. "And my Step Mum's over in the UK for quite some time with some big accountancy firm."

Lilly placed her arm around his shoulders and kissed him. *Well we know what your Dad's up too.*

"Well if you need a hand mate give me a shout seeing as I'm back for a week," Alex said. "I'm sure Chloe won't mind if I go missing for a few hours."

Chloe squeezed his hand tighter. "Don't be too sure about that kiddo ….. You only got back on the island last night and you're already trying to get rid of me."

The six friends laughed.

"Anyway, don't forget it's my birthday this week. I hope you've got me something I've been wanting for some time," Chloe joked.

"Sorted," Alex replied as he flashed a pack of condoms to the group and winked cheekily at Chloe as he nudged her in the ribs.

Ben and Usha looked at each other embarrassed at what they were hearing.

"So changing the subject somewhat." Chloe turned to Luis. "Lilly's been telling me that your Grandfather is a Q'ero Indian and he practices Shamanic Journeying back in his home country of Peru."

"Err … Yeah …. He's a Shaman. I've actually been on some of his journeys. It's not easy and generally speaking, girls are more likely to succeed. My Grandfather thought it had something to do

151

with the feminine aura. He showed me how to do it but I haven't practised journeying for a long time. Not everyone is able to go on a journey 'cos they have to have an open mind. It's a bit like dream walking and some people just can't get the connection. Sometimes, you enter another sort of world. It's all about belief."

"Wow," Alex exclaimed. "That's really weird 'cos I've been studying Shamanic Journeying in my spare time. It's REALLY interesting …. I told you about it, eh Chloe?"

"Yes you did hun. But I just thought it was a load of old codswallop." Chloe gave Lilly a knowing look.

"Come on then." Lilly looked purposefully at Luis.

"What?"

"Let's give it a go."

"You sure about this Lilly?"

"Yeah, why not. What d'ya reckon guys?"

"Yeah, we're in aren't we Alex?" Chloe asked.

"Count me in Luis."

"And don't forget us two," Usha chimed in as she hugged Ben.

Luis sighed. "Right, okay then. We need to sit round in a circle and hold hands ….. We've got a problem though."

"What's that?" Lilly asked.

"Well normally someone would make a rhythmic beat. It helps to concentrate the mind."

"I can do that for you."

The six teenagers turned to see Richard. "Sorry guys, didn't mean to startle you …. I was passing in the van and I happened to see your scooters parked up so I thought I'd see what you was up too."

"Perfect timing Mr Morgan," Alex replied. "Luis was just going to show us, or maybe take us on a Shamanic Journey ….. We need someone to make a rhythmic style beat. You up for it?"

"Sure. I'll see what I've got in the back of the van. Must have something to make some noise with."

Two minutes later, Richard reappeared with a large empty paint tin. "This should do the trick." He tapped the base of the tin with his hand and it gave a hollow toned sound.

"Right, let's get started," Luis said with some sort of authority. "The six of us need to sit in a circle and hold hands whilst Mr Morgan slaps that tin with a steady beat."

Richard started to hit the tin with a steady rhythm.

"I want you all to close your eyes …. Empty your minds and concentrate on the sound of my voice and the sound of the beating that Mr Morgan is producing," Luis said. "It might work for some or all of you and it usually takes about ten minutes to tune in to my thoughts ….. Okay?"

The young friends nodded approvingly in anticipation as to what was about to transpire.

Richard watched intently as Luis started to hum …. And then he chanted in Quechuan, the traditional language of Peru ….

Richard glanced at his watch. *Been about fifteen minutes so far.* He looked around the circle. *Luis is still chanting. Lilly, Usha and Chloe look at peace and Alex….* "Alex."

Alex gasped as his eyes opened, "Shit …. Couldn't do it."

Seconds later and Ben opened his eyes.

Richard gestured to Alex and Ben to keep quiet ….

"Where are we?" Lilly asked.

"This is the realm of Hanan Pacha, you're on my journey," Luis replied. "Are you here Chloe?"

"I'm with you, yes, I'm here ….. What is this place? It's so serine …. It's wonderful."

"Usha?"

"I'm here. Where are we? Look at the sky, it's pink!"

"This place is what Christians call Heaven. The Upper World or Realm according to Inca Mythology, but as you can see, it's no myth," Luis explained. "This is your journey now." He sat down and closed his eyes.

"WELCOME." A powerful voice boomed towards the four teenagers. "COME CLOSER THAT I MIGHT SEE WHOM HAS DARED TO ENTER OUR REALM."

The three girls stepped forward slowly. Luis remained seated as if transfixed in his own dream walk.

"STOP." The voice boomed. "THE THREE MARYS ….. COME CLOSER THAT I MAY SEE YOU BETTER."

Lilly glanced at Usha and Chloe before taking each others hands and stepped forward.

There was an audible gasp as the girls drew closer. Three huge figures sat before them. Their appearance was akin to characters straight out of a Biblical story.

"STOP. SO THE THREE MARYS DARE TO ENTER OUR REALM …. I AM ILLAPA, THE GOD OF THUNDER AND LIGHTENING. TO MY LEFT IS MAMA KILLA, THE MOON GODDESS AND FINALLY, THIS IS INTI, THE SUN GOD. WE KNOW OF YOUR QUEST TO FIND THE LIMA TREASURE. IT IS OURS TO TAKE BACK IF WE SO DESIRE."

The girls looked at each other.

Inti, the Sun God stood up. "WE WILL HELP YOU …. BUT THERE MAY BE CONSEQUENCES ALONG THE JOURNEY AND …. THERE WILL BE GREAT DANGER AND THUS YOUR POWERS WILL BECOME STRONGER. THE HUNTER IN THE CONSTELLATION OF ORION CHOSE YOU THREE AND YOU HAVE ALREADY SHOWN YOUR WORTH IN DESTROYING DEMONS. BE OF NO DOUBT, MORE WILL COME."

"I am known as Mama Killa, the Moon Goddess." Her voice was soft. "Be it known that danger is all around, both in the human world and the spirit worlds, our three realms of Pacha …. And to that end I bestow to each of you, these light staffs which will aid you in your quest." She passed a two metre seemingly wooden staff to each of the girls. "You will find these at the place you love most in your world. Use these wisely as a cataclysmic event is on the horizon which could transform the entire order of your world. Be warned, a world changing event is possible …. This is what the Supay, the demons in Ukhu Pacha, the World Below, desire. One further thing that you must know before you enter each realm …. Use your imagination as to how you wish to appear, because remember, our worlds are your dream worlds so anything is possible."

Illapa stood up. "GO NOW. WE WILL HELP WHEN AND WHERE WE CAN, BUT BE IN NO DOUBT, THE FUTURE OF YOUR WORLD AS YOU KNOW IT LIES WITH YOU, THE THREE MARYS. GO NOW." The God of Thunder and Lightening pointed to Luis as he spoke.

154

Richard stopped beating the empty tin as the three girls and Luis opened their eyes and gasped for air.

"AWESOME," Usha shouted as she jumped up off the ground and danced around excitedly.

"Wow….. Excellent," Lilly and Chloe exclaimed.

Richard glanced at his watch. *Fifteen minutes. Strange. Wherever they've been, it's taken no time at all in real time!*

Luis sat there looking at the girls. "I take it then, that you enjoyed your journey? Shame you didn't manage to come with us lads. Perhaps next time. It really is all about believing."

"So what did you experience Luis?" Richard enquired.

"A Shamanic journey always leaves me at peace with the world. It's my escape from reality, it's my dream world. I can take people with me, such as I did today with the girls, but once they're there I don't always continue with them. I suppose it's a more personal journey for any individual. It's like today, I knew the girls were with me, but I have no idea where their journey took them. Sometimes I get to see someone's journey, but not often."

"Interesting stuff Luis …. Well I'm off guys. I'll take my empty tin and go. Perhaps I'll see you all later. Take care."

"Your Grandad's okay Usha," Ben whispered in her ear. "Bit of a screw loose though, don't you think."

"Ha …. Wouldn't change him for the world boy. Come on, are we going?"

"Yeah sure …. Scooter's over there gal."

"SEE YOU GUYS LATER." Usha climbed onto the machine with Ben. A wave of hands and the pair roared off into the distance.

"Looks like it's time to go then." Chloe turned to Alex and kissed him.

"Right you are then. Looks like I've got my orders, ha."

"Yeah, come on Luis, it's getting on a bit. We might as well go too. We'll follow Chloe and Alex round on the coast road." Lilly pulled Luis up from the ground.

The two young couples climbed on their scooters and waved to each other as they drove off down the road.

CHAPTER 24

THE UNDERGROUND

"Now lighting a cigarette, Now knowing I will regret, The way our love had to end, In her room, Standing all alone, All alone, Soon I will be gone....." Brilliant!

It was late afternoon and Richard was enjoying a bit of me time in the back garden listening to one of his fave rock bands of the seventies. The track playing was Soon I Will Be Gone by Free. There'd been a light shower of rain twenty minutes earlier and as he continued to listen to the music he looked in the distance. A double rainbow was visible. *Just perfect in every way.* The rain had softened the earth enough for him to guide his hoe between the rows of vegetables he'd grown from seed earlier in the year, to chop down the weeds that were gleefully encroaching on his plants.

Hmm, this row of peas could do with stringing up to support them as they grow. I'll have to put some stakes in to tie the string too. Let's have a look in the shed. Richard turned off his CD player.

Richard's shed was ..... "A bomb site! I really must sort all of this mess out. What are these?.... Don't remember having any stakes like this. Perfect, they'll do the job. Just need to cut them to size."

Lilly and Usha's scooter screeched to a halt on Richard's front driveway as Chloe's scooter pulled up beside them.

"You got the same idea as me?" Chloe asked.

"It has to be," Lilly replied. "If not here, then I give up."

"What's all that noise?" Usha covered her ears. "What a din ... Where's it coming from?"

The three girls walked around the house into the back garden to see Richard, man handling a chainsaw. Sparks were flying in every direction as the blade of the machine bounced off what he thought were wooden stakes.

The girls looked on in disbelief. Lilly took a step forward. *Jeez, Grandad's going to hurt himself in a minute.* She turned and nodded to Chloe and Usha. They each extended an arm out …. The three light staffs flew across the garden into the hands of the three teenagers.

"WHAT THE F…." Richard's chainsaw fell to the ground out of harms way and spluttered to a halt. "What's going on girls?"

"Sorry Grandad, we didn't have time to tell you earlier today," Lilly explained as she expertly spun the staff around through her fingers. "These three light staffs were given to us by Mama Killa, the Moon Goddess who we met on our Shamanic Journey."

Chloe and Usha then went on to excitedly explain what had occurred on their journey.

"It was awesome." Usha spun her light staff around above her head. She then slammed one end of her staff to the ground ……… "Whoahhh …. What the …." A power pulse rippled through the air as it emanated from the light staff and knocked Richard, Lilly and Chloe to the ground. It continued to pulse a glowing white light until Usha panicked, throwing it to the ground. "WOW!….. Is everyone alright?"

"Hmm …. Interesting," Richard mused as Chloe and Lilly pulled him up from the ground and he proceeded to dust himself off. He picked up Usha's light staff and inspected it closely as he handed it back to his Granddaughter. "I'm assuming, after that impromptu demonstration, that the three light staffs will have the same powers. What powers they hold will no doubt become evident when you use them. Either way, with the powers you already have, I wouldn't like to cross you three girls on a dark night!"

The young girls looked at each other in mild amusement. The thought of using the light staffs in battle heightened the thrill and anticipation. Lilly could feel the fine blonde hairs on her arms tingling as was always the case when she'd experienced static electricity. *Weird and wonderful. Mind you,*

I've had the same feeling more than once when I've been with Luis.

"So .... I don't know about everyone else, but I need to get this scenario round my head." Chloe had an enquiring voice. "We were given these light staffs when we were on our Shamanic journey, right?" The other two girls nodded. "When we were released from our journey we didn't have the light staffs, but instead found them here .... I get that, 'cos The Moon Goddess told us where they would be ..... In a fashion!"

Usha and Lilly looked at Chloe with smirking faces. *She's digging herself a hole here!*

"So what I'm asking is....."

"Come on Chloe, spit it out," Usha growled.

"Well .... What happens to the light staffs if the three of us go on another journey?"

"From what you three girls have told me, I guess your light staffs would be waiting for you in much the same way you found them here," Richard explained. "But I see what you're getting at Chloe. It's much like what Luis told me .... You have to have the belief and also the desire for it to happen. You may well be able to summon them to you, using your powers. In all honesty, you're not really going to know until you travel on another Shamanic journey. That's the best explanation I have."

"S'pose," Chloe replied.

"But picking up on that idea," Richard continued, "Luis told me that when he goes on a Shamanic journey he knows who's with him and he sometimes gets to see their journey, but not often. So that could present a problem for us."

The teenagers nodded.

"Grandad, there's something you need to know," Lilly said. "We're not a hundred percent sure about this. But the other day when we all disappeared after we had chanted Hanan Pacha, Ukhu Pacha, Kay Pacha and our eyes turned red, we think we physically visited Hanan Pacha, the upper realm, the world above .... Which is where we travelled to on our Shamanic journey with Luis, which of course, was in our heads, a bit like dream walking so to speak. If we're right, then we should be able to physically visit any of the realms providing that we chant in the right order and we wouldn't need Luis to take us there."

"Of course …. You could well be right," Richard replied. "But there's only one way we're gonna prove it ….. Eh girls?"

"Awesome," Usha exclaimed excitedly.

"So who's going?" Richard asked.

"Safety in numbers I think Grandad," Chloe replied. "Don't you think girls?"

"Which realm though?" Richard asked.

"We need to know what we're up against Grandad," Lilly replied. "So it's gonna have to be Ukhu Pacha, the world below."

"S'pose you're right, but I don't like it one little bit. You three must be really careful and look out for each other 'cos this is serious stuff."

"One question guys," Usha muttered. "How do we get back?"

"Yeah like …. To hell and back …. How DO we get back?" Chloe asked.

"Ha, that reminds me of the 1955 Second World War film starring Audie Murphy as himself, a US army soldier …. It was a true story and he was highly decorated. That was called To Hell And Back ….." Richard mused.

"GRANDAD," Lilly shouted. "That's not helping. Seriously, how DO we get back?"

"Sorry girls ….. Well in theory, to return you would need to find a cave, or mine, a cavern or perhaps a water source. That's the best I can offer you. None of you have to do this, but as you've said, we need to know what we're up against. They'll be demons there for sure. I mean, you're entering the Inca Underworld where the inhabitants are Supay, a group of demons controlled by the God of Death. Nothing more to say really."

The teenagers looked at each other.

"Come on girls, let's do this," Lilly said assertively. "Come on, we can do this."

"Hold it …. HOLD IT," Usha shouted. "One more thing girls. As we enter the realm, we need to use our imagination as to how we will appear, remember?"

159

"You're right gal," Chloe replied. "It was an obvious reference to what clothes and so forth we would be wearing .... Right, no more faffing. Let's get on with this."

The girls gathered in a circle clasping their light staffs and started to chant .... "Ukhu Pacha, Hanan Pacha, Kay Pacha .... Ukhu Pacha, Hanan Pacha, Kay Pacha .... Ukhu Pacha, Hanan Pacha, Kay Pacha .... Ukhu P....." Their eyes turned red and in an instant, the girls were gone.

Richard sat down to contemplate the seriousness of the situation. *My three Granddaughters .... Oh jeez, hope they'll be alright.*

Above and as far as the eye could see, the sky was a boiling red interspersed with black foreboding clouds that didn't appear to be moving. In the distance, vast craggy mountains cut across the horizon. The stench of sulphur filled the air as fireballs erupted from lava pits. Pools of acid like liquid bubbled and boiled. The infertile ground was crawling with prehistoric insects that seemed oblivious to the searing heat. Strange eerie shrieks and sounds could be heard intermittently from the huge, scorched tree like structures. No imagination was needed for the three girls .... This was hell.

"Everyone okay?" Lilly asked.

Usha and Chloe nodded. Their faces grimacing from the scorching heat as they looked each other up and down.

"Cool outfits." Chloe gawped at Lilly and Usha. "Wouldn't look out of place in the Chronicles of Narnia, ha! Thankfully, this armour feels quite light but strong, and it certainly hugs our figures eh Lilly?"

Lilly was preoccupied in making sure her breasts couldn't fall out of her armour. "Eh?.... Oh. Yeah you're right Chloe."

"You'd better recheck your size sis' for next time." Usha playfully nudged Chloe's arm and chuckled.

"We need to move Lilly," Chloe grunted as she pointed over to the left. Three yellow eyed demons were approaching at speed closely followed by a ten foot troll with long straggly hair, oversized nose and enormous hands and feet.

Lilly glanced around nervously. Yellow eyed demons were coming from all angles .... "We're going to have to stand and fight. I can't see any way out. You okay sis?"

"LET'S DO THIS .... BRING IT ON." Usha slammed her light staff into the ground creating a power pulse to knock the first wave of demons to the ground. The young girl jumped on the first demon and thrust a lightening bolt into it's chest in a cloud of dust as blood curdling screams could be heard all around her. Lilly and Chloe followed her lead in destroying the demons.

Chloe looked around as she destroyed another demon. "THERE'S TOO MANY LILLY." The young girl side swiped another two demons across their necks with her light staff. *We need to get out of here.* Through the increasing hordes of creatures threatening to overwhelm the three teenagers Chloe saw, what she thought was a huge crevice in the rocks ahead. She slammed her light staff to the ground dispersing the demons in front of her. "OVER THERE USHA." She pointed the way ahead.

Usha immediately thrust her hand forward firing an energy pulse at the crevice. The rocks split open to reveal a cave. "COME ON CHLOE .... NOW'S OUR CHANCE." The two girls ran to the entrance, destroying demons as they progressed. On entering the cave, Usha immediately threw up a power shield around the entrance as the demons attempted to follow them to no avail. "NOT SURE HOW LONG I CAN KEEP THIS UP FOR CHLOE ..... WHERE'S LILLY?"

Lilly was going for it big time. Her eyes were glowing black as she destroyed everything in her path.

Chloe watched on, in awe as her cousin created mayhem. *Boy, she's in control of her powers now!*

Lilly spun round for the umpteenth time. She'd quickly mastered the art of concentrating her powers through her light staff. Laser beams were cutting through the demons ..... But to no avail, she was slowly being overcome by the sheer numbers .... ***"You need to get out of there Lilly .... now!"*** A voice in Lilly's head. It was Chloe .... ***"Now Lilly. Over here in the cave."***

Lilly slammed her light staff to the ground creating a clear path to the cave. She threw a couple of lightening bolts at the troll as it drew closer …. It fell to the ground with an earth shattering crash. *Just a few more steps* …..

"DROP THE SHIELD USHA," Chloe shouted.

Usha gasped for air as she released the shield.

Lilly threw herself into the cave as another demon savaged her legs. "ARRGGHHH."

Chloe immediately created another power shield. "Take a quick look at Lilly, Usha."

Lilly groaned as her sister turned her over on to her back. "She's in a bad way Chloe …. She's going to struggle to walk and she's barely breathing."

The demons continued to attack Chloe's power shield.

Usha picked up her light staff and pointed it into the darkness of the cave. She concentrated to enable the implement to emit a shaft of light. "We have to move down the cave Chloe. Trust me …. It's our way out." *I've just got this feeling, this is the way.*

Chloe turned to Usha. "Okay, let's do this. I reckon the shield will hold for two more minutes. We'll have to try and move Lilly along the best we can."

The two girls grabbed Lilly from each side under her arms and slowly moved further into the cave using the light staff, a bit like a torch, to see into the darkness.

"The roof of the cave is getting lower Usha ….. A few more metres and we'll be crawling."

There was a deafening noise from behind them. Usha quickly spun round to light up the path they'd just taken. "Demons Chloe …. The power shield has failed. Jeez, we've had it."

"Not today gal." Chloe threw her hands upwards, releasing a power pulse to the cave ceiling causing rocks and rubble to crash down behind them. The cave was blocked and as the dust settled it became apparent to Chloe she could hear water. "Can you hear that Usha?"

"Yeah, sure can …. And I think I know where we are. Well ….. Pretty sure anyway. The roof of the cave gets lower further ahead. As it becomes more of a tunnel we're going to have to crawl. Good job we're not in our armour any more."

"Must admit Usha, I hadn't noticed. Must have changed after the rock fall 'cos we're not in the Underworld any more …. We're just in an almighty mess though and look at Lilly. She's in no fit state to go anywhere, never mind crawl. Any suggestions?"

"Well, I reckon there's another thirty metres ahead before we get to some stone steps and the trapdoor."

"Trapdoor ….. What trapdoor? What are you on about Usha?"

"Trust me Chloe, it's a long story which I'll tell you about later. Let's get hold of Lilly 'cos we're gonna have to drag her."

Lilly groaned as she felt the rock floor grind against her skin, and her legs were pouring with blood from five gaping wounds inflicted by the demons. Usha and Chloe slowly dragged her through the tunnel straining every sinew as their strength gradually drained away from their muscles. The roof of the tunnel then started to rise again and Usha's light staff highlighted the stone steps in front of them.

"Is that the trapdoor up there Usha?" Chloe pointed to the top of the steps.

"Yep, sure is …. Stay here, I'll just try it." Usha clambered up the steps to the trapdoor above her head and pushed ….. She tried again ….. "It won't budge Chloe. There must be another lever in here somewhere to release it." Usha sighed as she sat herself down on the bottom step and gave Chloe a soulful vacant look of resignation.

"There must be something gal. Perhaps Lilly knows, but we need to help her …. Heal her …. Anything. Where's your teddy?"

"Sorry Chloe." Usha shook her head. "We decided before we came not to bring it, in case I lost it. Lilly thought it might be a bit of a gamble."

"A bit of a gamble?… Lilly's dying and we can't save her. That's a really bad throw of the dice."

Usha burst into uncontrollable floods of tears.

"Oh Usha …. Sorry. Sorry, I didn't mean too ….."

163

"Chloe ….. LOOK." Usha pointed over her cousin's shoulder.

Chloe turned to see a wispy ghostly image. It was Mama Killa, the Moon Goddess…. "You, The Three Marys, our friends, have done well on this day." She glanced at Lilly struggling to breathe. "It is sad to see the suffering of one so young and beautiful." She turned to Chloe. "Look to your heart young one, to heal the ones you love. Remember…. You are the healer." The ghostly image evaporated before the two girls eyes.

"What the …"

"Your pocket Chloe …. Look in your breast pocket. The left one …. Over your heart."

Chloe rummaged around in her pocket and felt a small pebble sized object. She pulled it out of her pocket and held it in the palm of her hand. It was a crystal.

The two girls watched as it started to glow and then commenced to pulse ….. And then …. It was gone.

"What?" Usha muttered.

Chloe closed her eyes and, as if by instinct, placed her hands on Lilly's legs.

Usha watched as Lilly's legs healed and her older sister sat up and smiled.

Chloe opened her eyes to see the two sisters hugging and kissing each other. The two girls turned to Chloe who heaved a sigh of relief and the three girls held each other lovingly.

"Awesome …. You okay sis'?"

Lilly nodded as she looked around getting her bearings. "Is this the tunnel below Mr Allens' store?"

"Yep, sure is. Ben's Dad's store. We need to find a lever Lilly to open the trapdoor."

"Okay." Lilly's eyes turned black and immediately she was in control of Chloe's movements.

It was cramped in the tunnel but Chloe crawled forward and then reached out to a crack in the stone wall to the left. Chloe grabbed hold of some sort of object …. Lilly released her control.

"What have you got there?" Usha threw the light from the light staff to highlight Chloe's hand.

164

Chloe pulled on the lever and the trapdoor above burst open. "YES .... Right, let's get out of here."

"Hang on you two," Lilly said. "Pull the lever from the wall Chloe. It will be an Inca gold statue and if we leave it here it could be a possible way to our world for the demons from Ukhu Pacha. So we'll take it with us."

"Good thinking Batman," Usha joked. "Come on, let's go. Last thing we need is Ben or Mr Allens finding us here."

The three girls clambered up the stone steps, through the trapdoor, closing it behind them and into the dark and dusty store.

Lilly passed her hand over the lock in the heavy main door. The door creaked and groaned as the girls stepped out into the welcoming warmth of the sunshine and the sound of waves breaking on the nearby beach.

Lilly locked the door and joined Usha and Chloe as they strode off down the lane, already reminiscing about their latest adventure.

"Birthday party tonight eh Chloe," Lilly remarked.

"Too bloody right gal. Are we gonna have some fun or what girls?"

The three girls high-fived and then burst into song as they strolled along .... *"I'm ready for love, Oh baby, I'm ready for love, ready for love, oh baby, I'm ready for love, yeah, ooo, for your love ...."* It was one of their Grandad's favourite tracks by Bad Company.

CHAPTER 25

PARTY POOPER

The music was loud, REALLY LOUD.

Richard and Bea had managed to find seats at the back of the pub away from the speakers which were bouncing with the vibrations of the music. The lights were dim but Richard could occasionally glimpse a view of the karaoke stage through the gloom and the seemingly hundreds of people packed into the bar. They were in their local, the Campania, or the Camp, as most Alderney residents called it, to celebrate Chloe's sixteenth birthday.

Wonder where she is?.... In fact, come to think of it, I haven't seen Lilly and Usha, or any of their boyfriends, thought Richard.

Richard spotted Alex's parents, Beth and Frank Bean, as they stood at the bar, glasses in hand. They were chatting to one of the barmaids, Tessa. Richard had known her for years. She was a kindly, smiley lass who would help anyone out in their time of need. *She's a buxom girl these days, bless her.* Tessa leant over the bar to pass Frank his change, giving Richard an eyeful of cleavage. She playfully winked at Richard as she caught sight of him gawping.

"Ouch, what's that for?" He felt an elbow dig into his side.

"You know what for," Bea snapped. "You're always flirting."

Richard shrugged his shoulders and rolled his eyes. *Nothing wrong with flirting missus.* He raised his arm to acknowledge the mouthed hellos and smiles of Irene and Albert Allens, Ben's parents, as they entered the Camp and made a beeline for the bar to order drinks. Richard knew Irene well. She was a teacher at St Annes School and both Usha and Ben were students in her class. Irene had also taught Richard's daughter, Susan, many years before. *Good teacher. Well respected.* Albert was a decent carpenter, self taught, but nonetheless very good. He'd done work for Richard many times over the years with pleasing results.

"OY!" Tessa's voice boomed from behind the bar. Everyone looked in the direction Tessa was pointing. "GET OUT ..... YOU'RE BARRED. YOU KNOW THE RULES, GET OUT." Tessa's voice could be heard quite clearly above the music, still pounding a loud beat.

"Who's that?" Bea asked.

"It's Diego Garcia and his missus, Lucy. They're Luis' parents. Look at his face. He's been barred from every pub on the island after that incident with our Lilly at the football club. He's a dangerous man .... Err, where d'ya think you're going Bea?"

"Look at his wife Richard, she needs a friend right now, don't you think?" Bea pushed through the crowd and introduced herself to Lucy, as Diego was manhandled out of the pub accompanied by drunken cheers from the crowd.

Jeez, what's Bea doing now? Richard moved across a seat as Bea guided Lucy to where he sat and invited the woman to sit down with them.

"You're Richard aren't you? Lilly's Grandad?...."

Richard nodded. *This woman is well fit. Look at those muscles.*

"Luis has told me so much about you."

"Err, all good I hope."

"Oh yes. Luis talks about you and Lilly, especially Lilly, all the time."

"That's nice."

There was an awkward silence as Bea approached the bar .... And returned with drinks.

"There you go Lucy .... That's right isn't it. Rum and coke." Bea sat down next to Lucy.

Lucy nodded and smiled appreciatively.

"So. What do you do Lucy?" Bea asked. "Don't seem to see much of you around town."

"Oh, err .... I'm an accountant. I work for myself so I don't really get out much. Shame really 'cos it's a lovely island."

167

Richard sensed that Lucy was overly nervous. *I wonder why she's so twitchy?* "One of the kids told me you was off island a few days ago. Visiting relatives eh?"

"Err …. No ….. No, I wish. Business unfortunately. I have a lot of clients in the UK. I used to live there until I got married to Diego two years ago. I don't know why, but he was adamant that he wanted to live here."

"So you're not L….."

"No. Oh no, I'm not Luis' Mother. I'm his Step Mother. His Mum died about five years ago when the family lived in Peru. Apparently she was a perfectly fit woman when she suddenly died during the night in her sleep."

I bet she did.

"Diego doesn't talk about his late wife and young Luis is the same. Mind you, you've probably noticed, there's no love lost between Luis and his Dad."

"That's a shame." Bea placed a comforting hand on Lucy's shoulder.

Richard took another long swig from his glass of beer as Bea and Lucy continued to chat. He realised that the music had stopped as he spotted Alex peer round the main entrance to the pub and give Tessa a thumbs up signal. Immediately *"The Fanfare To The Common People"* by Emerson, Lake and Palmer echoed around the pub and as the sound of the regal fanfare faded away, the main door into the pub flew open. *"Highway To Hell"* by ACDC burst forth from the stage speakers as the six teenagers marched in to cheers and clapping from the punters in the pub ….. All dressed as Roman Centurions except for Chloe who looked to be impersonating Cleopatra wearing a long flowing white dress with a coronet sat on her head. Lilly and Usha were up front carrying makeshift standard bearers.

Richard glanced at Beth, Alex's Mum, who was still stood at the bar. She mouthed, *"Do you like the outfits?"* He nodded, smiled and raised his glass in approval because Beth had obviously made the outfits. Richard felt Bea nudge him in his side ….

"Those outfits are a bit tight don't you think? And look how short Lilly and Usha's skirts are ….. You can see the cheeks of their arses .... And just look at the top that Lilly's wearing. If she breathes any harder, everything she's got will fall out for all to see."

"Oh come on gal, it's just a bit of fun." Richard smirked to himself.

Albert, Ben's Dad, moved through the crowd to help the three lads who were, by now, struggling to carry Chloe on their shoulders and as they reached the karaoke stage they gently lifted her down onto the floor to a generous round of applause.

Chloe took hold of one of the microphones as the music of ACDC faded. "CAN I JUST SAY .... THANK YOU ALL FOR COMING. I HOPE YOU ALL ENJOY YOURSELVES. SO COME ON YOU LOT ..... LET'S ALL WALK LIKE AN EGYPTIAN." The music started and everyone in the pub started dancing and singing to the track by The Bangles .... *"All the old paintings on the tomb, They do the sand dance, don't you know? If they move too quick (oh-way-oh), They're falling down like a domino....."*

The karaoke was proving popular as the night moved on. The drinks flowed freely as the crowd enjoyed the party atmosphere.

"TIME FOR THE CAKE." A shout from behind the bar. Tessa placed the large birthday cake on the bar and lit the sixteen candles. "WHERE'S THE BIRTHDAY GIRL?" Chloe stepped forward and the whole pub started singing .... *"Happy birthday to you, Happy birthday to you, Happy birthday dear Chloe, Happy birthday to you".*

"BLOW THE CANDLES OUT!" .... A shout from the crowd and Chloe duly obliged accompanied by a huge cheer.

Chloe turned to be hugged and kissed by Beth. "Happy birthday Chloe."

"Thank you Mrs Bean." Chloe then stood on a chair. "THANK YOU ALL." She climbed down to be hugged and kissed by her boyfriend Alex.

Richard smiled to himself as he watched on.

As the party night began to wind down, relatives and friends were saying their goodbyes. Richard made his excuses to Bea and her new friend Lucy and joined the teenagers who were laughing and joking about how the evening had gone ....

"Come on Grandad. Come and join us." Lilly slid to the side on the bench creating space between herself and Chloe.

"No, no, it's okay thanks. Just thought I'd come over to say goodnight 'cos we're going now." Richard kissed his Granddaughters on the cheeks and said his goodbyes. "Stay safe everyone." He waved as he turned away and left the pub with Bea. Lucy had got herself a taxi ten minutes before.

Time to get home. It wasn't far to walk. It would take about fifteen minutes. It was a still, calm, moonless night with all the stars in the sky in full view.

"Not a cloud in the sky Bea. Look at all the stars."

Bea held Richard's hand as they walked across the cobbled street. "Is everything okay Richard?"

"What?"

"Are you alright? Only you seem to be a bit preoccupied these days."

"Yeah. Course I am. What a silly thing to ask." *Why the sudden interest in me?*

"Only Lucy was on about how you and our Lilly had taken an interest in her husband, Diego."

"Well ..... He's a nasty piece of work. Wouldn't trust him as far as I could throw him. Don't worry about it Bea. I'm just watching our Lilly's back. Besides, if I was in Lucy's shoes I'd be more concerned about looking after herself."

Richard and Bea turned the corner onto their driveway.

"What the ...."

A figure ran past, brushing Richard's shoulder and knocking Bea to the ground. He immediately knelt down by Bea's side as he noticed the figure quickly disappearing into the darkness of the night down the street.

"You alright luv?... Can you get up? Are you hurt?"

"I think ..... I'm alright. What was all that about?"

"Don't know Bea .... Here, let's get you up on your feet ..... Steady."

Richard helped Bea get to her feet and then noticed their front door to the house was open.

170

"Come on gal, let's get you inside ….. Looks like we've had an unwelcome visitor 'cos the door's been forced open ….. Shit!"

Bea placed her arm around Richard's shoulders and hobbled into the house.

"Here you are gal, sit here and I'll phone for an ambulance to come and check you out."

"You'd better phone the police as well Richard. Look at the mess."

Richard hadn't noticed the chaos around them. He'd been too preoccupied with helping Bea.

"Try not to move Bea. The ambulance and police are on the way …. I'm just going to have a quick look around."

The kitchen looked as if the Swedish Chef out of The Muppet Show had been let loose! A bomb had hit it. Ingredients spilled all over the floor and cupboard doors were open which had obviously been emptied hurriedly.

The lounge, dining room and conservatory were in a similar mess. Furniture tipped over and ornaments broken.

Richard climbed the stairs to face a scene of devastation. A scene of the film Die Hard sprung to mind. *And it isn't even Christmas!* The door to his computer room was slightly ajar. Richard pushed the door further open …. He sighed as he realised that whoever the intruder was, he, or she, knew what they were doing. All the hard drives had been ripped out and all his floppy disks had gone along with his collection of usb memory sticks. "Memory stick!" He glanced around the visible destruction and spotted the vase in which he'd concealed the usb memory stick with a video of Lilly using her powers at Fort Tourgis, shattered on the floor …. *Crap! The bastards!….* The usb memory stick was gone. Richard's heart sank at the thought that Lilly's secret was now in the wrong hands.

"RICHARD." …. Bea shouted from downstairs. He stomped down the stairs feeling annoyed with himself. *How could I be so naive to think hiding the usb memory stick in a vase was a good idea. Hells bells. How stupid!* "Richard, the police are here. Can you pick me up from the hospital later? The

171

ambulance crew are taking me down there now as a precaution, just to check me over."

"Yeah sure, I'll see you later Bea." Richard stumbled through the chaos on the floor to be greeted by the local police Sergeant, Peter Cordy, who was busy making notes.

"Oh hello Richard. Bit of a mess you've got here."

Richard nodded in agreement.

"Any ideas who might be behind this?"

"Err .... No .... Not really Peter. I do know that it was just one individual. He or she brushed passed us in an almighty hurry. It was too dark though to see who it was."

"Can you tell if anything is missing?"

"Err .... Well I've had a quick look round. Difficult to tell with all this mess but no ..... I don't think anything's missing." *I can't tell you anyway!*

"Looks like a case of mindless vandalism then. Let me know if you discover anything's missing. In the meantime, I'll get forensics to call round to dust for fingerprints and so forth. That's all I can do for now Richard. We'll step up the patrols around the area in the meantime. Right, I'll move on. I hope Bea's alright. You take care Richard."

Richard grumbled to himself as the police van sped away into the darkness. *Better go and see how Bea is.*

CHAPTER 26

SLINGS AND ARROWS

"So what was it like? Lilly asked.

"Okay," Chloe replied. *Just perfect. Just how I had always imagined.*

The two girls were sat in the café in town waiting for their boyfriends to arrive that morning. Alex was flying back to Guernsey later in the day to return to study at the college. The one week holiday had flown by so today was a mixed day of feelings and emotions for Chloe.

"So just okay then?" Lilly asked firmly. Diplomacy wasn't one of her strengths. Say it how it is, she was always told at home. She could see that Chloe's face was glowing. You could tell this girl was in love in a big way. *She obviously had sex last night.*

"Well …. Yes. What d'ya want me to say Lilly? It's personal don't you think? But yeah, we had a great night and it ended perfectly."

"Oh, okay then. Sorry gal. I'll get us a couple of lattes then while we're waiting." Lilly went to the counter and asked Usha for a couple of drinks. Usha had the day off school and she was helping out at the café with her boyfriend Ben. They chatted amongst themselves at the counter as Usha made the drinks.

Chloe's thoughts drifted back to the previous night with Alex …..

Can't believe I let it get out of hand last night. Chloe smiled as her thoughts became increasingly self indulgent. *We'd promised ourselves that it wouldn't happen …. Hell it was good. The way I arched my back as I sat astride Alex, sweat running between my breasts as Alex worked me into a frenzy. My whole body was alive …. Tingling.* As her thoughts continued Chloe could feel her nipples coming alive as they strained and pushed at her blouse unashamedly. *Moisture oozing from between my thighs as my love juices ran freely with every thrust from Alex. He'd been gentle and loving as he seemingly explored every inch of my young body with his tongue and hands. And then that moment .... There was no going back ......*

"Chloe .... CHLOE." Lilly pushed a latte across the table in front of her cousin. "You was away with the fairies gal."

"Um .... Oh was I? Sorry." Chloe was still smiling to herself as Lilly sat next to her. "Lilly .... We didn't take any precautions," Chloe whispered as she leant towards Lilly.

"Chloe?"

"I know, I know. We just got carried away .... It just happened." Chloe shook her head.

"So, what are you two talking about?" Usha walked from behind the counter and sat herself down at the table.

"Oh, err, nothing special sis'. Anyway, shouldn't you be helping Ben prep for lunch," Lily replied.

"Nah .... Ben's okay. He'll manage for a few minutes." Usha gave her usual impish grin.

The sound of two scooters pulling up outside the café broke into the girl's conversation.

"That'll be Alex and Luis." Chloe stood up to peer out of the windows. The two lads stepped into the café and Chloe immediately flung her arms around Alex and kissed him passionately. Alex instinctively held the cheeks of her arse and squeezed gently, oblivious to the questioning looks of Lilly and Usha.

"Cheeky!" Usha called out as she winked at Lilly.

Chloe broke off their passionate embrace as Alex patted her bum and immediately felt himself blushing as his friends smiled and unknowingly stared at him.

"What?" Alex exclaimed.

The friends laughed hysterically.

Luis kissed Lilly on the cheek and placed his arm around her waist. "Have you heard about your Grandad and Grandma girls?"

The three girls shook their heads. "No. Why?" Lilly asked in a concerned tone.

"Surprised you haven't heard anything." Luis continued. "It's all around the island. Everyone's talking about them."

"What?" Usha interrupted.

"Their place was broken into last night whilst they were at Chloe's birthday bash. They arrived home just as the intruder was fleeing the scene."

"Oh shit. That's terrible," Chloe muttered.

"Apparently the police reckon it was just mindless vandalism."

"Umm ….. Wouldn't be too sure about that … Eh girls?" muttered Usha. "Are they both alright?"

"Your Grandma's in hospital I believe. Not sure about your Grandad. Right, anyway, I've got to get to work. You giving me a hand today Ben?"

"Yeah sure Luis." Ben turned to Usha and kissed her. "I'll see you later gal. You take the scooter and I'll hitch a ride with Luis."

Usha smiled as her boyfriend turned to go.

"Good to see you Alex. Have a good flight down to Guernsey mate and take care of Lilly today. Come on Luis, let's get going."

"I'd forgotten you was going to Guernsey college today as part of your apprenticeship." Luis hugged Lilly and kissed her passionately.

"Thought you had. Ha! I'll be back this evening on the last flight. You'd better be waiting for me."

"Come on mate. We'll never get anything done at this rate." Ben was getting agitated.

"Okay okay! Good to see you again Alex. I'll see you this evening at the airport Lilly."

Luis and Ben stepped out of the café, climbed on the scooter and sped off up the hill.

"You two had better get going or you'll miss your flight," Usha said. "Don't worry about Grandma and Grandad. Me and Chloe will drop down to the hospital when we've finished here."

"Okay sis'. Come on Alex we'd better get off up to the airport."

175

"Yeah, right Lilly." Alex lovingly embraced Chloe. "Bye luv. I'll ring you tonight."

Chloe's eyes filled up tearfully as she smiled and kissed Alex before he turned and headed for the door.

The two teenagers climbed onto Lilly's scooter and waved as they moved away.

"I'LL SEE YOU GUYS LATER," Lilly shouted.

"Come on Chloe, let's clear up here. Then we can go and see what's happening with Grandma and Grandad at the hospital."

Chloe nodded approvingly. "I've got a bad feeling about today Usha. Call it intuition, but I just know something bad is going to happen."

"Don't be silly cuz', how could you possibly know or even think that? Come on, the quicker we get done here, the sooner we'll get down to the hospital. Everything will be fine ....
Believe me."

"S'pose."

The departure lounge at the airport was busy. Well, inasmuch there was twelve passengers including Lilly and Alex who were queuing to go through security! Their flight had been called and as usual Alex was nervous.

"You're not exactly the bravest when it comes to flying are you?" Lilly joked.

"I hate it. I really do. And I just don't like these Dornier aircraft."

"Well at least it's only a fifteen minute flight mate ..... Go on, it's your turn through the scanner." Lilly nudged him forward in the small of his back.

She followed her friend through and the pair smiled at each other as they walked across the tarmac to the waiting Dornier and climbed the steps into the aircraft.

The two teenagers sat opposite each other.

"Here, let me help." Lilly leant across. *He's so nervous he can't even fasten his seat belt!* She took hold of the seat belt around Alex and clicked it into place. "There you go. All safe."

"Thanks Lilly. I feel such a fool, but I've always been the same."

"No probs' mate."

The Dornier started to vibrate as the engines built up their revs and then suddenly the take off run commenced down the runway.

Alex gripped the armrests of his seat tightly as the aircraft lifted from the ground.

"Alex …. Alex! Just think about last night with Chloe." Lilly winked. "That'll take your mind off the flight."

Lilly smiled broadly as Alex gave her a disdainful look as he gritted his teeth in panic.

Lilly held his hand. "You'll be okay … Promise." She placed her earplugs into her ears from her phone and listened to Firework, one of her favourite songs by Katy Perry… *"Cause baby you're a firework, Come on, show 'em what you're worth, Make 'em go oh oh oh, As you shoot across the sky-y-y…."*

As Usha and Chloe parked the scooter in the car park at the hospital they spotted Richard coming out of the main entrance.

"GRANDAD," Usha shouted, as Chloe waved frantically.

Richard walked over to his Granddaughters.

"Hi girls."

"You okay Grandad? How's Grandma?" Chloe asked.

"Yeah … I'm okay thanks. Your Grandma's in the wars though. She's broken her ankle. Quite a bad break as well, so she's not happy. Not only that, she's got to stay here for a couple of days so it settles down enough to have a cast put on."

"So what happened last night then Grandad?" Usha asked.

"Some low life cretin broke into the house and ransacked the place while we were at Chloe's birthday bash last night. We arrived at the house as the intruder was leaving in a big hurry. Obviously didn't see your Grandma 'cos she was knocked to the ground. Whoever it was knew what they were looking for."

"How's that Grandad?" Chloe asked.

"The usb memory stick has gone …. The one with the video of Lilly using her powers at Fort Tourgis."

"Oh shit!"

"You got that right gal. Someone out there knows too much for my own liking and it could prove to be dangerous for all of us, especially Lilly."

"Does Lilly know the usb memory stick has been stolen?" Usha asked.

"No. I just haven't had time to talk to her and she's in Guernsey today. I'll send her a message in a bit to let her know."

The two girls nodded.

"When Lilly gets back we need to come up with some sort of plan to find the Lima Treasure. We have to move pretty quickly on this to stay one step ahead of whoever is showing an unhealthy interest in what we're doing."

Richard climbed into his van and fired up the engine, which coughed and spluttered into life. He grabbed his phone and sent a message to Lilly ....

Usb memory stick stolen
Secret is out there
Be careful
Love Grandad x

"I'm sure your Grandma will be pleased to see you both. I've got stuff to do so I'll see you both later. Bye girls."

"Bye Grandad."

Chloe and Usha entered the hospital as Richard drove away, waving to the girls.

Lilly glanced at her phone. *Message from Grandad .... Oh bugger. Oh well. Not a lot I can do till I get back tonight.* A jolt of the aircraft as it landed shook Lilly out of her thoughts. She glanced over at Alex, "You okay?"

Alex nodded and briefly smiled as he released his grip from the armrests and sighed with relief that his flying ordeal was over. *Jeez. Thank Christ for that.*

The two friends disembarked and walked across the tarmac and through the arrivals lounge, discussing their anticipated day ahead at college. They left the terminal building to see a bus pulling way.

"Damn, just missed the bus." Alex pointed over to the taxi rank. "And there's no taxis in either."

"No worries Alex." Lilly glanced at her watch. "We've still got time. There's bound to be a taxi in a few minutes."

"S'pose."

Lilly walked over to the taxi rank followed by Alex.

"Have you noticed Alex? We're the only ones around. Where is everyone?" *Something doesn't feel right.*

Alex shrugged his shoulders.

"Here we go. Here comes a taxi and it looks like one of those posh jobs. All the windows look black."

It was a black Mercedes. As it pulled up in front of the two teenagers, they were roughly grabbed from behind …. Lilly screamed.

Her screams were quickly stifled by a black hood being forced over her head and the sound of tape being wrapped around the hood and her wrists. A forceful hand on top of her head pushed her down and forward as she was manhandled into the car. She heard the boot close. *Alex must be in there.* Lilly listened intently, her senses heightened as she figured out there was two people sat in the front seats. The doors slammed shut and the Mercedes sped away.

Stay calm gal. Lilly could hear Alex kicking the interior of the boot. *He's alive at least. I could easily escape from this situation but, hmm …. Let's see what happens though. Just stay calm and keep your wits about you.*

A few minutes later and the car screamed to a halt. Lilly listened as the boot was opened ….

"YOU. You stop noise." An unfamiliar voice in what seemed like broken English.

"LOSE HIM." A voice shouted from inside the car.

That's the driver, Lilly thought. *Sounds foreign.*

Alex felt a punch to his stomach and he doubled up in pain. A pair of hands grabbed him and dragged him out of the boot. His assailant threw him like a sack of potatoes into the ditch on the roadside.

"KILL HIM!" The voice shouted from inside the car. "Here. Take this gun."

Alex was barely conscious as he lay on the roadside.

Christ they're going to shoot Alex .... Concentrate .... Jam the gun.

Lilly listened as the assailant stood over Alex. "Click .... Click .... DAMN! ... The gun's no good. Shit. It's your lucky day punk."

Alex passed out as two brutal kicks were launched into his ribs.

The car door slammed shut.

"GO! JUST GO!"

As the car sped away from Alex, Lilly's thoughts wandered. *Jeez, what a mess. I do hope Alex will be alright. I'm not sure what to do now, do I wait to see what happens? Do I tackle them once I'm out of the car?*

"My eyes! The light!"

Alex was barely conscious as he felt the hood being removed from his head. He could make out flashing blue lights and about a dozen people milling around him as he was gently lifted onto a stretcher.

"Lilly .... Where's Lilly?" Alex croaked.

"Who's Lilly?..." A voice in his ear.

"My friend .... Lilly. Where is she?" Alex tried to sit up.

"Steady on mate. What's your name?"

"Err ... Alex. Alex Bean. I'm supposed to be at college."

"Okay Alex, let's get you in the ambulance and then I'll let one of the officers talk to you. They've got a few questions they want to ask you."

Alex held his chest tight as the stretcher was lifted into the vehicle.

"Your ribs hurting Alex?"

Alex grimaced as he nodded.

"Okay mate, we'll give you a couple of shots to help the pain and you'll definitely need an x-ray at the hospital. There you go, that didn't hurt did it?"

"Hmm." Alex gave the paramedic a wry smile.

"Right then. Five minutes with the police and then we need to get you to hospital."

"Cheers mate. Thanks."

"Right then young sir. Perhaps you could tell me exactly what happened?" Asked the constable.

Alex recalled the events of the abduction of himself and Lilly to the officer.

"So let me get this right." The constable read from his notebook, "You think there were four attackers that were possibly foreign. You didn't get the car reg. It was a black Mercedes with dark tinted windows. No witnesses at the airport other than your friend Lilly who is now missing. I have to say …. Not a lot to go on."

"You're kidding me aren't you?" Alex snapped. "How many black Mercedes are there on island? Two, maybe three. And what about the gun you found at the scene? Thank Christ it jammed or you'd be talking to a dead body! There must be fingerprints so don't give me that crap."

"No need to take that tone with me sir."

"How do you expect me to react? Lilly's out there somewhere, possibly dead, and you've got officers here directing traffic instead of being out there looking for her." *What a plonker! Typical PC Plod!*

Alex waved to the paramedic who was stood by the ambulance doors. "Can we go now?"

The car had stopped some time ago. Lilly's two assailants had left her tied up and she hadn't heard a sound for what seemed like an age, after she'd been locked in the car and left by herself. *Gotta do something about my situation.* Lilly concentrated all her thoughts to contact Usha ….

Chloe and Usha were leaving the hospital after visiting their Grandma.

"Grandma didn't look too good eh Usha?….. Usha? Usha what's wrong?" Chloe just managed to catch her cousin as she became unconscious and collapsed to the ground.

Usha …. Don't panic. I'm in trouble. A thought from Lilly. Usha could see a blurry black and white image of her sister tied up in the back of a car. *A couple of guys have abducted me and they've got guns. Can't see where I am though.*

Usha looked closer at the images she was getting. The car was parked by the Little Chapel, a Guernsey tourist attraction …. *You're at the Little Chapel Lilly. Can't see anyone else around. I'll get help to you. Don't do anything stupid sis'.*

Gotta stop now Usha, someone's coming.

Usha took in a huge breath of air and sat up, still in Chloe's arms.

"Usha, you okay? You had me worried there. What was all that about?"

"Lilly's in big trouble. You'd better phone Alex to see if he's okay. I'll phone the police in Guernsey to let them know where Lilly is. Sounds like they're going to need their firearms unit as well." *Bloody hell Lilly.*

Lilly heard voices immediately outside the car. They were talking in Quechuan, the language used by Incas in Peru …. And she could make out three distinct voices, the two she'd heard earlier and a woman's voice.

"Clunk." The car was unlocked.

"GET HER OUT." The woman's voice bellowed.

I'm sure I've heard that voice before.

Lilly felt a rough pair of hands grab hold of her and she was manhandled out of the car, banging her head on the door frame.

"TAKE HER ROUND THE BACK OF THE CHAPEL," the woman shouted.

The two men dragged Lilly by her arms up the slope into a secluded area amongst the trees to the back of the Little Chapel.

"Take this rope and secure her to that tree," the woman ordered.

Lilly felt the rope digging into her body and arms as she struggled to resist the strength of the two men ..... And then the blinding light as her hood was removed. As her eyes adjusted she could make out the features of her three attackers. They all wore balaclavas to hide their faces, but the two men were quite distinct. Short, stocky, big hands, arms covered in tattoos and definitely had the appearances of South American origin. Plenty of muscle and probably mid twenties. They both had holsters with guns. *Bloody hell!*

One of the men also had a large bowie style knife which he pulled from his belt as he stood close to Lilly ....

"Now, my blonde beauty. Let's have some fun." Lilly grimaced as he ran the blade down the side of her face and across her neck. She could feel his other hand groping her body and then lifting her dress as he grabbed the top of her panties. The man cut the top buttons around her cleavage exposing her unfettered breasts. "Jackpot!" His mouth and tongue writhed across her nipples as he drooled over her breasts.

Lilly saw her chance as the man drew in closer to her ..... "TAKE THAT YOU BASTARD!" Her knee came up sharply and connected with his groin ....

"ARRGGG!!" The man stumbled backwards in agony and slumped to his knees as Lilly kicked out and her foot connected perfectly with his chin and left the man sprawled on his back as he dropped the knife.

The other man approached Lilly. He had a menacing look about him.

"ENOUGH! We don't have time for this." The woman stepped forward and grabbed the amulet on Lilly's arm. "This is what we came for." She roughly pulled the amulet from Lilly's arm and clasped it in her fist as she struck Lilly across the face drawing blood from her mouth and nose. The woman stared into Lilly's eyes. "And you're going to tell us EVERYTHING we need to know, or I'll let these goons have their fun before they kill you." The woman punched Lilly in the face twice more as the two men laughed.

I can hear sirens. Must be the police. Lilly's eyes turned black as she created a force shield around herself. *The amulet.* Her thoughts concentrated. She could see the amulet pulsing stronger in the woman's hand.

"ARRGGHH!.... MY HAND IS BURNING." The woman dropped the amulet as her skin began to melt. "THE PAIN."

The two men rushed at Lilly, knives in hand and they were flung to the ground by the young girl's shield. The woman fled the scene as the men pulled their guns out and took aim at the teenager. The first shots rang out as the police appeared from through the trees. "TAKE THEM OUT." More gunfire as the police firearms unit brought the two guys down in a hail of bullets.

Lilly relinquished her shield as her head dropped in sheer relief and exhaustion as she passed out, blood dripping from her head wounds.

"Lilly .... Lilly."

Lilly's eyes struggled to focus on Alex who was sat beside her holding her hand. "Is that you Alex?" she croaked.

"Thank goodness gal, how d'ya feel?" *Stupid question.*

"Hmm, I've felt better and my head's bangin'. Where am I? Christ, how long have I been out of it?"

"You've been admitted to Guernsey hospital. I was already here when they brought you in. I overheard a nurse say that you'd been unconscious for about ten hours."

"Really? Wow!" Lilly glanced down at her arms. "My amulet .... It's gone." She sighed and shook her head.

"You mean this bracelet?"

Lilly's eyes lit up .... Her sparkle was back. *Nice one!*

"One of the police constables gave it to me when they brought you in. He knew we were friends and figured out it must be yours when they found it at The Little Chapel when they rescued you. By all accounts, they got there in the nick of time. You was in a pretty bad state when the ambulance brought you in."

184

Lilly struggled to sit up as Alex propped her up in bed with some spare pillows. "Pass that mirror over please Alex."

Lilly held the mirror up to her face. "That's not a good look is it? I look as if I've been hit by a train .... Sorry Alex. I meant to ask. How are you doing?"

"Well, looking at you, I reckon I got off lightly with three broken ribs and a punctured lung ... Ha! But I don't get it Lilly. Why would any of these people want to abduct us, let alone, kill us? I just don't get it. This is Guernsey for gawd sake. Stuff like this just doesn't happen here in the islands."

Lilly shrugged her shoulders. "I don't know Alex. I'm sure the police will be all over it though." *Wish I could tell you mate. Gonna have to talk to the girls and Grandad about this.* "Have you been in touch with anyone back in Alderney?"

"Yeah sure. I'd just got off the phone with Chloe when you came round. She's spoken to your Mum and Dad. Usha, Ben and Luis know we're both alright .... And your Grandad knows."

"That's good then."

"There's something else you need to know."

"What's that?"

"Carol Mollins, Chloe's Mum, walked out of the psychiatric ward at this hospital yesterday morning."

"She just walked out?"

"Well .... Yes. I'd promised Chloe that I'd visit her Mum whilst I was here .... But she'd gone. Apparently some guy signed her release forms and escorted her to a car. The nurses watched them leave and ...."

"Let me guess .... They got into a BLACK MERCEDES." *I knew I'd heard that voice before.*

"Absolutely spot on. I clocked the connection straight away. But I still don't get it Lilly. Why attack us .... And in broad daylight?"

"I don't have any answers mate." *I hate lying.*

CHAPTER 27

MAYBE JUST MAYBE

Lilly gingerly stepped off the fishing boat onto the solid foundations of Alderney harbour. *Christ. I wish everything would stop moving up and down. And that smell of fish, yuck!* "Thanks Mr Bean. Love the boat." *Not!*

It was five thirty in the morning and the gentle rays of sun from the early morning sunrise danced across the rippling water in Braye Bay. *Just beautiful.* Lilly was still feeling tender and a little fragile after the events of the abduction a week ago and the boat trip had been far from smooth from her viewpoint, with her stomach complaining in no small way as it grumbled audibly. She was no sailor. Frank Bean, Alex's Dad, was a local fisherman who'd often visit Guernsey with his catch and had offered Lilly a 'lift' home after it had been decided that Alex was well enough to remain in Guernsey and attend college.

"LILLY." A shout from a familiar voice from behind the teenager.

"Oh hi Mum … Dad. Jeez it's good to see you both." Lilly squirmed as her Mum Susan hugged her tight. *Oooo! Steady on Mum, I'm still hurting.* Chris, her Dad, kissed her tenderly on the cheek and stroked Lilly's hair.

"Let me look at you." Susan held Lilly at arms length and then hugged her again. "We were so worried. How d'ya feel?"

"Well apart from everything moving up and down as if I'm still on that boat and I'm sure I smell like a fish…" Lilly smelled the air.

Chris smiled to himself.

"I'm fine. Just a few odd bruises here and there but I'll be okay. Where's Usha?"

"She's still in bed …. You don't expect your sister to be up at this God earthly hour of the day do you?" Chris motioned them to start walking as he turned and waved to Frank on his fishing boat. "She'll be over the moon to see you. Mind you, she seems to spend more and more time with her boyfriend Ben, or your Grandad than she ever does with us."

Lilly giggled as the three of them walked hand in hand away from the harbour.

"How's Grandma now?" Lilly asked.

"She's back at home, driving your Grandad round the twist I shouldn't wonder. Her one leg's in plaster now and they have a wheelchair if she needs to go anywhere." Susan smiled. "In fact I'm going up there this afternoon to keep her company and to give your Grandad a rest. Your Grandma can be a bit demanding sometimes. Believe me, I know from experience."

"Does Chloe know about Carol, her Mum?" Lilly asked.

"Yes she does luv. She's taken it badly 'cos she thought her Mum was on the mend. Something doesn't feel right about the whole situation. Best not to broach the subject with her just yet. Just try and give her a bit of time to come to terms with it."

Lilly nodded and smiled.

Chris gave Susan a knowing look as they walked into their house.

"Right young lady, give me your bag. I'll take it upstairs and pop it in your room," Susan said. "I'll give your sister a nudge as well …. I'm sure she'll be pleased to see you."

Chris turned to Lilly, "You hungry?".

Lilly nodded as she turned the radio on and tuned it into the local station, Quay FM.

"Right, I'll cook you some breakfast then. I'm sure the smell of bacon wafting up the stairs will stir some resemblance of life from Usha."

Chris and Lilly chuckled to themselves.

"Hello …. HELLO." A shout resonated from outside.

"I'll get it." Lilly rose to her feet and sauntered to the front door and opened it. "Hi guys …. Come on in."

Ben and Chloe kissed Lilly on her cheek as they entered the house leaving Luis stood on the doorstep.

Lilly threw herself into his open arms and kissed him passionately. A long and lingering kiss that would melt any teenager's heart. Luis held his girlfriend tightly, seemingly not wanting to let her go, Lilly wincing in pain as he hugged her.

"Didn't think I'd see you ever again hun'," Lilly whispered in his ear.

Luis wiped away her tears and kissed her gently on her wet cheek. "Love you ..... Come on gal, let's join the others. Hmm, that bacon smells good." As they turned to walk to the kitchen, Luis patted Lilly on her bum and squeezed gently.

"Cheeky!"

The sound of heavy footsteps on the stairs broke into the conversation as Usha bounded down every other step and leapt at Lilly.

"Where have you been sis'... Ha!" Usha couldn't contain her delight. "Thought you was a gonna."

"Be careful what you say," Lilly whispered in her ear as she kissed Usha on the cheek.

"Really good to have you back sis'..... Come on, let's grab some breakfast."

The country style kitchen had traditional oak beams that ran unevenly across the low ceiling that added to the charm. A compact room that gave little room for manoeuvre at the best of times, let alone five teenagers sat around the table with Susan watching on as Chris juggled with the cooking. The smell of bacon, sausages and eggs wafted through the air as Susan poured out glasses of orange juice.

"Here we go then." Chris placed three huge dishes in the centre of the table. "Dig in guys .... And be careful, everything's hot."

"Thanks Dad," said Lilly.

"Yeah thanks Mr Gat," added Ben enthusiastically.

"You're very welcome." Chris acknowledged the appreciation. "Shout up if you need more."

The friends dug in as they chatted amongst themselves.

"Shush everyone," Chris said. "Listen to the news on the radio. They're on about our Lilly and Alex."

"..... And the police have confirmed that the two men killed by the firearms unit last week were of South American origin and it's also believed that they had Mafia connections. Units from Interpol and the FBI are currently making further investigations into the whereabouts of two other men who may be able to help with their enquiries. The police have also

given out a description of a local woman who they would like to talk to in connection with this serious incident. According to local sources, the two teenagers involved in the incident are recovering well after their ordeal. Anyone with any further information are advised to contact Crime Stoppers or contact the local police ..... And now the weather forecast ...."

Chris turned the radio off.

Complete silence ....

Suddenly Chloe flung her chair back as she quickly got up from the table and ran out of the kitchen sobbing.

"CHLOE," Lilly shouted as she followed her cousin out of the house.

Chloe was sobbing uncontrollably, tears rolling down her face.

Lilly sat down on the bench next to Chloe and gently placed her arm around her shoulders. *God, she's in a right state.*

"That's it gal, let it all out." Lilly tried to wipe away the tears from Chloe's face.

"It's just not fair," Chloe blurted.

"I know, I know it isn't." Lilly tenderly stroked Chloe's hair.

"What am I going to do Lilly?"

"You're going to get through this gal. We'll find out what's going off with your Mum. You can always count on your friends to help and you've got great support from Alex's Mum and Dad ..... And you've got a gorgeous boyfriend eh ..."

Chloe started to cry again.

"Chloe?"

"Oh Lilly ..... I'm ..... I'm pregnant."

"Jeez Chloe ..... Does Alex know?"

"No, no he doesn't .... What am I goin' to do?"

"Sorry gal. You're asking the wrong person here. I'll support you with any decision you make but I think you need to talk to his Mum, Mrs Bean. Being a nurse I think she will be sympathetic and if you want me to be with you when you tell her, just ask. You need to tell Alex though. The sooner the better."

"What's going on you two?" Usha poked her head round the front door. "Have you been crying Chloe? Is everything okay?"

189

"Err …. Yeah. No probs' sis'. We'll tell you later." Lilly squeezed Chloe's hand to try and reassure her. "Are we going up to see Grandad this morning?"

"Sounds good to me," Usha replied. "What d'ya reckon Chloe?"

"Hell yeah … Why not. Need to do something eh girls," replied Chloe.

"That's settled then. The lads will be off to work soon, so we can leave them to finish off breakfast. I'll go and let Mum know we're going." Lilly sauntered back to the kitchen.

"Everything okay Lilly?" Susan asked.

Lilly nodded. "Chloe's upset about her Mum so we're going out for a while. We'll probably end up at Grandads."

"That's fine Lilly, but try not to do too much 'cos you're not one hundred percent. Say hello to your Grandad for me."

Lilly kissed Luis. "Catch up with you later …. Don't spend all morning eating bacon butties!"

Ben chuckled … And nearly choked as he took another bite of his buttie, tomato sauce drooling down his face and luckily onto his plate.

Lilly waved as she left the kitchen and joined Usha and Chloe who were sat astride their scooters, engines revving.

"Let's go girls."

The three girls arrived at their Grandad's house. It was early morning with the dew still on the ground after the cloudless night before. Richard was making himself breakfast whilst listening to one of his favourite bands, Depeche Mode. He was taking advantage of the fact that Bea, his wife, wasn't around and so the volume had been turned right up with plenty of bass. Bea had been admitted into hospital over night as a precautionary measure as the local doctor thought perhaps she might have an infection in her broken ankle. Richard had invited Annie round for part of the night and as always the sex had been great and Richard was feeling on top form this morning. So Depeche Mode was the order of the day! The track playing was Enjoy The Silence…. *"All I ever wanted, All I ever needed, Is here in my arms, Words are very unnecessary, They can only do harm …"*

"HELLO ….. HELLO …." Usha shouted as the music reverberated around the house.

The teenagers walked into the huge kitchen and stood staring. Richard was singing at the top of his voice as he played his air guitar oblivious to the fact his Granddaughters were watching.

Lilly mouthed *"Let's have some fun"* to Usha and Chloe. They crept up behind Richard. Stood either side of him playing their air guitars and sang along to the track …. ***"Words like violence, Break the silence, Come crashing in, Into my little world …."***

The track ended in hysterical laughter as Richard realised what had just been happening.

"Oh very funny girls …. And very good taste I might add."

"Awesome," Usha exclaimed.

"Anyone for breakfast?" Richard asked.

The kitchen filled with laughter again.

"Am I missing something here?"

"Sorry Grandad," Usha explained. "We've already had breakfast. My Dad was up early this morning cooking."

"Of course. Am I stupid or what?! I'd forgotten Frank was bringing Lilly up on his boat from Guernsey early this morning ….. Sorry I wasn't there Lilly." Richard hugged Lilly affectionately. "Thought we'd lost you gal."

"No probs' Grandad …. You gonna have your breakfast?"

"Yeah …. Come on then you lot, sit down round the table and tell me what happened. I'll have my breakfast and listen. Ideal while your Grandma isn't here."

As Richard tucked into his breakfast he listened intently as Lilly recalled the incident in Guernsey involving herself and Alex. *This is getting serious and just look at Chloe, she's suffering. All because of her Mum,* he thought.

"You were both very lucky gal. I mean, those guys would have raped and killed you if you hadn't been able to get in touch with Usha to get help …. You did really well Usha."

"Awesome."

"And I mean, Alex could have been killed if you hadn't jammed the guy's gun Lilly. Quick thinking eh gal?"

191

Lilly shrugged her shoulders. "I did what I had to do. Besides, I wouldn't have forgiven myself if Alex had died ..... Talking of which, I need to say something about Alex."

Lilly held Chloe's hand.

"He's starting to ask me serious questions about what's going on and I'm struggling to give him straight answers, that is .... Without lying to him. I think it's about time we told him our secrets. What does everyone think about this?"

"Can I just say something." Chloe stood up. "I fully understand where you're coming from Lilly and I for one, would love to tell him ..... But ..... I just feel it would be too dangerous for so many reasons."

"I agree with Chloe," Richard said. "We will all know when the time is right, but now, today, is not the right time. Alex was just unlucky the other day when he was with Lilly. Ordinarily he wouldn't have been involved and we need to try and keep it that way for his own safety. Agreed?"

The three girls nodded in agreement.

"There's something else I need to tell you all. Lilly already knows." Chloe squeezed Lilly's hand firmly. "You see .... Err .... I'm pregnant ..... Which is another reason I want Alex kept out of this."

"AWESOME." Usha couldn't conceal her delight.

Chloe continued, "No-one else knows yet. Not even Alex. Sorry guys, I'm in another mess. What with this and my Mum."

"So you've done a 'Maybe Baby' then?" Usha asked.

"A what?" Richard asked.

"You know .... A 'Maybe Baby'..... Come on guys, get with it .... A pregnancy test ..... Jeez."

"Well you learn something new everyday!" Richard said. "Seriously though, have you?"

"A pregnancy test?..... Yeah of course I have."

Richard placed his arm around Chloe and kissed her forehead. "Whatever you decide we will all support you. Right girls?"

Lilly and Usha nodded approvingly.

"Right girls, back to our current situation. The Mafia are obviously on to us. Someone out there has the usb memory stick. Chloe's Mum obviously knows the importance of Lilly's amulet and we don't know if she's working by herself or being coerced by the Mafia. Any suggestions?"

"It's about time we started investigating the locations we were given by the Orion Constellation don't you think?" Lilly asked. "They're obviously important."

"I totally agree sis'. We need to find out what ties these locations together," Usha said, as Chloe nodded in agreement.

"That's settled then. I'll finish up here and we'll meet up at the navigation marker on Tourgis Hill above Fort Tourgis in two hours. Is that okay with you girls?"

"Awesome."

"Let's do this." Lilly rose from her chair. "Come on girls, let's go. We'll nip down to the hospital to visit Grandma for an hour or so before going to Tourgis."

"BYE GRANDAD, WE'LL SEE YOU LATER," Chloe called out as the three teenagers left Richard's house.

CHAPTER 28

LILLY`S DESTINY

Richard had forgotten how exposed to the elements of the weather Tourgis Hill could be on a windy day. The westerly wind was gusting up to sixty kilometres an hour. Sat there on the grass bank, basking in the strong rays of sunshine it was difficult to believe that it was the start of summer as the cool wind took the edge off the temperature. *Could easily get sunburnt without realising* he thought.

The sound of scooters approaching interrupted his thoughts.

"Hi girls. How's your Grandma?"

"She's okay Grandad," replied Usha. "A bit bored I think, but she was pleased to see us. Apparently she's got to stay in for another day."

"Oh, okay," Richard retorted and shrugged his shoulders.

"So anyone got any ideas what we're supposed to do now that we're here?" Chloe asked.

Lilly was standing next to the navigation marker. It was a brick and masonry cone shaped structure standing approximately four metres high. About two metres across at the base gradually reducing in diameter until, at the top it was about twenty centimetres across. The structure had been rendered with sand and cement, and then painted white every year to make it more visible to passing mariners so they could use it as a navigational aid to plot their course at sea.

Chloe, Usha and Richard watched as Lilly walked around the structure, looking up and down as if searching for a clue. Lilly stopped and placed both hands on the white masonry. *Gonna try something,* she thought.

The swirling wind suddenly dropped .... There was complete silence as the steely blue eyes of Lilly changed to dazzling ice white.

"Lilly .... LILLY," Chloe called out as she collapsed to the ground at Chloe's feet.

"Looks like she's gone on a Shamanic journey," Richard said. "Wherever gone is! Looks like she's in some sort of trance. We're just going to have to wait here and keep an eye on Lilly until she's back with us."

Usha and Chloe sat down on the grass bank next to Richard as he kept a watchful eye on Lilly, waiting for any sign of life in her young body.

Usha suddenly lost consciousness.

"Usha .... Usha ... You okay?" Chloe leant over her cousin to see that she was in some sort of trance. "Grandad .... What d'ya think?"

Richard quickly glanced over at Usha. "Just keep an eye on her gal .... She's probably being contacted by Lilly some how."

Usha .... Usha .... I'm okay. Tell the others I'm in the realm of Hanan Pacha on a Shamanic journey.

Usha sat up sharply from the ground with an audible gasp of air.

Chloe hugged and kissed her in relief to see her cousin was okay. "I just can't get used to you having these episodes Usha. It's not good for my health!"

Usha gave her an impish grin as she told Richard and Chloe that Lilly was on a Shamanic journey.

"WELCOME." A deep powerful voice reverberated through Lilly's body. The teenager stepped forward slowly. "STOP."

Lilly dropped to one knee as she realised she was facing Inti, the Sun God.

"SO YOU HAVE FOUND A GATEWAY TO THE UPPER REALM OF HANAN PACHA. IT ALSO CONTAINS A MYSTICAL DOORWAY TO ONE OF THE MOST POWERFUL WEAPONS IN THE UNIVERSE, AN ANGEL BLADE THAT ONLY YOU CAN USE. YOU WILL NEED THIS WEAPON TO SUCCEED IN YOUR QUEST. THERE WILL HOWEVER, BE CONSEQUENCES. IF YOU DECIDE TO ENTER THIS DOORWAY THERE IS ONLY ONE WAY TO RETURN. YOU MUST DRINK THE BLOOD OF THE GODS FROM THE CHALICE YOU WILL SEE ON THE PLINTH. YOUR POWERS WILL BECOME MUCH STRONGER AND MORE VARIED BUT YOU WILL NO LONGER BE WHOLLY HUMAN. YOU WILL BECOME A SERVANT OF GOD. SO WHAT IS YOUR DECISION?"

"I believe it's the right thing to do. So yes, I am ready to be your servant."

A huge gold door which was covered in intricate carvings of mythological creatures and gods materialised in front of Lilly.

"ENTER." The Sun God raised his arms and the door swung open to reveal a small candlelit chamber. A bronze plinth stood in the centre of the dimly lit chamber, upon which was a silver chalice.

As Lilly tentatively entered the chamber the huge gold door closed behind her. A moment of panic dawned on Lilly. *Shit!*

The teenager stepped up to the plinth and picked up the silver chalice. Her eyes glanced down at the contents. *Oh Jeez, that looks disgusting.* Lilly lifted the chalice to her lips. She closed her eyes and started to drink the blood. The blood was thick and warm. As it passed down her throat she momentarily gagged and choked and then …. It was gone. She licked her lips without a thought and placed the silver chalice on the plinth which in turn slowly descended into the floor. Moments later, the plinth rose up from the floor with a silver triple edged dagger approximately sixty centimetres in length balanced precariously on top of the plinth.

Lilly grasped the dagger. *So this is an angel blade.* She held it up to admire the craftsmanship.

The huge gold door opened to release Lilly from the chamber and as she stepped out she felt an overwhelming sense of power within her whole being. *I feel different. Stronger. Even more ruthless and yet, somehow more at peace with the world.*

"LILLY." A booming voice cut into her thoughts. It was Inti, the Sun God. "YOU ARE NOW OUR SERVANT. YOU ARE AN ANGEL HYBRID WITH ALMOST LIMITLESS POWERS. YOU AND YOUR FRIENDS NOW HAVE THE POWERS TO DEFEAT YOUR ENEMIES AND SAVE THE WORLD FROM THE IMPENDING CATACLYSMIC EVENTS THAT COULD CHANGE THE WORLD ORDER .... USE YOUR POWERS WISELY. PROTECT YOUR LOVED ONES AND ABOVE ALL REMEMBER, YOU ARE OUR SERVANT."

Lilly knelt on one knee and nodded. "My heart is yours."

"GO NOW. THERE IS MUCH TO DO."

Lilly sucked in a huge gulp of air as the navigation aid relinquished it's hold on Lilly as she became fully conscious once more in the real world.

"Lilly!" Richard, Chloe and Usha crowded around the teenager with concerned looks on their faces.

"Look at this." Richard picked up the angel blade.

"WOW!" Usha gasped.

"It's beautiful." Chloe gushed with admiration.

Lilly awoke abruptly ... "GIVE IT TO ME." Lilly grabbed Richard's arm firmly. "THE BLADE BELONGS TO ME."

Richard passed Lilly the angel blade.

Lilly stood up, holding the angel blade up to the sky, glinting in the rays of the sun causing rainbows to dance across the sky.

Chloe and Usha stood in awe as they watched Lilly.

Richard gasped as his brain tried to decipher what he was witnessing. His Granddaughter was stood there in the sunshine proudly posing with her arm aloft holding an angel blade. Not only that, a strange shadow of Lilly was being cast over the grass bank .... Richard put his hand to his mouth as he realised Lilly's shadow appeared to include wings spanning four metres across. *How can this be? Something has changed. My mind is playing tricks on me surely?* Richard glanced again at his Granddaughter standing before him. *She looks normal .... And yet? My eyes aren't deceiving me .... Lilly's shadow has wings! She's .... She's an angel .... How can this be? Why? What has she done?*

Richard stood there open mouthed staring at Lilly whilst Usha and Chloe chatted excitedly with her, unaware of the apparent change in the teenager.

"LILLY," Richard shouted.

A split second passed by as Lilly disappeared .... "LILLY, WHERE ARE YOU?"

"I'm right here Grandad."

Richard spun round. Lilly was stood behind him. She laughed and disappeared in an instant.

"And here." Lilly laughed again as she stood next to Chloe. "Take my hand gal." Chloe held Lilly's hand.

The two girls were gone .... And back again in an instant, this time standing behind Richard. Before he could react, they were standing next to Usha. Chloe held her hand and the three girls instantly reappeared standing next to Richard.

"ENOUGH .... STOP IT LILLY. What is going on?"

"Okay girls, that's enough fun for now. I need five minutes alone with Grandad. Usha, go for a quick walk with Chloe please. I'll catch up with you both. Okay?"

Chloe and Usha wandered off down the hill.

"So what happened Lilly?"

"I met Inti, the Sun God and to cut a long story short he has given me the ultimate weapon of this angel blade to help defeat both ours, and their enemies."

"And?"

"And what?"

"You're not telling me something."

"Such as?"

"You're not fully mortal any more are you? In fact, he's given you the power of being an angel hasn't he? There has to be a catch Lilly, so what sort of deal have you done?"

"How do you know that? I've done what I had to do to help us sort out this mess that we're in."

"Maybe Lilly, but I reckon the feeling of having more power has clouded your judgement. Why else would Inti make you an angel? I'm right aren't I? You're now an angel." Richard sat down on the grass bank and rested his head on his hands with a sigh.

Lilly sat next to Richard and put her arm around his shoulders. "You're right Grandad. But I felt it would help us solve the mystery at a quicker pace and to be honest, what with the increasingly violent situation with the Mafia and Supay, the God of Death and his demons from the Inca Underworld, I thought we needed extra protection. Think about it, Alex and I were both nearly murdered the other week."

"But being an angel means that you're no longer a mere mortal or am I missing something?"

"I realise that Grandad."

"What about your wings? I mean …. If I can see them in your shadow, surely everyone else …"

"No-one else can see them, only you. In fact, as far as everyone else is concerned, I now don't have a shadow here on earth because …"

"Because you're not a mortal human being. I get it Lilly, but I'm not happy about it. What happens when this is all over?"

"I honestly don't know Grandad. One thing you need to know is that Inti can call on me at any time to help him in any of the realms, above or below."

"So you're at his beck and call?"

"Yes. I am now a servant of God. I am in fact, an angel hybrid."

"What do we tell Usha and Chloe?"

"Nothing. They know I've now got extra powers and I have this angel blade. That's all they need to know don't you think?"

"Yeah. Sure. It's one thing we agree on. So what next?"

"I need to go, Inti needs me."

"But…"

" I'll get the girls first."

In the blink of an eye Lilly vanished and reappeared with Chloe and Usha. Richard heard the faint sound of flapping wings as Lilly disappeared again.

"Awesome," Usha said.

"My head's spinning." Chloe stood holding her head. "Hope Lilly doesn't do that too often."

"Where's Lilly gone?" Usha asked.

"Er, she had something important to attend to," Richard explained. "Come on girls. Get your scooters. Let's get out of here." *I hope you know what you're doing Lilly.*

CHAPTER 29

ONE MAN`S BOAT

"Come on Ben, pull your finger out or we'll never get this roof finished."

"It's all right for you Luis. You do this sort of work all the time. I'm not used to all this heavy lifting up and down ladders."

"Sorry mate. Tell you what, let's take a break."

Luis and Ben were working on the new roof at the Nunnery on Longis Road. It was one of the oldest sites on Alderney. Archaeologists had recently discovered that at one time it used to be a Roman Fort and was now being rejuvenated as a visitor attraction. The whole site was a strange mix of Roman and German Second World War fortifications and which also included two private residences.

The two teenagers sat on the bare rafters of the roof they were tiling, looking out over Longis Bay which is on the south east coast of Alderney. A huge crescent shaped bay with a flat sandy beach which was flanked by an anti tank wall standing three metres high, which had been built by slave labour during the Second World War. Across the bay they could see the causeway that stretched four hundred metres out into the centre of the bay to Raz Island and another fort which was built in the 1850's.

"What a view eh Ben?" Luis grabbed a bottle of beer and took a few gulps.

"You're right there mate …. Hey, look out there." Ben pointed over to the far side of the bay. I'm sure that's Alex's Dad's fishing boat."

"He's probably putting some lobster pots down," replied Luis.

"Nah! Frank never fishes this side of the island. Wonder what he's up to?"

"No idea Ben. It looks like he's travelling with the tide though. He's heading west along the coast."

"Hmm, he's out of sight now. That's strange seeing him out here. I'll have to ask Alex about his Dad next time I phone him. It just seems out of character." Ben took a couple of swigs from his bottle of beer and wiped his sweating brow. "So how's things with Lilly these days?"

"Yeah …. Good mate. I have to say, I feel one lucky guy you know. I don't seem to 'ave been living here for long and I've landed one of the most intelligent and good looking girls on the island. Not only that, she seems to be able to look after herself. Don't you think?"

Ben nodded in agreement as he gulped on his beer.

"I mean, take the other week when she and Alex were abducted in Guernsey by those foreign goons. It didn't seem to phase her and apparently she gave the one guy a right good pasting."

"Yeah …. Haven't you ever wondered about that though Luis?"

"How d'ya mean?"

"Well. Come on. Be honest. She's got a great figure I know, but she's not exactly built like Arnie Schwarzenegger is she? I mean, some of these guys that she's taken out were big guys. Know what I mean? Doesn't it bother you?"

202

Luis smiled and finished his beer off with a couple of big glugs. *He could be right. Maybe she watched Buffy The Vampire Slayer as a kid ... Ha!*

"Hi Luis."

"What!!" Luis looked round to see Lilly sat behind him. "What the ..."

Lilly kissed him passionately on the lips. *That feels SO good.*

"Err .... How long have you been here?"

"Just got here. Saw you both up here so I climbed up the ladders." *Actually, I've been here all the time you've been talking about me and I didn't need to climb any ladders.* Lilly was now able to appear in any place instantly either visible to the naked eye or not. She'd been listening for some time, but she hadn't been visible until now. "I was just passing and I thought I'd pay you both a visit. You're doing a good job up here."

"Luis .... We'd better get on with this roof," Ben interrupted.

"Oh ... Err .... Yeah. Okay Ben." Luis was clearly shaken. "Actually Lilly, you shouldn't be up here. If anyone spots you, we'll be in big trouble."

"Right guys, I'll let you get on. I'll see you later Luis." Lilly clambered over the roof to the nearest ladder and disappeared out of sight. *Looks like I'm gonna have to be careful how I fight when the lads are around,* thought Lilly. She smiled to herself.

"We come from the land of the ice and snow, From the midnight sun where the hot springs flow..."

It was the ring tone of Ben's phone. It was the Immigrant Song by Led Zeppelin.

"Great track Ben. Good choice. When the band were at their best I reckon .... Who's on the phone mate?"

"Ha! That's just weird. It's Alex .... Hi Alex. How 'ya doin'?..... Oh right ...... Okay, I'll get her to ring you as soon as possible ...... Yeah I think they've had problems here on and off all morning ..... I use a different telecom network, that's why. Whilst you're on the phone mate can I ask? Does your Dad ever use his boat around Longis Bay and the rest of the south coast?….. No ….. Oh right …… No, no big deal. Just wondered that's all …… Okay Alex. I'll make sure Chloe rings you ….. No probs' ….. Catch up with you later."

"What did Alex want?"

"Oh he'd been trying to ring Chloe this morning but I think there's something wrong with the phone network. Seems okay this end so I'll let her know. I'll ring her now 'cos there's something I want to ask her."

"What is Love? Baby, don't hurt me, Don't hurt me no more…" Chloe's ring tone, What is Love by Haddaway broke into her conversation with Usha.

The two girls had just arrived at their Grandad's house.

"Hi Ben, what's up?…. Oh has he? Thanks for letting me know, I'll give Alex a ring later ….. His Dad, Frank? No, haven't seen him today. Mind you, I overheard him talking to Beth, Alex's Mum yesterday, that he'd be away for two days in Guernsey ….. What?….. Yeah, he went down on his fishing boat ….. Yeah I'm sure ….. Shouldn't worry about it Ben, it's probably nothing ….. Okay, I'll catch up with you later, byeee!" *That sounds a bit strange.*

"What did Ben want Chloe?"

"Err …. Just to let me know Alex had been trying to ring me. I'll ring him later when I know he's finished college for the day." Chloe frowned.

"But?"

"Don't know. It's probably nothing, but the lads spotted Frank's fishing boat cruising down the south coast past Longis Bay …… He NEVER takes the boat out around the back of the island. Something doesn't feel right."

"What are you two up to?" Richard appeared from around the back of his house. "Hey …. Deep in conversation …. Both looking quite serious. What's up?"

"Chloe's worried about Frank Bean, Alex's Dad. Luis and Ben spotted his fishing boat cruising past Longis Bay this morning."

"And?"

"He just doesn't take the boat around the south coast Grandad. And anyway, he's supposed to be in Guernsey for a couple of days. I overheard him telling Beth last night that he'd be in Guernsey," Chloe explained in a breaking voice. "It's just not like him."

"What d'ya think Grandad?" Usha placed her arm around Chloe's shoulders.

"Well there's only one way to find out girls. We'll go and take a look shall we?"

"Awesome!"

"Hop in the van girls, it'll be quicker to get to the south cliff footpaths. We'll just have to walk when we get there. Won't be a minute, got a new gizmo in the house that should help us and I've been dying to try it out."

The two girls climbed in Richard's van.

"Wonder what Grandad's got?" Usha asked.

"Soon find out, here he comes."

"Hold this Usha. Don't drop it."

"What is it?"

"Wow! You've got a drone," Chloe drooled. "It's a drone Usha."

"Cool."

Richard reversed out of the drive, the engine spluttering as per normal. "Yeah, it should save us a lot of legwork. Some of those cliff paths are a bit dodgy. I'll park the van up at the Giffaine."

"You mean The Guns, Grandad?" Usha asked.

"Yeah, up past the bunkers where they have the bunker parties. We can follow the cliff footpath from there."

Richard drove the van past the airport and turned left which took them past the local pig farm.

Two minutes later and Richard turned on to the rough track that would take them up to The Guns in the south west of the island.

"Hold tight girls."

The van rocked and rolled, bumped up and down as the rough terrain took its toll on the suspension.

"That's as far as I'm taking the van. Let's stop here before the van falls apart," said Richard.

The two teenagers literally fell out of the back, just managing to keep hold of the drone.

"Right girls, let's go. If we follow this path we'll get to the cliffs."

It was quite a walk. Even though it was a well trodden path after years of visitors, local families and dog walkers using it, it was unsafe in places as landslips had eaten into certain areas of the ground above the cliffs. They eventually reached a relatively flat plateau of grass.

"We'll stop here," Richard said as he caught his breath. *Not as young and as fit as I used to be.*

"I've been studying the drone Grandad." Usha held the controls of the drone and fired the small motors into life and tested the cameras to make sure she was getting images on her screen. "It looks easy enough to control. Very much like playing a video game."

"Okay. You can take the controls Usha. Just make sure we don't lose sight of it and keep it at a good height. We need to guide the drone over the cliff edge and along the shoreline," replied Richard.

"Awesome."

"Chloe, you keep hold of the extra video screen for the drone. You know Frank's boat better than most, so you know what you're looking for."

"Gotcha Grandad."

"I've got these binoculars just in case we need them. Right Usha …. Send the drone up," said Richard.

The revs of the four small motors increased and the drone lifted into the air above their heads and glided out over the cliff edge.

"That's it Usha. Send it out a bit further, away from the cliff edge and then drop it down gradually. About thirty metres I reckon …. You've got it." Chloe adjusted the focus on her video screen.

"Let's move along down the path girls. We should be seeing Telegraph Bay soon." Richard pointed ahead of the girls. "Are you getting the hang of it now Usha?"

"Sure thing Grandad …. Is this Telegraph Bay coming up?"

Richard looked at Chloe's video screen.

"Yeah, that's Telegraph. Been down there a couple of times. Wouldn't fancy getting down there now though, look … You can see some of the path that goes down there. Visitors used to walk down that path but some of it has now eroded away due to landslip and erosion by the weather over the years. It's really steep and rugged. The best way to visit the bay now is by boat."

"Look in the distance." Chloe pointed at the horizon. "You can see Guernsey and Sark."

Richard lifted his binoculars to his eyes. "Sure can gal. Good spot …. Come on girls. Let's keep moving along the path."

The three walked steadily eastwards along the coastal cliff path as sea birds flew overhead. They stopped to admire a kestrel hovering above, looking down to the ground for prey and then watched as the chattering swallows swooped to catch insects on the wing.

Usha sat down momentarily and studied the screen on her controls. "What bay is this Grandad?"

Richard glanced at Chloe's screen. "That's Bluestone Bay. It's beautiful down there. The beach gives the impression of being blue because it's made up of blue grey slate …. Hold on. What's that?…. Take the drone a bit further down Usha."

By now, Usha was competent with the controls and skilfully guided the drone down to the bay. "There's a couple of guys on the beach ….. And it looks like they've got guns." *Shit!*

"Look Grandad." Chloe pointed to the screen. "There's a fishing boat about twenty metres out in the bay. That's Frank's boat, definitely."

"Are you sure Chloe?" Richard stepped closer to the cliff edge and looked through his binoculars. "You're right gal. Looks like there's four guys on board. Can't make out if Frank is one of them. Bring the drone up Usha before they spot it."

The drone responded quickly to Usha's controls as it climbed above the cliff face and landed a couple of metres in front of the teenager. *Wicked!*

"What now Grandad?" Usha asked.

"We need to get closer to see what's going on. Got to be up to no good 'cos they've got guns. Come on girls, let's see if we can get down to Cachaliere Pier. It's easier to climb down to the pier on the headland rather than take our chances trying to get down to Bluestone. I think the tides going out, so we can get to Bluestone from the pier ..... Just keep your eyes open you two. Let's go." *Jeez, where's Lilly when you need her?*

Richard took the lead as the three of them left the path and started to scramble down a steep grass bank which gradually gave way to rocky outcrops with loose gravel and slate.

"Be careful girls, it's getting steeper so watch your footing. Let's rest here for a mo' and get our breath back."

"We're about half way down I think Grandad." Usha felt Chloe sliding away from her. She grabbed her hand. "You okay Chloe?"

"Yeah, thanks cuz. Thought I was on my way then."

"You alright Chloe? I mean, you're a few weeks gone now. You don't have to do this." Richard was well aware of Chloe's condition and was rightly worried about her.

"I'm fine Grandad. Quit worrying."

Richard sighed. *Where the hell is Lilly?...* "Usha, see if you can get hold of Lilly whilst we sit here."

Usha nodded. The young girl concentrated all her energy and powers ..... *Lilly .... Lilly .... Can you hear me?.... Lilly. We really need you.....*

A huge gasp of air and Usha collapsed into Chloe's arms and then quickly sat up. "Sorry Grandad. She's not answering and I've no idea where she is."

"It's okay Usha. You tried …. Could have done with her help but we'll have to manage."

The two girls smiled.

"Either of you got a signal on your phones?" Richard glanced at his phone. *No signal. Damn. Always the same over on the south cliffs.* "I've got nothing …. Could have done with being able to phone the police …. Oh well. Shit happens."

Chloe and Usha shook their heads as they checked their phones.

Richard gingerly rose to his feet trying desperately to get some sort of purchase on the rocks. "Come on girls, let's get down to the pier before we're spotted."

The girls tentatively followed their Grandad down the cliff face, slipping and sliding as they grabbed hold of any protruding rocks to steady themselves. They were now about ten metres above the pier ….

"OY!" A shout from below.

Richard waved to the two teenagers behind him to take cover as he ducked down behind a rock. He could feel his heart pounding in his chest as he felt they'd been seen. Richard grabbed the binoculars and scanned the bay below. The two guys they'd seen earlier in Bluestone Bay had obviously scrambled over the rocks around the headland and were now having some sort of altercation as they stood on the pier. *At least they haven't seen us.*

Chloe and Usha crept down the rocks to join Richard.

"What's going on?" Chloe asked.

"Not quite sure gal," Richard replied.

"It's the two guys we saw earlier isn't it Grandad?" Usha asked.

"Yeah. And it looks like they're having some sort of argument. Look there, the one guy has just pushed the other one onto the ground and he's giving him a real good kickin'. Nice people!"

"Here comes Frank Bean's boat, over there." Usha pointed out to just beyond the pier. "Looks as if they're going to bring it alongside."

Richard and the girls watched as the fishing boat struggled to find a mooring on the pier negotiating between the remains of the original pier submerged below the waterline. Cachaliere Pier had been constructed in the early nineteen hundreds to handle quarry stone and the like, but the work was abandoned in the nineteen thirties. Local rumour has it that the Germans tried to blow it up during the occupation of Alderney in the Second World War to deter any possible allied landings, but there are few remains nowadays, looking eerily spooky with rusty girders amongst the concrete structure.

"Christ, I've counted six guys that's just got off the boat," Richard muttered. "And they're all armed."

"BANG!" A gunshot echoed around the bay. The girls covered their ears with their hands as their faces grimaced in shock.

Richard watched as a lifeless looking body was thrown from the boat into the water. *Oh no .... Surely not Frank. My God.* Richard was feeling angry. *Got to do something.*

"Usha .... If you use your shield, d'ya reckon you can climb down to the pier and get into the water?"

Usha nodded reassuringly.

"Try to locate Frank. If you can, swim round to Bluestone Bay and pull him up onto the beach. Once you've done that, try and join up with us at the pier. Hopefully me and Chloe can take these evil bastards out before we even reach the pier."

"How are you and Chloe going to manage that?"

"Well Chloe can summon her light staff to use .... And if you summon yours now, I can use your light staff. It's the only way that we can take them out from a distance. They've got guns so we don't want to get any closer than we need to. Right Chloe?"

"To bloody right Grandad."

"Awesome." Usha closed her eyes and in an instant the light staff was in her hand. She handed it to Richard.

"Right gal. Get going. And Usha ..... Be careful." Richard kissed her gently on her cheek.

Chloe hugged Usha and whispered in her ear, "Everything will be just fine. You'll see."

Usha smiled as she drew on her powers to form a shield and clambered over the rocks down towards the pier.

"You ready Chloe?"

"As I'll ever be Grandad."

"Remember, don't get too close. Try to pick 'em off with your light staff. The lightening bolts will definitely kill 'em." Richard climbed further down using the rocks to hide behind with Chloe following closely.

"UP THERE!" A shout from the pier.

Shit. We've been spotted.

Gunshots rang around the bay as bullets ricocheted off the rocks around Chloe and Richard.

"I'LL DRAW THEIR FIRE CHLOE. TRY TO GET SOME CLEAN SHOTS IN." Richard scrambled further down the cliff edge, ducking and diving as he tried to use the rocks for cover. He managed to see two of the men fall as they were hit by lightening bolts fired by Chloe.

Richard felt a sudden gush of wind brush past him. *That's Chloe. She's using her shield to get closer to the pier without being seen.*

Richard used his light staff to take out two more of the attackers. He caught sight of Chloe firing another lightening bolt from below the pier and as the guy fell dead into the water she felt the presence of Usha in her head …. ***Chloe …. It's Usha. Frank's alive …. Just ….. I've managed to swim round to Bluestone Bay ….. I daren't leave him or he'll bleed to death.***

Chloe had briefly stopped as Usha connected with her.

Move Chloe. What are you doing? Richard fired two more lightening bolts with deadly accuracy. Two men fell dead from the pier directly past Chloe shaking her back into action as she realised she needed to climb on to the pier to tackle the last man.

Richard watched helplessly, as if in slow motion, as Chloe lifted herself up on to the platform. She ducked as the assailant fired his gun and she slid along the pier firing lightening bolts, hitting the man fatally in the chest as he fired his last round ….

The bullet ripped into Chloe's ankle and she felt her bones shatter.

"ARRGGHHH." Her blood curdling screams of agony cut through the fresh sea air.

By now, Richard had managed to reach the base of the pier. He looked up to see Chloe slumped over in agony, blood pouring from her shattered ankle .... And then realised there was yet another attacker disembarking the fishing boat.

Richard desperately started to climb on to the broken staging of the old pier.

"HEY! BITCH!" The gun toting guy sauntered over to the slumped body of Chloe. He stood over her, his face distorted with rage. "YOU PAY FOR THIS!" he screamed. He kicked her viciously in the face and then lashed a second sickening blow to the pregnant girl's stomach. He spotted Richard clambering onto the pier and without hesitation, raised his gun and fired twice. The first bullet grazed Richard's head and the next one missed.

Chloe momentarily stirred and looked up at the man who aimed menacingly at her head .... He laughed hysterically as he squeezed the trigger .....

"WHOOSHHHHH!!" The guy dropped to the ground dead, his guts spilling out caused by an angel blade.

Lilly stood there, blood dripping from the blade. Her wings barely visible even to Richard.

"You alright Grandad?" Lilly asked as she knelt down beside Chloe.

"I'll be okay. Can you do anything for Chloe?"

"Li ... Lilly .... Is that you?" Chloe stuttered weakly. "Where was you when we needed you?"

"Yeah, it's me Chloe. I'm going to help you."

"Tell Grandad that Frank's alive and Usha needs help."

"Yeah okay Chloe. Need to sort you out quickly."

"My baby Lilly, my baby." Chloe clutched her stomach and sobbed uncontrollably.

Lilly scooped Chloe up in her arms with the power of four men. "I'll sort Chloe out Grandad .... And I'll send help for Usha and Frank." She disappeared in a blink of an eye, save for the faintest sound of wings.

Richard blinked his eyes and raised his hands to his head as he felt the warm blood trickling from the bullet wound on his forehead. *I'm a lucky old bastard eh? Ha! Gonna have a banging head tomorrow.* The sound of a helicopter above broke into his thoughts. Richard waved frantically to the crew above to encourage them to move across to Bluestone Bay.

Frank was in a bad way. He'd been shot three times and Usha was covered in blood from Frank's wounds as she tried in vain to stem the flow. The young girl heaved a sigh of relief as the Alderney Lifeboat appeared round the headland and immediately launched a small outboard with two crew. Within minutes, Frank was being winched upwards to the helicopter for an emergency flight to Guernsey. Usha had joined Richard for a boat ride on the lifeboat which had also managed to get a crew on board Frank's fishing boat, which was now following them to Braye Harbour.

"Are you alright gal?"

"Yeah. Sorry I couldn't get back to help you and Chloe Grandad. But Alex's Dad was in such a bad way I couldn't just leave him. How is he?"

"The paramedics told me it was touch and go but he'd pull through. So I'm really proud of you Usha. You saved Frank's life." Richard hugged his Granddaughter and kissed her on the forehead.

"There was two other guys on the beach Grandad."

"Who's that? How?"

"Diego Garcia, Luis' Dad and that doctor person who was being investigated by the FBI. You know, the guy who was drugging Chloe's Mum before he fled to America. You told me he had Mafia connections in South America. Remember?"

"Yeah I remember. You mean Dr Perez. He's a nasty bugger. What the hell were they doing down in Bluestone Bay?"

"Don't know Grandad. As I dragged Mr Bean up onto the beach I caught sight of them disappearing into a cave."

"Hmm. Well we're coming into the harbour. Look, there's an ambulance and quite a few police cars kicking about. Try not to say too much Usha 'cos I'm sure they'll have plenty of questions for us."

Usha had her impish grin back.

CHAPTER 30

LOVE AND HATE

Chloe's eyelids flickered as she struggled to regain consciousness. She felt a soft warm hand on her forehead with another hand gently stroking her swollen belly.

"Steady Chloe, try to remain calm." The softly spoken voice was Lilly's.

"Where …. Where are we?" Chloe struggled to talk as she tried to sit up.

"Somewhere safe," whispered Lilly, trying to reassure Chloe. "Stay still cuz."

Chloe peered through half open eyes trying to focus on her surroundings. Everything seemed to blend together in shades of white. *This is surreal,* she thought.

Lilly moved slightly away from her cousin. Chloe could vaguely hear voices in the background. Calming voices. Quiet voices. Concerned voices.

"Hello Chloe." A voice the young girl didn't recognise. "So … You are the child of the stars. In fact you are the one the Gods call Alnitak from the Orion Constellation. Our angel hybrid, Lilly, has spoken highly of you since she became a servant of God."

"Wh …. What?"

"Shush my child. Please, stay still …. My name is Mama Killa. You probably know me as the Moon Goddess." Her hands moved over Chloe's shattered ankle. "You might feel a slight twinge. Do not worry. That is normal in the healing process."

Chloe's previously shattered ankle was healed. *I can feel a warm sensation.* She sighed in relief from the pain as she relaxed a little in the strange surroundings.

Mama Killa stepped back and turned to face other figures in the light. "I can't save the baby." She had a soft yet

214

commanding voice as she consulted with other silhouettes that Chloe was unable to bring into focus. "If I try to save the baby we will lose our child of the stars." Further voices could be heard in the background of light as the Moon Goddess returned to Chloe and knelt beside her.

The Goddess placed her hand gently on Chloe's face. "My child, you must stay strong," she whispered. "I cannot save your baby. You ..."

"ARRGGHHHHH!!" Chloe screamed uncontrollably and started to sob and shake. "NOoooooo!!"

"Shush my child .... Shush." Mama Killa stroked Chloe's stomach tenderly. "The pain will go .... I know it's difficult but you have to believe that all will be right with the world. Your dreams will come true." The Goddess continued to soothe Chloe quietly until the teenager drifted off into a deep sleep ....

"Hello Mr Morgan and I take it this is Usha is it?" The paramedic put his hand to Richard's head. "That's a nasty wound, let's take a look at that." Richard winced in pain as the paramedic touched the bleeding wound. "Take a seat in the ambulance and I'll clean it up for you."

Usha climbed into the ambulance and sat down next to Richard. "Seems like your Grandad has been very brave eh Usha," the paramedic said. "Looks like he was very lucky. "The bullet has literally bounced off your Grandad's skull."

Richard winked at Usha as she grinned like a Cheshire Cat.

"There you go Mr Morgan. Keep the bandage on for a couple of days and here's a couple of pain killers to help ease the headache that you'll no doubt get later."

"Ha! Cheers mate."

"Hi Richard. Okay if I interrupt?" It was the local police Sergeant, Peter Cordy.

"Yeah, course you can Peter. I think we're done here." The paramedic nodded in agreement. "How can we help Sergeant?"

"Looks like you've had a pretty rough time so I'll keep it brief. We can always catch up later if the higher ups need to know more .... If you get my drift."

Richard nodded and gave an ironic smile. *Yeah right, that won't happen.*

"Firstly, what was you doing out at Cachaliere Pier and Bluestone Bay?"

"Just giving the girls a look round." *Shit ... He only knew about Usha.* "They'd never been down there before."

"Girls?"

"Yeah, Usha and Chloe."

"Right then. So where's Chloe?" Peter asked.

"It got too much for her, so she walked home earlier."

Richard glanced at Usha.

"So how come you got involved with those thugs?"

"Er, well." Richard hesitated. "We'd spotted Frank Bean's fishing boat in the bay with some guys aboard that were armed."

"And just how did you know they were armed?"

"Usha had seen them on the drone we were using .... That's right isn't it gal?"

Richard turned to see that his Granddaughter had collapsed. *Bet she's contacting Chloe or Lilly.* "Usha!"

Lilly .... Chloe ..... No questions asked. Chloe needs to be at home ..... NOW!

"Usha! Usha! You okay gal?" Richard grabbed her hand.

"What .... Oh .... Yeah ..... Sorry must have dozed off," Usha mumbled.

"So is the drone still up on the cliffs Richard?"

"Yeah sure. We didn't have time to retrieve it. Hope it's still there."

"One last thing Richard. Apart from one guy, all the others had some strange markings on them. It looks as if they've had an electric shock."

Richard shrugged his shoulders. "No idea Peter. Can't help you with that .... One thing I can tell you. I reckon they were Mafia .... And not only that, we spotted Dr Perez amongst them, one of the FBI's most wanted I believe. Diego Garcia was involved as well. If I was you I'd be requesting reinforcements from Guernsey ..... But hey, that's only my humble opinion."

"Constable." Peter beckoned one of the police officers over. "Get yourself up to Chloe Mollins' place to make sure she's alright and report back to me immediately. If Dr Perez is on the island, she could be in danger. He's already tried to kill her before."

"Sir." The officer nodded and walked quickly away to a waiting patrol car.

"Don't forget she's staying at Beth and Frank Bean's place up near the golf course," Richard reminded the constable as he climbed into his patrol car. *I hope Lilly's managed to get Chloe back there. Wonder how they are.* "Can we go now Peter?"

"Yeah sure Richard. Thanks for the info. But like I said, we may need to talk to you again." *Something doesn't feel right about all this.*

"By the way, have you heard how Frank's doing?"

"Last I heard he was 'serious but stable' Richard."

"That's good to hear. Come on Usha, we'll walk to your Mum's house and then I'll borrow your scooter to go and pick up my van up at The Guns."

"Don't believe in fear, Don't believe in faith, Don't believe in anything, That you can't break ...." Usha's ring tone, Stupid Girl by Garbage blurted out ..... "Hi Lilly, everything okay?...... Where are you?..... At Chloe's, that's good ..... How's the baby?..... Oh, oh no!...... What about the police? Have they called round?..... They've just left have they? ..... Okay ..... See you soon."

"The police have just left Chloe's place. Everything was okay Grandad but...."

"But what Usha?"

"Chloe's lost the baby ..... Oh Grandad." Usha started to cry.

Richard held the young girl tightly and wiped away her tears with a tissue. "I know it's sad gal, but sometimes things aren't meant to be. The most important thing is, Chloe's alright. When the time is right Usha, Chloe will have a baby. It just wasn't to be this time. Thankfully there was only us and Lilly that knew she was pregnant ..... It's probably for the best gal." *Bloody hell!*

Usha nodded, smiled and composed herself as she held Richard's hand. They walked into the front garden to be greeted by Susan and Chris .... "USHA! ..... We've been sick with worry. Are you okay?"

"I'm fine Mum, Dad." Usha hugged her parents.

"We knew something was going off," Susan said. "We saw the lifeboat leave the harbour and the helicopter seemed to be flying around for ever."

"Safe to say, we've had an eventful day," Richard commented to Chris as they followed Susan and Usha into the house. "I can't stay long 'cos I need to pick up my van."

Usha sat with Chris in front of the television which was broadcasting the national news.

"Have you seen our Lilly today Dad?" Susan asked.

"Err, no I haven't. Why?"

"Well she's been out all day and we haven't seen her. She's not even phoned either of us which is strange."

"MUM .... I spoke to Lilly on the phone about half an hour ago," Usha interrupted. "Remember Grandad?"

"Oh yeah .... That's right. I forgot about that. She's up at Beth and Frank's place with Chloe."

"Shush you lot. The local channel news has just come on." Chris turned the volume up .....

"Good evening and we start our news tonight with Breaking News from Alderney (video clip starts) .... This is the moment that a young girl risked her life to save a local fisherman from drowning. This video, taken by visitors out walking on the south cliffs of Alderney earlier today, shows how she dived in and managed to pull the man to safety under a hail of bullets. The local man involved is allegedly fifty three year old Frank Bean who'd been shot three times on his fishing boat by, we now believe to be, South American members of the Mafia, and he was then thrown overboard. He was later picked up by a rescue helicopter and flown to Guernsey Hospital where we have been informed he is now in a stable condition. Happily, the young girl, Usha Gat, was unscathed during her ordeal and is now safely at home (video clip ends). A big well done to Usha.... On to our next item which involves...."

Chris turned the television off.

There was a stunned silence.

"What?" Richard gasped. "Why are you all looking at me?"

"Why is it whenever our Usha is with you something seems to happen?" Susan asked.

"That's unfair to say things like that."

"It's true though Richard," Chris added. "What was you doing up on the cliffs today?"

"We just went for a walk and we were trying out my new drone. Anyway, you should be very proud of Usha."

"We are. We're always proud of her. But you know what, she could have been killed today." Susan hugged Usha.

"But she wasn't …. And I don't hear Usha moaning about it." Richard winked at Usha. "Anyway, I need to go and pick up my van so I'll see you all later." Richard turned and walked towards the door.

"Wait Grandad." Usha ran up to Richard and hugged him. "Love you Grandad."

Richard kissed his Granddaughter on her forehead. "I love you too gal and I'm very very proud of you. I need to go. See ya'."

Chloe's eyelids flickered open to see Lilly sat on the side of her bed, deep in thought and visibly upset. She could feel one of Lilly's hands stroking her stomach as she lay there. Chloe lifted her head from the pillow slightly... "Li Lilly …. It's okay. I understand."

"Oh … Chloe. Thank goodness you're awake ….. Sorry, what did you say?"

"I understand Lilly. Honestly I do."

"But the baby?"

"It wasn't to be. I just have to believe that my dreams and hopes will come true." Chloe held Lilly's hand. "Tell me. Where did you take me?"

"To a better place," replied Lilly as she wiped away tears from her own face.

"Did I hear a voice call you an angel?"

"You probably think you heard and saw many things Chloe. You was in great pain and delirious. They say people see unbelievable things when they're close to death. I'm just so glad you're alright and I'm so sorry you lost the baby." Lilly kissed Chloe tenderly on the cheek.

"HELLO!" A shout from the kitchen downstairs. "HELLO!"

"UP HERE MRS BEAN," Lilly responded.

Beth walked into the bedroom to see Chloe lying on the bed. "Oh dear. Someone not very well?"

"I'm not bad Beth, I feel better than I did earlier. I've just felt tired all day. Lilly's been keeping me company." Chloe gave Lilly a knowing look.

"That's nice love. Thank you Lilly."

"Right, I think it's time I went." Lilly placed her hand on Chloe's forehead giving her cousin an overwhelming sense of happiness. Chloe smiled as if she had suddenly found peace with the world.

"Thank you for staying with Chloe, Lilly."

"My pleasure Mrs Bean. I'll say goodbye then."

Richard had made it up to The Guns on Usha's scooter to where he'd left his van. He lifted the scooter into his van. *Right, let's see if I can find the drone or the spare video screen.* He turned. "What the ..."

Lilly stood immediately in front of him.

"Jeez gal. Stop appearing like that. You'll give me a heart attack!"

"Sorry Grandad .... Anyway, what the hell are you doing back up here?"

"Well, if you must know, I came back for the van ...."

"Oh."

".... And the drone or the spare video screen. It could have recorded something that we missed."

"Right. Come on, I'll help," Lilly replied.

Lilly and Richard followed the same path that Richard had taken earlier that day. Whilst they walked, they discussed the events of the day.

"Just so you know, your Mum and Dad have been wondering where you've been all day," said Richard.

"Yeah?"

"I'm just giving you the heads up. They weren't too pleased when I turned up at their place with your sister .... Especially

220

when there was a news feature on television which included Usha."

"I bet sis' was chuffed?"

"She was very brave you know. Without a doubt, if she hadn't have been there, Alex's Dad would be dead now. A cool head on young shoulders."

"Usha would never let anyone down. You know that."

"I think you need to listen to yourself gal. We really needed you today and you went missing."

"I know Grandad. I'm really really sorry but I was needed elsewhere by other angels. It's extremely difficult to explain but the short story is that the order of the world is changing in a way that mere mortals couldn't even imagine. There are evil and corrupt powers trying to get a foothold here on earth. Disruption of the equilibrium is their aim, to create mayhem and destruction. What we are seeing here in Alderney, with demons and the like, is happening elsewhere in the world. It's the first step to anarchy and the armies of angels are at full stretch to keep incidents as limited as possible. I don't have an easy answer for you Grandad."

"Hmm. Try telling that to your Mum and Dad ….. Or Chloe!"

"Chloe's alright now and she fully understands. I know she lost the baby which is unbelievably sad, but her dreams will come true. You have to believe me Grandad."

"Here we are. This is where we left the drone. It's gone though unfortunately." Richard huffed.

"Looks like the police have been quite thorough." Lilly peered down over the cliff. "All the bodies have been recovered and removed."

"That's something you can probably deal with."

"What's that?"

"Sergeant Cordy asked me about the peculiar marks on their bodies. As he put it, 'markings caused by electric shocks'. I assume the marks are caused by the lightening bolts?"

"Yeah I can sort that, 'cos they're bound to do autopsies. Basically they die of a heart attack due to the immense electrical surges. But I can easily make their skin almost perfect so no-one will be none the wiser. You don't need to know how I can do it but yeah, I'll sort it."

The pair walked a little further.

"Here we go Lilly." Richard bent down to the ground. "That's a stroke of luck."

"What have you got there?" Lilly asked as she looked over Richard's shoulder.

"It's the spare video screen for the drone. The police aren't as good as we thought. Ha!" *They never let me down!*

"Does it still work Grandad?"

"Yep. I've got it running now."

Richard and Lilly sat watching the video intently.

"There Grandad." Lilly pointed to the screen. "Freeze the frame. Who's that?"

"That's Dr Perez and Diego Garcia. Usha spotted them on the beach earlier today at Bluestone as they disappeared into a cave."

"So Dr Perez is, or was on island again?"

"Sure is. You'd think the FBI would be crawling all over the island but I've seen no evidence of that," replied Richard.

"Run the video again. In slow mo' .... to the point where you can see the cave ..... Just there Grandad." Lilly pointed to the screen again. "Can you see it?"

"See what?"

"Well for starters, there's four shadows .... And look .... There, on the ground .... What's that?"

Richard strained his eyes to focus on the small area of beach Lilly was pointing at on the screen. "That's err ..... It looks like a chest. What d'ya think gal?.... Lilly .... What the...." *Shit. She's gone.*

Lilly stood on the beach, her eyes scanning around looking for the cave. *There it is.* She stumbled across the thousands of stones that made the beach until she reached the entrance. It was a narrow but tall cave. *No chest. No surprise. Gonna have to move further into the cave.* She stepped forward and then heard the faintest of sounds about ten metres in front of her. Lilly froze. *Just listen gal.* Her heart was racing and the adrenalin pumping as her senses acclimatised to the darkness.

"AARRGGHH." A blood curdling scream as two thugs rushed out of the darkness and knocked Lilly to the ground. She felt knives slash deep into her flesh as she pulled herself up from the ground. The two thugs rushed at Lilly once more, but she was prepared this time. With the power of four men she lifted the evil thugs off their feet and threw them against the cave wall. With one sweep of her arm the angel blade sliced both attackers in two and the bodies fell lifeless, with blood and guts spilling out onto the cave floor.

"Well done." A man's voice emanated from the darkness as he sarcastically applauded the young girl. "You've improved your skills." The voice was closer and the man came into view.

"Dr Perez. I should have known." Lilly raised her angel blade and she could feel all her emotions and powers building up inside her.

"So what are you going to do Lilly? Kill me?...."

The thought had crossed my mind, thought Lilly.

"How's that little bitch, Chloe? You can't protect all the people you love you know ..... There are thousands more like me fighting for control of the world."

Lilly's eyes turned black and the rage inside took over as she thrust the angel blade deep into his chest and drew downwards slicing him in two. "THAT'S FOR CHLOE." She grabbed his hair and without hesitation sliced his head off in one movement. "AND THAT'S FOR DAVE AND PHILIP YOU BASTARD!" Lilly casually dropped his head to the bloody cave floor before heading further into the cave.

Using her amulet to illuminate the way ahead, the narrow cave opened out into a huge chasm, hewn out over many centuries by the sea and underground streams. She noticed several empty cans strewn around on the cave floor which indicated recent human use but no sign of Diego Garcia. *Strange. There was definitely four shadows on the video screen.. Where is he?*

A glint of light from the far end of the cave caught her eyes. She moved forward slowly. *I'm being watched.* Lilly stretched out her arm to the glint of light. *I heard that .... Behind me.* The teenager spun round to see Diego Garcia skulking in the shadows making for the cave entrance.

"HEY!.... YOU!" Lilly raised her hands ready to use her powers.

"I wouldn't if I was you." He had a menacing tone in his voice as he showed Lilly the detonator in his hand.

Lilly quickly realised the cave entrance had been primed with plastic explosives. *He knew I was coming. Bastard.* She lowered her hands.

"That's better girl. You don't learn eh? I warned you I would catch up with you and I warned you to stay away from my son Luis. This WILL BE your final performance. SEE YOU IN HELL." Diego pressed the detonator as he threw himself through the cave entrance onto the stony beach, the rocks falling behind him completely blocking the opening.

Amongst the clouds of dust and debris everything was still. Not a sound in the darkness of the cave ....

As the clouds of dust cleared, Lilly emerged through the darkness, her amulet glowing and pulsing strongly, emitting a beacon of light that lit up the vast chasm. The young girl realised for the moment, she was trapped. Her 'teleporting' power was useless below ground, particularly when surrounded by granite rock formations. *Ha, Grandad would have said 'You're only supposed to blow the bloody doors off' like Michael Caine in the movie The Italian Job.* Lilly smiled to herself. Her thoughts immediately drew her back to the glint of light in the cave wall. Lilly reached out to what she thought would be just a natural fault in the surrounding rock allowing sunlight to pierce through the darkness ....

Oh! Didn't expect that. It's another Inca gold statue that's been used for a lever. Lilly pulled on the lever and a huge slab of stone in the cave wall rolled to the side revealing a chamber with hand hewn stone steps that climbed upwards in a steep spiral through the rock above. The teenage glanced around the huge chasm. *No chest .... Bugger! Garcia must have hidden it outside of the cave and took it with him. Damn it.*

Lilly pulled the Inca gold statue from the rock. *No-one will be able to enter this cave from the beach so I'll take this with me.* The young girl climbed up the steps. The walls were cold and damp to the touch from the penetrating water in the rock and it was a hard steep climb even for a fit teenager, but eventually she reached the top to be faced with a heavy iron style grill above her. It was locked and looked as though it hadn't been moved over many years. Lilly grabbed hold of two of the thick, heavy rusty bars in the centre of the grill above her head and as her amulet glowed with power, the bars bent apart creating enough space for Lilly to squeeze through. She pulled herself up through the bars and stood there studying her surroundings. *A circular stone built room with two broken windows .... Interesting. Looks like it hasn't been lived in for some considerable time.*

Lilly made her way outside and realised where she was. *It's Telegraph Tower which was built in the early eighteen hundreds and used for communicating with the other Channel Islands. Wow! I'm only a couple of hundred metres from where I left Grandad.*

Wonder how long Lilly's going to be? I need to get back to the van. Richard lifted himself from the ground where he'd been sat and as he turned to go he felt a rush of wind.

"Hi Grandad."

"Lilly. Where the hell have you been? I'd given up on you."

"Sorry about that Grandad, I've been a little preoccupied." Lilly stood there with the Inca gold statue in one hand and the angel blade, still dripping with blood, in the other. "Here, look what I found." She passed him the fifteen centimetre high statue.

"Wow! It's pure gold. And it's identical to the other one you found in Albert Allens' store below Fort Tourgis," said Richard.

"Yep!"

"If you think about it Lilly, you may have stumbled upon something that's highly significant. We're looking for the Lima Treasure right?"

Lilly nodded. "Yeah obviously .... And so is everybody else it seems, with the Mafia, Diego Garcia, the Inca Gods and knowing our luck, the FBI."

"No. You don't understand. The gold statues could well be the Lima Treasure, or perhaps they are the key to finding the treasure."

"Arrhh .... Okay, I'll buy that," replied Lilly.

"If I'm right, our problem is how many statues are there? Any other treasure we find is a bonus so to speak and could be like a trail of clues."

"Could be Grandad. Out of interest, where did you hide the first statue we found? Surely not at home."

"No, no. I've learnt my lesson on keeping anything at home that relates to the Lima Treasure. I got Chloe to hide it at the library. She's assured me that no-one will find the statue. I'll give this statue to Chloe next time she's working at the library."

"I should be able to find out how many statues there are. Might even rope Chloe in for a Shamanic Journey. Could be interesting," replied Lilly.

"Good idea …. Can I ask, those wounds you've got. They look really bad. Don't they hurt?"

Lilly glanced at her bloody shoulder and legs. "These? They did at the time but they'll be gone in about half an hour. There's a positive being an angel hybrid."

"Hmm …. And dare I ask. Is that blood dripping from your blade?"

"Hell yeah. The bastards deserved it and let's just say, we don't have to worry about Dr Perez any more."

"What?"

"He went to pieces on me Grandad. What can I say. He deserved everything he got." Lilly gave Richard a piercing look with her steely blue eyes.

"He's dead then?"

"Too right he is. I missed out on Diego Garcia though and I think he took the chest we saw. So we still don't know what's inside it."

"Okay. Well I need to get back to the van with this video screen in case the police come back and I've still got to go down to your place to drop Usha's scooter back before going home. You want a lift?"

A faint sound of fluttering wings disturbed the still air surrounding Richard.

That's a no then ….. Damn it!

CHAPTER 31

EMOTIONS

"Take a look into my eyes, Tell me what you see, Take a look into my eyes, Tell me is it true? Take a look into my eyes, Oh when I look at you, Take a look into my eyes, Tell me is it me? Is it really me?..." The local pub, The Campania, was bouncing as Mirror Mirror by Def Leppard was being performed by a local band, Gone Tech. And it was standing room only.

"So how d'ya think we got on today Luis?" Ben asked as he grabbed another bottle of beer.

"Yeah, okay I think .... D'ya know, I seem to have done nothing today other than think about Lilly. I haven't been able to get her out of my head. The thing is though, apart from seeing her on the roof down at the Nunnery site earlier today, no-one's seen her around the island at all. Bit unusual considering what's gone off today down at Bluestone Bay and Cachaliere Pier. She usually has the knack of being involved in those sorts of incidents don't you think?"

"I've told you before mate, there's something really weird going on. I've said before."

"Yeah I know, I know. But when I think I'm getting somewhere close to the truth it seems to go straight out of the window. I mean, I trust Lilly, but I always feel that something's not quite right."

"Hmm."

"But what about your girlfriend eh?" asked Luis.

"Usha?"

"Obviously, you plonker. Saving Alex's Dad, Frank Bean. I hear he's going to be alright and you know, it was all over the news. Even a video clip provided by some holidaymaker. Brill eh?"

"Yeah, it was well good," replied Ben. "Everyone's been going on about it .... But you know, you have to ask yourself what the hell was she doing down there in the first place? She's always with her Grandad, Mr Morgan. Why didn't he dive in to rescue Alex's

Dad? I mean, Usha's a fit girl, but she's only a slip of a thing so how was she able to drag Frank Bean up onto the beach? It's like, when she saved me and those two girls from the fire at the school. Come on Luis, how does that work for you? I find the whole scenario is quite strange with Lilly and Usha. You have to admit something's not quite right."

"I get what you're saying mate, but …. Oh hang on. Speak of the devil, I spy Lilly and Usha. They've just walked in."

The two sisters immediately spotted Luis and Ben. Lilly ambled over to the two lads and threw herself into Luis' arms and kissed him passionately on the lips as she grabbed his torso tightly and manoeuvred herself between his legs, writhing in a steady up and down motion. *Jeez, I want him,* she thought.

Luis struggled to contain his passion as his manhood awoke and strained to release itself from his jeans. *She's been drinking.* He gently eased Lilly away from his body as best as he could. "Steady on gal, people are watching. You're embarrassing me. Slow down."

The young couple's sexual chemistry was suddenly interrupted by the sound of people clapping, whistling, woo wooing and cheering Usha. The crowd in the pub slowly parted as Usha made her way over to her friends.

Ben pulled Usha close to him and kissed her on the lips. "I'm proud of you gal. I really am." He kissed her again as the local band began to play There She Goes by The La's …. *"There she goes, There she goes again, Racing through my brain, And I just can't contain, This feeling that remains…."*

There was a clinking of bottles as Tessa, the local barmaid passed the young friends four bottles of beer. "There you go guys, on the house." She winked. "Just bear in mind though, you're all underage so I know nothing, if you get my drift. Well done Usha for saving Frank earlier today. He's a popular guy in Alderney so I think you've managed to make a lot of friends here today." Tessa strolled back to the bar collecting empties as she chatted to the punters.

"Awesome."

"By 'eck, Tessa sure has a great pair of tits," Luis joked. "Don't know how she keeps them in there!" He nudged Ben in the ribs.

"Typical man comment," Lilly snapped. "Sexist."

"Yeah, but he's right. She'd make two of us Lilly and it's the sort of thing Grandad would have said," Usha replied.

The four friends laughed hysterically and continued to enjoy their beers.

It was late as the four teenagers left the Campania. They were all a little tipsy .... Not drunk. Just happy with each other's company as they sauntered down High Street.

Ben and Usha walked hand in hand occasionally stopping for a kiss and a cuddle.

Lilly and Luis were twenty metres behind .... Lilly suddenly grabbed Luis and pushed him into an open doorway and without hesitation tore at his shirt. *I need you now.* "I've got to have you Luis, I can't control my feelings any more."

Luis tried to push Lilly away. *Bloody hell. She's so strong.* "Stop it Lilly ..... Not here, not now."

It was no use. Lilly pulled her top off revealing her unfettered breasts. Her nipples pert and upright in the cold night air. She breathed heavily as her passions quickly rose to the surface and her emotions became uncontrollable. "Don't fight me Luis. I WILL have my way with you or I'll kill you." There was a look of menace in her eyes. She grabbed his hands and forced them down her skirt as she locked her lips on his.

Luis struggled, not only with his own feelings, but he knew this wasn't the girl he loved. Something was so wrong, so very wrong. *Wow... Shit ... Lilly's eyes are black.* Luis tried to resist his girlfriend's strength as he struggled and kicked out desperately.

Lilly could feel her love juices soaking her thighs as she became more powerfully aroused. "Oh Luis, this is the time ... I will have my way with you." There was a intimidating tone in Lilly's voice as she forced herself upon her boyfriend ....

Lilly suddenly collapsed to the ground with an almighty thud as a stunned Luis looked down at her .... "Lilly. What the? What's wrong?"

Chloe stepped out of the shadows with Richard stood behind her. "Sorry Luis. Don't worry, she'll be alright in a little while." Chloe bent down and gently stroked Lilly's blonde hair.

Richard wrapped a blanket around Lilly as he heard footsteps approaching at speed .... It was Usha and Ben.

"What the hell?!" Usha exclaimed. "What's happened?"

"It's okay gal, I'll explain later." Richard gave Chloe a knowing look. "Are you two guys going to be alright making your own way home?.... 'Cos I'll take the girls in my van."

"Yeah, yeah Mr Morgan," Luis stuttered, still in shock. "We'll manage .... Come on Ben. Let's get the hell out of here." *Bloody hell!*

Ben kissed Usha tenderly on the cheek. "Night luv."

Richard and Chloe picked Lilly up from the ground. She was still unconscious as they gently placed her in the back of the van. "Right girls, hop in and try and sort Lilly out. Make her look a bit more respectable as well." He passed Usha, Lilly's top and a few tissues before climbing behind the steering wheel.

The engine spluttered into life and Richard drove away from the scene.

"So what's just happened Grandad?" Usha asked.

Richard pulled the van over and stopped out of sight of prying eyes. "Did you see anyone out of the ordinary at the pub? Anyone you wouldn't normally see?"

"Don't think so". Usha thought for a moment. "No wait. I did see Mrs Garcia. You know. Luis' Step Mum, but I didn't think anything of it. Why?"

"You mean Lucy Garcia? That would explain a lot. Look, there's something you need to know. Chloe already knows, but without going into a lot of detail, your sister is an angel. She's actually an angel hybrid," explained Richard.

"Who? Our Lilly?.... Really? ..... Honestly?..... AWESOME!"

"No, actually, it isn't Usha. It's causing all sorts of problems and it's effecting Lilly in ways she, or any of us couldn't possibly imagine."

Chloe interrupted. "Lilly took me somewhere, I don't know where, when she saved me on Cachaliere Pier. I thought I was hallucinating when I saw the Moon Goddess, Mama Killa and I began to realise that I was probably in Heaven. It sounds crazy I know, but when Lilly got me back home after I lost the baby, she laid her hand on me and everything suddenly seemed to make sense. Lilly knew she was in great danger even though she has all these powers and the power of an angel, so she chose me as her Protector, to protect her soul. I only have to touch her on the shoulder and her emotions collapse. That's what you witnessed earlier tonight. I've been getting this voice in my head that I'd been chosen and it warned me that Lilly would be in danger tonight so I phoned Grandad to pick me up."

"Now then girls," Richard continued. "Lilly knows that Chloe is a Protector of her soul because she gave her that power. Lilly is also fully aware that she is in constant danger but she has the added responsibility of protecting all of us which throws certain spanners in the works. There has become a dark uncontrollable side to Lilly that makes her vengeful, which is being exploited by our enemies. Lucy Garcia obviously spiked Lilly's drink earlier this evening knowing full well the drug would trigger her emotions. Most people would have dealt with it, but Lilly's powers survive on emotions so she becomes a loose cannon, so to speak. Until this evening, Lucy must have thought that Lilly was dead 'cos Diego Garcia would have told her, thinking he'd killed her in the cave at Bluestone Bay, not knowing that she'd escaped later. Not only that, he must have let her know that Lilly had killed Dr Perez."

"WHAT?.... REALLY?... That's really heavy stuff! Couldn't have happened to a nicer guy!" *Yes!!*

"Totally agree with you Chloe. Especially how he treated you and your Mum." Usha high-fived Chloe.

Richard fired the engine into life and continued to drive to Lilly and Usha's house.

"OOo my head." Lilly sat up in the back of the van to be greeted with hugs and kisses. "What happened?"

"Let's just say that you've got a bit of explaining to do with Luis." Chloe nudged Lilly.

"What?"

"I'll explain tomorrow after you've had a good nights sleep. You'll feel better."

"I doubt that."

"Why?"

Richard glanced in his rear view mirror to see his three Granddaughters. "Because angels don't sleep. Do they Lilly?"

CHAPTER 32

HOME TRUTHS

Chloe stirred in her bed as she struggled to convince herself it was time to get up. She'd got in late the night before, after dealing with Lilly's issues ….

"Well good morning young lady. Welcome to the land of the living." Beth opened the curtains allowing the bright sunlight to flood the bedroom.

"Whooooaaa." Chloe squirmed in the blinding sunlight and pulled the duvet up and over her eyes.

"Should have been up a couple of hours ago. The dog's been waiting for you to take her for a walk." Beth pulled at the duvet in an effort to loosen Chloe's grip. "Come on Chloe, I need you up. Remember?"

"What? …. Remember what?"

"You are hopeless sometimes Chloe. I'm flying down to Guernsey today to visit Frank 'cos if all goes well, we're hoping that the hospital might let him come home with me today …. And that's only because I'm a nurse."

Chloe threw the duvet off and leapt out of bed. "Yeah, of course. Sorry Beth, it completely slipped my mind."

"Looks like it's not the only thing you forgot!"

Chloe caught a glimpse of herself in the full length mirror. *Oopps!* She grabbed the duvet again, but this time, to hide her modesty. "Err, late night Beth. I was SO tired." Chloe yawned.

Beth gave a wry smile. "Just get yourself dressed and come down for breakfast." She closed the bedroom door behind her as Chloe dropped the duvet and studied herself in the mirror as she ran her hands over her soft young skin. *Not bad girl. Not bad at all if I say so myself.*

Chloe sat down at the kitchen table and poured herself an orange juice. Dapper, the retriever, sauntered over to the young girl and rubbed herself against the young girls legs. "Hello girl." Chloe stroked the dog affectionately. "Just give me a few minutes."

Beth sat down at the table with a cooked breakfast for Chloe. "There you go. That should keep you going for a while."

"Thanks Beth." Chloe felt her face redden up. "Sorry about earlier. I, I don't normally sleep in the buff."

"I've seen it all before gal. No worries, but please remember when Frank's in the house, try to keep your appearance a little more respectable."

Chloe nodded. "How is he anyway?"

"Apparently he's made good progress. The consultants at the hospital told me on the phone yesterday, that he'd been extremely lucky 'cos two of the bullets narrowly missed a couple of arteries. Mind you, he wouldn't be alive today if it hadn't been for the quick thinking of your cousin Usha. Not only did she save him from drowning, but she managed to stem the flow of blood from the bullet wounds. So we will be forever grateful." Beth glanced at her watch. "Right, I need to go. Don't forget to take Dapper out for her walk."

"Hope everything goes alright Beth. Don't worry about Dapper, I'll take her with me when I go to the library. I'm working there this morning and Mrs Dodds won't mind Dapper being with me providing she behaves herself."

"Who, Mrs Dodds?" Beth had an impish grin.

"Ha! I won't tell her you said that. Besides, the walk will do us both good."

"Okay then." Beth kissed Chloe on the cheek. "I'll see you later then …. Oh by the way, I'm supposed to be meeting up with my lad Alex as well so I'll give him your love shall I?"

"That would be lovely, thanks Beth. Bye then."

Beth walked out of the house and climbed into the waiting taxi to take her to the airport.

"Right Dapper, I'll get some shoes on and we'll get going …. Go and fetch your lead."

"Richard, what are you doing this morning?" Bea asked as she hobbled to the sofa and fell back gratefully into the soft furnishing.

She still had a cast on her ankle which was due to be taken off later in the week.

"Not sure luv …. I hadn't really given the day ahead much thought. I might get out in the garden 'cos they've given bad weather out for later in the week. Why?"

"Well I've got these three library books that need returning. D'ya mind taking them Richard? I'll give Annie Dodds a ring to let her know you'll be calling in at the library. She knows what sort of reading I like so I'll ask her to choose something for me. Saves you looking for me, besides which, you'd choose something that I didn't like anyway."

"Hmmm …. Yeah that's fine." *Anything to keep the peace …. Actually, I've just remembered the statue. I'll take it with me.*

"Thanks."

"I'll see you later then. Shouldn't be too long." Richard leant over and kissed Bea on the cheek as he picked up the library books. "I think I'll walk. I need the exercise."

Richard entered the library and immediately spotted Annie on the far side of the building through the numerous shelving units. *The library's empty. That's unusual at this time of day.* She was standing on a small step ladder sorting books on the top shelf. *Looking good as always gal.*

Annie was an old school friend of Richards and at one time in their younger years, they'd been engaged to be married. She was a good looking highly sexed woman who prided herself on her sexuality. Annie was slim and petite with a good figure that she had proudly looked after over the years and she was always immaculately dressed. Today was no exception. Her cleavage strained beneath the figure hugging top which was suitably colour matched with her mid thigh skirt which clung to her well tanned legs.

Annie spotted Richard approaching behind her in one of the security mirrors. He was watching her every move. She smiled warmly to herself as she felt the goose bumps rise on the back of her neck. *Richard. My long time love. Oh if only.* Her auburn hair bounced around on her shoulders as she moved the books from side to side. She pretended not to notice him as Richard walked up to the step ladder. *God, the very sight of him turns me on.*

234

"Hi Annie."

The step ladder wobbled as the librarian turned to look down at Richard who instinctively put his hands firmly around Annie's legs to steady her.

"Oh hi Richard." *Ooo his hands feel so good on my legs.* Annie took a step down on the ladder as Richard's hands slid further up her legs sending a tingle of passion and lust through her body.

They stood there momentarily lost in their lustful thoughts, oblivious to any probable distractions.

"Here, err, let me help you down Annie." Richard grabbed her waist with both hands and lifted her down to the floor and held her tight to his body as their passions raged inside. He could feel his jeans bulging between his upper thighs ....

Annie looked up into Richard's eyes. "Oh Richard, we made the biggest mistake of our lives all those years ago. You know I've always loved you." Her emotions rose to the surface and she kissed Richard lovingly on the lips as tears ran down her face.

Richard's heart was racing. Annie had been his first love and his feelings hadn't faded over the years. "And I will always love you too girl." He wiped Annie's tears away and then continued to kiss her, a long smouldering kiss. Both of them unaware that Chloe and her dog had entered the library a few moments earlier and had been watching discreetly.

Annie pulled Richard down to the old wooden floor behind a shelving unit as she deftly undid his jeans. "I need you now Richard. I love you. I love you .... I know it's wrong, but I want you and I need you."

As Richard's hands pushed her skirt up, Annie pulled her top off revealing a skimpy bra that barely held her ample breasts and pulled Richard's face into her cleavage. She groaned as Richard ran his hand between her now wet thighs .....

Dapper suddenly barked once.

"Ssshhh Dapper," Chloe whispered.

"Did you hear that Richard?" Annie whispered with a stutter.

"Yeah I did." *Shit .... Clothes ..... Bugger!*

The flustered couple struggled to re-arrange their clothes as Chloe got a little closer.

"HELLO," shouted Chloe, Is anyone here?" *Try and give them some warning. Ha!* "HELLO!"

235

Richard stood up from behind the shelving unit. "Oh, err, hi Chloe." *This is embarrassing.*

"Hi Grandad. You okay?" *Look at the colour of his face. Ha!* Chloe stepped closer.

"Yeah. Yeah sure." Richard tried to compose himself. "We're just trying to find some books for your Grandma."

Annie's head popped up from behind the unit looking completely flustered, with her seemingly wind blown hair. She was still on her knees as Chloe joined them. "Hello Chloe .... Yeah just sorting some books out for your Grandma." *Where are my knickers?*

"What? In the woodworking section?!.... Perhaps advice on splinters!" Chloe grinned impishly as she pointed to the books. She spotted Annie's knickers precariously hanging from one of them. Chloe diverted her eyes as Annie grabbed her skimpy underwear and stuffed them in her pocket.

"What's this?" Annie picked up the gold Inca statue off the floor. "It looks valuable."

Richard felt his pockets. *Damn it. Must have dropped out of my pocket.*

Chloe took the statue out of Annie's hand. "That belongs to Grandad. He's helping a friend with a restoration project, that's right isn't it Grandad?" Chloe passed Richard the statue with a knowing look.

"Err :.... Yeah. That's right Chloe. Mustn't lose it eh?" Richard put the statue in his pocket as Chloe gave him a dissenting look.

Time to change the subject. "It's alright if Dapper here, spends the morning in the library isn't it Mrs Dodds whilst I work? She won't be any bother."

"Yeah yeah, that's fine Chloe. Will you both excuse me for a couple of minutes. I need the bathroom." *And I need to get my knickers back on. Damn it!* Annie disappeared sheepishly into the back.

"Chloe. I ....."

"Don't Grandad .... Just don't go there. I do NOT want to discuss it."

"But Chloe...."

"Sorry Grandad. I thought we told each other everything. I trusted you. But now look. Don't worry, I won't say anything, but

236

jeez. And not only that, you let Mrs Dodds see the statue. What was you thinking?"

"It's complicated Chloe and all I can say is, I'm sorry."

Chloe fastened Dapper's lead to a chair. "Stay girl .... I need to get on with some work Grandad so...."

"Before you start Chloe," Richard took the statue out of his pocket and passed it to Chloe, "can you hide this with the other statue whilst Annie's not here."

"Yeah sure." Chloe walked over to one of the tables and moved it slightly. She placed her hand at one end of a short floor board and applied pressure which pushed the one end down, lifting the other end of the wooden floor board up and placed the statue carefully underneath, then repositioned the table back on top of the floor board. Dapper watched intently as if she was about to play her favourite game. "All done .... Now I must get on with some work."

Annie called to Richard as she reappeared and they both walked to her counter.

"Richard." Annie spoke quietly, "I don't know what to say." She was visibly upset and moved her hand across the counter to hold Richard's hand. "I can't deal with this any more. All these years Richard ..... And I've wasted them with another man. I care for him and he's always treated me well, but .... You know Richard that you were the only one for me. The only man I truly love." The tears poured down her face as she sobbed uncontrollably.

We were so young Annie. Oh shit. "Annie." Richard tried to wipe away her tears. "Annie, you are always in my heart and in my thoughts. You know I love you and I do try to see you when I can, but......"

"Ssshhh!" Annie placed a finger across Richard's lips, "Don't Richard." The sobbing continued.

Chloe walked over to Richard and held his hand. "Grandad, she needs to go home. She's in no fit state to work, take her home." *They're like two love struck teenagers!*

"Chloe?"

Chloe nodded. "Go on Grandad, do the right thing and walk her home. I'll hold the fort here and lock up at lunch time. Then

I'll drop the keys off at Mrs Dodds' place so she can come to work this afternoon."

"You sure?"

"Just go Grandad …. And don't forget these." Chloe handed Richard, Bea's library books.

Richard held Annie around the waist and left the library. Annie's head turned briefly to mouth an emotional thank you to Chloe.

Chloe smiled in contentment. *Wow. Something serious must have happened years ago to throw them apart.*

Annie and Richard were stood hand in hand just round the corner from Annie's house out of sight from prying eyes.

"Richard, I can't do this any more. Every time I see you with Bea it breaks my heart."

"I know luv, but what can we do? You've got your family, your Grandchildren, the same as me. If we decided to up sticks and live together we would have to leave the island."

"Would that be so bad? We only need each other …. Just how it should have been all those years ago."

"Is that what you really want Annie? To live the rest of your life not seeing your family? To not see your Grandchildren grow up or maybe Great Grandchildren?… Sorry, I could never do that. As much as I love you … And always will." Richard kissed Annie tenderly on the cheek. "You never know what the future holds. All we can do is treasure every moment that we have together, however fleeting."

Annie hugged Richard tightly. "I'm always here for you. Come what may." She kissed Richard passionately on the lips and wiped away her tears as she reluctantly pushed herself away from him. "I'd better go luv before someone sees us. You take care Richard. I love you." Annie slowly turned and walked round the corner and out of sight.

Richard sighed. *Bloody hell! Jeez what a mess. All that bullshit of following your heart all those years ago …. And for what?*

Richard slammed the door behind him as he entered the house.

"Is that you Richard?"

"Yeah it's me. Why? Was you expecting someone else?" Richard walked into the lounge and dropped the library books on the table in front of Bea as he tried to keep his emotions in check.

"Of course not. It's just that you've been a long time. S'pose you've been chatting up that woman down at the library. That's what you're usually up to eh?"

"What d'ya mean by that?" Richard snapped.

"You've always fancied Annie, ever since you was at school. Don't deny it."

"Annie's a friend. A good friend, that's all. You believe what you want to believe and anyway, I've actually been chatting to young Chloe …. Are the books alright?"

"Yes of course." Bea shuffled the new library books. "Annie's made some good choices here …. Hmm, apart from this one."

"What's that?"

"Woodworking for beginners" replied Bea.

Ha! You wait till I see Chloe. Richard smiled to himself.

"Hello dear. How are you?" Beth leant over Frank, kissed him and sat in the chair next to the hospital bed.

"Actually, I feel pretty good. Still a bit sore where they dug the bullets out, but other than that, good. It's great to see you luv." Frank held Beth's hand.

"So it looks like they're letting you go home today. I've spoken to the doctors and they're quite happy to discharge you."

"Thank Christ for that. I couldn't have put up with any more of their so called meals."

Beth smiled and squeezed Frank's hand as Alex walked into the room.

"Hi Mum … Dad. How are we doing?"

Beth rose from her chair and hugged Alex. "It's really good to see you son. Just look at you, are they not feeding you here? Have you lost a bit of weight?"

"It's fine Mum, stop fussing. I've taken up running to keep myself fit, that's all."

"Good for you son." Frank gingerly climbed out of bed and placed his arm around Alex's shoulders.

"I'm pleased to see you're alright Dad …. So come on then, what exactly happened that day?"

Frank sat on the bed. "It's the same as I told the police, I don't really remember a lot. I got a call out of the blue from some woman in Guernsey who wanted to hire the boat for a couple of days."

"A woman? That's odd."

"Yeah well. She was offering big money, I mean BIG money which I couldn't afford to turn down, 'cos as you know, the fishing has really dropped off thanks to those EU trawlers. So anyway, I took the boat down to Guernsey and met up with this woman."

"Who was she?" Alex asked.

"I don't know, she never gave her name. She was local I'm sure of it, but anyway, she gave me this bundle of money, must have been a couple of hundred thousand pounds."

"How much? Woaahh, no wonder you took the job on Dad."

"And then she disappeared after telling me to wait for eight men who wanted to come up to Alderney and take a look around the south coast. She told me they were a group of developers."

"So what happened luv?" Beth asked.

"Well, these guys turned up. They all appeared to be South American which made me feel rather uncomfortable to say the least and all spoke in broken English, that is, apart from two of them who I vaguely recognised. One of them was young Luis' Dad, Diego Garcia and the other guy I knew was Dr Perez."

"Wow! Are you sure it was Luis' Dad?" Alex asked.

"Absolutely. He's a miserable sod and I know he treats Luis very badly …."

"The police told us that they only found six bodies and none of them showed up on their records," Beth interrupted. "and they're fairly certain they were connected to the Mafia. The police and FBI have been crawling all over the place."

"So anyway," Frank continued, "we arrived up in Alderney and I dropped Diego Garcia and Dr Perez off at Bluestone bay. They said they were going to be testing the rock formations, to see if it would be suitable for building material. And then I moored on Cachaliere Pier just round the headland. That's when it all kicked off."

"Jeez Dad. So they just shot you."

"Yeah. They wanted me to wait for them when they got off the boat but I refused. I told them I couldn't stay there because of the tides but they were having none of it. That's when this one guy pulled a gun out and shot me three times and pushed me overboard."

"Christ …. The bastards …. So what happened to the money Dad?"

"I'm assuming that Garcia has it. He told me that he'd put it in a chest so the other guys didn't see it. As he put it, 'keep it out of sight of the other greedy buggers'. The police told me there was no chest on board when they searched the boat so I've lost out all round."

"But you're still alive luv. That's the main thing." Beth kissed Frank on the cheek. "And that's all due to young Usha pulling you out of the water and having the knowledge of how to stem the flow of blood."

"I know. I still don't know how she managed to pull me up onto the beach but hey, I'll never be able to thank her enough."

"Mr and Mrs Bean?" A nurses voice broke into the conversation.

"Yes."

"If you'd like to sign these papers you can go home whenever you're ready …. Just there on the dotted line, thanks." The nurse pointed to the paper as she handed Beth a pen.

Beth glanced at her watch. "Come on then luv, get yourself sorted. We've got time to catch the last flight back up to Alderney …. And it's been really good to see you son. You'll have to let us know when you're due to come home."

"Sooner than you think Mum. I'm coming with you both. The college has given me a week off as compassionate leave."

"Oh that's really good of them Alex. Mind you, I know someone who'll be pleased to see you …. Chloe."

"Me too Mum. I've missed her."

241

CHAPTER 33

A LIFE FOR A SOUL

"Come on Dapper, pick your ball up. Let's go home."

The retriever bounded across the golf course to Chloe who immediately fastened the lead to the dog's collar.

"Good girl." She stroked the dog affectionately, picked up the bag of golf balls that she'd collected for Alex's golf ball box and turned round to walk the two hundred metres or so to home. "Who's that up there Dapper?" The lone figure in the distance drew closer with every footstep and Dapper began to bark making Chloe feel a little on the nervous side.

Who is that? A little closer. *It's .... It's Alex.* "ALEX ..... ALEX." Chloe waved furiously and then broke into a trot.

"CHLOE." Alex walked quicker until he reached his girlfriend and flung his arms around her. *You smell great gal.* "Oh Chloe, I've missed you." He kissed her passionately on the lips as Dapper rubbed herself against the young couples legs. Alex bent down and patted the dog, "Yes girl, I've missed you too."

"It's great to see you Alex. I've SO missed you." Chloe pulled him closer and smothered Alex in kisses. "So how come you're home?"

"Come on gal, let's talk on the way home. I've got so much to tell you." *Good to see you're keeping my golf ball fund going, ha!*

"Me too. I've got loads to tell you." *Not too much mind!* "Come on Dapper. Keep up."

"I would like to climb high in a tree, I could be happy, I could be happy, Or go to Skye on my holiday, I could be happy, I could be happy ...." by Altered Images played out on Usha's phone.

"It's Chloe 'sis. She's just messaged me to let me know that Alex is home."

"That's cool ey?" Lilly replied.

"She's wanting to know if we all want to meet up at Saye campsite behind the sand dunes of Saye Bay. She says to bring some bottles and something to eat 'cos they're going to have a barbecue. What d'ya reckon Lilly?"

"Hell yeah. Why not. We'll have to go the conventional way though on the scooter if we're taking beer."

"Ha! Yeah …. Losing bottles mid flight on the wing wouldn't be very environmentally friendly," Usha replied.

The two sisters laughed as they got ready to leave.

"Are you changing your outfit Lilly?"

"Yeah. Of course. Got to look my best for Luis. D'ya think this dress is too revealing? What d'ya think?"

Usha glanced at Lilly as she stood in front of the mirror applying her make-up. *A bit tarty gal.*

Lilly squeezed and pushed her young breasts up in her tight fitting dress to create more cleavage. "What d'ya reckon 'sis?"

"It doesn't matter what I think Lilly. It's what Luis is going to think eh?" *Still think the outfit makes you look like a tart.*

"You look nice Usha. Are you going to put some make-up on?"

"Nah …. Ben always says he likes the natural look. Anyway, I feel comfortable without make-up."

"Oh okay …. I have to say, I'm a bit nervous about seeing Luis again after the other night."

"You'll be okay. Just apologise and tell him what happened. I'm sure Grandad will already have told him."

"Hmm. Hope so Usha. I don't want to lose him."

"You'll be fine gal. Come on, let's get going. Who's driving the scooter?".

Sparks flew up into the night air as Ben stirred the embers of the fire with a stick he'd found. The young lad had always loved playing with bonfires. Luis placed a couple of logs strategically on the coals and checked to see if he'd remembered to bring a pan to fry the sausages and onions for hot dogs.

Meanwhile Chloe and Alex sat together on the ground wrapped in a blanket, soaking up the heat of the fire, occasionally drinking from a bottle of beer as they discussed the comings and goings of the past few weeks. Chloe snuggled up closely as they soaked up their teenage love for each other.

The unmistakeable sound of a four stroke scooter over revving in the distance cut through the still night air ....

"I take it Lilly's driving that machine tonight," Ben joked. The four friends turned to see the headlight of the scooter getting closer as Lilly steered it down the gravel track to the campsite and slithered to a halt in a cloud of dust.

"That's definitely Lilly driving." Ben ran to Usha as she clambered off the scooter and kissed her on the lips. "Glad you came gal. You okay?"

"Yeah I'm good. Help me with these bottles will you 'cos I think Lilly wants a moment to herself with Luis."

"Sure, that's cool. Come on, Alex and Chloe are over there next to the fire."

"Awesome."

Lilly stood next to her scooter trying to make out she was sorting her hair out. *I don't know what to say to Luis ... I'm so nervous .... Here he comes .... Smile girl.*

"Hi Luis."

Luis took hold of Lilly's hand and kissed it. "Hi gal ..... You look stunning .... You also look cold .... Here." Luis threw his jacket around Lilly's shoulders.

"Thanks Luis .... Luis, I need to explain about the other night ...."

"No you don't. You really don't have to do this ..."

"But ...."

"Ssshhh. No you don't. I understand .... Really. Your Grandad told me your drink had been spiked."

"Did he?" *It was your Step Mum.*

"Yeah. Someone in the pub, right?"

"Yeah that's right Luis. But even then, I'm so, so sorry about the way I acted .... It wasn't me at all."

"I know luv, come on .... Let's go and join the others. I'm starving."

"You're always hungry. Ha!"

"Can you hear that?" Alex stood up and looked towards the light emissions in the sky over the town in the distance. "Can you hear it?…. Listen ….. Sirens ….. Lots of 'em."

Even though Saye campsite was about two kilometres or so from town, the sound of sirens cut through the still air of the night.

"That sound always sends a shiver through my whole body" Ben said as he put his arm around Usha's shoulders.

"I've got a bad feeling about it." Chloe shivered as she stood up next to Alex and held his hand. "Something's not right." *I've got a really bad feeling.*

"Is this your intuition kicking in again gal?" Alex asked. "It could be anything …."

"It's obviously bad whatever it is," Lilly interrupted. "There are three different types of sirens blaring out which means all the emergency services are out." Lilly could feel her amulet pulsing on her wrist …. She glanced over to Usha and Chloe …. They looked back at Lilly whilst holding the pendants around their necks indicating that they understood they needed to somehow separate themselves from their boyfriends.

In an instant Lilly disappeared. The faintest sound of wings fluttering for a moment dissipated in the night air ….

"Where's Lilly?" Luis asked.

"Look …. Over there." Alex pointed to the hill in the distance. "A really bright light …. It almost blinds you."

"Yeah look. There's another, about fifty metres to the right of the first." Ben indicated with his hand. "And another ….. Maybe forty metres or so further up. This is getting weird. What d'ya reckon you lot?"

"Why don't you go and check it out guys." Chloe nudged Usha.

"Yeah, better safe than sorry," Usha said, as Lilly appeared from the shadows.

"Where have you been luv?" Luis turned to his girlfriend.

"Been for a pee …. Had to go, I was busting."

"Oh … Err … Right luv. What d'ya reckon. Should we check those lights out?"

Chloe smirked at Lilly. *You've used a light staff to heat up some stones. They should throw light out for a couple of hours or so. Clever girl.*

"Yeah, you three guys go and take a look. Could be connected to all the commotion in town. You never know," Lilly replied. "Us girls will stay here. We'll even keep the fire going."

"You sure girls?"

The young friends nodded in unison.

"Come on then guys." Ben started to walk in the direction of the lights followed by Luis and Alex.

"HAVE FUN GUYS," Usha shouted.

"AND BE CAREFUL," shouted Lilly and Chloe in tandem, much to their amusement.

"What now?" Usha asked.

"Well I'm guessing because our pendants and Lilly's amulet are pulsing we need to take a look at the arch 'cos it's the image I remembered after being in contact with the Orion Constellation up at the bunker party" Chloe said. "But I don't like the idea. What d'ya think Lilly?"

"I have to say I'm not overly keen on doing this. I mean, there's a lot of history from the Second World War that encompasses the campsite and the arch. This whole area was a labour camp for prisoners of war who were very badly treated. Some of the prisoners were either shot or beaten to death under the arch in the tunnel through to Arch Bay. I've even heard of prisoners being bricked up in the tunnel …. The very thought turns my stomach."

"Come on you two, it'll be too late to do anything if we're just gonna stand here talking," Usha interrupted, "and the lads will be back soon."

The three girls walked to the front of the arch. The tunnel ahead was about ten metres in length, constructed entirely of bricks which resembled a tunnel you'd find in the Victorian sewers. The teenagers shuffled along in the sand on the ground which had been blown in from the beach ahead at Arch Bay.

"It's pitch black in here ….. In here ….. In hear." Chloe's voice echoed in the tunnel as they moved slowly forward towards the moonlight at the other end. "And what's that smell?"

"Are we being watched?" Usha whispered.

"Concentrate," Lilly snapped. "Keep your wits about you."

The sound of the waves breaking on the beach ahead was slightly reassuring as they reached the other end of the tunnel.

"Come on girls, let's take a look around," Chloe said. "I've never been on this beach at night." She took a step forward and …….

"CHLOE!"

"What the …… Lilly …. Where's Chloe?" Usha sunk to her knees.

"CHLOE!"

"Oh shit!". Chloe looked all around. *The arch and tunnel have gone …. And where's the beach and sea?..... Ooopps! Where the hell am I?* Chloe concentrated and tried to contact Lilly or Usha. *Lilly. Are you there?.... Usha …. I don't know where I am.* "That's obviously not going to work ….. Hmm." Chloe stood there in a totally different landscape. Devoid of grass or trees as far as the eye could see, the rough rocky ground seemed recently scorched, unable to sustain any form of life. The heat was unbearable from the two red suns high in the cloudless yellow sky. Far away on the horizon, Chloe could just make out, what she thought were huge mushrooms. As she watched, Chloe realised more of the shapes were appearing and as they did, the ground beneath her feet shook violently accompanied by sudden surges of hot air.

"SO YOU ARE CHLOE …. THE SOUL PROTECTOR."

Chloe stepped back as she studied the huge biblical type 'man' in front of her. *What the f...!*

"DO NOT BE AFRAID .... I am here to help you and your friends."

"Who .... Who are you?"

"I am Inti the Sun God. You have passed through into my realm. I know not why, for it is Lilly, the angel, who I summoned."

"Why d'ya need Lilly?"

"She is an angel, an angel hybrid actually ..... She is the servant of the Gods. Look around. My realm, Hanan Paccha, is being destroyed by both the Supay and also your so-called intelligent civilisation."

It suddenly dawned on Chloe that she was in fact, in the Upper Realm. *Heaven.* "The horizon. Those 'mushrooms'.... Are they....."

"Nuclear explosions? Yes. They will ultimately destroy mankind and the world as we know it. We need Lilly's help to overcome this evil .... This madness."

"Right."

"So Chloe, will you release Lilly's soul so that she may once again fight against our common enemies?"

"But how?.... It was Lilly that gave me the power of controlling her soul."

"For the moment, there is only one way to relinquish that control. It's dangerous, and you, and you alone, have to make the decision."

I knew today was goin' to be a bad day. "Come on then, spit it out .... What do I have to do?"

"Lilly must strike you down with her angel blade."

"WHAT?".

"She must strike you down."

"You mean like .... DEAD?!"

"Yes, it is the only way."

"No, no, no, no ..... You can't be serious. I'm not ready to die just yet."

"Of course ..... You are our only hope Chloe .... We would anticipate that Usha would be able to resurrect you."

"And what if she can't?"

"She will, believe me ….. You have to believe Chloe that anything is possible."

"Hmm." *Not happy about this, AT ALL.* She reminded herself that Lilly was needed to save the world. "Okay then, let's do this."

"There is one other thing you must know before you return to your world …."

Of course there is.

"Your friend …. The keeper of books is in grave danger. Evil surrounds her as we speak. All is not well."

"You mean Annie don't you?…. The librarian."

"I know not her name. I do know that all is not what it seems…. REMEMBER THAT CHLOE."

"But …."

"CHLOE." Usha swept forward and hugged her cousin. "We thought we'd lost you."

"I … I'm fine Usha. Honestly. Where's Lilly?"

"She's at the other end of the tunnel keeping a look out for the lads."

"Good. We need to talk to her before the lads get back. Come on."

Usha and Chloe walked back through the darkness of the tunnel to find Lilly watching the hillside intensely for any sign of the lads.

"CHLOE …. Thank goodness. I was SO worried about you." Lilly kissed Chloe on the cheek. "So where did you go?… What did you do?…. What happened Chloe?"

"Yeah c'mon Chloe," Usha snapped.

Chloe told her story of meeting Inti the Sun God in the Upper Realm and how life as they knew it, was in imminent danger of becoming either total anarchy or total annihilation of the world.

"Wow," Usha exclaimed. "That's a bit extreme."

Lilly had stood quietly listening to Chloe.

"Lilly ….. Say something." Chloe looked directly into Lilly's eyes. "You know what I'm going to say don't you?"

Lilly nodded.

"What the hell is going on girls?" Usha asked.

"The Upper Realm is in dire trouble Usha. Inti the Sun God needs every angel possible to help defeat the evil before more demons spill into our world," Chloe explained.

"And he wants me to help." Lilly broke her silence. "But I can't."

"Why?" Usha asked.

"Because Chloe is the protector of my soul which prevents me from leaving our world ...."

"There is a way Lilly," Chloe interrupted. "You must kill me with your angel blade which will then release your soul."

"NO! ABSOLUTELY NOT .... That's madness. There has to be another way Chloe. I could never kill you."

"Lilly .... Listen to me. THERE.. IS.. NO.. OTHER.. WAY." Chloe held Lilly's shoulders and looked directly into her eyes. "Believe me Lilly, if there was another way I'd take it. You have to have faith that anything is possible. I've already decided that this IS going to happen." Chloe shook Lilly. "WE HAVE TO DO THIS."

Usha hugged both Chloe and Lilly. "I believe in both of you and I'm ready to do my bit."

Lilly pulled out her angel blade. "Usha, do you have a bottle of water to hand?".

"Yep!... And yeah I have my teddy." Usha turned to Chloe. "Chloe I ...."

"Just believe Usha .... I trust you." Chloe turned to Lilly. "You ready gal? Just make sure you ..... AARRGGHHH."

Lilly's angel blade glinted in the moonlight as it sliced into Chloe's torso .... The faintest sound of wings flapping and Lilly had disappeared.

"Oh Chloe." Usha knelt down by the side of the crumpled bloodied body of her cousin, tears rolling down her face as she gently cradled Chloe's head on her lap. "Come on gal. Drink this." The young girl soaked the teddy stuffed with shavings from the Nanteos Cup, with water from her bottle and squeezed. The water trickled into Chloe's lifeless mouth. "Come on Chloe ..... Please ...... Come on. You have to live."

It seemed like a lifetime as Usha cradled Chloe's lifeless body. She tried to stem the flow of blood from the gaping wound. *It's not working. Oh God. Come on Chloe.* She poured more water onto the teddy and squeezed it over the wound ..... *It's working .... The wound's disappearing ..... Come on gal!*

"Haaaaaaah." Chloe gasped for air as she sparked into life, coughing and spluttering.

Usha rubbed Chloe's back to help clear her airways as she struggled to sit up. "Oh Chloe, don't do that to me ever again." The two girls hugged.

"I promise you Usha, it's not my favourite pastime ..... I take it Lilly's gone to fight her wars?"

Usha nodded. "My sister's changed hasn't she Chloe? She's not my Lilly .... She's not my big sister any more is she?"

Chloe placed her arm around her cousin's shoulders and kissed her on the cheek. "No she isn't gal ..... Lilly has a dark side to her that none of us can control. But if we're going to defeat the Mafia and find this treasure we need her big time. So for the moment we allow her to help the Gods defeat the evil forces and in doing so, save the world."

Usha started to cry.

"Believe me Usha, we WILL get the Lilly that we all know back. I don't know how yet but it'll happen. You must believe that ..... C'mon gal, pull yourself together, I can hear the lads approaching."

"Helloooo ..... Hi girls ..... We're back."

"Did you find anything?" Chloe asked.

"Nah .... Bit of a wild goose chase I reckon," muttered Ben, as he hugged Usha. "You okay gal? You look a bit pale and flustered."

"Yeah .... Yeah I'm okay. Can you take me home Ben?"

"Course I can hun. You sure you're alright?"

Usha nodded. "I'm fine .... Just tired."

"Where's Lilly?" Luis asked.

"Oh, err ..... She's gone home. She wasn't feeling very well," Chloe explained. "No doubt she'll catch up with you tomorrow." *Another lie!*

"Hmm .... Right ..... Might as well pack up and go then."

"Looks like it's just us two then." Alex held Chloe's hand. "What d'ya reckon gal?"

"We might as well go luv. Tell you what, we'll get off home, pick Dapper up and take her for a walk. What d'ya think?" *Hopefully we can swing past the library.*

"Yeah okay, we'll do that then ….. See you guys later."

Chloe hugged Usha as they all clambered aboard their scooters. She whispered in her ear, "Don't worry gal, everything will work out. Remember what I said, 'just believe'."

"Oh hello you two. Wasn't expecting you back for a while."

"Hi Beth. We packed in early so decided to come home and take Dapper out for a walk didn't we Alex."

"Yeah. Is that okay Mum?"

"Course it is son."

"What's all the commotion in town Beth?" Chloe asked.

"Not sure luv. It seems all the emergency services are out in town this evening. Must be serious."

"Dapper …. Dapper. Come on girl." Alex called the retriever and fastened the lead. "You ready Chloe? ….. See you later Mum."

"Bye son …. Enjoy your walk you two."

It was a good twenty minute walk into town as the two lovers held each others hands. Occasionally they would stop to admire the stars in the late evening sky as Dapper strained on the lead.

Chloe and Alex had noticed that there seemed to be more people out and about than usual in town. The young couple turned the corner to be faced with police barriers across the road opposite the library.

"Jeez gal, what the hell's going on?"

Flashing lights blurred the crisp night air as policemen patrolled the area. Two paramedics were busy walking back and forth from the library.

Chloe felt a cold shiver down her spine as she caught a glimpse of the inside of the library through a side window, before it was abruptly covered up from inside. *Christ, it looks like a bomb's gone off in there.* She could feel herself starting to panic and her forehead was bursting into a cold sweat. *The statues!…. Oh shit!…. I wonder if? ….. Let's see how clever you are Dapper.* Chloe discreetly slipped the lead from Dapper's collar and whispered "Fetch."

"OY! STOP THAT DOG!" A shout from one of the police officers cut through the evening air.

"DAPPER," Alex shouted. "How did she get off the lead Chloe?"

Chloe shrugged her shoulders. "Don't know luv."

The retriever ran into the library amid confusion and shouts from the police officers.

Come on Dapper. Do your stuff.

Two minutes later Dapper ran out of the library entrance and bounded up to Chloe. "Good girl," she muttered under her breath as she patted the dog's head. Chloe quickly took the two statues out of the dog's mouth and deftly dropped them in her coat pocket.

"Is that your dog sir?" Asked Peter Cordy the local police Sergeant, as he approached the young couple.

"Err ... Yes she is," Alex replied as Chloe fiddled around with the collar and lead.

"Well just keep it under control. This is a crime scene."

"So sorry Sergeant, she managed to slip her lead. Sorry, it won't happen again."

"Hello Chloe, haven't seen you for some time."

"Hi Peter. No I've been busy with stuff just lately ..... This looks pretty serious. What's happened?"

"They'll be a statement released later, but seeing as I know you work here, you ought to know."

"Know what?"

"It looks like it's a case of a burglary gone wrong. Serious stuff."

"Why?"

"We've found the body of Annie Dodds."

"Wh .... What?" Chloe gasped and held her hand to her mouth as she fell to her knees.

"It looks like she's been murdered ..... Now I don't know the circumstances so don't go jumping to any conclusions. The authorities may want to question you Chloe at some point just to clarify any queries."

Alex lifted Chloe to her feet and placed his arm around his girlfriend's shoulders. "That's just terrible officer."

"Who would want to kill Annie?" Chloe sobbed and collapsed to the ground again.

"Right …. Well I need to get on. I'm really sorry about Annie, Chloe." Peter turned to Alex. "I suggest you take Chloe home sir. This is not the place to be right now …. And keep that dog under control eh?"

Alex grabbed Chloe's hand and helped her to her feet. "Come on gal, we need to go."

"No wait …. Look." Chloe pointed over to one of the police cars. "Look, it's my Grandad …. And he's in handcuffs. They've arrested him ….. They've arrested my Grandad! Bloody hell! What the hell is going on?"

"C'mon gal, there's nothing we can do here for the mo'. They're probably just following a line of enquiry, but yeah, can't understand why they would arrest your Grandad."

"But Alex, I …" *What the hell have you done Grandad? Something's not right.*

"What?"

"Nothing …. It's nothing Alex. C'mon, let's go. Here Dapper. C'mon gal." Chloe gently pulled on the dog's lead.

The young couple started to walk back home. They walked in silence, in their own thoughts as to what they had witnessed.

"Let's sit here for a minute Chloe." Alex indicated to a bench on the roadside. "Sit Dapper!"

"Alex, I …."

"It's okay Chloe. I need to ask you something."

"Go on then".

"What did Dapper give you earlier on tonight?"

"Nothing." *Oh shit!*

"So if I look in your pocket I won't find anything then?…. Chloe, I'll ask you one more time and don't give me any more crap …. Or else we're finished. What's the point of being my girlfriend if I can't trust you?"

"Alex …. I ….." *Bugger it!* Chloe reached into her pocket and pulled out the two Inca statues and placed them in Alex's hands.

"Are these what I think they are?"

Chloe nodded.

"They're gold aren't they?"

"Yeah."

"What the hell! Why have you got 'em?…. What's this all about Chloe?…… Chloe?"

254

"Sorry Alex. We've been wanting to tell you for a long long time. It's, shall we say …. Complicated."

"We? Who's we?"

"Err ….. Well me obviously. And then Lilly, Usha and my Grandad ….. I'm so sorry Alex. We were trying to protect you."

"Protect me from what? So no-one else knows?"

"No." Chloe shook her head. "Listen carefully luv, I know I probably should have told you sooner, but you really need to trust me on this. Here is not the time or place to explain everything to you. I'll phone Usha and arrange a meeting, especially considering what's happened this evening." Chloe kissed Alex on the cheek.

Alex looked at the statues in his hand. "So I know these are gold, but what are they?"

"They're part of an Inca treasure trove which I'll tell you about later. In the meantime, can I have them back?" Chloe held out her hands.

"Yeah …. Sure. C'mon, let's make a move. You can tell me more on the way home."

Chloe put the statues back in her pocket and held Alex's hand as they walked further down the road. *Hope I've done the right thing. Better ring Usha.*

"'Cause I like you, Yeah I like you, And I'm feeling so Bohemian like you, Yeah I like you yeah I like you…" Usha's ring tone by The Dandy Warhols stopped as Usha picked up her phone ….

"Hi Chloe, you okay?….. Yeah I can do ….. You've done what?….. Grandad? Yeah I heard …. I'll be round at yours in about an hour, okay?….. Catch you later."

Bloody hell ….. Alex!

"So Lilly's an angel?…. Wow!... I mean, that's just incredible."

Chloe and Alex were getting close to home.

"And she prevented the Mafia killing me in Guernsey? She bloody well saved my life? Jeez."

Chloe nodded and smiled. *He's taking this better than I thought.* "So you're pretty much up to speed now ….. Here comes Usha."

Usha pulled her scooter over. "Hi guys."

255

"Sorry about your Grandad gal." Alex kissed Usha on the cheek.

"Something's not right eh Chloe?" Usha asked.

"Got that right gal …. Inti told me that Annie was in danger."

"That's the Sun God, right?" Alex interrupted.

"Yeah that's right. He also told me that I 'had to believe'…. You see, what both of you don't know is that Annie is Grandad's secret lover. They were a serious item at school all those years ago and for whatever reason, they split up and married different partners. I've got a feeling that Grandma has known about their affair for years."

"Awesome …. Well sort of!"

"Wow! Your family don't do things by halves do they?" Alex exclaimed.

"D'ya think Grandad's being framed?" Usha asked.

"It's possible gal 'cos he wouldn't murder his long time lover would he? The trouble is, we don't know how Annie was killed for starters. My money is on Diego Garcia but we can't prove it."

"Luis' Dad ….. No way. I know he's probably got a screw loose but no, surely not Chloe?"

"Alex, you have to realise that Luis' Dad is not to be trusted. He was mixed up with Dr Perez and the Mafia. That's for certain and a word of warning, don't trust his Step Mum Lucy either."

"Was?"

"Well let's just say that the good doctor is no longer with us. Not in this world anyway."

"Wow!… So what about Luis?" Alex asked.

"The honest answer is we don't know if we can trust him either, even though he's Lilly's boyfriend," Usha continued. "I've never told Ben either, even though he's my boyfriend. The less they know, the safer for all of us … And them."

"S'pose …. So what's next?"

"Me and Usha will visit Grandad tomorrow. They should let us into the police cells and we'll take it from there."

"Right."

"Looks like I need to go." Usha clambered onto her scooter.

"ALEX! CHLOE! IT'S LATE. LET'S HAVE YOU IN," Beth shouted from the house.

"See you both tomorrow guys." Usha waved as she drove away.

256

CHAPTER 34

TIME'S UP

"Ten minutes girls." Sergeant Cordy closed the cell door behind them.

"Hi girls." Richard hugged and kissed Chloe and Usha before slumping back into the chair.

"What's going on Grandad?" Usha asked.

"They've got it into their heads that I murdered Annie." Tears welled up in Richard's eyes. "But it's not true. You've got to believe me."

"We believe you Grandad," Chloe said as she held Richard's hand. "I know the truth Grandad. You love Annie don't you?"

Richard nodded. "Always have."

"Did you see her body?" Usha asked.

"Yeah, they arrested me at home on suspicion of murder and they took me down to the scene. I was told that the two paramedics in attendance reckoned she'd been dead about six hours which I found odd."

"Why?"

"Well they let me kneel down next to Annie and when I touched her face as I pushed her hair away, she felt warm to the touch which isn't natural. She should have been cold. I mean, come on Chloe, you know as well as anyone that the library is always cold. It just seemed strange."

"Hmmm. So how did she die?" Chloe asked.

"Don't know. I honestly don't know. There was no blood. No marks. It's as if she was asleep."

"Okay Grandad. Has anyone else been to visit you?" Usha asked.

"No. Not even your Grandma. Can't say as I blame her though. I understand completely. We've had a happy life together surrounded by you and your families but yes, I admit, I did have my frailties when it came to Annie. No-one's perfect eh?"

"Well something's not right Grandad and we'll try to get to the bottom of it. Might try a Shamanic Journey with Alex to see if we can find anything out."

"Alex? But …."

"Don't worry Grandad. It's a long story but Alex knows everything. It seemed the obvious step and we can trust him implicitly. We had to trust someone else Grandad, with Lilly busy with the heavenly wars."

"But I thought we'd sorted that problem out with you protecting her soul Chloe."

"Yeah well, let's just say we had to change the arrangement."

"Right. Well I'm sure you'll manage without me. What happened to the statues Chloe?"

"I've got them safely hidden away and all thanks to Alex's dog Dapper, ha!"

"Guard them with your life, they are the key to all of this, I'm sure of it."

"Time's up folks." The prison cell door opened. Sergeant Peter Cordy stood there.

"Thanks for coming girls." Richard held his two Granddaughters tightly and kissed them. "I love you."

"Bye Grandad …. Try not to worry. We'll figure it out."

Alex had been waiting patiently outside the local police station with his Mum and Dad, Beth and Frank Bean. He glanced nervously at his watch before seeing Chloe and Usha emerge from the front entrance.

"How's your Grandad?" Frank asked.

"He's okay considering," Chloe replied.

"Right, I'll go and have a chat with him. I'll see you later Beth."

"Okay luv. Don't forget I'm down at the hospital all day today. I'm on the day shifts this week."

Chloe nudged Usha.

"Mrs Bean."

"Yes Usha."

"I don't like to ask, but ….. Annie Dodds. Could you…."

"I'm not getting involved, so I didn't hear that Usha."

"Mum …. C'mon." Alex wrapped his arm around Beth. "We know it's a risk."

"I can't Alex. You know I'd lose my job …. Sorry son."

"And how many times has my Grandad helped you out over the years Beth?" Chloe pressed her. "Doesn't that count for anything?"

"Well …… Well alright then. But I'm not taking any chances. I'll find out what I can."

"Yesssss!!" Usha fist pumped the air.

"Thanks Mum." Alex kissed Beth on the cheek. "It means a lot to all of us."

Beth turned and sat herself in her car. "You guys be careful and I'll do what I can, I promise. Bye." The car drove off leaving the three teenagers stood in the police station's car park.

"So what now guys?" Alex asked.

"That's easy," Chloe said. "We get ourselves down to the hospital. C'mon, I'll explain on the way down there."

Half an hour later and the three teenagers are hiding behind the mortuary at the hospital.

"So do we all know what we're doing?" Chloe asked. "Are you okay Alex? You look nervous."

"It's alright for you two, you've done this sort of thing before."

"Look, all you've got to do is keep a look out whilst me and Usha do our thing. You'll be fine."

"So you break the lock Chloe and I'll check for Annie's body in the mortuary. Remember, you can't use your shield when you're breaking the lock on the door. You'll need all your power for the lock so Alex will have to watch your back while you do that. Once we're in, I'll check the bodies …. Then we'll take it from there. Okay?"

"Yeah, fine Usha." Chloe grabbed her pendant and concentrated. Alex watched intently as his girlfriend seemingly disappeared as her shield powered up. A gust of wind ruffled his hair as Chloe quickly made her way to the main door of the mortuary.

"Alex …. Alex, get to the door and keep watch while Chloe breaks the lock. I'm right behind you." Usha grabbed her pendant and disappeared in an instant behind her shield.

Alex watched as Chloe placed her hand on the door lock and concentrated as her eyes turned red. "Wow," he whispered. The door burst open and Chloe pushed Alex away as she and Usha entered the mortuary. Alex hid by the doorway looking for anything out of the ordinary as the two girls inspected the bodies ….

"It's bloody cold in here Usha."

Usha nodded. "Check them over there gal."

Chloe lifted another sheet from a body. "Here Usha. Here she is. It's Annie …. Oh jeez. She's cold."

"Well you'd be cold gal if you'd been stuck in here for hours, ha!… Let me look." Usha reached in her pocket and pulled out a small pocket mirror and placed it over Annie's face. Watch ….."

"The mirror's steaming up Usha. That means she's..."

"SHE'S ALIVE …. YES. But not for much longer bitches." Celia Perez stood in the doorway with her arm wrapped around Alex's neck. She had a knife held to his heart. "You thought you'd seen the last of me eh, bitches?"

"Sorry girls," Alex croaked as he struggled to breathe.

"Stay calm Alex, everything will be alright, promise." Usha could feel her power growing inside her.

"I told you I'd be back bitches. And this time I'll destroy you and your families." Celia pulled her hand back to thrust the knife into Alex and in that instant Usha summoned her light staff and threw a lightening bolt to knock the knife out of Celia's hand.

"You can't win Celia, let go of Alex. Give up now." Chloe by now had her light staff.

"You fools. You think it's goin' to be that easy." Celia released Alex who collapsed to the floor and raised her arms as she shouted, "I CALL UPON MY SOLDIERS."

Chloe and Usha watched in horror as the sheets moved and the bodies rose from the tables.

"She's somehow possessed the bodies Chloe. We're surrounded by demons …. Jeez."

"KILL THEM AND BRING ME THE BODY OF THE LIBRARIAN," Celia screamed and ran out of the mortuary.

"GET OUT OF HERE ALEX," Chloe shouted as she was grabbed from behind.

Two demons dragged Annie's body out of the building as Usha's eyes turned black and pounded her light staff on the floor causing lightening bolts to ricochet around the mortuary destroying all the demons in clouds of dust.

Chloe rushed to Alex who was sat on the floor in a daze. "You okay luv?" He nodded.

"He's in shock Chloe. Are you okay?" Usha asked.

"Yeah sure ….. We need to get out of here ….. Fast."

The three teenagers ran out of the mortuary and disappeared down the hill, stopping only when they were out of sight of the hospital.

"Well you learn something new every day I s'pose." Alex breathed heavily. "So is this a sort of every day occurrence with you two?"

"Ha!… Not really Alex. We try not too. Honestly."

The two girls chuckled to themselves.

"My life is brilliant, My life is pure, I saw an angel, Of that I'm sure…." Alex's ring tone of You're Beautiful by James Blunt broke into the laughter. "It's my Mum. Ssshhh girls …. Hi Mum …… Yeah …. Right ….. Are you sure?….. Right, okay. Thanks for that."

"What did your Mum want?" Usha asked.

"Well, she managed to get a look at the paramedics journal and the initial doctor's reports. There's two things that stick out like a sore thumb …. Firstly there's mention of a drug, and I can't pronounce it. But anyway, they found this drug in Annie's system which basically slows the heartbeat and breathing right down so they're barely noticeable. They sometimes use it for transplant surgery."

"And what's the other thing luv?" Chloe asked.

"One of the paramedics who attended the murder scene was Celia Perez. Apparently they found the real paramedic tied up behind the ambulance station. Celia Perez ….. That's the girl who was going to kill me!"

"But what's she up to?" Usha asked.

"Well apart from wanting revenge on our family, whatever she's up to, she needs Annie Dodds .... And she needs her alive. The point is, where's she taken her?" Chloe replied.

"They could be anywhere. If Lilly was here she'd find them in an instant," Usha muttered.

"Well she isn't, so we need another option." Chloe turned to Alex. "How d'ya fancy doing a spot of Shamanic Journeying?"

"Who me?.... I know I've been studying the origins and how it works but .... I don't know if I can do it."

"Well we're going to find out aren't we .... Right now." Chloe sat down on the grass. "Come on guys, sit down and hold hands .... We have to try Alex 'cos we have very little time and no other options, so give it a whirl."

"Come on Alex. You can do this." Usha smiled at Alex.

"Okay girls .... Close your eyes and empty your minds of any impure thoughts. When you've achieved some sort of peace you need to hum in unison and hopefully we will enter a higher realm of reality ...." Alex started to chant in Quechuan, the traditional language of Peru .....

"This is the realm of Hanan Pacha, you're now on my journey. Can you see and here me girls?"

"We're here with you Alex, yes, you've done it. We're in Heaven. It's so wonderful." Usha purred as she soaked in the surroundings.

"WELCOME." A powerful voice boomed towards the three teenagers. "COME CLOSER THAT I MIGHT SEE WHOM HAS DARED TO ENTER OUR REALM."

The teenagers stepped forward slowly.

"STOP."

Alex gasped audibly as they drew closer. Three huge figures sat before them, Illapa, the God of Thunder and Lightening, Mama Killa the Moon Goddess and Inti, the Sun God.

Inti stepped forward. "Chloe .... You have done well. Thanks to your sacrifice, the angel known as Lilly, fights for us against the many evils. We believe we are beginning to see the light."

"Is Lilly alright?" Usha interrupted.

262

"Ahh …. You are the sister of our angel Lilly …. Yes she fights well little one …. And our thanks to you for helping Chloe."

"SO, WHAT IS IT THAT YOU REQUIRE FROM US?" Illapa boomed.

"We need to know where Celia Perez has taken Annie Dodds?" Chloe asked.

"Arh …. The demon and the keeper of books."

"The demon?"

"Yes of course. This Celia you speak of is possessed by the Supay."

"So why does she need the keeper of books …. Err, I mean Annie Dodds?"

"To enable her to resurrect her father, whom Lilly our angel, killed in the darkness of the cave found in the land of blue stones."

"You mean Bluestone Bay?" Usha interrupted. "But how?"

"The blood of the keeper of books is required in a sacrifice that will breathe life back into the Supay's father."

"Oh shit!" Chloe exclaimed. "Annie has an extremely rare blood type so it must be a match to Dr Perez, that's the only explanation. How do we get inside the cave 'cos Lilly sealed it?"

"Go to the talking tower of stone on the cliffs above. There you will find your answer Chloe."

"GO NOW. WE GROW TIRED OF YOUR PETTY QUESTIONS …. ILLAPA, THE GOD OF THUNDER AND LIGHTENING HAS SPOKEN. GO!!"

The three teenagers gasped for air as their journey ended abruptly ….

"Jeez ….. What the hell?!" Alex grunted.

"Wow Alex ….. You did it ….. Awesome!"

"Telegraph Tower …. It has to be," Chloe said. "C'mon guys, we need to get up there pretty damn quick if we're going to save Annie …."

The three friends walked around the perimeter of Telegraph Tower looking for any indication of activity ….

"Nothing …. There's nothing here girls. No-one's lived here for years, I mean, look, there's two broken windows."

"That means nothing Alex …. See, the vegetation around the old wooden door has been trodden down, besides which, the lock on the door is broken," Chloe explained.

"C'mon guys, stop faffing around." Usha pushed the door open and the sunlight flooded into the dilapidated building. "Look at all the footprints on the dusty floor."

"Yeah. And they all lead to that heavy iron style grill in the floor." Chloe walked over to the grill. "It's padlocked." She placed her hand on the lock. Her power ebbed through her hand as the padlock fell away. "The two middle bars have been bent apart but I'm not squeezing through there …. Give me a hand guys, the three of us should be able to lift this grill open."

The three teenagers heaved and lifted the grill open which fell away from the opening with an almighty crash as the intrepid friends cringed at the thought that the noise would be heard.

"Shit!…. They probably know we're coming now," Usha whispered.

"I'd guess they already anticipated that gal," Chloe replied. "Look, there's some sort of spiral staircase that's been cut out of the surrounding stone below ground. This must lead down to the cave. It looks really dark, we'll have to use our light staffs Usha."

"You're gonna have to stay here Alex to keep a lookout for us. If we're not back in an hour, phone the police." Usha smiled at Alex. "Try not to worry."

Chloe threw her arms around Alex and kissed him. "I love you so much. Don't forget that."

"But…"

Chloe pressed her fingers to Alex's lips. "We'll be fine luv ….. C'mon Usha. We haven't got much time."

The two girls climbed down through the opening and Alex watched as they disappeared into the darkness beneath his feet ….

"You okay Usha?"

"Yeah sure …. Bloody hell, it's a long way down Chloe… And the steps are getting steeper gal."

"Ssshhh." Chloe grabbed Usha's shoulder. "Dim your light staff," she whispered. "D'ya hear that?"

"Yeah."

"Just remember Usha, there were two demons that got away from the hospital mortuary. Keep an eye out for them as well."

"Okay …. C'mon, let's make a move further down." Usha led the way. "I think I can see some light ahead Chloe." Usha crouched down and listened intently.

"What is it Usha?"

"I can see the entrance to the cave …. It sounds as if someone is chanting," Usha whispered. "Listen."

"I can't make out the words. I guess it's Quechuan, you know that ancient Peruvian language …. We need to be closer Usha."

The two girls clambered down the remaining stone steps and stood either side of the cave entrance and gazed inquisitively around the chasm. Candles flickered from every crevice casting strange shadows around the cavern. Two huge flat boulders lay in the centre of the cave and Celia Perez stood between them holding a vicious looking hunting style zombie knife and chanting rhythmically. Her father, Dr Perez, lay dead on the one boulder, his head crudely attached to his body which appeared to be rotting away from the fatal wounds inflicted upon him by Lilly.

Annie Dodds was tied to the other boulder and the girls watched as she struggled frantically to free herself from the ropes, but to no avail. A flattish oval gold platter style dish was balanced on the boulder next to Annie's head ....

"Aarrgghh." Annie screamed as Celia playfully ran her knife down the side of Annie's face and across her neck before placing it across her chest. "Your time has come to play your part in the resurrection of our master." Celia pointed to her father. "In a few moments I will slice your throat open .... But first, my servants must have their reward." Celia stretched both arms out to the side. "YOU TWO." She summoned the two demons out of the shadows towards her. "You have five minutes to enjoy, whilst I prepare myself .... DON'T KILL HER .... I have to perform the sacrifice ha!"

"Aarrgghh." Annie let out a blood curdling scream as the two demons appeared from the shadows and stood either side of Annie. They tore at her clothes with their talons and sank their fangs into her bare flesh as they flung her torn clothing to the floor. Talons cut into her breasts. "Aarrgghh ....."

"ENOUGH!" Celia pushed the demons to one side, picked up the knife and ....

"NOW," Chloe shouted.

The two girls leapt through the cave entrance. Usha smashed her light staff to the ground and lightening bolts ripped through the two demons, dropping them to the ground in clouds of dust ... Dead.

Chloe somersaulted over the boulder, smashing Celia's head with her light staff. Celia's knife glinted as she slashed Chloe across the upper torso. Celia thrust out again, ripping Chloe's arm open.

Usha watched instinctively as she wrestled to untie the rope around Annie. *Finally.* "Can you make it to the entrance Annie?" She pointed to the stairs.

Annie nodded as she grimaced in pain.

"Go," shouted Usha as Annie limped to relative safety. Usha quickly summoned her powers as she held her pendant.

Chloe was pinned down by Celia who was sat astride her. Celia raised her knife. "GOODBYE BITCH!" Celia plunged the knife .....

Usha's eyes turned black as she pushed her hands forward and her powers threw Celia against the cave wall with a lightening bolt thrust through her heart. "AWESOME!....... CHLOE .... Are you alright?"

Chloe slowly staggered to her feet, covered in blood. "Yeah, I'll be okay gal. Jeez, that was a close call ..... You wanna check on Annie? I'll be with you in a mo'." Chloe gingerly walked to the boulders and picked up the gold platter dish. *Gonna take this. I reckon it's important. I've seen these shapes somewhere else.* Chloe ran her fingers across the dish. *Six indentations. I wonder.*

"You ready to go Chloe?" asked Usha, "'cos we've still got all these steps to climb and Annie's not looking too good."

"Yeah sure Usha." Chloe joined Usha and Annie at the cave entrance.

"How can I ever thank you girls?.... Don't worry, I won't say anything about what I've seen .... Besides which, who would believe such a story." Annie grimaced in pain.

"C'mon, let's get out of here," Chloe said. "Alex will be waiting for us."

267

CHAPTER 35

AND RELAX

Chloe nuzzled up to Alex affectionately as they sat, relaxing in the café in town. They'd forgotten about their coffees which had gone cold as they discussed the events of the previous days with Usha and Lilly. Their conversation was interrupted by the local Channel News on the television.

"Turn the volume up Usha. This could be interesting..."

"Our first item this afternoon is from Alderney where extraordinary events took place earlier this week. We'll now cross over to our reporter who is in Alderney. Over to you Duncan ....

Thank you Emily .... I'm stood outside the local police station and as you can see, I'm surrounded by hundreds of well wishers and supporters who have turned out to see Mr Richard Morgan released from jail after being wrongfully accused of murdering local librarian, Mrs Annie Dodds.

If you recall Emily, in our last broadcast we were able to release details of this sensational case which involved the Mafia and the Perez family. However, following the discovery of Annie Dodds alive, at the well known historical site of Telegraph Tower, all of the charges have been dropped and Mr Morgan is now a free man. I did ask him for his reaction to his release and this is what he had to say ....."

"I'm of course, very pleased and feel totally vindicated that justice has prevailed. I am also extremely happy that Mrs Dodds was found alive. I'd just like to thank everyone that has turned out today and to thank my family and friends for their support through, what has been, a difficult time. I've nothing further to say. Thank you".

"As you saw there Emily, Mr Morgan was quite emotional and I believe he's due to leave the island later today on a well deserved holiday ....

I can also report that the Telegraph Tower has now been secured and boarded up by the local authorities. I did request an interview with them but they declined, only to say it was a 'security issue'. Back over to you Emily ….

Thank you Duncan …. And before you go, I believe you have another piece of news for us ….

Err yes Emily. This is a breaking story here on Alderney …. The local police are helping the FBI with enquiries related to the alleged theft of eight bodies from the local hospital mortuary after a break-in was discovered. The police are stressing at this time, that this incident is in no way related to the discovery of Mrs Dodds and Mr Morgan's release …..

This is Duncan Wright reporting for Channel News in Alderney ….

Well thank you for that Duncan. It certainly looks like Alderney is the place to be at the moment. Moving on to our next item ….."

"Switch it off Usha. You really couldn't make this stuff up eh Lilly?….. LILLY!…………. LILLY!"

CHAPTER 36

WAKE UP CALL

Life is good eh? Richard breathed in the sensual aroma of her perfume as he rolled over on the bed to feel the soft warm skin of his lover as she lay naked in a provocative pose oozing pheromones. *Jeez, this woman is something else!* His hand gently caressed her inner thighs as she groaned and opened her legs to invite his hands to explore further as Richard gently nibbled her aroused nipples.

She pushed Richard over on to his back and knelt astride his body. He throbbed in anticipation as she held him firmly, before slowly sitting down on him. She felt him slide inside her and then pleasured herself with a slow and deliberate rocking motion accompanied with quiet erotic groans which increased with intensity. He gently caressed her breasts as his lovers movements intensified as she rode him. She arched her back in ecstasy as Richard succumbed with his final thrusts.

Annie relaxed as she regained control of her body and snuggled close to Richard beneath her as she felt their warm love juices run from inside her on to her inner thighs. *That was SO good Richard.* Richard kissed her on the cheek as he stroked her hair and then smacked her firm bottom playfully. "Think we ought to get up gal. That's the third time this morning and I could do with some breakfast. I'm getting hungry. What d'ya think?"

"What's that luv?"

"We should get up Annie .... Come on gal, we've been at it all morning. We should take a shower and go and have some breakfast before they close the dining hall."

"S'pose. But can't we just ...." Annie sat astride Richard's chest and pulled her knees up to pin his arms down with her legs as she pushed his face into her tightly knit auburn curls hoping Richard would stimulate her with his tongue. He kissed her delicate flesh as Annie gently moved herself closer ....

"No. Come on Annie, we'll do this later I promise." Richard gently pushed her off and sat up. *Christ gal. Give us a break!* "Go on, you take a shower first while I roll a cigarette."

Annie sighed as she rolled over on the bed and sat herself next to Richard. She kissed him on the cheek. "I love you Richard." She stood up as Richard playfully pinched her arse. "Cheeky!" Annie grinned to herself and casually crossed the room to the bathroom.

As he sat rolling his cigarette Richard gazed out of the open balcony doors which led out to their private infinity pool with an awesome view of the coastline in the distance. *What a gorgeous view.* Annie's voice interrupted his thoughts ...

"Can you pass me a towel luv?" Richard turned to see his lover through the open bathroom door, standing in the shower cubicle. *What a figure.* He strolled over and passed Annie a towel from the rail as she stepped out of the cubicle.

"I won't be long gal." He stepped into the cubicle and turned on the shower. *Ahh that feels good.* Richard closed his eyes as he soaked in the moisture falling from above and his thoughts strayed to earlier in the year .... *Best decision I ever made, coming here to France and getting away from Alderney and all the crap of the Mafia and the Supay.* Richard had left Alderney in a hurry after the publicity caused by the 'murder' of his lover. His long time relationship with his wife Bea, understandably, was under considerable strain even though she was seemingly still unaware of his long time love affair with Annie. She had her suspicions as always. As far as Bea was concerned, Richard had been admitted to hospital in France for a minor operation while he was on holiday. Annie had asked a friend who lived in France to contact Bea, pretending to be a doctor from the hospital after Richard failed to return from a two week holiday. *It's been four weeks of unadulterated bliss.* Annie had joined up with Richard after a weeks recuperation in Guernsey hospital, which she needed after she'd been injured by demons. Her husband was away on business in America. *I wonder how the girls and their boyfriends are? It's been a while ....*

"RICHARD .... NO. PLEASE DON'T...."

"What the ..." Annie's shouts of anguish cut through Richard's thoughts. He quickly grabbed a towel as he hurried out of the bathroom to be grabbed from behind around his neck. *Shit!* He felt the edge of a knife pressing into his back as his assailant tightened his grip round his neck.

"Richard, I ...." Annie was punched in the face with a sickening thud as she was sent sprawling across the floor by the second man, his eyes bulging with rage.

"ANNIE!... Leave her alone you bastard." *Bloody hell. Mafia.* Richard struggled in vain as he looked down at his lover, still naked and bleeding heavily around her face. "You bastards! What d'ya want?"

"THIS." The assailant grabbed Richard's arm and pulled the amulet off. "THIS IS WHAT WE WANT." The man held it tightly in front of Richard's face and then turned and knelt down next to Annie. "BUT WHILE WE'RE HERE, LET'S HAVE SOME FUN SHALL WE?" The attacker ran his hands down Annie's body.

"I wouldn't do that if I was you." Richard struggled again.

"And what are you going to do about it? .... Ha!" The attacker grabbed Annie's breasts and .....

"WHOOOOSH."

The two assailants fell dead in an instant to reveal Lilly standing over them, holding her angel blade as blood dripped copiously from the weapon onto the floor. "Look after Annie, Chloe."

Chloe stepped out from behind Lilly and knelt over Annie's naked body before holding her pendant over her heart. Chloe chanted ... "I am Alnitak the Healer and Child of the Stars." She passed her hand over Annie's bloodied face as a bright white glow hovered over Annie, until all her injuries were healed. The teenager gave Richard's lover a bath robe to cover her modesty as Annie sat up in a state of shock.

Richard rushed over to his lover, kissed her on the cheek and hugged her. "You okay luv?" Annie nodded as she pulled herself up from the floor and then hugged and kissed Chloe. "Hi Chloe, it's really good to see you .... But how? How did you know where to find us?"

Richard hugged Chloe. "Good to see you gal. So, it's a good question, how did you know Chloe?"

Chloe gave Lilly a knowing look as she explained that they'd discovered the precious stones in the amulets and pendants had some sort of signature alarm.

"Grandad." Lilly had a concerned look on her face. "Should we even be discussing this in front of Annie?"

"Now look here young lady, Annie suffered more than most in Alderney and that was due in part, down to us." Richard placed his arm around Annie's waist. "You can all trust Annie one hundred percent with anything. Annie knows everything that we're involved in and is willing to help in any way she can, especially with the research side of things …. So do either of you have any problems with that?"

"No Grandad," Chloe said.

"That's fine then," Lilly said. "Just so long as we all know about the possible consequences and so forth …. We've found out that when an amulet or pendant is separated from its rightful owner, they somehow send a signal to that gold Inca platter style dish Chloe and Usha recovered from the cave at Bluestone Bay."

"It vibrates Grandad. A bit like a mobile phone does when it's receiving a text or a call." Chloe was visibly excited as she explained to Richard. "It's as if they're communicating with each other."

"Fascinating …. So it's quite possible that the Mafia already have access to another Inca platter dish, 'cos how else would these two goons know we were here. Thinking about it, it's my fault they found us. Richard sighed. I have always kept my amulet on until the other night when I took it off to let Annie take a closer look at it."

"Yeah, we thought that maybe the Mafia had one of these dishes Grandad." Chloe rifled through the pockets of the dead men and pulled out a crumpled scrap of paper. She placed it on the table trying to flatten out the creases as they all gathered round. "Look. It's a rough sketch of the Inca platter that shows loads of numbers and letters written within the various Inca images. There's six hexagonal shapes around the edge of the platter, like indentations, which Usha thinks could be for the gold statues we're finding, to stand in."

"I'd totally agree with that Chloe." Richard nodded.

"So anyway, this is the interesting bit … When the platter vibrates, different letters and numbers glow in a set sequence. It was Usha that figured all this out …. The platter gives us map co-ordinates for anywhere in the world. If you look closely at that piece of paper, the co-ordinates for this place have been roughly written on the back."

"Really?"

"We've tested it Grandad, haven't we Lilly?"

"Yeah."

"I take it you've tested it on your angelic travels Lilly?"

"Sure have Grandad. But as we're pretty sure the Mafia have one of these Inca platters it leaves us with two immediate problems. You and Annie need to get away from here as soon as possible and secondly, we need to find this other platter, but that's gonna be tricky." Lilly screwed up her face in frustration.

"I may be able to help with that," Annie interrupted. "Apart from the obvious of translating the Inca symbols on the platter, we need to trawl the internet for anything that could be connected with it and find out if there are any more of these platter type dishes. I suspect the answer to that is hidden away in the symbols. I do know someone who can lend me some books which should help as well."

Lilly nodded appreciatively. "There is someone that could help Annie. Luis' Grandfather. He's a Shaman and one of the few remaining Q'ero Indians that still lives in the Central Andes in Peru near the ancient centre of the Inca Empire."

"So, going off subject. How's things back in Alderney Chloe?" asked Richard.

"Pretty much the same Grandad. We've had the odd skirmish with a few demons but nothing we haven't been able to handle. We haven't got any further in finding the Lima Treasure but that's partly due to not having enough spare time to do any research and Lilly being away, helping the angels to save humanity."

"Well hopefully when Annie and myself get back to the island, the research side of things can be left to us. How's everyone else?" asked Richard.

274

"Usha's been great and it's been a case of same old same old with the lads. That's right eh Lilly?"

"Yeah sure."

"How's your Grandma?"

"She's not been good Grandad. She's lonely and worried sick about you. So how are you going to deal with the situation?" Lilly asked.

"I know, I know. I haven't dealt with the situation very well. Everything had just got on top of me, what with the Supay, the Mafia and all the cover ups with lies to friends and family. I'd got to the point when I couldn't deal with it any more especially after being arrested for so called murder. My whole life seemed to be in a downward spiral so my answer was to escape from it all. But after what's happened today, it's proved to me that I have to continue with this adventure to not only protect myself, but everyone else involved."

"So what are you going to do?" Lilly asked.

"Well, first things first. I can't arrive back in Alderney at the same time as Annie as that would immediately attract attention …."

"I can take Annie." Lilly turned to Annie. "D'ya think you'll be alright 'cos it takes a bit of getting used to?"

Annie nodded. "Hopefully yes."

"Chloe could come with me …. It'll take a couple of days travelling," explained Richard. "I'll pick up a hire car and drive across to Saint Malo and get a local fisherman to bring us over to Alderney along with Annie's luggage. What d'ya think Chloe?"

"That'd be cool Grandad …. I'll phone Beth to let her know."

Annie pulled the bath robe tighter around herself. "I'd better get dressed then if we're going today."

"No need to Annie. I can drop you off inside your house, no problem. I have to take you home now 'cos I have other, more important things to do." Lilly grabbed Annie's hand and they disappeared in a heart beat, save for the faintest flutter of wings.

CHAPTER 37

THE JOURNEY

"Bit of a tatty car Grandad." The front bumper shook precariously as Chloe kicked it playfully.

"Yeah I know. Best I could do at such short notice but we'll manage Chloe. I have to say the guy at the car hire station seemed a bit dodgy to me, but I didn't really have time to argue with him. Pass me that other bag please …. Thanks."

"That's the last case, so I think we're ready to go."

"Yep, you're right gal. Fancy a coffee before we get going?"

"Would that be white with one sugar then Grandad?"

Richard spotted the wicked glint in her eyes. "Ha! You're not goin' to let me forget about that are you?"

Chloe smirked. "I was thinking about your figure Grandad!"

"Yeah if you say so." *I know what you was thinking about young lady …. Annie at the library a few weeks ago.*

Chloe handed a mug of coffee to Richard. "There you go, your usual, three sugars and not too much milk."

"Thanks gal." Richard lit a cigarette.

"Always somewhere, Miss you where I've been, I'll be back to love you again ..." The Scorpions track, Always Somewhere played on Richard's phone …. "Hi Annie, everything okay?…. Better than you thought? That's good then ….. Lilly? Yeah I know, it's something we've all got to deal with …. No, I'm not happy with her …. But as long as you're alright …. You take care luv …. I'll ring if there's any problems …. Oh, and don't forget what I told you the other day eh …. I love you too, see you soon …. Bye luv."

"I take it that was Annie."

Richard smiled as he drew on his cigarette. "Yeah. She's okay but she wasn't happy with Lilly just taking her home without any warning."

"To be honest Grandad, none of us are happy with Lilly. She's become a loose cannon and every time any of us see her, we don't know which Lilly we're going to get. It's like she's got an off and on switch. Know what I mean?" A look of annoyance on Chloe's face gave her feelings away.

"Yeah I know exactly what you mean gal. You can't trust her any more. This angel business is seriously messing up her head." Richard inhaled deeply on his cigarette before stubbing it out furiously, as if he was taking out his frustration with Lilly. *Damn it!*

It had been a long drive into Brittany and the hire car hadn't helped. With only a top speed of eighty kilometres an hour and a dodgy clutch, the journey had been arduous. As Richard and Chloe drove through the walled city of Saint Malo, it was difficult not to notice how busy the city was, with thousands of tourists enjoying the open air markets, restaurants, bars and shops, totally oblivious to the worldwide strife being caused by the Supay and the armies of demons around them. Oblivious to the heavenly wars and the angels battling for good over evil. *Probably just as well eh!* Richard thought. *There are enough troubles in the world without the added knowledge that the world as we know it could descend into mayhem and destruction, literally overnight.*

"Here we are Grandad. The marina. Look at all these boats." Chloe folded the tatty road map up and stuffed it into the glove box as Richard parked the car and turned the engine off. *What's that?* A small red light was steadily blinking .... Chloe spotted wires running across the back of the glovebox and as she glanced down to take a closer look, she noticed the wires passed through a roughly made hole in the compartment and ran down into the foot well where the wires disappeared through a hole in the floor. The flashing light turned green ….. *Oh Shit!* "GET OUT OF THE CAR … NOW GRANDAD!!…. BOMB!!"

Richard and Chloe struggled frantically with the door handles …. "They're jammed Chloe. We're locked in." Richard kicked the glass in desperation. "It's no good gal."

"COVER YOUR EYES," Chloe shouted as she quickly grabbed her pendant from around her neck and held it against the windscreen as her eyes turned black. She shielded her eyes as the pendant gave out a high pitched screech and the glass shattered into thousands of pieces. "CLIMB OUT GRANDAD!"

Richard clambered over the steering wheel and dashboard as Chloe pushed him through the gaping hole onto the bonnet of the car. "GIVE ME YOUR HAND CHLOE …. HURRY." Chloe grabbed his hand and pulled herself out …. "RUN CHLOE."

Richard rolled off the car bonnet and started to run, stumbling with every step …. He stopped and turned instinctively to see where Chloe was …. *What's she doing?… For fucks sake!* He ran back towards Chloe ….

Chloe was two metres from the car waving frantically at the gathering inquisitive crowd, trying to move them away from the car. She was shouting …. "GET BACK …. THERE'S A BOMB …. MOVE BACK."

Richard knocked Chloe to the ground with a sickening thud as he threw himself on top of her. A split second passed as the car exploded in a huge ball of flames sending a shock wave across the marina. The boats rocked back and forth, windows shattered and sails tore as thousands of mangled car parts flew through the acrid air, impaling and destroying as they hit the ground indiscriminately ….

Chloe slowly stirred as she lay on the ground. Her ears were throbbing. *My head …. The pain.* She lifted her head gingerly and tried to focus her eyes through the foul smelling smoke …. People screaming, shouting …. Mutilated bodies. Dead bodies. Carnage. *Oh God! Why?* The teenager tried to move. *Something heavy on top of me.* Chloe suddenly realised she was covered in blood. She turned her head. It was Richard's blood …. "GRANDAD!"

Richard didn't move as Chloe gently eased herself from beneath his shattered body and then knelt beside him. She gasped audibly. She moved Richard to the recovery position on his side and felt for a pulse …. *Nothing .... Oh God .... He's dead.* Tears rolled down her face as she struggled to comprehend what had happened. Numerous sirens could be heard as one by one, emergency service vehicles were beginning to arrive. The sound of screams and anguish filled the smoked drenched air as Chloe gathered her thoughts and senses.

Chloe, what's happened? My pendant is pulsing, what's wrong? Usha was in Chloe's head. *Chloe?*

Chloe glanced down at her pendant. *It's pulsing.* She checked Richard's wrist …. *Nothing, but his amulet's pulsing .... What's going on?*

Contact Lilly, Usha. It's Grandad, it's a matter of life or death. Get her to bring yourself and Annie here. Do it now ….

" WHOOOOSH." Lilly appeared. To her sides stood Usha and Annie ….

"Thank God," Chloe blurted.

They all gathered round Richard's lifeless body and knelt down beside Chloe.

"There is still time girls." Annie glanced at each of the stunned teenagers. *They're clearly all in shock, especially Chloe.* "Chloe, remove your Grandad's amulet and give it to me please."

"WHAT'S GOING ON? WHO GAVE YOU THE RIGHT TO GIVE OUT THE ORDERS?" Lilly snarled angrily.

"Calm down Lilly, Annie knows what she's doing." Chloe pulled the amulet from Richard's wrist and passed it to Annie who immediately placed it around her own wrist.

"YOU CAN'T DO THAT ...."

"Be quiet Lilly …. Just for once, trust us." Usha calmly smiled and then turned to Annie …. "Carry on Annie."

"Thanks Usha. We need to act fast now whilst the pendants and amulets are still pulsing so each of us must place a hand on Richard. You first Usha …. Now Lilly, place a hand on top of Usha's and then I put my hand on top …. And finally Chloe, as the

279

healer, you place a hand on top of mine …. Good. Now Chloe, do your stuff …."

Chloe held her pulsing pendant over her heart and started to chant as her eyes turned black …. "I am Alnitak the Healer and Child of the Stars." As the others watched in awe, a bright white light gradually built up to a dazzling glow of intensity, hovering over Richard and then totally engulfing his entire body …. A few anxious moments passed until Richard gasped with a raspy splutter of breath as the light dispersed …. "Don't move Grandad," Chloe whispered in his ear as she lifted her hand from his body.

"You've healed him Chloe …. Awesome." Usha fist pumped the air as Lilly looked at Chloe in disdain.

"No Usha, WE healed him. All our combined powers got us this far, but Grandad still has a long way to go to fully recover. We've only healed his internal organs. The rest is up to Lilly." Chloe looked at her cousin. "You ready Lilly?... Okay, take Grandad to Mama Killa the Moon Goddess. She'll know what to do."

Lilly gently scooped Richard up with the strength of four men and disappeared in the blink of an eye, save for the faintest sound of the flutter of wings.

Chloe, Usha and Annie held each other closely in relief and as their adrenalin subsided they sobbed with tears of joy.

"So how did you both know what to do?" Usha asked.

Annie and Chloe smiled at each other as they explained to Usha that Richard thought an attempt on their lives by the Mafia was only a matter of time, so he'd warned Chloe of the possibilities and that he'd told Annie what to do if the situation arose.

"That's why your Grandad gave me his amulet the other day for a couple of hours just to make sure I didn't have any adverse reactions," Annie explained.

"Excuse z-moi."

The three girls glanced up to see a paramedic standing over them.

"Tun'as rien?"

"He's asking us if we're okay," Usha explained.

The three of them grinned and nodded …. "Oui, merci," Usha replied.

The paramedic nodded and smiled before walking to another group of people.

"We should try and help some of the injured, don't you think?" Annie asked.

Annie and the two girls stood up to survey the shattered remains of the marina. They had been so preoccupied with saving Richard that they hadn't realised the extent of the devastation caused by the car bomb. Billowing smoke filled the air and half submerged boats sat in the oily polluted water of the marina. Glass from shattered windows littered the ground with mangled car parts embedded in standing structures. They were surrounded by carnage and from amongst the destruction, cries of anguish and screams filled the air.

"C'mon, we need to help these people." Annie held Usha's hand. "We'll see what we can do over there." Annie pointed to a group of people over to the left. "See what you can do to help over there Chloe." Annie pointed to the right. "We'll meet back here in about two hours …. Okay?"

Chloe nodded and smiled as Annie and Usha walked away, hand in hand. *Annie's alright you know!*

Three hours had past by when Chloe found Annie and Usha knelt beside a badly injured boy they were comforting.

Usha looked up. "Hi Chloe. This is Andre and he's in a pretty bad way. Is there anything you can do to help him?"

Chloe knelt down and gently placed her hand on the young boy's forehead as he moaned in pain. "Schuss. There now. Hi Andre, my name's Chloe. Let's see what I can do for you." She held her pendant over her heart and chanted quietly. "I am Alnitak the Healer and Child of the Stars." As Usha and Annie watched, a bright white light hovered over the young French boy. Chloe released her pendant as the white light dissipated and Andre sat up smiling.

"Merci …. Merci." Andre stood up and blew kisses to the girls as he ran off into the welcoming arms of his distraught parents.

"Arh bless him," Usha said as Lilly suddenly appeared. "Right you three, ready to go?"

CHAPTER 38

THEY'LL BE TROUBLE AHEAD

"Good to be home again eh girls?"

Chloe and Usha nodded and smiled at Annie who was visibly upset. Tears were welling up in her eyes and she turned away ….

"Sorry girls, I just need to go to the bathroom." Annie hastily left the room as she struggled to control her emotions.

"Think I'd better go Chloe. My Mum and Dad will be wondering where I am." Usha sighed. "It's difficult enough at home having to cover for Lilly when she isn't there without having to explain myself. Know what I mean?"

Chloe nodded and hugged her cousin. "Try not to worry about Grandad, he's in good hands."

"Yeah I know. Are you staying here with Annie for the night?"

"Got to really. I've no options 'cos I'm supposed to be in France with Grandad. Gonna have to sort something out 'cos things could get awkward with Grandma."

"Yeah right." Usha raised her eyebrows. "Sounds like you're needed in the bathroom gal. Annie's sobbing her eyes out in there."

"To be honest, I don't know how she held herself together for this long …. Okay then Usha. Give me a ring tomorrow and we'll see where we go from here." Chloe hugged and kissed her cousin on the cheek as she opened the front door to let her out of the house.

"Bye then cuz."

Chloe closed the door. *Oh dear…. Poor Annie …. Listen to her …. She's in a right mess.* She walked to the bathroom where she found Annie sat on the side of the bath in floods of tears. Chloe knelt down in front of Annie and placed her hands on her knees as she tried to console Annie.

"What's this all about Annie?... Is is to do with Grandad?... If it is, he's in good hands. You know that don't you?... Come on Annie, what is it?... What's upset you so much?"

Annie sucked in the air as she tried to control herself. Tears continued to roll down her cheeks as Chloe gently used a tissue to try and stem the flow. "Oh Chloe," she sobbed. "My life just feels out of control at the moment." Annie took another gulp of air. "My husband ...." She gasped. "My husband's been killed."

Chloe tried to hold herself together as she consoled Annie. *Oh shit!* "Oh Annie, I am so sorry .... How?"

"He was ...." Annie began to cry again. "He was shot mistakenly by the police in New York .... He got caught up in one of those BLM protests on the way back to his hotel," she blurted. Annie dropped to her knees and threw her arms around Chloe. She rested her head on the teenager's shoulders and continued to sob.

Poor woman.... I know how she must feel right now. Jeez! Chloe held her tight and moved her hands back and forth across Annie's back as she tried to comfort the older woman. "Annie .... I'm so, so sorry for your loss." Chloe kissed her tenderly on her wet cheek ....

Annie responded by kissing Chloe near her ear and then again on the teenager's cheek. "Oh Chloe, I ..." Annie kissed her on the cheek again. "I need your ...."

Chloe turned her head slightly as she felt Annie place her hand on the back of her head and run her fingers through her hair. Their noses touched and Chloe could feel the wetness of Annie's tears on her face. Their feelings of lust, passion and the need to be loved began to take control as their lips met momentarily .... Chloe pulled herself away hesitantly and then in a moment, Annie pulled her back into a loving embrace. Their mouths seemingly devouring each other as Annie's tongue entwined with Chloe's.

The teenager's blood flowed faster as she felt her heart pounding harder in her chest. She felt euphoric, almost out of control, as Annie deftly unbuttoned her top and unclipped her bra. Chloe felt Annie's warm, gentle hands on her soft skin as she slowly manoeuvred them to cup her young pert breasts.

Lost in their desires for much needed affection the pair undressed as their moist lips smothered each other, oblivious to any consequences. They lowered themselves to the bathroom floor as they pleasured each other and then drifted contently into a dream like sleep, their naked bodies entwined ....

"I didn't hear you leave, I wonder how am I still here, I don't want to move a thing, It might change my memory ...." Chloe lifted her head from Annie's ample breasts as she heard her phone playing, Here With Me by Dido .... *It's Usha ....* Chloe felt Annie's hand run through her hair. The young girl turned to see Annie smiling up at her. "Who was that on your phone Chloe?"

"Err .... It's Usha, she's sent a message." *What the ....What have I done?* Chloe quickly grabbed a towel from the bath rail and wrapped it round herself to cover her modesty as she felt herself blushing.

"Chloe." Annie pulled the teenager towards her ....

"Don't .... Just don't touch me Annie." Chloe pulled herself away. "It was a mistake .... It shouldn't have happened."

"Why? Why was it a mistake Chloe?... We're both adults .... We needed each other. We wanted to be loved."

"But .... But not like that Annie .... We went too far .... Our emotions got carried away."

"You can't deny that you felt something Chloe. You enjoyed it as much as me didn't you?"

"Well .... Yeah .... I s'pose .... But Alex?... Grandad?... What about them?"

"Let's put it this way, it can be our little secret eh? No harm done and besides, it doesn't mean you're gay." Annie kissed Chloe on the cheek. "Anyway, let's get dressed and then you can see what Usha wants."

Chloe looked at Usha's message ....

I think we've got trouble coming.
Take a look at the International
News on SKY.
Call me.
Usha xx

"Where's your television Annie?"

"There's one in the kitchen. Why, what's up?"

Chloe rushed into the kitchen, grabbed the remote and switched the television on. "What channel is Sky News on Annie?"

"Give me the remote …. There you go. What exactly are you looking for?"

"Usha reckons there's something on that we need to see …. There it is, breaking news …. Turn the volume up Annie."

".... Thank you Alistair …. Welcome back to Saint Malo in France where earlier today a huge car bomb tore through the marina complex. As you can see behind me, the emergency services are still working frantically to secure the area. Since we last reported we have managed to unearth this footage of the exact moment this massive car bomb exploded with devastating consequences …. If we slow the footage down you can clearly see a man selflessly throwing himself on top of a young girl to protect her from the blast. The authorities here have been unable to confirm the identity of this man but have issued a statement to say that the man's body hasn't been found and it is highly unlikely that he survived. The police are appealing for anyone that recognises this man to come forward …."

"That's Grandad Annie …. Shit!"

"Shush! There's more gal …."

".... There's a certain unease here Alistair that this is more than just a terrorist attack. I've been talking to some of the people who were caught up in this terrible incident and they are convinced that an angel or even an alien has been amongst them. Now I know that many of you at home and in the studio might be checking the calendars to make sure it's not April Fools Day, but I have here at least forty different accounts of miracles being performed here today by a young girl. Stories of healing and resurrection is rife amongst the many hundreds of people who were here at the time of the explosion and the aftermath. Suffice to say, if any of the stories are true the death toll could have been a lot worse.

The latest figures we have is twenty five dead and approximately one hundred and forty seven injured.

This is still a developing story Alistair and we'll have another update in about an hour, so it's back to you in the studio ...."

"CHLOE?!.... WHAT THE HELL!"

"I er .... I ...."

"What was you thinking? I know we said we'd try and help, but this takes us into deep doo-doo territory," snapped Annie.

"What .... What was I supposed to do? I mean .... All those people dead or dying and I have this gift of healing. I couldn't just walk away you know and I felt partly responsible. If I hadn't have been there with Grandad, all those people would still be alive."

"I get it Chloe, I really do. But how the hell do we deal with this? I mean, by now most of the world will have seen this news item and I can pretty much guarantee there's worse to come yet. Someone will have filmed you."

"I need to phone Usha."

"And what's she going to do about it? .... Eh Chloe? What the hell can she do?"

"I ... I don't know Annie. I'm going to phone her now." Chloe stomped out of the kitchen muttering to herself. "Bloody hell Chloe, what a mess."

"In your head, in your head, Zombie, zombie, zombie, hey, hey, What's in your head, in your head, Zombie, zombie, zombie, hey, hey, hey, oh ...." Usha picked up her phone as Zombie by The Cranberries played ....

"Usha."

"Hi Chloe. I take it you've seen the news then?"

"We've just finished watching it .... Annie's not very happy about the situation. Can't say that I blame her."

"Yeah I know where she's coming from, so basically we're in the shit."

"I know that Usha."

"Right .... So d'ya have any ideas?" asked Usha.

"What about Lilly? Couldn't she ....."

"No Chloe. You know as well as I do, that's not going to happen."

"There must be something we can do Usha."

286

"Look, there's obviously no way we can cover this up other than to try and bluff it out. We have to come up with a story that places us here in Alderney when it happened." Usha paused for a moment as she ran scenarios in her head. "In other words, we couldn't possibly be in two places at once, if you get my drift."

"Yeah I get that but …."

"Jeez Chloe, get your head together," snapped Usha. "First things first. We need to call in a couple of favours. As soon as we've finished talking, I'll get my scooter and come round to Annie's place to pick you up. Then we need to get up to Mr Bean's house to talk to Alex's Mum and Dad. We'll have to convince them to give you and Grandad a cover story. We don't have to tell them why, I mean, Frank owes me big time for saving his life."

"Annie reckons there's a good chance that people will have taken pictures and videos."

"I guess so, and we've got about forty five minutes before the next news bulletin. Look, I don't know if Grandad's well enough but he's our only chance if, and it's a big if. If he's able to hack into the internet, social media and the phone networks before any videos or pictures are posted."

"But he's not at home."

"Yeah I know it's a big ask but I have no other ideas. If he's well enough to travel, Mama Killa the Moon Goddess would have to instruct Lilly to take him home immediately. Luckily I do know that Grandma's in Guernsey today so Grandad wouldn't have any awkward questions to contend with. So you must get Annie to contact Grandad straight away to explain. She probably doesn't even know she has that power, but she does. Chloe …. You need to move …. NOW!... I'll pick you up in five minutes. Byeee."

"ANNIE!!... WHERE ARE YOU?"

Chloe opened the door as Usha frantically knocked ….
"You ready cuz?"
"Yeah …. Sure Usha. I'll just get my jacket."
"Oh hi Annie." Usha waved to the older woman who was standing in the kitchen doorway down the hall. "Are you

feeling any better?" *Am I seeing things? The reflection in the kitchen mirror? There seems to be a very faint ghostly, wispy image standing by Annie's side and she appears to be surrounded by a black mist.* Usha blinked. *Nah, I must be imagining it. Can't see it now.*

"Yes thanks Usha. I feel much better now after Chloe helped me relax." Annie passed Chloe her jacket as she tenderly ran her hand down the side of the teenager's face. "There you go Chloe."

Chloe scowled at Annie as she grabbed her jacket. "This isn't finished …. We'll talk later." The young woman ran to Usha. "Come on gal, let's get out of here." Chloe slammed the front door behind her.

The two teenagers clambered onto Usha's scooter and accelerated away.

"What was all that about?"

"Nothing," snapped Chloe.

"Didn't look like nothing from where I stood gal." *That's weird. Chloe's reflection in the wing mirror has a faint black mist. That's twice now in the last few minutes. Maybe I need to get my eyes tested.*

"Long story. I'll tell you about it later. *Maybe!* We've got more important things to do. C'mon, hurry up Usha."

"Oh just so you know, Grandad's back home and working out how to deal with the phone and internet networks. He's never tackled this sort of hacking on a worldwide scale before so it's going to be touch and go."

"Usha, I really am sorry about all this. You do know that don't you?"

"Yeah, of course I do."

"I just couldn't stand back and watch people die."

"Honestly Chloe, I totally get it, but it just goes to show you that we all have to be vigilant when using our powers …. Anyway, forget it. What's done is done and we'll deal with it …. Here we are, Frank and Beth's house."

"So that's all you need me to say if anyone asks?" Frank gesticulated with his hands and had a quizzical look in his eyes.

"Yes please Mr Bean," Usha replied. "That you picked up Annie Dodds, Chloe and my Grandad from Saint Malo yesterday and brought them here on your boat .... That's it, nothing else." Usha smiled.

"So just so I'm clear in my head, you've definitely done nothing wrong?"

Usha and Chloe shook their heads. "Scouts honour."

"Okay then girls. Just this once, no questions asked eh?"

The teenagers hugged and kissed Frank, much to his embarrassment.

It's up to you now Grandad, thought Usha.

"Hello, darkness, my old friend, I've come to talk with you again ...." Richard's ringtone played on his phone. It was Sound of Silence by Simon & Garfunkel. Richard stopped what he was doing and answered ....

"Hello."

"Oh hi Grandad, it's Usha. How are you?"

"Pretty good considering gal .... Look, before you ask, I haven't been able to hack into all of the networks. It's just been too big of a job, sorry, and I was running out of time."

"Bugger! Oh well, thanks for trying. We'll just have to deal with any consequences but hopefully our cover story with Frank Bean will throw any inquisitive enquiries off our scent."

"I reckon you should be alright Usha, providing everyone sticks to the same story. Try not to worry too much. By the way, how's Annie?"

"Er .... You don't know then?" Usha hesitated and stuttered.

"What?" You'd better tell me Usha."

"Well er .... Her husband's been killed in America. I don't know the full story, you'll have to ask her yourself. Chloe stayed with her for some time to keep her company. She said Annie seemed okay but I got the feeling that something's not right between the two of them. Something weird was going on, I couldn't put my finger on it, really strange. Anyway, I left Chloe at Mrs Bean's place and I'm just on my way to meet Ben up at the Campania pub."

Jeez Annie. "Oh. No, I didn't know about her husband. I'll try and call round to see her later, after your Grandma and I have sorted a few things out if you get my drift."

"Right okay Grandad. Say hello to Grandma for me and I'll see you soon .... Byeee!"

Luis stubbed his cigarette out and casually threw it to the ground as he pushed on the door and walked into the bar room of his local pub, the Campania. *Christ I'm knackered. That's been a long, hard day's work. Think I deserve a drink .... Or two. Ha! There's Ben over there.* Luis slumped over the bar as he spied Tessa the barmaid in the back room preparing food for the darts team, who were playing a match later on in the evening. "HI TESSA .... ANY CHANCE OF A DRINK?"

Tessa glanced up and sauntered to the pumps at the counter. "Hello luv, looks like you've had a hard day. The usual is it?"

Luis nodded appreciatively as he watched the buxom lass pull on a pump, filling a pint glass. "And whatever Ben's drinking please m'dear .... There's a tenner there Tessa." He slid a ten pound note across the counter. "You can keep the change .... I've had a good day."

"Arh, cheers luv."

Luis picked up the two glasses and took a hefty slurp out of his drink before wandering over to the table that Ben was slumped at, watching the television that was fixed precariously to the adjacent wall. "There you go mate, get your mouth round that." Luis pushed the glass across the table. "Hellooooo! Earth to Ben. Anyone there?" Luis dragged a chair out from under the table and sat down.

"Eh?.... Oh cheers Luis. Sorry mate, I've been watching this coverage of that car bomb in France earlier today."

"Oh right, why? What about it?"

"I can't make my mind up about it. I've watched the actual blast loads of time and THERE, LOOK." Ben pointed to the television as it showed the blast in slow motion. "What d'ya reckon?"

"Well .... Er .... Apart from the quality of the footage, I'd say that guy is the spitting image of Richard Morgan. Mind you, after an explosion like that, whoever the guy is, he'll be dead now." Luis had a wry grin.

"But don't you think it's weird though?"

"No not really. It's just a coincidence mate. They reckon that everyone has a double somewhere. I must admit, it would really feel strange to bump into someone else that looked identical to yourself. Christ, I've just had a terrible thought ...."

"What's that?"

"There could be two of you!... Oh my God .... The very thought of it is sending shivers down my spine, ha!"

Ben thumped Luis on the arm making him spill his drink. "You bugger .... Ha!"

The two friends laughed out loud as Usha entered the pub and waved to the two lads. As she waited for Tessa to pour out a glass of cola she noticed the television was on .... *Damn it! The news channel is still covering the car bomb incident in France.* Tessa broke into her thoughts.

"That's just terrible eh gal?"

"Eh? Oh, yes it is."

"All those poor people killed."

"Yeah, awful, yeah."

"Mind you, it could have been worse you know."

"How's that Tessa?"

"Well they reckon there's been reports of a girl healing and resurrecting people after the explosion. No idea if it's true or not. I mean, these days folks will say anything to get attention for themselves. Mind you, the news channel reckons it's got hold of some social media recording showing this girl in action. You know how it is, they like to make sure it's the real deal before they broadcast it, if you know what I mean."

"Yeah, yeah sure, I know what you mean." *Jeez .... Chloe!*

"Mark my words though, I can guarantee the incident will be all over the national newspapers tomorrow."

"I s'pose you're right. Thanks for the drink Tessa, I'd better go and see what my boyfriend's up to." Usha sauntered over to where Ben and Luis sat, still laughing. "Budge up guys. Make room for a little one." She sat next to Ben and kissed him. "So what you up to guys?"

"Ben's been on about that guy in France, you know, involved with that car bomb. I must admit it's the spitting image of your Grandad Usha." Luis shrugged his shoulders and rolled his eyes.

"Yeah I've seen the pictures. S'pose it does. Shouldn't think it'll bother my Grandad." Usha stood up. "Anyway, you coming Ben? I thought you was taking me for a meal."

"Yeah sure gal." Ben stood up and held Usha's hand. "I'll catch up with you tomorrow Luis."

Luis sat there in his own thoughts staring at his drink as his two friends left the pub. *Christ. Where the hell is Lilly these days. I wonder what she's up to?* He sighed and held his empty glass up to order another pint as Tessa caught his eye. *It's gonna be a long night.*

"Right luv, I'm just popping out. I'm meeting up with one of the lads for a spot of fishing. I should be back by midnight latest so don't bother waiting up for me." Richard pulled his thick jacket over his shoulders and headed for the front door as Bea handed him his woollen hat.

"It's cold outside tonight Richard. You'll need the hat to keep your ears warm."

"Thanks luv, I'll see you later." Richard closed the door behind him leaving Bea in the warmth of the house.

The van spluttered into life. *That's a novelty, first time of asking! Right, let's get round to Annie's place. I must remember to get my amulet back ....*

Richard stood back into the darkness of the deserted driveway as he spotted Chloe stepping out of Annie's house. His heart pounding ever faster in his chest as he peered through the gloom of the night to see Chloe turn and kiss Annie passionately, as she squeezed the older woman's bum underneath her skimpy see through negligée, before saying goodnight and climbed on to her scooter.

What the hell is going on? Richard held his breath and took another step back into the darkness as his Granddaughter drove past, oblivious to the fact that her Grandad was there in the shadows …. Watching …. Wondering …. Bewildered. Richard shook himself as he digested what he'd just witnessed.

Richard walked up to Annie's front door and stood on the step wondering whether to knock or simply walk away. The adrenalin was pumping as his heart pounded seemingly louder every second. *Something's terribly wrong. How can my Granddaughter possibly be Annie's lover? I'm losing the plot here* .... The thought of them making love sent a shiver through his whole body. *I'm going.* Richard took a step back and turned to go. The door opened ….

"Richard." Annie stood posing in the doorway still wearing the negligée, her nipples accentuated by the cold air in the moonlight.

He half glanced …. "Annie I …."

"C'mon luv. Don't just stand there gawping at my tits. Come on in …. You know you want to."

Richard entered the house without thought, as if on some sort of auto pilot. "Annie I …."

"Shush luv." Annie pressed her finger against Richard's lips. "Let's get your jacket and hat off."

Richard duly obliged and fleetingly came to his senses as he spotted his amulet on Annie's wrist …. The crystals were glowing and pulsing rapidly. "Annie I …." His thoughts and questions dissipated as Annie led him to the bedroom ….

"Feeling better now luv?" Annie sat on the edge of the bed as she combed her hair.

"Wh …. What?" Richard lifted his head from the pillow and focused his eyes firstly on the bedside clock and then on Annie as he struggled to recall what had happened over the last two hours. *I can't remember a thing!... I just can't! Not a bloody thing …. Something's wrong with me. I'm sure.*

"You getting dressed luv? Bea will be wondering where you are." Annie manoeuvred her ample breasts into the cups of her flimsy bra and fastened the clips as she stood up and faced Richard as the amulet on her wrist pulsed steadily.

"Er …. Yeah, of course." Richard sat up and turned towards the wall mirror as he put his feet to the floor." *What the hell?* He could see a faint ghostly, wispy image in the reflection of the mirror standing by Annie's side and his lover was enveloped in some sort of black mist. *This is weird. What the hell is going on?*

293

Richard half turned as his lover walked round the bed and pushed him on to his back across the bed and sat on him.

"Annie .... No!" Richard tried to push her away. *Her eyes ....They're black .... Shit .... She's too strong.* "ANNIE." Richard could feel that he was aroused as Annie gyrated her whole body on top of him, seemingly out of control. "ANNIE." He shouted again as he tried to push her away when suddenly, his lover was seemingly engulfed in a black mist which took the shape of a deformed skeleton with a huge skull. Huge twisted horns protruded from the creature's skull.

"Aaarrrggghhh ...." The evil looking apparition growled directly into Richard's face as Annie pounded away bringing Richard to the ecstasy of an orgasm and then she collapsed on top of him as the apparition dissipated.

"Bloody hell." Richard pushed Annie away from him across the bed as he caught his breath. *She's out of it. Time to get out of here.* He quickly dressed. *The amulet.* He reached for the pulsing amulet on Annie's wrist .... "NO!" Annie's mouth moved involuntary as an unworldly voice shouted once again. "NO!"

Bloody hell .... I'm out of here. Richard threw a quilt over Annie and quickly grabbed his hat and coat as he left the house, stumbling in his haste.

CHAPTER 39

FOG

"Lock your door, switch the light, You'll be so afraid tonight, Hide away from the bad, Count the nine lives that you had. Death walks behind you, Death walks behind you ...." Usha reached for her phone that was playing Death Walks Behind You by Atomic Rooster. *Jeez, who's phoning me at half past five in the morning!*

"Hello."

"Hi Usha, it's Alex. Sorry, I know it's early ...."

You got that right mate!

"When did you last see Chloe?"

"Er, yesterday Alex. Why?"

"How did she seem to you?"

"She was okay .... A bit concerned about what had happened at Saint Malo in France but other than that ...."

"Nothing weird then?"

"Er, depends what you mean by weird, Alex. I mean, when I picked her up at Annie Dodds' place she was definitely not herself, you know. There was some sort of tension in the air between them but Chloe seemed okay. Mind you, having said that, there was one thing I thought was strange at the time, but I thought I was seeing things."

"What d'ya mean Usha?"

"Well it's probably nothing and this is going to sound daft, but I could have sworn I saw some sort of black mist, or presence if you like, surrounding Chloe .... But I only saw it in her reflection .... You're gonna tell me I'm going crackers now eh?"

"No, no, not at all. I thought it was me that was losing the plot," replied Alex. "When she came home last night she was acting really aggressively, not like her at all and yes, I thought I saw something but then I just dismissed it."

"Where's Chloe now?" asked Usha.

"She's still in bed asleep thankfully."

"Right." *I WAS asleep mate!*

"Probably just as well I s'pose."

"What d'ya mean Alex?"

"My Dad's just got home from a fishing trip. While he was down at the harbour, another boat was offloading the national newspapers," explained Alex.

"Yeah, and?"

"He was telling me about the headlines. They're all about Chloe in France and get this .... They've printed photos. I mean, my Dad knew he would be covering for Chloe at some point but he didn't realise what the story was, so to say he's peeved is an understatement."

"Yeah but Alex, it's no big deal providing everyone sticks to the same story. He knows that, so I don't really see a problem."

"You're right I know, but the pictures of Chloe whilst she's healing people are really clear and the headlines are the usual sensational bullshit."

"Like what?"

"Oh stuff like .... *'ET's home'*, *'Alien encounters'* and what was the other one? Oh yeah, *'God's work'*.... You know, that sort of thing .... Are you laughing Usha?"

".... Ha! Er, sorry Alex .... Like I said, they're nothing to worry about but yeah, I understand what you're saying. Anyway, this other 'ghostly' thing could be a problem so I suggest, just you and me meet up at my Grandad's place later this morning to see if he can help out, say about nine thirty."

"Yeah, sounds good Usha. I'll make my excuses to get away from Chloe and I'll see you there .... Right I've got to go. I think I just heard Chloe coming down the stairs. Catch you later."

"Okay. Byeee."

"When you said you looked a mess, I whispered underneath my breath, But you heard it, darling, You look perfect tonight ..." Usha grabbed her phone. It was playing Perfect by Ed Sheeran ....

"Hello."

"Hi Usha, it's Ben."

"Oh hello hun, you okay?"

"Yeah, yeah. More to the point, do you feel alright?"

"Course I'm alright Ben why? …. C'mon, what's up?"

"I don't know to be honest. It's just that I've been in the cafe and then walked up through town this morning …. And this is goin' to sound really strange, but nearly everyone I passed totally ignored me as if I wasn't there. At first I thought maybe it was me 'cos everyone I passed appeared normal, but when I glanced in the shop windows, their reflections looked to have a black sort of mist surrounding them. It really spooked me."

"That does sound kind of weird." *I think the shit is gonna hit the fan if we don't figure this out soon.* "All I can say Ben, is to try and keep away from people for the mo'. Try and avoid any physical contact. I don't know what else to tell you. You keep safe hun and I'll catch up with you as soon as I can …. Promise."

"Yeah okay gal. I'll see you later."

What the hell is goin' on? Usha glanced at her watch. *Need to get up to Grandad's place.* She grabbed the keys for her scooter and ran out of the house.

Usha drove her scooter onto the driveway at Richard's house to be greeted by Alex.

"Hi Usha."

The teenagers hugged and kissed each other on the cheeks before entering the house.

"HELLO," Alex shouted.

"GRANDAD …. Anyone here?" Usha asked as the two friends walked into the kitchen to see Richard and Bea sat at the table staring at each other in total silence.

Usha and Alex looked at each other in bewilderment.

"This is weird gal."

Usha nodded. "Grandad …. Grandma …. What's wrong?"

Alex nudged Usha in the back as he whispered in her ear, "Look at their reflections in the upright freezer."

Usha gasped as she saw the black mist that was surrounding her Grandma and Grandad. *Oh shit!* Without any hesitation she banged the kitchen table with her fists to get a reaction ….

Nothing. Usha and Alex grabbed the shoulders of Richard and Bea and shook them furiously .... "HELLO!!"

The black mist engulfed Bea and Richard and suddenly took the shape of two deformed skeletons which had huge skulls with horns .... They turned to face the teenagers .... "Aaarrrggghhh." The evil looking apparitions growled and hissed as they reached out for the teenagers ....

"WHOOOOSH."

Lilly appeared. She grabbed Alex and Usha. "HOLD ON," the angel shouted as they disappeared in an instant, save for the faintest sound of wings as the evil dark apparitions dissipated.

"You guys okay?" Lilly asked.

"Yeah .... Yes I think so," Alex replied. "That was a close call. What the hell are we dealing with?"

"They are ghosts, lost souls .... Or to be specific, fallen angels. We call them The Gloaming."

"Right."

"Oh Lilly, where have you been?" Usha hugged her sister and kissed her on the cheek.

"Hi sis', it's really good to see you. I've missed you SO much over the past few weeks." Lilly hugged Usha tightly as she explained to the two teenagers how she'd been helping other angels to fight demons and the Supay all around the world and in both the Upper and Lower Realms. "It's been really tough at times but we are slowly beginning to see progress. Well, that is until now."

"How's that Lilly?" Alex asked.

"Well ever since the dawn of creation, heaven has had to deal with the odd angel they had to cast out because they'd sinned, but it never caused many problems because heaven has a tracking system. That's the only way I can describe it in basic terms. Anyway, just lately, heaven has noticed a sudden surge of fallen angels and they are latching on to mortal beings such as Grandad, Grandma, Chloe and Annie ...."

"And there are others on the island according to Ben 'cos he's seen them around town apparently," Usha interrupted.

"Yes I know and it's only gonna get worse as The Gloaming takes over the persona of individuals, because the evil temptations control their emotions and so forth. We knew that the Mafia had found a way of persuading demons to help them achieve their evil ambitions. But we've only just discovered that these same creatures from hell are recruiting fallen angels to create The Gloaming. It will have terrifying consequences unless we can find out how the fallen angels are being converted, so to speak."

Usha had been listening intently whilst she'd been exploring various possibilities in her head. "Just a thought .... We know the Mafia have an Inca platter style dish, that's possibly identical to the one we retrieved from the cave at Bluestone Bay and that they've been using it as a sort of radar to locate anyone who's wearing an amulet or pendant. That is, anyone that is wearing one, but shouldn't be, if you get my drift."

"Such as Annie," Alex said.

"I'm sorry guys, but where is all this going?" Lilly asked. "I'm not following you at all."

Usha rolled her eyes in disbelief. "Think about it. Annie is wearing Grandad's amulet so the Mafia know exactly where she is and therefore they were able to target her first with The Gloaming. She's been alone with Chloe and no doubt Grandad has been there alone with her, so we can be fairly certain that Chloe will have targeted Mr and Mrs Bean just like Grandad has with Grandma."

"And so it goes on unless we can find a way to stop the 'infection'," Alex said.

"Precisely. Annie is the source of The Gloaming because of the amulet she's wearing so we either have to destroy The Gloaming that's possessing Annie or find a way to take the amulet from her .... Or both." Usha pondered for a moment .... "The other scenario is to find the other gold Inca platter dish that the Mafia have in their possession."

"Finding the other dish would be the perfect solution, but it would take too long I reckon," Alex said.

"Either way, we don't have time for all this," Lilly said. "Hold on tight you two, I'll take you to the Upper Realm, Hanan Pacha. They will know what needs to be done." In the blink of an eye the three teenagers arrived in heaven....

"You two okay?" Lilly asked as she waved to another flock of angels passing by.

"I can't get used to this," Alex gasped.

"WELCOME ONCE MORE TO LILLY, OUR MOST FAITHFUL SERVANT." A powerful voice boomed through the air. "HOW MAY WE HELP?"

"Awesome isn't it Alex," Usha whispered as Alex stood open mouthed in disbelief. He stared at the three huge figures sat before them.

"They look like characters you would find in a Biblical story," Alex replied. "And I've just realised that I can see Lilly's wings …. They're amazingly beautiful and so big."

"Yeah, you can see her wings because we're in heaven," Usha replied.

Lilly knelt down on one knee. "Oh mighty Gods, we have come to ask for your help. The earth below is becoming infected with The Gloaming."

Illapa, the God of Thunder and Lightening stood up. "YOU DARE TO ENTER THIS REALM FOR SUCH A TRIVIAL MATTER …. WHAT NEWS OF THE LIMA TREASURE?"

"We are unable to continue our quest for the Lima Treasure because of The Gloaming. It has infected Alnitak the Healer and Child of the Stars, Annie Dodds, the librarian and ….."

"STOP!" Mama Killa, the Moon Goddess stood up. "THE HEALER AND THE KEEPER OF BOOKS?"

"Yes," Usha interrupted. "We think Annie, the keeper of books is the source."

"WE CANNOT ALLOW THIS TO HAPPEN …." Mama Killa boomed. "AND THE HUNTER IN THE CONSTELLATION OF ORION WILL BE VEXED IF HARM SHOULD COME TO ALNITAK, THE CHILD OF THE STARS."

Inti, the Sun God rose to his feet. "THE KEEPER OF BOOKS, DOES SHE WEAR THE AMULET BY DEFAULT?"

"Yes she does," Lilly replied.

"SO OUR FALLEN ANGELS ARE BEING RECRUITED THROUGH HER."

"It would appear so," Usha replied.

Inti turned to Lilly. "YOU MUST GO TO ORION THE HUNTER AND COLLECT HIS SWORD WHICH HAS THE POWER TO DEVOUR THE GLOAMING."

"What exactly does that mean?" Alex asked.

"The sword of the Hunter comes from the Orion Nebula which has a mass two thousand times greater than our sun," Lilly explained. "When used on earth it will act as a magnet for any fallen angels. The souls of the fallen angels should, in theory, be absorbed by the sword and without the souls, the demons cannot survive …."

"And I assume, without the souls of the fallen angels and the demons powerless without them, The Gloaming will dissipate instantly," Usha said.

"Ha …. Well that's the theory," Alex replied. *Bloody hell!*

"But what happens to the souls of the fallen angels?" Usha asked.

"I will return the sword to the Hunter in Orion …." Lilly explained. "…. Whereupon the souls will be released to form more stars in the Orion Nebula."

"Sounds simple eh?" Alex joked.

"ENOUGH!... I GROW TIRED," Illapa's voice boomed angrily.

"BEFORE YOU DEPART, THERE IS ONE THING YOU MUST KNOW. THE SWORD CAN ONLY BE USED ONCE …. INTI, YOUR SUN GOD, HAS SPOKEN."

Lilly rose to her feet. "Thank you. I am, as always, your servant." She turned to Usha and Alex. "We need to go …."

"Before you leave …." Mama Killa, the Moon Goddess spoke softly, "To ensure you collect all the souls of the fallen angels you must use the sword at night when the Orion Constellation is framed in stone …. God speed Lilly."

Lilly grabbed hold of Alex and Usha …. In an instant, the three teenagers were stood outside Richard's house next to their scooters they'd parked earlier.

Alex was still recovering from his angelic trip as Usha spoke to her sister Lilly ….

"Framed in stone sis'? What's that all about? And how the hell are you going to get the Hunter's Sword? Even with your powers of an angel you can't possibly travel to the Orion Constellation. It's thousands of light years away."

"What's going on?" Alex asked.

"I was just saying to Lilly, that even with her powers, I don't see how any of this is possible," Usha explained.

"Oh, I see …. Usha does have a point Lilly."

"Don't you two get it," Lilly said impatiently. "Orion framed in stone refers to the bunker up on The Guns where they hold the bunker parties. The same bunker we all experienced the Orion Constellation phenomenon, when we found out that Chloe was in fact The Healer, a Child of the Stars and was known as Alnitak. Somehow, we have to get Chloe up to the bunker tonight and trick her into summoning the power of the constellation. That'll be your job Alex."

"What about Annie 'cos she's the source?" Usha asked.

"Well I'm hoping that Chloe will be suspicious enough to contact her and Annie will come to the bunker to meet up with Chloe." Lilly continued. "You two need to make sure you're there before either of them arrive. Okay?"

"I s'pose," Alex replied. "I don't like any of this, but we don't have any options eh?"

"What about you Lilly?" Usha asked.

"Don't worry sis', I'll be there at the right moment."

Usha and Alex stood nervously in the blackness of the night. The two friends had been in the cold, dank bunker for about two hours and it was bitterly cold. The only visible light was from the starry night above, which could be seen through the two metre diameter hole in the concrete roof above them casting the occasional strange shadow. Alex stepped carefully to the centre of the bunker and looked up through the gaping hole ....

"I reckon it's about five minutes before the Orion Constellation moves over us into full view," he whispered.

"Get back over here Alex, against the wall. You're making me feel nervous. Just make sure you remember the plan."

Alex stood back in the shadows, his back against the cold damp wall. "I don't like this plan Usha."

"Well, it's all we've got. I had to lie to Chloe to persuade her to meet me here, so I just hope Lilly's timing is right." Usha stepped into the centre and looked up. "It's time Alex." She nervously lay down on the dusty concrete floor as Alex approached and bent over her. He pulled a hypo out of his inside jacket pocket and carefully gave her an injection in her arm.

"Don't worry gal, I've got the resuscitation drug here. I'll bring you back." Alex kissed her on the cheek as Usha appeared to stop breathing and her head dropped to the side.

"So Chloe, what exactly are we doing up here?"

"Bloody hell Annie, this is our chance to take the bastards out. Usha sent me a text on my phone earlier today, telling me that she was willing to lose her soul to help our cause. She knows that we can control the world."

Alex shuffled backwards into the shadows against the bunker wall as he heard Annie and Chloe's voices echoing in the corridor as they approached the main bunker room in which Alex was waiting silently. He clutched the hypo he'd taken from the hospital the day before, which contained the antidote, Narcan, tighter. *Whatever happens I mustn't lose this .... Usha's life depends on it. Stay calm .... Stay calm .... Breathe ....* Alex watched as Chloe and Annie entered the room. They were completely surrounded by The Gloaming which snarled and growled as the black mist contorted into hideous creatures of the night ....

303

Annie bent down over Usha's lifeless body and felt her neck for a pulse. She turned to Chloe …. "The bitch is dead. DAMN IT! She's no good to us dead 'cos we needed her alive to get her soul, to infect her." Annie stood up and pulled Chloe close to her body ….

Alex stared in disbelief as his girlfriend and Annie caressed each other intimately, working themselves up into a sexual frenzy as The Gloaming swirled around, howling until suddenly, Chloe threw Annie across the room, inadvertently crashing into Alex, smashing the hypo as it dropped to the floor.

As Chloe hissed and growled, Annie quickly stood up and grabbed Alex tightly, pulling him up from the floor and forcing his arms around his back …. "Well look here Chloe, another plaything. HA!"

Alex grimaced with pain as he struggled in vain. *Oh Usha ….*

"ENOUGH," Chloe growled. "I'll bring this bitch back to life." She knelt over Usha and began to chant …. "I am the Child of the Stars …. I am Alnitak the Healer …." Chloe looked up to the Constellation of Orion above her and held out her hands and shouted. "HEAR ME ORION, FOR I AM ALNITAK …. GIVE ME THE POWER …."

"WHOOOOSH." Lilly appeared armed with her light staff. A piercing beam of white light from the Orion Nebula, which forms the sword of the Hunter in the Constellation, passed through the opening in the roof of the bunker and hit the light staff, transforming it into a one metre sword which glowed brightly, so bright that Lilly's outstretched wings could be seen.

"YOU FOOL," Chloe shouted. "Do you think a sword will destroy us? HA!" The Gloaming slowly filled the room growling and hissing as the black mist surrounded Lilly ….

With the strength of four men, Lilly lifted the heavy sword above her head and pointed it towards the sky above as the beam of white light continued to hit the sword until suddenly it ceased …. The sword shone like a beacon in the night, and like moths to a flame, The Gloaming was absorbed into the sword releasing its pervasive hold on Chloe and Annie as they collapsed to the floor of the bunker. Lilly continued to hold the sword aloft as the invasive black mist from all parts of the island were sucked into its powerful influence. For a few eerie moments, the island was

304

engulfed in the black mist as The Gloaming succumbed to the power of the sword and then finally, Lilly dropped her arms to her side, resting the sword on the ground and turned to Alex ....

"ALEX .... Alex remove the amulet from Annie's wrist before she comes round .... NOW! Then check to see she's okay. I'll take a look at Chloe."

Alex slid the amulet off Annie's wrist and placed it in his pocket as she awoke and sat up holding her head ....

"Ooh .... I feel like I've been hit with a sledgehammer. What happened? Where have I been?... And what's up with Usha?"

Alex turned to see Usha still lying motionless on the floor in the centre of the room .... *Oh shit!* "LILLY." Alex rushed to Usha's side.

"Give her the antidote Alex," Lilly said as she tended to Chloe, who had just come to her senses. "The antidote .... Give it to her, quickly or we'll lose her."

"I .... I can't Lilly, the hypo was smashed .... Oh God!" Alex was physically shaking.

Lilly turned to Chloe. "Are you strong enough gal?"

"I think so." Chloe crawled over to Usha's lifeless body and started to chant as she held her pendant with one hand and held the other over Usha. "I am Alnitak the Healer, the Child of the Stars." A white light surrounded Usha and then she stirred slowly and struggled to sit up with the help of Alex ....

"Did we succeed?" Usha spluttered.

Alex looked around as the others smiled at him. "Yes gal. Er, not quite as planned, but everyone's okay." He hugged Usha and then helped her to her feet as the group of friends huddled together in the centre of the bunker room.

"One last thing," Lilly said as she strained to lift the heavy sword above her head .... "HEAR ME ORION." A shaft of white light from the Orion Nebula instantly hit the sword which disappeared in the blink of an eye, leaving Lilly holding her light staff.

"Come on guys, let's get out of here. Time to go home," Alex said.

CHAPTER 40

REVELATIONS

"So how long has it been since the last sighting of The Gloaming?" Richard asked as he fiddled with the amulet on his wrist. He kept looking at the amulet as he wondered what might have been if it hadn't have been for the heroic actions of his Granddaughters, Lilly and Usha, assisted by Alex. *Doesn't bear thinking about.*

"I s'pose about six weeks Grandad," Chloe answered. She placed the tray of drinks on the table and sat at the only remaining seat next to her boyfriend Alex and wrapped her arm around his shoulders as she kissed him gently on the cheek. "Help yourselves guys."

It was a hot day, a very hot day and the friends had met up in the gravelled gardens of The Old Barn Restaurant close to Longis Bay, to discuss a possible plan of action. Annie and Richard sat opposite each other, occasionally playing footsie under the table like a couple of lovestruck teenagers whilst Lilly and Usha were catching up on Lilly's heavenly battles as an angel. Their boyfriends, Luis and Ben were due to meet them at the restaurant later that afternoon.

"Cheers Chloe." Usha picked up her glass of shandy and took a couple of gulps. "So come on guys, we need to get back on track here. We need to have some sort of plan to find the rest of the Lima Treasure."

"Shush Usha," whispered Lilly. "Tourists."

There was the sound of crunching gravel as a group of six visitors wandered through the archway into the gardens. The group slowly walked past Lilly and her friends and headed towards the door to the restaurant. They opened the door and filed in, one by one. "I won't be a minute." It was a woman's voice .... She turned and headed directly to the table that Lilly and her friends were sat around .... The woman stood staring directly at Chloe. She glanced down at her phone and then stared unashamedly at Chloe ....

"COME ON JOANNA, THE OTHERS ARE WAITING." A shout from the door of the restaurant.

Chloe was feeling decidedly uncomfortable at the unwanted and intrusive attention.

"You're that girl aren't you? The one in France?" Joanna asked as she looked directly at Chloe. She held her phone up which had a photo of Chloe healing a young girl after the bombing in France. She pushed the phone into Chloe's face .... "That's you isn't it? Don't deny it. You've still got that blonde streak in your hair as well."

"I, er .... No it's not what you ...." Chloe stuttered.

"I think you need to stop harassing my cousin, lady," Usha said as she stood up and grabbed hold of Joanna's arm ....

"Take your hand off me girl," snapped Joanna.

"Or what?" Usha's grip on the woman's arm tightened causing Joanna to grimace in pain as Richard passed a discerning look at Usha.

"I'll report you to the police. Let go of my arm, now."

"Fine .... Fine .... Whatever!" Usha let go of Joanna's arm and held up her hands.

"That's better .... You've not heard the last of this. Mark my words."

307

Richard stood up. "Sorry about that miss, do you mind if I take a look?" He pointed to Joanna's phone.

"I s'pose." She passed her phone to Richard .... She swayed from side to side and collapsed to the ground as Lilly touched her on the back of the head.

"Sort the phone out Grandad, quickly. She won't be out for long," said Usha, as she placed her hand on Joanna's forehead and concentrated .... *You will forget everything that has happened here and the photo on your phone never existed.*

Joanna came around as Richard finished doing 'his thing' on her phone and dropped it to the ground.

"Are you alright?" Richard helped Joanna to her feet. "You went a right pearler there miss and it looks like you've bruised your arm." He gave Usha a knowing look.

"Er, thank you." Joanna brushed herself down. "I seem to have lost my phone."

"Here you are." Usha bent down and picked the phone up off the gravel and placed it into Joanna's hand. "You don't want to be losing your phone 'cos it looks an expensive model."

"Well thank you young lady. Now then, what was I doing?"

"Your friends went through that door there," Richard said, as he pointed to the restaurant.

"Oh yes. Yes of course, silly me. Well thank you again for your help. I'd better go and catch up with my friends. You all have a nice day." Joanna walked across the gravel and entered the restaurant, oblivious to the events of the last ten minutes.

"Sorry guys," Chloe said. "That's the second time that's happened this week. I'm getting a little fed up of it now. I reckon it's occurred on about a dozen occasions since the actual event."

"The price of fame, ha! Sorry Chloe," Alex joked. "Maybe you should cut your hair short, or perhaps bleach your hair blonde so it's the same colour as Lilly and Usha's. I mean, you've already got a blonde streak in your hair so why not go the whole hog? I'm sure it would help."

"Actually, that's not a bad idea Alex," Annie said. "Even if it's just for a few weeks Chloe, until the interest generated by that TV footage of the bomb blast eases off. You can always revert back to your normal colour anytime you want."

Chloe nodded. "I'll think about it guys."

"Ha! That would make us the three blondes," Lilly joked.

"Nah ….. More like The Three Blonde Marys, eh girls." Usha threw her head back and ran her fingers through her blonde curly hair which sparkled in the sunlight." She laughed as Lilly and Chloe copied her actions.

Richard interrupted the laughter. "Usha, what the hell happened earlier with Joanna?"

"What?"

"You did something to her memory didn't you?... And what about the force you used on her arm. What's that all about eh gal?"

"Er, well …. It's ever since that night in the bunker when we defeated The Gloaming. I've discovered that I can alter or erase parts of people's memories when they're unconscious or asleep. And not only that, the strength in my hands and arms has increased dramatically. The thing is, that night, I was pretty much unconscious the whole time. I told Lilly about it weeks ago and since then I've been learning to control both powers, especially the strength 'cos I can crush pretty much anything. I mean, I tried not to hurt Joanna which worked up to a point, but to be honest I thought I did quite well considering I could have easily tore her arm off."

"Wow! Just …. Wow!" Alex couldn't control himself. "That's just totally awesome."

"Well, yeah sort of," Usha replied. "A bit of a worry though."

"I'll say it is. How the hell has that come about?" asked Richard.

"It may have something to do with the Hunter's Sword," Lilly explained. "When the shaft of light from the Orion Nebula hit the sword I was holding aloft, it's quite possible the light refracted and at some point hit Usha. She wouldn't have known anything about it at the time as she was unconscious. If I'm right, the sword has passed on these powers to sis'. Who knows, she may even have another power that she doesn't know about yet."

"So exactly how strong are you Usha?" Annie asked.

Usha glanced around to ensure no-one was watching and then picked up a piece of granite stone the size of a tennis ball and without straining herself, squeezed ....

"Wow!" Chloe gasped as the granite disintegrated to dust.

"To be honest guys, I'm not entirely certain how strong I am, but for the moment, it's all about learning to control my strength. Time will tell I s'pose," Usha said.

"Remind me not to challenge you to an arm wrestle," Richard joked.

Usha rubbed the dust from her hands as she sat down and gingerly picked up her drink from the table. "So back to my original question and the reason why we're all here .... What's next for us?"

"Well Annie and I have been busy trying to translate the symbols on the gold Inca platter style dish using the internet and trawling through loads of books that we've acquired," Richard explained.

"And we are beginning to see some progress," Annie added. "We all know how important it is to understand it's power and we're all aware that the Mafia are in possession of an identical dish. So myself and Richard are concentrating all our efforts to find out how to locate it."

"Yeah, and we've organised a Zoom call with a professor of Inca curios who's based in Oxford," Richard explained. "Actually, I think that's happening tomorrow isn't it Annie?"

"Yes it is my love. We're using the computer at the library."

"That's good then," Lilly said.

"Yes it is," Richard replied. "But as I've said before, the Inca gold statues are by far the most important items to find as the hexagonal bases of the statues fit perfectly in the indentations around the edge of the platter dish and there's six in total. Not only that, I firmly believe the statues ARE the Lima Treasure and once located in the platter dish in the correct indentations, all will be revealed so to speak."

"Well so far we have two statues," Chloe said, "and they're carefully hidden away for now."

"Know the secret of the ancient desert lands, You are the keeper of the mystery in your hands ...." Lilly grabbed her phone as it played The Nomad by Iron Maiden ....

"Hi luv. You okay?.... Yeah, of course we're still here .... Hmm yeah .... That's alright .... Five minutes. We'll see you then .... Bye Luis." Lilly put her phone away and quickly brushed her hair. She then grabbed a small mirror out of her bag and held it to her face as she checked her makeup. She ran her hands down her dress trying to eliminate any creases and quickly patted and pushed her breasts to accentuate her cleavage.

"I take it that was Luis on your phone Lilly?" Annie asked.

Lilly nodded, slightly embarrassed as she realised everyone had been watching her. "Er yeah. He'll be here in a couple of minutes with Ben. Apparently they had to help his Dad move a heavy chest before they could get away."

"A chest you say? I wonder," Richard mused. "I wonder if that's the chest we saw at Bluestone Bay."

"Maybe," Usha replied.

"You mean the one my Dad saw on his boat," Alex said. "If it is, it had a lot of cash in it .... And I mean, a lot."

"Right then. The decision has been made for us I'd say," Richard said. "When the lads arrive, we need to find out what they've been up to with that chest and then decide how we're going to tackle the situation 'cos we all know that Luis' Dad is working with the Mafia."

The friends nodded their approval as the sound of crunching gravel behind them gave way to the voices of Ben and Luis ....

"Hi guys," Ben said as he made a bee line for Usha and kissed her on the cheek.

"Yeah, hi guys." Luis wrapped his arms around Lilly and kissed her passionately on the lips, as she responded by squeezing his bum. "Sorry we're late, we had to do an extra job for my Dad out at Mannez Quarry."

"Here you go lads," Alex said as he stood up and nodded to Chloe to follow his lead. "You two sit together here whilst Chloe and I fetch you a couple of drinks." Alex winked at Lilly and Usha as they walked to the restaurant.

Ben and Luis sat down whilst Usha and Lilly stood behind them with their hands on the boys shoulders .... "A COUPLE OF BEERS PLEASE ALEX," Luis shouted.

311

"So what have you been up to lads?" Richard asked.

"We've been busy with a big plumbing job," Ben replied.

"Yeah, but then my Dad wanted that chest moving eh Ben," Luis said. "Bloody typical ….. There's always something extra to do for him. It was strange really, I'd never seen the chest in the house before but the weird part about it, was the fact that he wanted it moved to Mannez Quarry."

"But there's nothing at Mannez Quarry other than the train and the train shed," Richard said.

"Yeah well, that's what we thought," Ben replied. "But there's a tunnel in the rock face. It's one that the forced labourers dug out for the Germans during the occupation of Alderney in the Second World War."

"I didn't even know about the tunnel until today," Luis said. "I'd guess it's about one hundred metres in length and there's a couple of offshoots as well. We had to carry the chest all the way to the end of the tunnel. Christ knows why, but that's my Dad for you. Well weird eh Ben?"

"Too bloody right. Plain stupid if you ask me, but who cares as long as we get paid for the job."

Luis nodded in agreement as Lilly touched both of the lads on the back of the head and they lost consciousness ….
"Quickly Usha, do your 'mind thing' before they come round."

Usha placed her hands on Ben and Luis' foreheads and concentrated …. *You will forget everything that has happened in the last ten minutes.* Usha moved her hands away as the boys came round to the sound of clinking bottles as Alex and Chloe approached.

"There you go guys, a couple of beers. Looks like you need them, a busy day eh?" Alex asked.

"Er, yeah. A big plumbing job and then we had to move a chest eh Luis."

"Hmm, yeah sure," Luis replied, as Lilly decided having heard this conversation before, sat on Luis' knee and kissed him passionately. *Hmm, that's rather nice.*

"Right guys, we're going now," Richard said as he helped Annie out of her chair and held her hand, giving her a loving look. "Does anyone need a lift?"

The teenagers looked at each other and shook their heads. "No thanks Grandad," Usha said. "We've all got our scooters."

"Okay then, we'll see you all soon. Phone me to let me know how you get on". Richard and Annie sauntered away hand in hand down the gravel path and through the rustic arch to the van in the car park.

"What was your Grandad on about?" Ben asked inquisitively.

"Oh, er, before you arrived we'd been discussing my homework for school, that's all," Usha replied. *Sorry luv, can't tell you.*

"When's Bea expecting you back home luv?" Annie asked.

Richard quickly glanced at Annie whilst trying to keep his eyes on the road ahead as he drove past the lighthouse …. "Well actually, she isn't, 'cos she flew to Guernsey this morning with one of her friends. She's not due back until tomorrow night …. Something about 'no available return flights today'. I was going to ask you if you wanted to stay the night gal. What d'ya think?"

Annie leant over and kissed her lover on his cheek. "Let's go to my place instead." She ran her hand across Richard's leg to his inner thigh and rubbed gently.

"Yeah, er fine." Richard could feel the anticipation building up inside him.

Annie nibbled and licked Richard's ear knowing full well he was trying to concentrate on his driving. She ran her fingers through his hair .… "You'll be gentle with me won't you," she said teasingly.

"Ha! Speak for yourself gal .… And when you've finished with me, we can take a look at our notes that we've collected so far about the Inca platter dish. What d'ya think?"

"Yeah, you're right, we need to be on the ball for that Zoom call tomorrow. Actually, there's quite a lot to collate so it'll have to be a quickie tonight luv." Annie grinned.

"Ha! Yeah right. Your interpretation of a quickie doesn't relate to any known time scale."

The two lovers laughed out loud.

"C'mon, let me concentrate on the driving luv otherwise we'll never get to your place."

"Your Grandad seems to be in a better place these days, you know, happier," Luis said as he grabbed his bottle of beer from the table. "I'm guessing that Annie is the new woman in his life."

"C'mon Luis, say it as it is .… Yes, he's having an affair. What of it?" snapped Usha. "If he's comfortable with the situation and if it makes him happy, so be it. He still loves our Grandma, but in a different way. Who are we to judge. Grandad's worked all his life whilst loving and protecting all of his family, including us. We are all here on this planet once, so I think he's decided to make the most of the rest of his life." Usha rose from her chair and stormed off in the direction of the restaurant trying to hide her tears.

"Now look what you've done." Chloe stared at Luis as Lilly nudged him with some annoyance.

"What?" Luis shrugged his shoulders. "I haven't done anything."

"No, but you know how fond Usha is of Grandad," Lilly said. "It's a tricky subject Luis, and the relationship between Annie and our Grandad is not common knowledge. So a word of warning, keep it to yourself."

"Yeah, yeah. Okay. I get it. Sorry luv." Luis kissed Lilly on her cheek.

In the meantime Chloe had followed Usha into the restaurant. *Where is she?* Chloe's puzzled look drew the attention of one of the waitresses. "Are you looking for your friend?" Chloe nodded and smiled as the waitress pointed to the ladies toilets.

Chloe pushed the door open and walked into the rest room. She immediately heard sobbing from one of the four cubicles opposite the wash basins and mirrors. "Usha .... Usha, it's me, Chloe." The sobbing continued. Chloe pushed on the cubicle doors in turn, each swinging open. *Well she must be in this one, it's locked!* "Usha, let me in." Chloe thumped her fists on the door as the sobbing suddenly stopped .... "USHA, USHA .... LET ME IN .... COME ON GAL!" Chloe tried to look under the cubicle door and immediately realised blood was running along the tiled floor from inside the cubicle .... "OH SHOOT! USHA!" .... Chloe raised her hand to the lock. The teenager concentrated and the bolt of the lock slid across. Chloe pushed the door open and gasped audibly ....

Usha was slumped forward on the toilet seat, thick red blood seeping from a self inflicted gash across one of her wrists ....

Without thinking, Chloe instinctively pulled her belt from around the waistband of her jeans and quickly wrapped it around Usha's upper arm and pulled it tight to act as a tourniquet. *Come on Usha, let's get you out of this cubicle.* She slid her arms under Usha's and dragged her onto the tiled flooring of the restroom laying her cousin down carefully and placing her head on her jacket that she'd removed minutes earlier. *Jeez! She's been secretly self harming. Look at all the scars on her arms .... Bloody hell.* Chloe knelt down, holding her hand over Usha's body whilst holding her pendant with the other and began to chant .... "I am Alnitak the Healer and Child of the Stars." A bright white light enveloped Usha as Chloe moved her hand across the length of Usha before the light dissipated and Usha sat up completely healed.

"Oh Usha!" Chloe held her cousin tightly and rocked her back and forth. "Why? Why Usha?"

Usha burst into tears .... "Chloe ...." She stuttered as she tried to gulp air into her young lungs.

"Come on gal, try and calm down .... Take this tissue."

"I'm .... I'm so confused Chloe." Usha sighed as she wiped tears from her face. "Why .... Why is Grandad seeing Annie? I

315

love him to bits and I love Grandma as well. Does he still love Grandma? And what about me? What's going on Chloe? I don't understand."

"Is this what it's all about gal? Why didn't you say something?"

"I can't talk to Mum and Dad about it 'cos it's supposed to be Grandad's secret and I can't say anything to any of the teachers at school. It's awful Chloe, what am I going to do?"

"What about talking to Lilly about it."

"You've gotta to be kidding me. She's never around 'cos there's always another heavenly battle to deal with and I daren't tell Ben in case something slips out about what we're doing, you know."

"Look, I know it's a difficult situation but you can't continue to cut yourself. It doesn't achieve anything. I've had to deal with plenty of crap deals over the last few years and believe me when I say, taking your own life is NOT the answer. No-one or anything, is worth that sort of crap."

"But …."

"But nothing missee. You're one of the toughest and bravest girls I know, so take some of your own medicine and fight your way through this. I promise you, it gets better. It's all about life and growing up …. Well now is the time to grow up and take charge of your life. Got it?"

Usha nodded. "You won't tell the others will you?"

"Of course not gal, but I think you need to have an honest chat with Grandad. He needs to know that you're struggling with the situation that he's created by having an affair with Annie. But you have to understand Usha that they've been in love for years, before we were around. That's not an excuse, but it's something you need to bear in mind when you talk to him …. Okay?"

"Yeah, okay Chloe. Thanks."

"No probs'." Chloe helped Usha to her feet. "We'd better clean this mess up before we go."

CHAPTER 41

MAY THE FORCE BE WITH YOU

It was a cold dark night and the rain that had been promised earlier in the day had just started ....

"Brilliant, that's just typical. We're gonna get wet through standing here waiting for Lilly," Chloe moaned.

"What about Usha? Is she not coming then?" Alex asked.

"Er .... No," Chloe replied hesitantly. "I told her to spend the evening at home with her Mum and Dad. Besides, this shouldn't take long."

Alex gave Chloe an enquiring look.

"Don't worry luv," Chloe said. "Usha's got issues with herself at the mo'." *Which I'm not goin' to tell you about.*

"Oh okay."

"C'mon, let's get inside the tunnel. It's just over there." Chloe pointed across the quarry floor to what looked like a cave entrance in the surrounding granite rock face. "I'm not standing here any more, getting wet through." Chloe took hold of Alex's hand and encouraged him to walk with her ....

"Are you sure about this gal? Shouldn't we wait for Lilly?"

"We'll be fine luv. We're only interested in the contents of the chest .... C'mon, watch your head luv."

The teenagers crouched down as they stepped through the entrance to the tunnel which had been hewn out of the surrounding granite rock. Once inside, they were able to fully stand up.

"Did you bring your torch Alex?"

"Yeah sure .... There you go." The beam of light from his torch briefly blinded Chloe. "Oops, sorry gal .... There you go." Alex pointed the torch down the tunnel revealing the floor to be covered with about ten centimetres of water. "It looks like we're still goin' to get our feet wet anyway gal."

"Hmm. Well my feet are already wet and it looks like the level is rising luv. Look at the roof and walls. All this rain is permeating through the rock so we don't want to be hanging around for long."

Alex nodded in agreement. "Are you sure about this? The tunnel appears to be on a slight gradient falling away from us so the water is gonna' be deeper the further we go, which means it's not really safe to go any further. I mean, we could do this at another time don't you think?"

"Yeah we could, but aren't you curious as to what's in that chest?"

"Well yeah, of course, but ...."

"C'mon Alex, let's get this done and stop being a wimp .... Shine the torch ahead, slightly pointing to the floor so we can see where to step 'cos there's rocks and all sorts of rubbish under the water."

"Okay gal." *Don't blame me if this all goes tits up!*

The water level was slowly rising as the pair carefully waded further down the tunnel passing two other smaller openings in the walls that Alex casually directed the beam of light down. *Intriguing,* he thought.

A sudden crash from behind startled the couple causing them to momentarily halt ....

"What d'ya think Chloe?"

She shrugged her shoulders. "Perhaps some of the roof has fallen down .... I really don't know. C'mon, it can't be much further." Chloe gave her boyfriend a gentle nudge.

"Have you noticed? If you look carefully in the water, there seems to be tracks of some description." Alex stopped and shone the torch to the floor around where they stood .... "Look, there. See what I mean. They look exactly the same as railway tracks."

Chloe took the torch from Alex and crouched down to take a closer look. "You're right, definitely railway tracks but a smaller gauge than what you'd normally see. I'll ask Grandad about it next time I see him." Chloe passed the torch back to Alex as she stood up. "C'mon, let's make a move 'cos this water is getting deeper."

Alex shone the torch ahead as he stepped forward .... "There Chloe. Look, the chest. It's nearly submerged in all this water."

The teenagers struggled to paddle the last few steps to the end of the tunnel as water continued to run down the walls as it permeated through the ground and rock above them ....

"Two padlocks gal, sheesh!"

"No problem." Chloe held her pendant whilst placing her other hand on the two padlocks.

Alex watched as his girlfriend's eyes turned red and the padlocks dropped into the water. "Good job gal." He reached forward and lifted the wooden lid of the chest back on its hinges, and shone the torch inside ....

The teenagers looked inside excitedly and then glanced at each other with despondent faces. "Well that's a total let down," Alex grumbled. "I don't know about you luv, but I was expecting to find a huge stash of money and the missing gold platter dish."

"Damn it," Chloe growled. "I reckon we've been set up. All we've got is a good soaking and a chest with nothing but a lump of rock in it. What a load of crap." She picked up the tennis ball sized rock in disgust ....

"Chloe, the rock is starting to glow."

"Yeah and I can feel it vibrating .... Weird."

"I think you should put it down Chloe, the green light is getting brighter."

The green pulsating light was mesmerising, almost blinding in its intensity.

"Chloe, let it go ….. Chloe, NOW." A huge surge of light lit up the tunnel and then …. Nothing. Total silence. Chloe had gone. "CHLOE!.... CHLOEEEE!!" Alex sank to his knees in total despair.

"Alex …. ALEX. ARE YOU THERE?"

Alex turned his head slightly as he heard a familiar voice echoing from further up the tunnel.

"ALEX …. WHERE ARE YOU?"

"IS THAT YOU LILLY? I'M HERE, AT THE END OF THE TUNNEL." Alex directed the beam of light from his torch up the tunnel to help Lilly find him …. And there she was, paddling towards him.

"Why didn't you wait for me as we arranged?" Lilly asked.

"We did for a while, but Chloe was getting impatient. You know how she is."

"Hmm yeah. Talking of Chloe, where is she?"

Alex began to tear up as he told her what had happened. How his girlfriend had seemingly just vanished into thin air. "All I know Lilly, is that she picked the rock up out of the chest, it started to glow green and then there was a blinding flash …. She's gone Lilly …. We've lost Chloe."

Lilly placed her arm round Alex's shoulders. "Come on mate, pull y'self together. I know it's difficult, but we'll find her …. I promise. Now then, is this the rock Chloe took from the chest?" Lilly pointed to a rock on the ground submerged in the water.

"Yeah, that's the one," Alex replied as Lilly bent down to pick it up. "Be careful Lilly."

Well here goes nothing! Lilly grabbed the rock and pulled it up out of the rising water and stood with her arm outstretched. "Nothing, I don't feel anything Alex."

"Give it to me."

"Are you sure mate?"

Alex nodded as Lilly passed the rock to her friend. He held it for a few moments and then dropped the rock in his jacket pocket. "I don't understand Lilly. Why would it react with Chloe but not with either of us?"

Lilly shrugged her shoulders. "I have no idea Alex. We'll get the rock home and see if any of the guys have any suggestions. In the meantime, I'll put this other rock in the chest, close it and make good the padlocks 'cos we need to get out of here. The water level is rising quite rapidly now."

"Yeah okay Lilly, let's go …. But what about Chloe?"

"We'll figure it out mate, we always do. She'll be okay Alex. She knows how to take care of herself …. Come on, before we both drown in here."

"Just there luv …. Ooh that's so good."

Richard ran his hands across Annie's naked breasts as she straddled him and slowly moved up and down, arching her slender back ….

"Confusion will be my epitaph, As I crawl a cracked and broken path, If we make it we can all sit back and laugh, But I fear tomorrow I will be crying …."

"Jeez, is that your phone?" Annie panted as she rolled away from Richard.

"Er, yeah, sorry luv." Richard picked up his phone that was playing Epitaph by King Crimson. *Usha, what does she want?* "Hi gal, what's up?"

"Just letting you know that I'm on my way round to your place Grandad."

"Er, well I'm at Annie's house, but you're okay to call round."

"Oh, right. I won't be long. I'd better let Lilly and Alex know 'cos they were on their way to your place," Usha replied.

"What's this all about?"

"I'm just passing a message on. All I know is that it was urgent. Something to do with Chloe."

"Alright Usha. We'll see you soon."

"I take it that was Usha," Annie said.

"Yeah, sorry luv. You'd better get dressed 'cos it looks like we might have 'trouble at mill'."

Uurgh! Christ, where the hell am I? Chloe's eyes slowly opened as she tried to lift herself up from the ground. She glanced around trying to decipher her surroundings. The only light was coming from a low arch in the curved stone wall that surrounded her. She looked up to see that the whole structure was in fact made of stones of various shapes and sizes which bizarrely gave her the impression of being inside a bee hive. She stood up and walked to the opening in the wall and stepped out. "WOW!" *I'm on an island. I'm surrounded by the ocean.* Chloe stood perfectly still, soaking in the views of the crashing waves below her and a number of other stone structures that looked identical to the one she had, somehow, arrived in. *All this looks vaguely familiar. I've seen these structures somewhere but I just can't remember,* Chloe thought. *One thing's for sure, I'm by myself. The only sounds are birds calling and the waves crashing onto the rocks below. I'd better take a good look around before darkness descends.*

The faintest flutter of wings disturbed the air in Annie's kitchen as Lilly appeared, accompanied by Alex who looked quite unwell after his flight.

"Hi guys …. You don't look too good Alex," remarked Annie.

Annie smiled coyly to herself. She'd experienced travelling with Lilly herself. *It was frightening and yet exhilarating as Lilly's wings propelled us through the air as I held her hand in flight. A bit like being on a fairground ride at altitude. Ha!*

"You'll be okay in a minute Alex …. Is Usha here yet?" Lilly asked.

"Not yet. She should ...." Richard's reply was interrupted by the sound of frantic knocking at the front door. "That'll be her now. Let her in Annie please."

"Hi Annie, thanks. Have Lilly and Alex arrived yet?" asked Usha as she removed her coat and hung it up on the last remaining coat hook on the back of the door.

"Yeah they're here gal. Come on, they're all in the kitchen," Annie replied.

The friends hugged Usha in turn before Richard pulled a chair from under the table and sat down, indicating to the others to do the same ....

"So .... What's this all about?" Richard asked.

Alex immediately started to explain what had happened earlier in the evening in the tunnel at Mannez Quarry and how Chloe had disappeared in the blink of an eye.

"I picked the rock up but nothing transpired and I certainly didn't pick up or feel any mystical properties," Lilly said. "And when I gave it to Alex, again, nothing happened."

Alex shook his head. "Nothing, I felt absolutely nothing. I've got the rock here." He took the rock out of his pocket and placed it on the table. "And just so you all know, we put another rock in the chest and Lilly reattached the two padlocks just in case Luis' Dad or whoever returns."

Richard picked the rock up nervously and gave it a cursory inspection. "Well it obviously doesn't react with me and to be honest I don't see anything that makes it special."

"Let me have a look luv," Annie said, as she took it out of Richard's hand. "It's just a rock eh? Oh hang on, look at this." She turned it ninety degrees and held it up to show everyone. "What d'ya see? Apart from the fact that it's highly polished on that one side."

"It's a six sided polygon .... In fact, it's a hexagon," Usha said.

"Quite right," replied Annie, "and I've seen that shape before on something else. Excuse me guys, I'll be back in a mo'." She rose from her chair and left the room only to return almost immediately. "Recognise this guys?"

"Of course," Richard replied. "The Inca Platter dish." He picked the rock up and placed it in the hexagon shaped indentation in the centre of the dish. "It fits perfectly …. Well that's solved that mystery but we still have no idea what it's for or how it helps Chloe."

"Maybe not luv, but it's something else we can discuss tomorrow in that Zoom call with the Professor," Annie replied.

"Yeah that's true. Look, we're not getting anywhere at the moment. Does anyone have any ideas?"

Alex turned to Lilly and Usha. "Have either of you tried contacting with your mind controls?"

"I've already tried Alex and strangely I've got nothing, which is worrying 'cos normally it's never a problem," replied Lilly. "What about you Usha?"

Usha didn't answer. It was if she was somewhere else, far away. She was staring at the rock in the centre of the dish ….

Lilly was about to give her sister a nudge, when Richard intervened and indicated to everyone to sit still and stay quiet as Usha continued to stare at the rock without blinking....

I can feel some sort of force drawing me to the rock. This is well weird. It's as if it's talking to me …. It's a bloody rock gal! Hang on, I'm starting to get an image ….

The group of friends watched intently as Usha's eyes turned green. She reached out slowly and placed both hands on the rock which instantly started to glow green …. Usha moved her hands away from the rock and as she remained in a trance like state, the glowing rock produced an arc of green light about a metre in height.

"Look at that guys," Richard said. "It's a hologram."

The green arc of light flickered as the images became clearer.

"There's Chloe, look," Alex exclaimed. "This is weird. You can see her walking between those huts …. Are they huts?"

"Not sure Alex. I thought they looked a bit like oversized bee hives," Annie replied.

"I think I know where Chloe is," Lilly interrupted.

"Where?" Richard asked.

"The huts that we can see in the hologram are the bee hive monastic huts on Skellig Michael off the west coast of Ireland," Lilly explained. "The only reason I recognise the sixth century huts or cells as they're also known, is because they were featured in the Star War films, you know, The Force Awakens and so forth."

"Of course Lilly, spot on," Richard replied. "If I remember rightly, that's where they went to train to be Jedi Knights. How weird is that."

"So what the hell is Chloe doing there?" Alex asked. "She's hardly training to be a Jedi Knight is she? The Star Wars franchise is pure fiction."

The friends looked at each in bemusement as they continued to watch the hologram until ….

A huge explosion of green light filled the room and Usha disappeared, seemingly sucked in by the light which dissipated in a blink of an eye leaving the rock in the centre of the platter dish ….

"Noooooo!!!" Lilly screamed. "Usha's gone," she sobbed.

"Get after her," Richard said. "Follow her now you know where to go."

"I can't Grandad …. Even with my powers of an angel I'm not allowed to set foot on Skellig Michael."

"Why's that Lilly?" Annie asked.

"There are certain places in this world where angels fear to tread."

"Hmm, that's a title of a novel by E.M. Forster. It was also made into a film you know," Richard mused.

"That's not helping Grandad," snapped Lilly. "I was going to say that angels aren't allowed to visit UNESCO World Heritage Sites for fear of any interference."

"Oh I see, but it would take any of us weeks to get there, so we're going to either have to find another way or …."

"Or we wait to see if Chloe and Usha can figure it out," Alex interrupted. "At least they've now got each other for support."

"What the hell?" Usha exclaimed. She picked herself up off the granite stone which at first glance appeared to be a quay of some sort for the disembarking of sailors or fishermen. The tell tale signs of boats having moored there were lying all around. Fishing nets and rope were lying on the ground with a couple of old lobster pots that had seen better days. The crashing of waves thundering against the quay shook Usha out of her thoughts …. She turned round to face a seemingly endless steep climb of ancient stone steps which twisted and turned, upwards through the craggy outcrops of stone to what looked like stone structures some two hundred metres above her. The teenager checked her phone .... *No signal. No surprise there, seeing as I seem to be in the middle of nowhere.* She concentrated on her powers to connect to anyone's thoughts .... *Nothing ....*

Oh well, onwards and upwards .... It's starting to get dark, I'd better have my light staff. Usha concentrated momentarily and held her hand out as her light staff materialised. "CHLOE!" she shouted. And again, "CHLOEEEE!" *She can't hear me. Oh well, I'd better start climbing these steps before the darkness sets in and makes it dangerous.*

Usha was about half way up the steps. *Sheesh! Take a breather.* She sat down momentarily and looked out to sea. *Nothing but the crashing of waves and the stars in the sky.* "CHLOE .... CHLOEEEE!" Usha shouted. *Better make a move.*

Thirty minutes later and Usha was standing at the top of the steps admiring the seven bee hive huts. "CHLOE," she shouted, but again there was no reply. *It's too dark to go any further. I'll spend the night in this bee hive and start again in the morning.* Usha entered the structure and sat down on the stone floor totally exhausted.

"Well there's nothing else we can do tonight," Lilly said. "Let's wait to see if your Zoom call tomorrow turns anything up Grandad."

"I suppose you're right. Hopefully, Annie and I can get some answers."

"Yeah. Hope so," Lilly replied. "D'ya want a lift home Alex?" She put her arm around his waist and before he could answer they had disappeared in an instant save for the faintest flutter of wings.

"Right luv, are we going to bed?" Annie asked as she slid her hand between Richard's thighs and kissed him tenderly on his cheek. "I've got a feeling it's going to be a long day tomorrow .... And to be honest I'm feeling decidedly horny tonight." Annie could feel Richard's jeans were at bursting point.

"Yeah okay gal, you've convinced me."

CHAPTER 42

ALL THAT GLITTERS

Chloe stirred as she heard the screeching of seagulls as they flew overhead in the early morning light ....

"What the hell?" The teenager opened her eyes slowly as they adjusted to the light. She shivered as a cold gust of wind blew through her long dishevelled hair. "Christ, I ache all over." She stood up with a struggle, as she twisted her young aching body from side to side to encourage the circulation of blood. *I need to warm myself up,* she thought, and started to jog on the spot, quite gingerly at first before being a little more enthusiastic with the speed. Chloe stopped for a breather and rubbed her hands together to ease the pain in her aching cold fingers. *I really could do with making a fire of some sort to keep myself warm. But how?*

Chloe .... Chloe. Where are you? Usha was in Chloe's head. ***I'm here .... On the same island as you .... Where are you?***

Usha .... Thank God. I'm in, what I think is a small church on the plateau at the north-eastern summit.

Okay, don't move. I reckon it'll take me five or ten minutes to reach you. Usha smiled to herself in relief to know that she would see her cousin once more. She stepped out of the bee hive that had been her shelter for the night and made her way around the dry stone walling, until she found an opening which gave way to what used to be a small garden. "CHLOE .... CHLOE, ARE YOU HERE?" Usha turned full circle for any sight of her cousin.

"OVER HERE."

Usha spun round to see Chloe stood in a stone archway about ten metres away from where she stood. "CHLOE," she shouted as she ran to her cousin and embraced her lovingly.

"It's so good to see you gal. You're shivering. Are you okay?" Usha took a step back. "You don't look too good Chloe."

Chloe shook her head. She could hardly speak as she was shaking violently from being so cold.

"Sit down cuz, I'll get you warm." Chloe sat and watched as Usha quickly wandered around picking up pieces of granite, twice the size of bowling balls with ease .... Her newly acquired power of super human strength was coming in handy as she built a pile of stone in front of her cousin and then proceeded to squeeze each piece of granite .... They glowed with heat as Usha exerted pressure on the stones before she sat down next to Chloe and placed her arm around her shoulders.

"So .... so h how did you f find me? How d did you g get here?" Chloe asked as she shivered.

"Hmm, well I think it was the stone in the middle of the Inca Platter Dish."

"What? The stone fits in the dish?"

"Yeah it fits perfectly. But what I don't understand is, why or how it transported you here Chloe? I mean, I barely touched it but in a strange way I felt I could control it as it produced a hologram. It was if it was showing me where you was but then, wallop, I was here .... You any warmer?"

"Yeah, a little bit thanks. It's all a bit weird gal, 'cos when I picked the stone up from inside the chest, it immediately glowed with an intense green colour and in an instant I was here. By the way, where is here?"

"Ha, thought you'd never ask. We are off the west coast of Ireland on the island of Skellig Michael. Apparently it's a UNESCO World Heritage Site and very few people visit the island and that's only during good periods of weather during the summer."

"Oh," Chloe groaned. "But surely Lilly could wing her way here in an instant."

"That isn't going to happen," Usha said as she shook her head. "From what I could make out from Lilly, angels aren't allowed to visit World Heritage Sites for fear of the damage their powers can do. I suppose you can understand up to a point, I mean, these monastic bee hive huts were built in the sixth century."

"Wow, really? So we're all alone then?"

"Yep .... Are you feeling any better?" asked Usha. "We should take a good look around and see if we can figure out this mystery."

"A lot better now thanks. You're right of course." Chloe struggled to her feet. "Come on, let's go. Let's start in this small graveyard."

"I'm assuming this graveyard must have been for the monks that lived here all those years ago," Usha remarked as she studied one of the roughly made crosses.

"Probably gal, although these other three graves have headstones made of wood and it sort of looks as if they've each been roughly carved, to look like a person. They've got very faint inscriptions .... That's strange, if I'm reading these correctly, these graves belong to women. That can't be right. The monks that lived here all those years ago would have been grown men."

"Well obviously Chloe ...."

"No I mean, there wouldn't have been any women living here."

"Hmm, does sound a bit weird. C'mon, let's take a look on the other side of that stone wall. There's a gap in the wall over there."

329

The two teenagers followed each other as they criss crossed the cemetery trying not to walk upon any graves. They reached the gap in the stone wall. It wasn't very wide so the girls squeezed themselves through sideways and immediately held each others hand as three vertical columns of flames appeared two metres directly in front of them ....

"Bloody hell Usha. What's going on?"

"Awesome!"

The flames quickly died down to reveal three slim, pretty young women who looked to be about one and a half metres high and around twenty years old. Usha immediately observed that they were probably triplets as they looked identical in every way. Long red hair, brown eyes and hour glass figures. Even their clothing was the same, shamrock green ankle length dresses with boots to match!

"And what have we got here girls?" The women on the left pointed at the teenagers.

"It looks like these two are lost eh?"

The three women laughed amongst themselves as Usha and Chloe watched in bewilderment.

The woman turned to the other two and whispered .... "Let's practice some magic on them." She quickly spun round to face the two cousins. The three women blurted out a couple of unrecognisable words as they raised their hands .... A searing bright white light filled the air which surrounded Usha and Chloe and rebounded, hitting the three women, knocking them to the ground.

"What's wrong Lilly? You look as white as a ghost," Alex asked.

"I just felt this sudden surge of energy. Something's happened to Usha and Chloe, I can feel it. I'm going to have to go Alex. I realise that I can't physically set foot on the island of Skellig Michael but I'll feel a lot happier if I'm close by, if you know what I mean."

"Yeah sure gal. I totally get it. You go. Let me know as soon as you find the girls."

Lilly kissed Alex on the cheek and save for the faintest flutter of wings, Lilly disappeared.

Chloe and Usha burst into laughter as the three women struggled back to their feet, brushing themselves down and looking decidedly annoyed and bemused ....

"Okay, who didn't say the right spell?" The women on the left snapped and then they started to argue with each other.

"Er .... Hello." Chloe said as the three continued to disagree with each other.

"Jeez, sod this for a game of soldiers," Usha grumbled. "OY YOU THREE!"

"I think you got their attention gal," Chloe said with a big grin as the three women stopped arguing. "Who ARE you and WHAT are you?"

"Well my name is Lola and this is Ruby, my sister and the stroppy cow on the end is my other sister, Samantha."

"The name is Sam thank you very much and I want to know why our magic doesn't work on you two eh. Why?" Sam stomped her feet and placed her hands on her hips in disgust.

Chloe and Usha looked at each other, giggled and smiled in the knowledge they'd found someone else with the same sort of attitude as Usha.

"Why should your magic work on us?" Chloe asked.

"Because," Ruby said, "it should."

"That's not a good reason," Usha replied as the sunlight hit her pendant causing it to glint.

"Arh, the blonde one has a pretty," Ruby said. "That's why the magic doesn't work." The other two women nodded in agreement.

"You mean this?" Usha grabbed her pendant and held it so that the women could see it better.

"Yes yes. A pretty." Lola smiled.

"I have a pretty, er ... pendant too," Chloe revealed as she held it up. "So come on then, if you can use magic, what are you?"

"One moment," said Lola. The three sisters turned away from Usha and Chloe as they whispered argumentatively between themselves. After a few minutes they turned around to face the teenagers ....

Ruby stepped forward and nodded her head as she offered her hand to Chloe who gently shook it as she introduced herself. "My name's Chloe and this is my cousin Usha." Ruby shook Usha's hand who squeezed it tightly, not too tight as she didn't want to crush Ruby's hand ….

"Ah, Usha is all powerful in strength," Ruby indicated to Sam and Lola as they both stepped forward, nodded their heads and shook the teenager's hands.

"So where do the three of you come from and what are you?" Usha asked.

"We are Fae," Lola said. "I suppose you know our species better as fairies."

"Awesome."

"Oh wow," Chloe said. "But I thought fairies had wings and I'm not being funny, but aren't fairies supposed to be incy wincy tiny tiny."

Usha smirked and giggled.

"You've obviously watched too many Disney films and read too many fairy tales," Sam said. "I mean, come on, the likes of Cinderella has done us fairies no favours at all. Fairies come in all shapes and sizes from a few centimetres in height and a few do have wings, but they're in the higher order who live in Fairy Land. Myself and my sisters are about the average height for where we live."

"And where's that?" Usha asked.

"We're from the Isle of Man. We live at the Fairy Bridge in the south of the island." Ruby explained.

"The three of us moved there about two hundred years ago from the west coast of Ireland, just across the water there." Ruby pointed across the sea to the Irish coastline that was clearly visible from their vantage point."

"Two hundred years ago? So how old are you?" Chloe asked.

The three sisters muttered to each other ....

"We were born on this island in the sixth century," Lola said. "Our mothers are buried here in the small graveyard."

"Whoa, whoa," Usha interrupted. "But you're triplets and you don't look a day over twenty. How can that be?"

"Fairies get to a certain age and then our appearance doesn't alter as we get older. We don't know why we had different mothers but we're definitely triplets. The three of us were born here on this island at exactly the same time on the same day. The honest answer is, we don't know," Sam said. "We've always been told that fairies have only ever been born as a single baby. Maybe that's why our mothers were brought here to Skellig Michael to keep us safe. Our mothers all sadly died giving birth to us and the monks who lived here raised us as their own."

"I think we actually left here when we was sixteen years old," Ruby explained. "It's all a bit vague, but we've since found out from our friends on the Isle of Man that fairies become aware of their powers of magic once they turn sixteen."

"It seems reasonable to assume that we couldn't have left Skellig Michael before then," Sam said, "as there was no other way of leaving."

"So why are you and Chloe here?" Lola asked Usha.

"That's a very good question. It's something we'd like to know isn't it Chloe?"

"It sure is. There has to be a reason," Chloe said as she quickly continued to explain their story of the search for the lost Inca treasure in Alderney, their powers and their continuing fight for good over evil as the three fairies listened intently.

"So we don't know how we arrived here other than finding a granite stone which glows an iridescent green. Chloe found it in a chest and is connected in some way to the golden Inca platter style dish that she mentioned earlier. It generates some sort of transportation power, but we have no idea why it would bring us to this island," Usha said.

Lola and Ruby turned to Sam who had suddenly gone all coy ....

"What?"

"Don't give us that look Samantha. What have you been up too?" Ruby asked.

"We told you not to play with that dish we found didn't we," Lola said.

"Yeah I know, but ...."

"But what?" Lola snapped. "You know not to play with things that you don't understand."

"Whoa, hang on a minute," Chloe interrupted. "Are you telling us that you have a golden Inca platter style dish?"

Sam looked to the sky and mumbled "Er ... Yes."

"Sorry girls. We didn't know that Sam had been playing around with the dish. To be honest, we didn't even know what it was until Chloe explained earlier, about the one you already have," Lola said.

"It's a fairy trait," Ruby explained. "We collect pretties. Anything shiny. We collect pretties because our magic doesn't affect them, we have thousands."

"Really?" Usha asked.

"Oh yes," Sam replied. "Thousands .... D'ya want to see them?"

"Hell yeah." Usha replied.

"It's not far," Ruby said. "We'll take you to where we keep our pretties. Just hold our hands."

Chloe and Usha held hands with the three fairies to form a circle and instantly disappeared in a ball of light ...

"Here we are then," said Lola as the light dissipated. "All safe and sound."

"Where are we?" Chloe asked.

"This is our pretty room," Sam replied.

"It doesn't look very pretty to me .... Ha!" Usha giggled. "It looks more like a dungeon, or even a crypt." Usha glanced around the huge stone room. The ceiling was low. *Okay, maybe not for fairies!* What light there was, came from eight wooden torches hanging precariously around the stone walls. What struck Usha was the fact that there was no visible doorways or windows and the damp smell indicated that they were underground. *We could easily be trapped in this place.*

"We are beneath the monks church," Ruby said. "The monks used to hide us in here whenever they thought it was too dangerous for us to be seen on the island. They were frightened that the Muki would find us."

"Hang on a mo'," Chloe interrupted. "What's Muki?"

"A Muki is a pale goblin. They can be nasty pieces of work. Very malicious and they crave pretties," Sam replied. "They usually work and travel by themselves as they like to keep everything they find to themselves."

"They're quite powerful as well," Lola explained. "They have magical abilities second only to fairies. Mind you, at least they're smaller than us, here, I'll show you." Lola rubbed her hands together and clapped as she muttered a couple of words in fairy tongue ....

An image of a Muki goblin appeared as a hologram in the centre of the room. "He's an ugly critter," Usha said. Chloe nodded in agreement as they studied the hologram. The pale brawny goblin stood about half a metre high with a large hairy head, with two horns which protruded from it's skull just above it's pointed ears. It's reddish head seemed to blend into it's body with no neck to speak of, but maybe that was down to the long white beard and long blonde hair! "Look at the size of it's feet, they're huge," said Usha.

"Ha, never mind it's feet, look at the blonde hair." Chloe laughed. "It's exactly like yours Usha."

The three fairies joined in the laughter as the hologram disappeared.

"Humph, that's not funny guys," Usha said. "So where does this grumpy looking git come from?"

"Well they generally live in caves and the Muki come from the caves in the Andes according to Quechuan legends," Sam replied.

"You are joking, right? Chloe, did you hear what Sam just said?"

"Er, yeah gal. Are you absolutely certain Sam?"

"Of course we are girls, we've known about the Muki for centuries 'cos they're our biggest enemies. They try to steal our pretties," Sam replied. "We hadn't seen one for a hundred years or so until …."

"Until what?" Usha asked.

"Until a couple of months ago,"Lola replied. "About the same time Sam found the golden Inca platter dish."

"Shoot! All this time Chloe. I don't believe it."

"Ruby, can we take a look at your pretties?" Chloe asked.

"Of course." Ruby extended her arm and slowly moved it above the floor as she spoke in fairy tongue ….

The ground shook as five huge stone coffin style containers rose from the ground and as the fairy clapped her hands, the stone lids of the containers slid to the side, to reveal thousands upon thousands of every type of jewel and treasure anyone could imagine. Usha and Chloe looked on in astonishment as the three fairies ran their hands through the treasures.

"That's …. That's just incredible." Usha gasped.

"Unbelievable," added Chloe. "This lot is worth an absolute fortune."

"Here is the Inca dish girls." Sam picked the dish up from one of the containers. "Is it what you've been looking for?" She passed it to Usha.

"Oh yes, yes indeedee, it certainly is," Usha replied as she ran her fingers around the indentations. "I don't suppose for one moment that you have any of the statues that stand in these indentations?"

"I don't remember seeing anything," Ruby replied. "Hang on, let me do a search spell on the containers." The fairy clapped her hands and held them over her head as she spoke in fairy tongue. A few moments passed …. "No, sorry girls. There's nothing here."

"Worth a try," Chloe said. "So where did you find the Inca dish Sam?"

"Well er, I was on one of my hunting trips with Lola, you know, for pretties and er, we was in France …. Did you ever hear about that incident in St Malo involving a car bomb?"

"Yeah, only too well Sam. I was caught up in it." Chloe sighed.

"Oh …. Well any way, amongst all the confusion I came across the two cretins who set off that car bomb with a remote control. They had this pretty with them, you know, the dish, so I put them under an enchantment and truthfulness spell and took this dish, along with this stone that fits in the centre. They then handed themselves into the police as I left to find Lola."

"I was injured in the blast," Lola said. "But you healed me Chloe didn't you? I remember as if it was yesterday."

"I er, healed a lot of people that day Lola. It was the right thing to do. I had no idea who you was, obviously."

Lola burst into tears and hugged Chloe. "You saved me from certain death Chloe and for that I will be forever grateful."

"We are all eternally grateful Chloe," said Ruby.

"Awesome." Usha grinned like a Cheshire cat.

"You are more than welcome to take the dish and the centre stone girls if it helps in your quest. Plus it will throw the Muki off our scent, although you will now have that problem to deal with," Sam said.

"I think we'll manage, eh Chloe?"

"I reckon."

"Right, that's settled then," Sam said. The fairy closed the containers which then sank back into the ground as she waved her hand from left to right, murmuring in fairy tongue. "We need to get back above ground. Form a circle everyone and hold hands." A ball of white light engulfed the five friends and immediately they were standing close to one of the bee hive structures as the cold wind blew through their hair.

"Wow, I can't get used to the way we are transported," Usha said. I've travelled with Lilly many times and it's a totally different experience."

"It's not very pleasant for humans," Ruby replied, "and we can only move you short distances, whereas we can travel anywhere when we use our magic pillars of fire."

"So what you're telling us, is that you three can leave this place anytime but it's impossible for myself and Usha," Chloe said.

"There is a way Chloe," Lola replied. "When the three of us shook your hands earlier today we all sensed the power of strength in Usha. We also know about your hidden gift Chloe."

"Which is?" Chloe asked.

"We believe you are a shapeshifter," Sam replied.

"Yes, without a doubt," Ruby said as Lola nodded in agreement.

"No. No that's not possible," Chloe replied. "I've never, ever changed my living form. That can't be."

"You may not have felt the need to shape-shift because of your other, more dominant powers," Lola explained. "But you do have that power and it's probably due to having a near death experience. Have you ever had one?"

"You've actually died gal, remember?" Usha said. "That day in the arch, at Saye Beach when Lilly killed you to release her soul."

"Er, yeah, I remember. But you brought me back Usha."

"Ah, the Phoenix Syndrome," Ruby interrupted. "It's more than likely that when Usha brought you back from the dead, she awoke the Phoenix within you. That is also why you was chosen to be the Healer by the stars of Orion."

"You look confused Chloe," Sam said. "Let me show you how fairies shape-shift."

"You can shape-shift as well?" Usha asked.

"Yes we can," Sam replied. "A lot of fairies can but it's generally the bigger and older ones. It seems to be a trend that's dying out. Anyway, I'll show you how we do it." Sam took one step back with her arms to her side, closed her eyes and shouted "MORPH!" as she quickly threw her arms up over her head and clapped, as her clothes dropped to the ground …..

A Siberian Tiger sat in front of the friends and roared.

"Whoa!" Usha and Chloe stepped back nervously as the tiger padded forward and rubbed itself against the girl's legs.

"Awesome. It's purring. Sorry, Sam's purring," Usha chuckled.

"How lovely." Chloe stroked the tiger as it shape-shifted back into Sam. "Oh, that's embarrassing," Chloe said as she moved her hand away from Sam's naked bottom.

That's a bit of a turn on .... Sam's body is just gorgeous.
Such soft skin, Chloe thought.

"Of course," Lola explained. "The downside is, as you've seen, when you change back you're totally naked so you need to try and pick your moment."

Chloe couldn't resist the urge after seeing Sam naked, it had re-awoken her hidden sexual feelings towards women. She fastened the clips on Sam's bra and helped her with her dress. "So is that all there is to it Sam?"

"Pretty much. Changing back is a natural occurrence. You just need to control when you change, obviously." Sam could feel Chloe's attraction to her. "Come on, give it a go. As you clap your hands just concentrate on what animal you want to shape-shift into."

Chloe took a step back with her arms to her side, closed her eyes and shouted "MORPH!" as she quickly threw her arms up over her head and clapped as her clothes dropped to the ground .....

"Wow!" Usha exclaimed, as a black raven flew up from the ground and landed on her shoulder and pecked her ear.

"Ha! Well done Chloe," Lola said. "You even have two blonde feathers just like the streaks in your hair."

The raven flew to Sam's hand and shape-shifted back into Chloe who kissed the fairy on her cheek. "Thank you Sam." The fairy smiled affectionately and licked her lips sensually.

"Er, Chloe," Usha said. "Your clothes .... You need to get dressed."

"Yeah okay gal." *I think Sam fancies me. Cool.* "Actually, there's not much point in getting dressed if we're leaving Usha."

"Chloe, I think your best chance of getting off this island with Usha," Ruby explained, "is to shape-shift into a Phoenix. That bird is seriously powerful and will be able to carry Usha with ease. I reckon it will take you about an hour to fly down to Alderney."

"Well there's no time like the present," said Chloe. "Make sure you've got the Inca dish and my clothes Usha."

"Right. Well girls, it's been lovely to meet you," Usha said to the three fairies.

"Yeah, thanks for everything," Chloe said. "We'll see each other again, soon I'm sure."

The friends embraced each other.

Chloe took a last look at Sam as she put her arms to her side and shouted "MORPH!" as she quickly threw her arms up over her head and clapped as she shape-shifted into a magnificent Phoenix. Usha laid down with a tight grip on the Inca dish as the giant bird hopped over and cradled Usha in it's huge claws. The Phoenix flapped it's wings and took off into the sky and quickly disappeared into the distance.

Lola turned to Sam and Ruby. "I hope they succeed in their quest. We need the world to be a safer place."

"I hope I see Chloe again girls," Sam said. "She was really nice." *I haven't had these feelings of love for a long time.*

"Let's go girls," said Ruby. The three fairies held hands and chanted in fairy tongue as three magical pillars of fire appeared and in an instant, Sam, Ruby and Lola disappeared.

CHAPTER 43

WOULD I LIE TO YOU?

"Ben … BEN! ARE YOU GETTING UP BOY?" Irene shouted up the stairs.

"Er, yeah. I'll be down in a few minutes Mum," Ben mumbled and then glanced at his clock through bleary eyes. *Jeez, it's only half past five. Who the hell wants me at this time of the morning?* Ben moved his legs over the edge of his bed and sat up. He pulled at the curtain hanging rather precariously in front of his bedroom window and peered out ….

Police car! What the hell? Ben picked up his clothes from the floor which he'd 'hung' there the night before and quickly dressed before stomping down the stairs.

Ben stepped into the kitchen and immediately felt all eyes were on him as he pulled out a chair from underneath the table and sat down opposite his Dad and the local police Sergeant.

"Well it took you long enough to surface my lad," his Dad, Albert said. He took another slurp of tea from his huge ceramic mug.

"It's okay Albert, er, Mr Allens, no need to upset your lad. Good morning Ben, I know it's early but your Mum and Dad have given me their permission to take you down to the police station to answer a few questions."

"What? You're kidding me. About what Sergeant Cordy?"

"We'll go through all that at the station Ben. Come on, let's get going." The Sergeant ushered Ben through the front door and towards the waiting police car. "Get in the back Ben and strap yourself in."

Ben opened the rear door of the car to reveal Luis sat in the back on the far side ….

"Hi Ben."

"Er, hi Luis." Ben sat next to his friend, pulled the car door shut and fastened his seat belt. "What's this all about mate? Do you know?"

Luis shook his head and shrugged his shoulders as the engine roared into life and the police car pulled away towards town.

"Here we are guys," the Sergeant said as he opened the rear door to the car. "Follow me. We'll use the interview suite." The two friends followed Sergeant Cordy into the police station and he opened the door to the interview room ….

"Hi guys." It was Alex. He was sat at the only table in the middle of the windowless room, coffee in hand.

"Take a seat lads." The Sergeant pointed to the chairs at the table as Ben and Luis wandered into the interview room looking somewhat shell shocked as to what was happening. Two further cups of coffee were placed in front of the two friends as they sat down.

Sergeant Cordy sat down opposite the three friends. "I suppose you're wondering why you're all here this morning."

Alex, Ben and Luis nodded in unison as the Sergeant continued …. "Well we are concerned about the whereabouts of your girlfriends, Lilly, Usha and Chloe."

The friends glanced at each other.

"They are your girlfriends? Yes?"

"Well, yes of course," Luis replied as his two friends nodded. "Why? Has something happened?"

"Well I was hoping one of you might be able to tell me where they are." The Sergeant's tone of voice was more serious than usual.

The three friends started to chuckle. "Is this what this is all about? Ha! Seriously?" Ben chortled.

"This is no laughing matter guys. Their parents are extremely concerned about their whereabouts, so, I'll ask you again. Do you know where they are?"

"I'm sorry Sergeant but, we don't know. We have as much idea as you. The girls are always missing so I don't see how we can help you," replied Alex. "I mean, I haven't seen Chloe for about three days …. And that's not unusual is it guys?"

"Nope," Luis agreed. "I can't remember the last time I saw Lilly."

"Same here Sergeant," Ben added. "It must be three or four days since I last saw Usha."

"They've always been a rule to themselves," Alex continued, "and they come and go as they please. We can't help you Sergeant so can we go?"

"Well …"

"Sorry Sergeant, unless you have any proof of any us having done anything wrong, then you have no legal grounds to detain us any longer," said Alex. "Come on guys, let's go."

"I'll be watching the three of you," the Sergeant replied.

"We don't care," Ben said.

The three friends strode out of the police station as Sergeant Cordy looked on in frustration and watched the lads disappear out of sight as they turned the corner into town.

"CONSTABLE," the Sergeant shouted. "Get out there in the patrol car and keep an eye on those three lads …. Something's going on and I will get to the bottom of it."

"Sir."

"DOWN THERE CHLOE," Usha shouted from her precarious position inside the talons of the Phoenix.

The great bird looked under it's wings towards Usha on hearing her voice through the rush of wind and flapping of wings.

"OVER THERE CHLOE. PUT US DOWN OVER THERE." Usha pointed towards the small uninhabited island of Burhou which lies just two kilometres off the north west coast of Alderney.

The huge bird squawked in acknowledgement as it spiralled down and landed on a grassy bank. The Phoenix released Usha and as she stood up, the bird gave a final squawk amid a flurry of wing flapping and shape-shifted back into Chloe, who's naked body glistened with sweat in the sunshine.

"Looking good Chloe. You'd better give Chloe her clothes sis'," Lilly said as her wings came to rest.

343

Chloe turned as Lilly appeared behind her. "Good to see you cuz'. A tad embarrassing but, whatever." The girls kissed each other on the cheeks as Usha flung her arms around them both.

"I've been following both of you since you left the island of Skellig Michael. Nice touch, shape-shifting into a Phoenix Chloe. How long have you been able to do that?" Lilly asked.

"It's a long story gal. I'll fill you in with the details later," Chloe replied.

"Okay. Well get y'self dressed and I'll take you both home," Lilly said.

"That's not a good idea sis'," said Usha. "We've been missing for a few days. That's why I thought, that if we land here on Burhou, we can tell folks that we've been camping here. Lilly, if you can drop in on Alex and let him know where we are, he can get his Dad to use his boat to pick us up. I know it's a bit of a long winded way of doing things, but at least it will give us a cover story. What d'ya think girls?"

Lilly and Chloe nodded approvingly.

"Yeah, that makes sense," said Chloe, "and in the meantime, myself and Usha can watch the Puffins and the other sea birds."

"That's a plan then," said Lilly and with barely a flutter of her angel wings, she disappeared.

The two friends sat down at the table as Alex walked over to the cafe counter and poured out three cups of coffee from the pot that had been sat on the hotplate.

"Do you want anything else to go with your drinks Alex?" Sally asked. She was a slim petite lass who had only started working at the cafe the week before and had known Alex for a number of years. She was eighteen, slightly older and had always fancied her chances with him. Sally smiled as she passed Alex the jug of milk. Their hands touched momentarily and milk lapped over the edge of the jug onto Sally's fingers and across the counter ....

"Oopps, sorry Sal, my fault," said Alex.

"No, no, it's fine, I'll clean it up in a mo'." Sally slid her fingers in and out of her mouth as she suggestively sucked the spilt milk from her fingers and ran her tongue across her lips.

"Funny how this white stuff always goes sticky, ha!" She winked.

Alex could feel he was blushing. *Talk about giving me the come on!* "Er, yeah. Sorry Sal, I'll also have three lots of bacon sarnies with plenty of sauce on please."

"No probs'. They'll be ready in about five mins'."

"Thanks Sal. I'll just take these drinks over to the lads." *Have to say, Sal's a seriously hot piece of stuff these days!* Alex placed the coffees on the table.

"Jeez Alex, how long does it take to get three drinks?" Ben asked, as he nudged Luis with his elbow.

"What you on about?" Alex replied.

"We saw you up there with Sally," Luis said. "She couldn't take her eyes off you, eh Ben?"

Ben grinned. *Wait till I see Chloe!*

"Don't know what you're on about …. I'm just gonna' get the bacon sarnies." Alex spun round to walk back to the counter when he spotted Lilly outside, tapping on the window. Alex walked over to the open door …. "Lilly. Where the hell have you been?"

"Well hello to you too. Listen, never mind all that. Can you get your Dad to take his boat out to Burhou and pick the girls up?"

"You, you've found them. That's great news. Do you want to come with me 'cos I can phone my Dad now?"

"No, no that's fine. So long as I know he's coming."

"But …."

"Honestly Alex, It'll be fine. Just get your Dad to come over to Burhou on his boat and I'll explain later. Okay?"

"Er, yeah, I s'pose."

Lilly disappeared with barely a flutter of her wings.

"Alex …. ALEX. Where's those sarnies?" Luis called. "And who was that at the door?"

"Yeah, sorry mate. Sarnies on the way." Alex quickly walked to the counter and picked up the three plates piled high with bacon sarnies and carried them to the table. He sat down next to his friends and quickly typed a message to his Dad on his phone.

"Who was you talking too at the door Alex?" Ben asked.

"Oh, er …. Just a friend letting me know that the girls have been found on Burhou which is good news eh guys?" *Better not tell Luis it was Lilly. He wouldn't be impressed.*

"Hell yeah," Luis replied. "Perhaps the police will give us a bit of space now."

"Guys …. Guys." Sally bent over the table giving Alex an unhindered view of her young voluptuous breasts under her loose top. "I forgot the sauce." She shook the bottle vigorously as Alex watched her breasts move back and forth with the motion, before pouring the brown sauce over the bacon sarnies. "There you go. Nice and thick." Sally passed her finger over the nozzle to catch the dribble and placed it in her mouth and sucked suggestively knowing full well that Alex was well and truly hooked.

"Thanks Sal," Ben said as he watched her saunter back to the counter, as if she was a model strutting her stuff on a fashion catwalk.

"Well I don't know about you Alex, but myself and Ben have to get to work. Thanks for the sarnies. We'll catch up later no doubt, when the girls are back." The two lads stood up and made their way to the door. They waved to Sally as they left, leaving Alex to pay the bill.

"Thanks Sal. How much do I owe you?" He reached into his pockets as Sally smiled and made her way from behind the counter. She stood behind Alex and placed her hands on his front trouser pockets ….

"Here, let me. I'm good at pocket billiards," Sally whispered in his ear, as she pulled his hands from his pockets and slid hers in to feel his aching hardness between his thighs.

His heart was racing. It had been so long since his passions had been aroused by his girlfriend Chloe. He craved for the touch of a young woman's flesh on his. "The door Sal," he gasped. "Close the door."

Sally pulled her hands away, made her way to the door and pushed it shut. She turned the sign to 'CLOSED', locked the door and walked back to Alex, grabbing hold of his hand and led him through to the preparation area at the rear of the cafe, out of sight from prying eyes.

Alex could feel the anticipation building up inside as Sally deftly unbuttoned his belt and jeans, pulled them down and knelt before him and began to pleasure him. *Oh my God,* he thought.

Alex reached down to Sally's shoulders and lifted her to her feet. He kissed her passionately on the lips and then pulled Sally's top off to reveal her soft voluptuous breasts before lifting her up and sat her on the work surface.

No words were uttered. This was pure sexual lust. Sally deftly released the two buttons on the waist of her skirt as Alex slid his hands around her bottom and lifted gently to remove her panties.

She smiled and then pouted suggestively as she ran her hands between her thighs and opened her legs to reveal her delicate curls. Alex pulled her in onto his hardness and with every thrust their lustful craving was satisfied as the two lovers cried out with pleasure.

"A vacation in a foreign land, Uncle Sam does the best he can, You're in the army now, oh-oo-oh you're in the army now ….."

"That's your phone Richard," Annie said. "Sounds like Status Quo."

"Hmm, yes it is. Good track eh?" He picked the phone up. "Oh hi Susan, what's up?"

"Hi Dad. I just thought I'd let you know that the girls are back at home."

"That's great news. I bet you're relieved aren't you?"

"Yeah of course, but I just don't understand why they didn't tell me that they were going on a camping trip over on Burhou Island. They didn't let you or Mum know did they?"

"Er, no …. I would have told you if I had known." *This is terrible having to lie to my own daughter!* "Who picked them up?"

"Well Chris went down to the harbour to meet them on the quay. He said that Frank Bean brought them in on his fishing boat."

"That was good of Frank. So I take it he's taken Chloe home then?"

"Well I think that's what Frank wanted to do 'cos Beth had been so worried about her, but Chris reckons she ran off as soon as they landed, saying she wanted to find Alex."

"Right. Oh well, so long as they're alright. That's the main thing eh?"

"I s'pose Dad. Anyway I've got to go, the girls are starving. I'll see you soon."

"Alright love. You take care. Bye." Richard put his phone down and sighed.

"What's up luv?" Annie asked. "You should be pleased that all three of them are back safe and sound."

"I am darlin'. It's just ...."

"I know. You can't tell Susan the truth. It's a tough call, but what else can you do?"

Richard sighed again. "Well now that everyone is back in Alderney, we need to get together and figure out what to do next."

Annie nodded.

"Can I leave it to you to sort something out Annie?"

"Of course. Consider it done.

"That was great Alex," Sally whispered in Alex's ear. She leant back on the counter, propping herself up with her arms stretched out behind her.

Alex grinned with satisfaction. He unashamedly admired and lusted at Sally's body as she sat provocatively in front of him. All thoughts of Chloe had been lost in the mindless passion he'd just experienced.

The sweat on Sally's body glistened under the work lights. Alex ran his hands across his lover's breasts and she leant forward to embrace him once more. *I need to get into his head.* "If you like, we could do this more often Alex .... You know, away from here. Somewhere that I can seriously turn you on. I can teach you so many things it will blow your mind." Sally suggestively bit her bottom lip.

"What are you on about Sal?"

"I can give you everything that you desire. Incredible sex and all the money you can handle, there's no limit." Sally kissed and caressed Alex intimately. "I can give you all the

348

power you desire." She ran her hand through his hair and tweaked his ear lobe.

"And how can you possibly do that?" asked Alex. He groaned as Sally gently ran her hand down between his legs.

"I know people with certain connections who are interested in your friends, Lilly, Usha and their cousin Chloe, your so called girlfriend. They will reward you handsomely for information."

"Well, er ...."

"What have they done for you? They've done nothing, other than put your life in danger on more than one occasion. Think about it Alex. What are you getting out of it? They've all lied to you, especially Chloe."

"S'pose. So what d'ya want from me?"

He's hooked! "Information on a day to day basis, that's all. Shouldn't be too difficult for you to handle. All you have to do is phone or see me everyday."

"I'm not sure, let me think about it."

"That's not an option Alex." She kissed Alex and slid her hand between his legs once more. "I need an answer now," she whispered in his ear before playfully biting it.

"Okay," he blurted. "I'll do what I can." He kissed her passionately as he satisfied his lust once more ....

"We should get dressed Alex," Sally whispered again. "I need to re-open the cafe before anyone becomes suspicious." She reached for her top and slid it on as Alex passed her skirt and panties. Sally quickly brushed her hair. "Come on Alex, get yourself sorted 'cos I'm going to open up." She disappeared into the cafe.

The bell rang on the cafe door and Alex could hear voices as he finished fastening the belt on his jeans. *Jeez. I'm sure that's Chloe's voice.* He glanced around the work surface nervously and spotted a cloth which he grabbed and started to wipe the work surface.

"He's in the back," Sally said quite loudly, and Chloe walked through the cafe and into the preparation area ....

"Hi Alex."

Alex looked up. "Oh. Er. Hi Chloe. You're, you're back then," he blustered. His face felt like a furnace as his adrenalin pumped ever faster.

Chloe detected a hint of nervousness about her boyfriend and put her arm around him. She leant in to kiss him.

Alex turned his head slightly and kissed her on the cheek. "It's really good to see you again gal. I've been worried about you."

"Yeah? Right." Chloe stood back, as if questioning his reaction. "So what's all this then?"

Alex held up the cloth. "Oh this? I promised Sal I'd help her out this morning …. THAT'S RIGHT ISN'T IT SAL?"

Sally poked her head through the opening to the cafe. "What's that?" she asked.

"I was just telling Chloe that I was helping you out this morning. That's right isn't it?"

"Oh, er yeah. Helping me out …. Did you want a coffee while you're here Chloe?"

"No thanks Sally. I need to get going. Thanks all the same." Chloe turned to Alex. "I'll see you later then?"

"Yeah gal. Absolutely," Alex replied. "I'll see you later."

Chloe wandered out of the cafe. *Hmm. Something's going off in there. Alex wasn't his usual self and they both looked all hot and flustered, especially Sally. Don't trust either of them.*

CHAPTER 44

QUESTION TIME (AND SOME ANSWERS!)

Miguel paced around the dingy windowless room that was below a cafe situated on the banks of the River Seine in Paris, France. It was a cold morning and the atmosphere was one of evil foreboding as the group of Mafia terrorists gathered round. "So, we all meet at last." He thumped the wall viciously, drawing blood from his fist.

"So what the hell are we going to do about the situation in Alderney?" Miguel asked. He had a low gravelly voice which was filled with menace and directed towards Diego Garcia. He gesticulated angrily as the others watched. "You've got your son, Luis, over in Alderney and this bitch." He pointed to Carol Mollins who was cowering in a corner. "But you've still not managed to locate the Lima Treasure."

"I ...."

"And not only that," Roberto interrupted, "you've got someone on the inside and the situation has not improved at all. No information, no nothing." He turned to face Esteban. "So what's the current status around the world?"

Esteban took one step forward and studied his laptop. He browsed through the pages .... "The North American territory is generally doing well with good advances being made by our demon allies. Society in Washington in particular is seeing a deterioration in law and order and the state of Louisiana has seen an upsurge in vampire activity, so that bodes well for us. Most of South America is in chaos, due to our Muki goblin friends and the cartels are ahead of schedule in tearing down the Amazon rain forests with the help of the Supay demons." He paused as he flicked through his files and then looked up .... "Asia is making progress, as is Australia where we've managed to create plagues of rodents and as an added bonus, raging wildfires. I haven't received many details from Russia which is to be expected as they continue their war in Ukraine. Europe and Africa seem to be our biggest success at the moment, with us funding the movement of terrorists, who are infiltrating the surge of migrants and using the Covid pandemic as a means of de-funding the defence structures of many of the European countries. We did have a blip in France with a car bomb in St Malo, but we have more than achieved a foothold there."

"Yes, the incident in St Malo was unfortunate," Roberto said. "Our target, the self-styled leader of the resistance, Richard Morgan, unfortunately survived, but we managed to create some chaos within the French security services. We still have plans for Morgan, be assured of that."

"But in all the chaos you caused, your men managed to lose the Inca gold platter dish which was our only way to track Morgan and his band of young fighters." Miguel banged the table violently. "Where is it now?"

"It was on the island of Skellig Michael just off the coast of West Ireland," the Muki growled.

"WAS? So where is it now?" Miguel asked.

"The last report we have is that the shapeshifter in Alderney possesses it," the goblin replied.

"Which means Morgan will have it now. YES?"

"I s'pose, yes."

Miguel paced around the room, anger etched over his wizened face. "Is there anything else I should know?"

"As I see it," Carol raised her head and spoke nervously, "we need a concerted push of action to quell the upsurge of Morgan's young warriors in Alderney and the Isle of Man if we are to have any chance of finding the Lima Treasure."

"Am I missing something here?" Miguel snapped. "Do we also now have a problem in the Isle of Man? Esteban?"

"Er ...."

"WELL?"

Esteban lowered his head. "Fairies sir. The fairies have pledged their allegiance to Morgan and his followers."

Miguel stopped pacing .... "FOR FUCK'S SAKE." He grabbed Esteban around the neck and pinned him against the wall as the others looked on. Miguel pulled a knife and held it against Esteban's face as he struggled to breathe. "Think very carefully before you answer the next question." The blade dug into Esteban's face as Miguel's grip around his throat tightened.

The steel door creaked open .... "ENOUGH! Release him."

Esteban slumped to the floor as the hooded, masked figure grabbed Miguel's arm forcing him to drop the knife.

"How many times do I have to tell you?" The masked figure twisted Miguel's arm around his back.

"So sorry master," Miguel hissed and dropped to his knees as the hooded figure released the grip.

"Master." The evil gathering knelt before the hooded figure.

"Get up," the hooded figure spoke. "No more of these pointless disagreements. You, the Muki. Call your clan together and get after the fairies."

"Yes master."

"Garcia."

"Master?"

"Take the bitch Mollins with you to Alderney and take out Morgan. I don't care how you do it, just make sure you wipe him out," the masked figure ordered.

"Yes master."

"The rest of you, and that includes you two," the hooded figure pointed to Esteban and Miguel, "will go now. You're gonna' kill yourselves an angel and find this treasure."

"Yes master."

"What do you wish me to do?" Roberto asked.

"Just keep us all up to speed as to who is doing what and where. Keep in contact with our informer and let me know the instant you hear of any plans made by Morgan and his crew. Got it?"

"Yes master."

"Now all of you, leave me." The hooded figure pointed to the steel door and as soon as it had closed behind the evil minions, the figure reached to a pendant around it's neck and chanted ....

Three columns of swirling white smoke appeared in front of the figure which gradually dispersed to reveal the archangels Michael, Gabriel and Raphael.

"My brothers, welcome." The figure drew the hood of the cloak down and removed the mask to reveal a heavenly woman's face, the face of an archangel. Her thick curly auburn hair fell down over her huge shoulders to her waist and she clasped a gigantic sword with ease in a powerful grip.

The three archangels knelt in front of the woman .... "Abaddon, we praise you."

"It is good to see you again my brothers. Be upstanding to join together in our quest as we join our king, Lucifer, in his fight to become the king of heaven and the universe. Be assured, I will become the queen of all angels and mankind. Nothing can stop us."

"All power to Abaddon," the archangels chanted.

"Abaddon, if I may?" Gabriel stepped forward. "None of us here doubt your powers but how are we to defeat God and why do we concern ourselves with trivial humans?"

"This is the answer." Abaddon pulled a pendant from her neck and held it up. "I took this many many years ago from an ancient Inca tribe and although I can draw on some of its powers, it is not truly mine to control at its full potential. The humans have two of these pendants and there is one other to find. They are part of the so called Lima Treasure and hold many mystical powers. Fortunately, we still have the six Inca statues hidden away here, that belong to the Inca gold platter style dish that Morgan and his gang took from us, so they are still unable to use its power. The humans are unaware of how much power they wield and it is this extra power from the missing pendant that I need, to make me totally invincible. I can be the ruler of heaven and earth, with your help of course."

"What of the angel they call Lilly?" Michael asked. "She could be dangerous."

"She is not aware of her potential. Because she is a hybrid, she still has her soul which is affecting her decisions as she tries to protect her human friends," replied Abaddon. "I am more concerned about the shapeshifter, the one they call Chloe, but have no fear, our minions will take care of these minor details, until the right moment arrives when we will destroy them all."

The three archangels nodded approvingly.

"It is time for me to go," Abaddon said. "Lucifer is calling me. Until next time my brothers." She disappeared in a column of swirling white smoke save for the faintest flutter of wings followed instantly by Michael, Gabriel and Raphael.

"So, you're a shapeshifter as well. How cool is that?" Richard said.

"Yep," Chloe replied.

"And the three fairies we met were really cool eh Chloe?" Usha added.

"For sure." *Especially Sam.*

"Are we all here then?" asked Annie, as she glanced around the library and double checked the doors to make sure the 'CLOSED' sign was in view from outside. "The security cameras are all switched off and all the doors are locked so we're all secure."

"Where's Lilly?" Usha asked.

"Right behind you sis'." Her wings came to rest as she appeared.

"What about Alex. Has anyone seen him?" Annie asked. "Did he not come with you Chloe?"

"No. I've no idea where he is," Chloe replied, "and to be honest I don't much care at the mo'." *Probably with that floozy Sally!*

"Oh …. Right." Annie said. *I'm not going to ask why. Judging by the look on Chloe's face, something's amiss.*

"So how did the Zoom conference go with that professor Grandad?" Usha asked.

"Not as well as we thought, eh Annie?" Richard replied.

"No. It could have gone better. Most of what he told us, we already knew about. However, he did warn us that the Lima Treasure will be of significant interest to certain heavenly forces according to his studies."

"What exactly does that mean?"

"We're not entirely sure Chloe but one theory that the professor has, is that it could involve fallen angels or indeed archangels as they've always wanted control of both heaven and earth," Richard explained.

"But surely Lilly would get to hear about something like that from the other angels," Usha replied.

"Not necessarily. Archangels are almost invincible so angels of Lilly's status tend to steer clear of them. Right Lilly?" Richard asked.

"Yeah, pretty much. I've met and witnessed the power of Abaddon just once and let's just say I wouldn't like to cross her. But I must admit that she appears to have another agenda other than protecting heaven. One thing I did notice, the one time I met her, she took a particular interest in my amulet. I didn't think anything of it at the time, but with the awesome power she has why would an amulet be of interest to her?"

"It's not about the amulet Lilly," replied Annie. "It's where it originated. It's about the Lima Treasure. Abaddon will now know you have an Inca connection. What she's after is the last pendant which the professor believes and according to legend, will double her power. Basically, because she already has a pendant, finding another would make her all powerful, strong enough to defeat God."

"Jeez, we know how to pick a fight eh?" Usha said.

"So there's three pendants then?" Chloe asked.

"Actually there's four, but the problem is no-one knows where the remaining one is," Richard replied.

"What?"

"The professor told us that a pendant with great powers had been made by the Inca tribes for Inti, their Sun God, but an archangel came amongst them and stole it. We therefore have to assume that Abaddon was that archangel," Richard continued. "What the archangel didn't know at the time was that when the Lima Treasure was made there was another three pendants of the same magnitude of mystical powers."

"So that's why the Gods of Hanna Pacha, the world above, are so desperate to help us in finding the Lima Treasure," said Lilly, "to help keep the equilibrium between themselves and the archangels thus saving the world and the universe I guess."

"Am I being a little slow on the uptake here?" remarked Chloe. "Does that mean that myself and Usha could have as much power as an archangel given that we each have a pendant?"

"No that wouldn't be possible, 'cos neither of you are angels," Annie replied.

"Right. Gotcha'."

"Schuss, someone's tapping on the front door," said Annie. She walked over to the front door of the library. "Oh it's okay, it's Alex." She smiled at him through the glass pane and opened the door. "Come in Alex. You're late." Annie closed the door behind him and locked it.

"Yeah, er sorry folks. I completely lost track of time," explained Alex. "Have I missed anything?"

"Course you have stupid," Chloe retorted.

Richard glanced with a discerning look at Chloe. *Looks like things are not good between them.*

"I'll fill you in with the details later," said Usha.

"Thanks gal."

"What if Chloe or me gave Lilly our pendant? Surely that would give her the power to defeat the archangels?" Usha asked.

"It's a nice thought," Annie replied. "But like the gold Inca platter dish, they each have their own signatures."

"Yeah, the pendants behave in a similar way to the wands in the Harry Potter books and films. I know that's fiction but the same principle applies, in that each wizard had a wand that only worked properly for them personally. The pendants 'belong' to Chloe and Usha," Richard said. "Therefore they only fully work for them."

"So not only have we got to find the remaining statues to fit in the gold Inca platter dish and the Lima Treasure, we also have to find the last remaining pendant. We're definitely out of our comfort zone now," Chloe said.

Bea stirred in her sleep. She'd dozed off whilst waiting for Richard, who'd gone to the library for her to pick up some books not fully realising his real intentions. Richard had promised to take her shopping on his return but as always he was running late. She was dreaming and one dream was becoming more lucid. She breathed deeply as memories and suspicions merged in vivid detail.

"Mother," Bea gasped as Mary hugged her tightly and kissed her on the cheek. "How can this be possible?" *I must be dreaming.*

"Schuss Bea, you called for me in your hour of need."

"I did?" Bea asked inquisitively. "I, I don't remember. But you died years ago …." Bea's thoughts drifted back momentarily to her early family life with her own Mum, Liz. Her Dad, Bill, had died when she was barely two years old and so, as an only child, life had been tough until she met Mary Morgan. Bea had always called her 'Mother' even before she'd met her son Richard and it wasn't too long before Bea and Richard married. Mary interrupted her thoughts once more.

"…. Your body died, yes. But I've always been with you. Surely you've felt my presence in your times of need?"

Bea nodded and smiled as Mary wiped tears from her daughter-in- law's face.

"I'm worried about Richard," Bea said.

"I know you are," Mary replied softly. "My son is having an affair isn't he?"

"Yes he is. I've known about Richard and Annie for a long time and strangely I can forgive him for that."

"What?"

"I know, you may think that's strange or just not right, but Annie is good for him. Richard has all the troubles of the world on his shoulders, quite literally. She is always there for him to back him up in any situation. It's his way of protecting me as he tries to unravel the mystery of the Lima Treasure, but I'm getting really concerned about his safety," Bea replied.

"You know about the treasure?"

"Of course I do. I've known for years, probably longer than Richard," Bea explained. "Back in my teenage years before I met your son Richard, I was dating Dave Haynes. I was with him at one of the bunkers when we found a pendant. If I remember rightly he gave it to my son, Philip, before he passed it on to Chloe. Do you remember Dave, Mother?"

"Yes I do dear. He was a lovely man. Perhaps you'd like to see him again?"

"Excuse me?.... He's dead."

"Hello my darlin' Bea."

"D, Dave, how can all of this be real?" Bea stuttered.

Dave leant in and kissed Bea as Mary smiled to herself.

"I was just telling Mother that we used to date."

"We most certainly did eh gal?" Dave grinned as he remembered the good times they'd had together.

"Bea was just saying how worried she is about Richard's involvement with the Lima Treasure," Mary said.

"Ah yes. It's intriguing isn't it? But involves a lot of danger eh?" Dave replied.

"It's certainly dangerous."

Dave spun round at the sound of a familiar voice .... "Philip my boy. Good to see you."

"Whoa, whoa. This cannot be right. Am I still dreaming or is this all real?" Bea asked.

"Does it matter Bea? It's whatever you want it to be gal," replied Dave.

"Hello Mum. You're looking good. How's my daughter Chloe these days?" Philip asked.

"She's turned into a fine young lady, one that you would be proud of. Chloe hasn't reached her full potential yet but I think that's partly down to her love life. It's been very confusing for her as she discovers her real gender."

"So you know she's gay?" enquired Philip.

Bea nodded. "Oh yes, the signs have been there for some time. Mind you, discovering that she was a shapeshifter was a game changer as well."

"You know about that as well then?" asked Mary.

"Oh yes. You'd be surprised what I know." Bea smiled smugly. "And it's mostly down to this woman ...." They all turned as the door opened. "I'd like you all to meet Lucy. This is Mrs Lucy Garcia, or should I say Agent Garcia."

"Thank you Bea."

"Well you're a sly one," said Dave. He grinned broadly.

"Ha! It goes with the job," Lucy replied.

"Lucy works for the CIA," explained Bea. "I've been assisting Lucy in her investigations into Diego Garcia and his connections with the Mafia with regards to people smuggling and the drug cartels, but as you all know this has now become an end of the world scenario."

"You mean the archangels and their minions defeating God and taking over the earth and heaven," Mary said.

"In a nutshell, yes," replied Lucy. "We have intel that they have instructed their followers to eliminate Richard and his group before they find the Lima Treasure and the last remaining pendant. They know the treasure will power up the gold Inca platter dishes, but as yet we have no idea what that power will be."

"And by having the additional pendant will give Abaddon, the archangel, absolute and total power to destroy God, creating anarchy in heaven and here on earth," Philip explained.

"So the time has arrived then," said Mary.

"What d'ya mean?" Philip asked.

"The time has now come for Bea to help her Granddaughter Lilly fulfil her destiny." Mary turned to Bea. "You know what you have to do." Mary opened up the display cabinet and took out an old battered hexagonal trinket box, that had seen better days and handed it to Bea.

The group of spirits and ghosts looked on as Bea opened the trinket box and took out a pendant. She held it up at arms length as a bright white glow filled the room and as the light dissipated Bea realised that she was alone .... And fully awake it seemed! *The pendant. Of course. All those years ago. I remember now as if it was only yesterday. Mother told me that she'd found a pendant buried at the site of the Madonna Stone, on the southern cliff path behind the airport ..... I'd forgotten about it.* "God bless you Mother."

"Who are you talking too Bea?" asked Richard. He closed the door behind him as he entered the room.

"Oh hello. Er, no-one. Just talking to myself," Bea replied.

"Right .... Sorry I'm late, got held up."

"That's okay luv. No probs'. We'd better get off out and do that shopping eh?"

"Sure, come on. We've got an hour before the shops close," said Richard. *It looks like Bea's had visitors!*

CHAPTER 45

CONSEQUENCES

"Good work Sally, I'll get this new information over to Diego and Carol immediately, 'cos they arrive in Alderney later today with fresh instructions to take care of Richard Morgan," muttered Roberto.

"Fine. I'm seeing my contact later, so if anything changes I'll let you know. Bye." Sally turned her phone off.

Richard turned the corner in the road onto the track that headed out towards the southern cliff path, to the west of Val du Saou . It was a still, calm, moonless evening with barely a cloud in the sky so it was difficult to navigate in the darkness. *Should have brought a torch. This phone of mine doesn't give out a great deal of light.* He'd walked the path many times over the years and seemed to know instinctively where to avoid the potholes and burrows dug out by the hundreds of wild rabbits in the area. It had turned eight o'clock in the evening when he'd left Bea at home on the pretence of visiting his daughter Susan and her partner Chris.

After discussing the situation with Annie, Alex, Lilly and Usha the day before about the urgency of finding the lost pendant and the remaining treasure, they had decided to visit the site of the Madonna Stone, but Richard had already made his mind up to check it out by himself first, to make sure they didn't miss anything. His instincts were telling him that the site was important and could be crucial to their cause.

Richard knew all the local stories that had been handed down through the generations about the Madonna Stone and in his mind, none of them really made any sense. One of the stories dated back to the eighteen hundreds involving an army officer and his wife who had just got married.

The officer lost his life in a shipwreck off the south cliffs, after which, his distraught wife would stand on the cliffs above for days, mourning his loss. She was apparently always dressed in grey and she was so grief stricken, she had thrown herself from the cliffs to the rocks below with fatal consequences. The story goes that the grey lady can be seen in the one and a half metre high granite standing stone looking out to sea. *That doesn't work for me 'cos I thought the stone had only been there since the 1960's. In fact, someone told me that it had once been a stone lintel in a house and had been put there to be used as a scratching post by the grazing cattle. Ha!*

"What the ...." Richard picked himself up from the ground as a rabbit bounded across the grass in front of him. "Bloody rabbits, digging holes everywhere." *Silly old sod. I could have broken my ankle!*

The sound of crashing waves ahead told Richard he didn't have much further to walk. *Can't be far now,* he thought. The granite standing stone loomed into view ....

"Stay still," Diego whispered to Carol as they knelt on the ground just two metres away from the standing stone. They were hidden from view by three low growing bushes. "Wait until Morgan's stood next to the stone with his back to us." Diego pulled out a large hunting knife.

"Okay," Carol muttered. She pulled her balaclava down over her face and took a twenty centimetre knife out from her waistcoat. "What the …." A rabbit startled her as it jumped in front of her and then quickly disappeared into the darkness.

"Schuss."

Richard placed his hand on the granite stone and used the light from his phone to study the nooks and crannies in the texture of the stone surface. *Nothing on this side. Let's have a look round here.* Richard turned ….

"NOW!" Out of the darkness two figures lurched forward towards Richard pushing him to the ground. "GET HIM!" Carol's arm swung, her knife slicing a deep gouge in Richard's arm as he desperately tried to defend himself against the two assailants.

Diego plunged his blade into Richard's stomach and twisted. Richard's agonising screams of pain cut through the night air as Diego raised his arm again to thrust once more and then ….

A brilliant bright light dazzled Diego and Carol momentarily as a rabbit, shape-shifted into Chloe, who instantly summoned her light staff and swung it around in a circular motion, knocking the two attackers to the ground. "COME ON THEN," she screeched. "LET'S SEE WHAT YOU CAN DO." Startled, Carol and Diego picked themselves up and ran off into the night.

"Chloe," Richard spluttered as blood began to run from the corner of his mouth, as he lay on the ground.

"Grandad." Chloe knelt down and placed her hand on his stomach wound to try and stem the flow of blood. *He's in a bad way.*

"Chloe. It was Garcia and Mollins. I recognised the voices. How did they know?"

"Schuss Grandad. Lie still and let me sort you out." Chloe clasped her pendant over her heart, and chanted … "I am Alnitak the Healer and Child of the Stars." She passed her hand over Richard's bloodied body as a bright white glow hovered over him until all his injuries were healed. Chloe leant over

Richard and placed her hand on the side of his face …. "How d'ya feel Grandad?"

Richard coughed as he struggled to sit up. "I'm okay …. I think. Thanks." He pulled himself to his feet. "How the hell did they know I would be here tonight?"

Chloe shrugged her shoulders. "I've no idea Grandad but let's be honest, you shouldn't have been here by yourself. They've already tried to kill you before."

Richard nodded. "Yeah I know. I've been lucky, perhaps too many times." He grimaced in pain and grabbed his stomach.

"You alright Grandad?" Chloe was seriously concerned.

"Yeah. Yeah, I'll be fine. I just feel quite sore."

"Right, that's it. You're going home right now. No arguments. I'll get Lilly." Chloe clasped her pendant and concentrated on contacting her cousin …. *Lilly I need your help at the Madonna Stone. Can you pick up Grandad? Er, and I need some clothes. Thanks.* She released the pendant and Lilly appeared almost immediately to the sound of beating wings.

"Hi Grandad, Chloe. Been in the wars again I see." Lilly handed Chloe some clothes.

"Thanks for coming Lilly," replied Chloe. "I've healed Grandad's wounds but he's still struggling. He's feeling rather sore, so I thought the best place to be was at home resting. We can pick up the trail tomorrow as we arranged, with all of us here. I just thought you could get him home easier and quicker."

"Yeah. Sure. No probs', and Chloe, just be careful out there tonight. There seems to be some violent incidents taking place and there's a few buildings that are on fire. They appear to be out of control." Lilly lifted Richard with the strength of four men and instantly disappeared, save for the faintest flutter of wings.

Chloe dressed herself and started to walk back down the rough track towards the main road. *We've got a problem I think. Someone's blabbing I reckon, but who? It doesn't make any sense and I just can't get my head round it.* Chloe reached the end of the track where it merged onto the back road into town. She'd left her Vespa scooter parked on the side of the road and thought nothing of the fact that she'd left her key in the ignition. She'd always done it, as many of the islanders did as well. Vehicle theft on Alderney just didn't happen. Chloe climbed on and turned the key. The engine started first time and she drove away. *I'm hungry. I'll be glad to get home,* she thought.

The scooter turned the bend in the road and began to pick up speed. *Downhill all the way now.* Chloe momentarily closed her eyes as the wind blew through her hair. *That feels SO good.* She opened her eyes as the scooter gained further momentum on the hill until the approaching bend in the road required Chloe to apply the brakes …. "OH HELL!" *The brakes. They've failed!* The scooter careered across the road and hit the grass bank throwing Chloe high into the air, with the scooter hitting the ground somewhere in the distance …. Silence.

CHLOE! Usha jumped out of her chair as she felt her cousin's pain. She immediately had a sense of impending doom. ***Chloe, where are you?*** Nothing, no response. Usha began to shake with emotion as she phoned Annie ….

"Tell me your secret, Sing me the song, Sing it to me in the silent tongue …." Will you? sung by Hazel O'Connor played on Annie's phone.

"Hello."

"Hi Annie, it's Usha. Something's happened to Chloe."

"What is it gal?"

"I don't know. I can just feel it," replied Usha.

"Right. Do you know where she is?"

"No I don't …. Hang on, I can hear the sirens of the ambulance …. I'm going Annie. I'm going to find out where it's going."

"Usha, wait. Usha …. Usha. Damn it, she's gone." *I'd better get out there. See if I can find them.*

"Richard, Richard." Bea knelt over Richard who'd collapsed to the floor holding his stomach and gasping for air. "Richard. What's wrong?" Bea held her husband's hand. *Jeez, he's cold but he's sweating.* She phoned for an ambulance, trying to

365

remain calm as she heard someone come through the door. Bea looked up ....

"Lucy."

"Bea. What's happened?" Lucy knelt down next to Bea.

"I've called for an ambulance. I'm not sure how long it will be 'cos they said they were receiving a lot of calls tonight."

Lucy nodded. "Yeah, all hell has let loose out there tonight." She placed her arm around Bea to try and reassure her. "He'll be okay Bea, he's a fighter." *This doesn't look good. Something's going down tonight, what with several fights breaking out in town and at least five major fires caused by explosions.*

Richard stirred and pulled Bea closer to him. "I'm sorry gal." He struggled to speak as he pulled the amulet from his arm and placed it in Bea's hand. "I'm so sorry about everything," he croaked.

"Best not to talk dear." Bea's tears rolled down her face. "The ambulance is on it's way."

"Give the amulet to Annie. She'll know what to do," Richard said with a faltering voice.

Lucy squeezed Bea's hand. "He's going fast Bea .... Damn it, where's that ambulance?"

Richard used what little strength he had left to pull Bea towards him as he lay on the floor. "I've always loved you gal, you know that, yes?" he whispered.

Bea nodded. "I know dear. I love you too. Save your strength."

"It's no good dear. It's my time." Richard coughed as blood began to run from the corner of his mouth. "You know about the treasure don't you?"

Bea nodded. Tears flowed more freely as she realised the life was ebbing away from her husband, her best friend and love of her life.

"Promise me that you won't blame Annie. The girls will need her strength and knowledge."

"I promise dear."

Richard coughed and spluttered again. "Make sure Lilly fulfils her destiny. She has to ...."

"Oh God, NO!" Bea sobbed uncontrollably as Richard's head tilted to one side.

"USHA .... USHA, WHERE ARE YOU?" shouted Annie. The darkness of the night was all the more foreboding. Blood curdling screams could be heard from every direction interspersed by sirens from emergency vehicles in the distance. Annie stood still momentarily to catch her breath and get her bearings. *Jeez, it looks like hell has come to visit us tonight. Look at all the fires. Bloody hell!* "USHA .... USHA." *Where is she?*

Usha back flipped to evade the demon's talons and summoned her light staff just in time to fend off the two demons behind her. She side swiped another hideous being to the ground before using her power of lightening bolts to destroy all of her attackers. *They're all over the island tonight. I hope everyone's alright.* **Lilly, where are you?**

Lilly felt her sister, Usha, connecting to her in her head. **Usha, I'm down at the harbour fighting off demons. What's up?** *I've lost contact with Annie and I can't locate Chloe.* **Sorry Usha, you're gonna' have to manage 'cos I've got my hands full. There must be at least thirty demons down here. Got to go ....**

"THERE SHE IS .... GET HER .... NOW!" A growling voice broke into Usha's thoughts as she fended off three menacing demons and then ran further on into the darkness to tackle another group of would be assailants.

"Chloe." A softly spoken voice.

She blinked her eyes.

"Chloe .... It's Sam. Chloe can you hear me?"

Her eyes started to focus on the shadowy figure in the darkness knelt over her .... "Sam, is it really you?"

"Sure is babe. How d'ya feel?"

Chloe sat up. She put her hand to her head. "I'll be okay I think. God, my head feels like it's been hit with a sledgehammer and my legs feel like jelly."

An explosion fifty metres away lit up the sky momentarily.

"You was lucky," Sam said. "I managed to catch you in mid flight."

"What?"

"You was thrown clear of your scooter just as I was arriving. I sensed where you was and as I flew in to land, you literally fell into my arms."

"But how come you've travelled here Sam?"

"A group of Muki goblins attacked the Isle of Man earlier tonight. Ruby and Lola agreed that they could deal with any incursions and they sensed Alderney was under attack so they sent me to help. They knew I'd want to be here with you Chloe."

"Do you?"

"Of course I do. Don't you feel it?"

Chloe smiled and nodded. "You know I do."

The couple fell into each others arms and embraced passionately.

"Bea …. Bea, let's close Richard's eyes shall we." Lucy moved her hand tenderly over Richard's face. "There, it looks like he's sleeping now." She helped Bea to her feet. "Come on gal, let's go and sit in the kitchen whilst the paramedics do their job. Come on, I'll put the kettle on."

Lucy and Bea sat at the table as they waited for the kettle to boil.

"I'm so sorry Bea." Lucy placed her hand on top of Bea's to console her. "What did he say to you Bea?"

"Eh? Oh, nothing. Nothing important." Bea squeezed the amulet in her hand.

CHAPTER 46

AFTERMATH

Susan and Chris sat down at the kitchen table for breakfast.

"Where are the girls?" Chris asked.

"They're still in bed luv. I wasn't going to disturb them this morning 'cos they were so upset last night when I told them about Dad," Susan replied. Her eyes immediately filled with tears as she spoke.

"Hmm, fair enough. I suppose it's gonna' hit them hard, 'cos they thought the world of their Grandad. How's your Mum holding up?"

"Well I phoned her this morning. She seemed okay 'cos her friend Lucy stayed with her last night. She said something about she'd got some important stuff to deal with today, so I left it at that," explained Susan.

"Bea, sorry, your Mum. She never changes eh?"

"Hmm."

Chris picked up the television remote and switched it on for the news ….

"Thanks Bill for the Covid update. On to other news and last night saw unprecedented scenes of violence all around the world which appeared to be premeditated and highly organised. The United Kingdom and the Channel Islands in particular appear to have seen high levels of violent disorder. We can take this opportunity to bring in our reporter, Desmond Giles, who I believe is currently in Alderney. Are you there Desmond?

Hello Geoff. Yes I'm here in Alderney and as you can see behind me the emergency services are still struggling to get some of the fires under control. I took a walk round the island earlier today and there is total devastation. It's quite remarkable the casualty figures are so low. Having said all that, there is a feeling of sadness this morning that one of the island's most popular characters, Richard Morgan, was allegedly murdered overnight. I might add that the authorities are still searching for five missing islanders and they are still refusing to release details of what is behind these atrocities. This is Desmond Giles reporting from Alderney.

Thank you Desmond. Now over to Gillian for the weather update …."

"Turn the telly off luv, I can hear the girls coming down the stairs."

Annie pulled back the curtains in her lounge as the seemingly huge, four by four vehicle drove on to her front drive. The deafening roar of the engine subsided as the car came to a halt and two women stepped out and walked to the front door. Bea knocked on the door, took a step back and stood next to Lucy who held her hand reassuringly. The door opened slowly ….

Annie stood in the opening, red eyed from crying. For a few moments, Bea and Annie looked at each other, but said nothing ….

"Come in Bea, please," said Annie.

Bea glanced at Lucy. "It's alright Bea. I'll stay here. You go on in."

Bea and Annie fell into each others embrace and sobbed unashamedly whilst Lucy went back to the car and sat down in the driver's seat. She watched the two women enter the house and the door close behind them. Lucy switched on her receiver that she had concealed in her jacket pocket and listened ….

"Bea, I have to say something …."

"No you don't Annie. No recriminations. Anyway, that's not why I'm here." Bea indicated to Annie not to say anything and pointed to the back garden through the open patio doors.

They walked out into the garden.

"What's going on Bea?"

"Your house is bugged."

"What? You're kidding me?" Annie gasped.

"Believe me Annie, when I leave here, get your house scanned by Lilly 'cos she can pick up the transmitter frequencies."

"Right, will do," said Annie. "Bloody hell, how long has that been going on?"

Bea shrugged her shoulders, smiled and gave Annie the amulet. "I promised Richard that I would give you this. Don't worry, I know what it is and what it's capable of doing. Lucy doesn't know about the amulet and it needs to stay that way. Okay?"

Annie nodded and slid the amulet onto her wrist. "What about Lucy. Can we trust her?"

Bea smiled. "She's an agent for the CIA and can be extremely useful to us. Your house is bugged! Can we trust her? Absolutely not!"

The two women laughed.

"So what do you plan on doing next Annie?"

"In one sentence, find the remaining treasure and save the world. We need to finish off the work that Richard started. That's two sentences, isn't it?" joked Annie.

"That easy eh? Seriously, you must have plans in place Annie?"

"Yeah well, I've a couple of things I need to deal with today to give us a fighting chance, but the most important thing is to find the missing fourth pendant to enable Lilly to …."

".... To fulfil her destiny," interrupted Bea.

"Well yes."

"In that case, Lilly is going to need this." Bea handed Annie the old battered hexagonal trinket box. "Open it."

Annie's hands shook as she opened the box. "The pendant, wow!... How?"

"Long story for another day and, it's complicated," replied Bea. *Thank you Mother.*

"Actually, I have a couple of things for you but I need to go into the kitchen to get them. I'll be a couple of minutes." Annie quickly walked back in the house and into the kitchen.

Bea sat down on the garden bench. *I wonder how many times Richard sat here?* She smiled to herself as her thoughts wandered to happier times ….

"Bea …. Bea, you okay?" asked Annie.

"Er, yeah. Sorry. I was deep in thought."

"Can you give this bag to Beth and Frank Bean please?"

"Yeah of course. What's in it Annie?"

"It's full of money …. One hundred thousand pounds to be exact," said Annie.

"Pardon!" Bea partially unzipped the bag and audibly gasped as she saw the bank notes.

"Richard found the money that the Mafia promised to pay Frank for the hire of his boat. Remember?"

"Well, yes. Frank will be thrilled," said Bea.

"When Richard found the money, we decided to give half the amount to Frank."

"And the other half?" asked Bea.

"Come with me," replied Annie. She took Bea by the hand and led her through the overgrown back garden.

"No disrespect Annie, but I think you need a gardener. Look at my legs now, they're covered in scratches."

"Sorry Bea, since my husband passed away, I've been too busy helping Richard, so gardening has been the last thing on my to do list. Here we are."

The two women faced a three metre high bank of earth that stretched across the total width of the garden and was covered with an impregnable forest of brambles. Slightly to the right was a partially visible, one metre high decorative concrete plinth with a sundial, mostly covered in ivy.

"Er, sorry Annie, what am I supposed to be looking at? Looks to me like a huge wall of brambles."

"Wait for it." Annie grabbed the sundial and turned it through ninety degrees. "Stand back Bea."

"What's happening?" exclaimed Bea, as a two metre width of the bank immediately in front of them steadily sank to ground level, revealing a huge steel door, about three metres inside the remaining bank. As Bea studied what was occurring in front of her, she noticed that each side of the bank that led to the door was held in place by steel plating. She could hear the hydraulics working below ground as a two metre square steel platform moved towards them from the doorway. It came to a halt with a shuddering clunk and Annie encouraged Bea to step onto the platform. They held hands as the platform travelled back across through the now, corridor of steel to the doorway. Annie held her hand up to a fingerprint scanner on the door and it slowly swung open.

"How? How is this all possible Annie?"

They stepped through the door and onto another platform. The door closed behind them as lighting flickered into life. Annie pressed a button on the side rail and more hydraulics could be heard as the platform lowered the two women four metres below ground, before it stopped at the bottom of the shaft with a slight thud.

Annie stepped off the platform. "Follow me Bea. Come on." She beckoned Bea through the dimly lit concrete tunnel which led them into a cavernous, well lit concrete space. "This is our command centre .... Are you listening Bea?"

"Oh, er, yeah, of course. This is just incredible Annie. All this equipment, look at all the screens, the computers, just, everything!"

"If you look up to your left at that monitor, you can see into the garden above us and you'll see that we are totally locked down. Everything has closed securely behind us."

"Yes, yes I can see. That's impressive Annie but how is this all possible?"

"When my husband and I bought the property many years ago, we found out it had a German Second World War underground bunker. There's a few on the island but this is the biggest. The idea of a command centre was Richards, but we never had the finances until he found the Mafia money. It paid for all this and more. We extended the complex which now has a bathroom, kitchen, a number of bedrooms and a gym. Through there is our weapons room and of course we have a library."

"Ha! A library, of course," Bea replied.

"Nothing and I mean nothing can get in here. All the exterior walls and ceilings are two metres thick and constructed with reinforced concrete, then lined with fifteen centimetre thick steel. Once we realised what we were up against we just knew that we had to play hard ball and last nights events proved us right. Richard didn't die in vain. This is his legacy Bea."

"But last night?"

"Last night we were compromised. This system you see in front of you wasn't live until three hours ago. You see, this will keep us all connected and we will know in an instant where any one of us is. Not only that, we know what's happening, anytime and anywhere in the world. We won't be isolated, unlike last night. The archangel's minions and the Mafia were able to spread confusion and used diversionary tactics to keep us all separated, therefore making us all vulnerable. It won't happen again."

Outside on Annie's driveway, Lucy was getting impatient and was pacing back and forth around the vehicle. *What are they up too? I can't get a damn thing on this receiver.* She banged and shook the receiver. *Nothing but interference, damn it! What are they doing?*

"I'm going to have to get going Annie 'cos Lucy will be getting suspicious."

"Before you go Bea …. I need to chip you and the girls so we can track everyone. It doesn't hurt, look …." Annie held her arm out and pointed to a barely visible small lump just above her wrist. "I've already chipped myself. If you look at that digital map of Alderney on this computer." She pointed to a flashing symbol on the map. "That's me. I'm going to chip the girls later. What d'ya think?"

"That's fine. Anything that helps." Bea held out her arm as Annie inserted the minute tracking chip using a hypo. "I tell you what gal, give me one of those chips and I'll drop it into Lucy's bag when I get a chance."

"Here you go. It's a good idea," said Annie "and just so you know, each chip is programmed so you can check on your phone where everyone is, just by using this app. Just download it onto your phone and it will be functioning immediately."

"Okay, that's great," replied Bea. "Oh, one last thing, if you see Chloe before I do, just let her know that Richard actually died of poisoning. I don't want her thinking that she didn't heal him properly. She did, but Chloe would have had no idea that the knife had been laced with poison. Richard had no chance."

The two women embraced.

"Right, let's get back to the house before Lucy throws a wobbly, ha!" Annie said as she led the way back to the lift.

Sam's skin is so soft Chloe thought, as her hands caressed Sam's body.

The two young women snuggled together under the duvet and kissed passionately as they pleasured each other, lost in their love making, oblivious to the calls from Beth standing at the foot of the stairs. She had been searching for Chloe most of the morning and had decided to call at her Mum's house on the off chance.

Beth was becoming impatient. Neither her son, Alex, or Chloe had come home the night before and she'd become increasingly worried as the violence throughout the island had escalated. Unbeknown to Beth, Chloe had taken Sam to her Mum's house in the knowledge that Carol wouldn't be there. In the meantime Alex had made contact with Sally and from there, they'd met up with Diego Garcia for further instructions following their successful elimination of Richard.

Beth started to climb the stairs and then stopped halfway ....

"CHLOE, CHLOE, ARE YOU THERE?"

Chloe stepped out hesitantly onto the landing at the top of the stairs, wrapped in a towel to protect her modesty. She peered down the stairs. "Is that you Beth?"

"You know it is young lady. Why the hell didn't you let me know you was staying the night here?"

"I ...."

"Who are you talking too babe?" Sam appeared on the landing.

"Who this?" Beth asked.

"This is my friend Sam," replied Chloe.

"So where's Alex then?"

The two girls looked at each other.

"We don't know Beth, sorry," Chloe replied.

"Jeez!" Beth turned and angrily stomped down the stairs. "I'll see you later Chloe .... AND PUT SOME CLOTHES ON

YOU TWO." The front door slammed shut as Beth stormed out of the house.

"Oopps," said Chloe. She was blushing.

Sam giggled as she pulled the towel from Chloe. The two young women playfully pushed each other back into the bedroom and fell onto the bed.

Sam stood in front of the full length mirror adjusting her clothes. Chloe stood beside her, brushing Sam's long red hair.

"Your hair is really thick Sam and the colour is gorgeous. It so matches your brown eyes."

"Thanks babe." Sam pointed to the mirror. "Er, Chloe. There's a man stood behind you."

"What?" Chloe turned her head to look behind herself. *Nothing.* She turned back to see their reflections in the mirror. *Bloody hell. Dad.* Chloe held Sam tightly. "Dad? How? This can't be real." *Jeez, I'm talking to a reflection of a ghost!*

"Chloe, I know this is difficult," said Philip.

"You got that right," Chloe replied.

"I've come to warn you Chloe. As you know, your cousin Lilly has a destiny to fulfil and that destiny means consequences for you and Usha. Consequences that will be irreversible."

"What's your Dad on about babe?" Sam gripped Chloe's hand tightly.

"We'll find the answers Dad. We have to. There has to be a way to defeat the archangels," said Chloe.

"There is a way," replied Philip. "Both yourself and Usha have to become angel hybrids."

"But what about the treasure? Dad? Dad?"

"He's gone Chloe. Come here," Sam pulled Chloe into a loving embrace. "Is this all real babe?" Sam whispered in her girlfriend's ear.

"Yeah, for sure gal. Let's get over to Annie's place," Chloe replied. She held Sam's hand as they disappeared in a magical pillar of fire.

Annie closed the front door behind her as Bea and Lucy drove away. The roar of the four by four engine faded away into the distance. She entered the kitchen to the sight of Usha and Lilly appearing, accompanied by the faintest flutter of Lilly's wings as they came to rest.

"Girls …. Oh girls." Annie held out her arms as the two sisters stepped forward and the three embraced, tears flowing down their faces. "It's so good to see you both." Annie pointed to the back garden and they walked outside.

"What's going on Annie?" Usha asked.

"The house is bugged," replied Annie. "Your Grandma told me you can sort it Lilly."

"No probs'. Give me a minute." Lilly stepped back into the house.

Usha and Annie watched through the windows as Lilly held her amulet and concentrated. "What's she doing Usha?"

"Lilly can pick up the radio frequencies of both the transmitters and the receivers. Once she's tuned in, she just frazzles them."

"That's pretty cool," Annie replied. "Here she comes."

"All sorted Annie," said Lilly.

"Great, thanks."

A magical pillar of fire materialised as Sam and Chloe arrived.

"Good entrance girls," said Lilly.

"Awesome!"

"So is this one of your fairy friends Chloe?" asked Lilly.

Sam stepped forward, bowed slightly to the amusement of the group of friends and took Lilly's hand in hers ….

"So, you are Lilly. The girl that everyone speaks of. You're quite famous in Fairy Land. All the Fae speak of you."

Usha and Chloe sniggered.

"You're obviously an angel, an angel hybrid actually," said Sam.

"How d'ya know?" Lilly asked.

"It's obvious isn't it? Apart from the fact that Usha and Chloe told me all about you when they were stranded on the island of Skellig Michael, I can see your wings."

"Really?" Lilly asked.

"Oh yes, quite clearly. Fairies and angels have many similarities," replied Sam, "including who are our enemies."

"So if anyone here has any doubts about where Sam's loyalties lye, they'll have me to deal with," Chloe said.

377

Sam kissed Chloe on the lips and placed her arm around her waist. *Thanks babe.*

"Right, now that all your egos are satisfied, we'll get down to business. Follow me, I've something of interest to show you all," said Annie.

Sally's flesh shuddered with each thrust from Alex. He lifted her knees higher over the arms of the chair as she screamed for him to push harder and faster.

"Yes, yes, that's it," she panted. Sally pulled Alex closer, his face buried between her ample sweaty breasts as his thrusts of lust overcame his teenage frailties and all thoughts of right from wrong were lost in his own ecstasy.

The door creaked as it opened ….

"Yes, yes, come on Alex, faster!"

Sally closed her eyes as Diego Garcia pulled Alex's head away from her breasts and viciously slit his throat wide open in one movement. He slumped forward onto Sally, gurgling and spluttering on his own blood, choking to death.

"Bloody hell, you took your time," muttered Sally. She pushed the bloodied dead body to the floor. "You didn't have to kill him though, I mean, look at the state of me now, disgusting. I'm covered in blood and who's gonna' clean this mess up? You said you was goin' to be here an hour ago. Jeez."

"We've had a few problems," growled Diego. "Besides, you obviously had a good shag," he sneered.

"Shut it. You got what you wanted, so now you can get out of here. And take the body with you."

Diego stepped over the dead body and grabbed Sally, pinning her to the wall. He slid the blade of his hunting knife across her breasts and dug the point of the knife into her neck. "Be very careful what you say, if you get my drift. You're nothing more than a trollop. Alex served his purpose. Get yourself cleaned up and dressed. I'll phone later. GOT IT?" he shouted in a menacing tone.

"Y, yes. Okay." Sally gasped for air as Diego pulled the knife away from her. He stormed out of the room as Sally slumped to the blood stained floor.

378

"So girls, what d'ya think of our command centre?" Annie asked.

"Very impressive," replied Lilly.

"Awesome."

The girls all nodded in agreement.

"So you're all chipped," said Annie, "and you've all got the tracking app on your phones. I want you all to try these headsets on. There's a good twenty or so different ones on the table and they all have microphones with video facilities and night vision."

"Wow gal. These are just brill," said Chloe. "Look up at the monitors girls. We're all there."

"That's the idea Chloe. I've got monitors here that I can observe each of you, wherever you are. So for instance, if one of you needs help I can contact any one of you instantly."

"Big brother eh?" asked Sam.

"I s'pose," replied Annie, "but it's for the greater good."

"Ha. We look like a special forces unit with this gear on," Lilly said.

"Maybe, but it'll save lives," replied Annie. "Right, I've got a couple of other things to cover. Firstly, there's this." She took out the hexagonal trinket box from her pocket and handed it to Lilly. "Open it Lilly."

Lilly gave Annie a quizzical look as she opened the box. "The missing pendant, wow!" Lilly fastened it around her neck and the friends watched as she hovered two metres off the ground, wings fully extended. Her blue eyes glowed a pure white as the power of the pendant pulsed through her body and aligned itself with the amulet on Lilly's wrist before her feet were once more on the ground.

"Bloody hell Lilly, you okay?" Usha asked.

"No probs' sis'. Everything's good." *I can feel the extra power immersing my whole body.*

"Okay guys, the shows over for now," Annie said. "Tonight the four of you need to take a look at the site of the Madonna Stone. Make sure you've got your headsets and so forth on, so I can keep an eye on things here. Please be careful."

CHAPTER 47

SEEING THE LIGHT

Sally shivered as the wind tore through the gorse and brambles on the southern cliff path. It was difficult enough sheltering from the bite of the blustery air without having to concentrate on the job in hand. Diego Garcia had tasked her with setting up an ambush at the site of the Madonna Stone, close to the spot where they had attacked Richard the previous fateful night. The thinking was, that a second attack at the same spot twenty four hours later would be more fruitful as Richard's team wouldn't be expecting another incident.

The tactic they were to use would involve an unsuspecting Sally as a decoy with Garcia and his minions set to pounce.

A twig snapped behind Sally ….

Garcia grabbed her arm and growled in her face. "No mistakes girl." He flashed his knife menacingly and punched her in the face, drawing blood from her now broken nose.

Sally recoiled backwards in pain, hand to her bloodied face. She felt the blade of his knife cut deep across her midriff as she doubled over in agony and slumped to the ground.

Garcia grinned at his handiwork. "That's more like it. Got to be convincing girl," he cackled and stepped back into the surrounding gorse to rejoin his minions.

"Take it nice and easy girls. About ten metres to go. Don't forget to keep scanning the areas to the left and right of you …. That's it, keep going." Annie's voice could be heard in the girl's headsets. *"Hold it! I'm counting at least twelve demon sources, plus one heat source, about four metres away slightly to your right …. And dead ahead is another heat source which doesn't appear to be moving girls. Be careful."*

Chloe indicated to Usha to move forward and to the right slightly as Sam moved away to the left. They both stopped and knelt on one knee as Chloe stepped forward. She spotted the bloodied body on the ground in front of her and bent over it. She pulled the seemingly lifeless body over …. *Oh shit, it's Sally!*

"What the hell is she doing here?"

"Chloe," Sally croaked, and pulled Chloe closer. "It's, it's a trap," she gasped. Chloe glanced left and right as Sam and Usha nodded to indicate they'd heard the warning on their headsets.

"Stay still Sally," Chloe whispered. She scanned the darkness for any sign of movement.

"Sam, take care of Sally. Chloe will cover you."

Sam moved over to Sally and applied pressure to the knife wound. "It's okay Chloe, I've got it. Do your stuff."

The crashing of the waves below gave way to screams and cries of terror as six demons lurched forward out of the darkness towards Chloe and Usha, talons and knives flailing.

Usha sidestepped one assailant before back flipping, kicking a demon in the head and using her light staff to decapitate two others.

Chloe crouched and shape-shifted into a Bengal tiger. It lifted it's magnificent head and roared as it stood back on it's hind legs and side swiped two demons with it's massive paws before leaping onto another demon and tearing it's head off.

"Behind you Sam."

Sam spun round and threw a magical fireball at the demon which disintegrated instantly into dust.

"Now Lilly."

Twelve demons rushed at Usha and the tiger …. They instantly disintegrated in a cloud of dust as a searing beam of white light from above burnt through them.

The tiger roared ferociously as Usha and Sam watched in awe. Lilly hovered in the dark night air above them, her eyes glowing a brilliant bright white, with her wings outstretched.

What a sight, thought Sam.

"Where's Garcia?"

"No sign of him Annie, sorry," replied Usha. "Wait, what's happening?"

A huge dazzling flash of blue light lit up the sky and the ground appeared to shudder ....

"I see it! It's …. It's Michael, one of the archangels …. Are you seeing this Lilly?"

A bolt of blue lightening flashed across the night sky, hitting Lilly, throwing her backwards, spinning uncontrollably over the cliff edge and out of sight.

Sam and Usha threw themselves to the ground as the archangel swooped down over their heads and landed six metres away on the cliff edge.

"Annie, where's Chloe?" asked Sam.

"Up in the tree directly in front of you. She's shape-shifted into a peregrine falcon."

Suddenly, Lilly soared high into the night sky from the cliffs below as the peregrine swooped down towards Michael the archangel and Sam disappeared in a magical pillar of fire ….

The archangel spotted Lilly and sent a bolt of blue lightening in her direction, narrowly missing, as the peregrine's talons tore at one of the archangel's eyes. Two magical fireballs from Sam found their target as the archangel reeled back ….

"Now Lilly."

The archangel lurched back and forth as Lilly's eyes emitted searing beams of white light until suddenly, a huge explosion of light and dust as the archangel disintegrated.

"Wow! Well done everyone. The area is now secure"

"Thanks for the help Annie, we'll take it from here," said Usha.

"Copy that."

"See you back at the command centre as planned. In the meantime, see if you can track down Garcia." Usha ducked as the peregrine swooped over her head and landed on the ground next to Sally. The bird immediately shape-shifted back to Chloe.

"How's Sally, Sam?" Chloe asked.

"She's in a bad way babe. Is there anything you can do?"

Sally moaned as Chloe placed her hand gently on the gaping knife wound and held her pendant as she closed her eyes. *No, it's too late. She's lost far too much blood.* Chloe cradled Sally's head in her arms as Sam, Usha and Lilly watched on ….

"Sally," Chloe whispered, "what was you doing up here?"

"Chloe …. Chloe, I …." Sally struggled to talk as her life slowly ebbed away. "Chloe, listen …. It's Alex." Sally choked as blood ran from her mouth.

"What about Alex?" Chloe's voice increased in volume. She grabbed Sally and shook her …. "WHERE'S ALEX?"

"He …. He's dead Chloe," Sally gasped. "Garcia, he …." Sally's head fell back.

"NO, HE CAN'T BE." Chloe shook her again. "SALLY."

"STOP IT …. PACK IT IN CHLOE, SHE'S DEAD," Usha shouted.

Lilly placed her hand on Chloe's shoulder. "That's enough Chloe. Sally's gone. There's nothing more you can do."

"But, but Alex," stuttered Chloe.

"Yes I know. We'll find out what happened cuz', I promise." Lilly lifted Chloe to her feet and kissed her gently on the cheek. "Get some clothes on and go with Usha back to Annie's. Sam and I will stay here and figure out what Grandad was looking for last night."

Usha nodded approvingly to Lilly and took Chloe's hand. "Come on Chloe, let's go. We'll see you two later at the command centre. Be careful."

"Keep an eye on them Annie. We'll see you in a while," said Lilly.

"Copy that."

Chloe and Usha disappeared into the darkness as Lilly and Sam gently moved Sally's lifeless body into the undergrowth out of sight.

"Can I ask you something Lilly? Who's Alex?" asked Sam.

"Hmm well, he was a good friend of ours and if you want me to be honest with you, he was Chloe's boyfriend before she met you."

"Oh."

"Just so you know, I believe their relationship had finished but I don't know all the details. Personally I would leave the subject alone Sam."

"Okay." *Jeez, I hope she's alright.*

"Did you hear that?" Lilly whispered.

Sam shook her head.

"Just listen …. There it is again. I can hear someone groaning, over there in those bushes," whispered Lilly. "Have you got anything Annie?"

"Yeah. I've detected a heat source to your right, three metres away. There's no movement."

"Okay thanks," Lilly replied.

The two girls stepped cautiously to their right ….

"Help me." A low voice gave the man's position away. "Help."

"Here Lilly." Sam tugged on Lilly's hand and they knelt down next to the injured man. "It's one of Garcia's minions. Looking at the state of him, he's not going to make it," said Sam.

"Leave him Sam. Just let him die. There's nothing we can do and to be honest, good riddance." Lilly rose to her feet.

"Hang on Lilly, let me try something." Sam clapped her hands and held them over her head as she spoke in fairy tongue. "I've put him under an enchantment and truthfulness spell." She looked into the injured man's eyes …. "What is your name?"

"My, my name is Esteban," the man stuttered.

"Who do you work for?"

"Garcia, Diego Garcia and our master …."

"Who is the master?"

"Sh, she is known as Abaddon," the minion choked.

"You mean the archangel?"

The man nodded as he gasped for air.

"Hurry up Sam, he's on his last legs," snapped Lilly as she paced impatiently back and forth.

"What do you know of the Lima Treasure?" Sam asked.

"We have the six Inca statues."

"WHAT? WHERE ARE THEY?" shouted Lilly.

"We, we have them in a safe, in Paris."

"Where in Paris?" asked Sam. She grabbed his shirt and lifted him slightly from the ground as she stared into his eyes.

"Below the cafe, Cafe Les Paris," he muttered.

Sam released him from the fairy spell as he drew his last breath and slumped to the ground.

"Did you get all that Annie?" asked Lilly.

"Yeah, I'm on it. Good work Sam."

"Yeah, good work Sam. Right, let's concentrate on the stone." They walked over to the Madonna Stone and Lilly summoned her light staff to enable them to study the surface of the stone. "Can you see anything?" Lilly asked.

Sam shook her head as she studied the undulating profile of the standing stone. "No, nothing. Perhaps we're looking at it too closely, you know. Maybe we need to look at it, as if we were studying a painting. From a few steps back."

"We can try," said Lilly. The two teenagers stepped back about two metres and began to walk around the Madonna Stone, which seemed to alter its appearance as the light staff created various shadows.

"There," Sam said as she pointed. "Stop Lilly. Take one step back. Just there, what d'ya think?"

"You could be right Sam. It certainly looks like a face of a lady. Annie …. Are you seeing this?"

"I see it girls. Hang on, I'm just running the image through a computer enhancement programme …. You're right, it's definitely an image of a lady, most probably the grey lady. I'm just getting the co-ordinates to see where she's pointing too, 'cos I guess that's what she's all about. She's looking at a location."

"Yeah, that would make sense," Lilly responded.

"Right, here we go. You won't be able to see it from the Madonna Stone, but the co-ordinates take you straight to the Casquets Lighthouse about 11 kilometres off the west coast of Alderney."

"Good work Annie. We'll go now, 'cos if memory serves me right the lighthouse is automated these days, so they'll be no-one there," said Lilly.

"Before you go Lilly, am I correct in saying that the base end of your light staff is a hexagon?"

"What ARE you on about Annie?"

"Humour me Lilly. Is the bottom of your light staff in the shape of a hexagon?"

"Well, actually Annie, it is. The first fifteen centimetres are carved in a hexagon shape and the remainder of the light staff is round. So?"

"Lilly, I'm guessing that your light staff has been carved to fit into something, perhaps as a marker. Think about it. When the grey lady was chiselled into the Madonna Stone, whoever did it would need to know the direction from there to the Lighthouse, so ...."

Lilly ran her hands across the top surface of the standing stone. "So they used a marker inserted in this hole I've just found Annie." Lilly picked up her light staff and pushed the base of it into the hole. "It's a perfect fit Annie, you're brilliant and the top of my light staff is now reflecting the beam of light from the lighthouse every time the lamp rotates. That's absolutely brilliant."

"That's okay. You're welcome. The wind has picked up tonight so watch yourselves on those rocks. The height of the waves will be troublesome. It'll be wild and rough."

"Thanks Annie," Sam replied, before disappearing in a magical pillar of fire.

The faintest flutter of wings and Lilly disappeared into the night sky.

"My apologies for disturbing you master."

"Come, enter Roberto. You have good news I hope?" Abaddon swung her cloak over her shoulders and walked over to the stained window and gazed out.

"Er, well. Not exactly my master," Roberto answered nervously.

Abaddon swung round to face Roberto. "Well out with it man. I don't have all day."

"The ambush on the er, angel, the one they call Lilly, failed."

"And the others that were with her?"

"They all survived master."

"DAMN IT!" Abaddon paced back and forth stopping occasionally to glare at Roberto.

"We lost fifteen demons master and we've also lost contact with Diego Garcia, not to mention our two inside contacts."

"That is of no consequence to me. What news of Esteban and my brother, the archangel Michael?"

Roberto bowed his head and remained silent.

"Did you not hear me?" Abaddon approached Roberto. "WELL?"

"So sorry master." Roberto stepped back. "They have both been killed."

"AARRGGHH!!" Abaddon pulled her sword from its sheath and swung it violently at the assorted, surrounding furniture. She suddenly stopped and grabbed Roberto by the collar. "The angel. The one they call Lilly. She must have found the missing pendant. How else could she have defeated Michael?" The archangel pulled Roberto closer. "Get back to Paris and double the security on the Inca statues. I will summon my brother, the archangel Raphael to meet you there ."

Roberto nodded.

"Do NOT let me down." She released Roberto from her grasp and he quickly scurried out of the room.

I will defeat you angel. Nothing is going to stop me ruling the world, thought Abaddon.

The waves of the ocean crashed violently over the rocks beneath them as Lilly and Sam appeared on the helipad, of the south west tower of the lighthouse buildings on the Casquets.

"You okay Sam?"

"Yeah, sure. Jeez it's wild out here Lilly. I can hardly stand in this wind …. And that noise." Sam covered her ears as the foghorn in the east tower bellowed twice.

"Ha, there must be some fog or mist around. You can hear that sound nearly six kilometres away. Come on, let's get off this helipad, there's a ladder here that'll take us down to the deserted accommodation buildings," said Lilly.

Lilly climbed over the edge and lowered herself onto the rusty ladder which was attached to the side of the tower. Sam watched as Lilly slowly descended, waves lashing her as they crashed over the rocks, whilst the steadily flashing light from the north west tower swung round every thirty seconds, illuminating the violence of the surrounding ocean ....

What was that? thought Sam, as the beam of light from the lighthouse momentarily lit up an object out at sea. The light swung round again .... *It's a fishing boat .... And it's in trouble.* "CAN YOU SEE THAT BOAT LILLY?" Sam shouted down to Lilly below, and she pointed in the direction of the boat.

Lilly stepped off the last rung of the ladder to stand on the rock. "I SEE IT SAM, BUT YOU NEED TO CLIMB DOWN NOW. THE WEATHER'S DETERIORATING." Lilly watched as Sam, who was eight metres above her, gingerly clamber onto the ladder and started to climb down. A huge wave crashed over the rocks swamping both girls as they held onto the ladder. The ageing metal of the ladder creaked under the strain of another huge wave and then .... Lilly let go as the ladder twisted in the power of the wave and tore itself away from the stonework. She knelt down and protected her face from the metalwork and stone as the water swept past her.

Lilly glanced upwards. *Can't see Sam.* "SAM," she shouted. "Annie, what d'ya see?"

"I've lost her Lilly. Just give me a mo'."

"Come on Annie, the storm's getting worse. Where's Sam?"

"I don't see her Lilly."

"What about that fishing boat we saw a few moments ago?"

"It's up on the rocks and looks like it's goin' to break up at any moment."

"Okay Annie. Any news from air sea rescue or the lifeboat station?"

"The lifeboat has tried to reach them but had to turn back because of the rocks. Air sea rescue couldn't even take off from the airport due to the extreme winds."

"Right Annie, I'll try to help them. We'll have to do this another day."

"Copy that .... WAIT! HOLD IT LILLY! Sam has just appeared at the command centre."

"Oh thank goodness."

"Lilly, are you there?"

"Yeah, I'm still here."

"Sam has disappeared again, but she's taken Usha with her. They said they were going to attempt a rescue on the fishing boat."

"Okay. In that case I'll stay here. Keep an eye on them Annie and let me know if they need my help."

"Copy that."

Lilly flapped her wings again in an attempt to keep them dry enough to fly. *Just in case I have to leave in a hurry,* she thought. She steadied herself against the rock wall as another huge wave crashed over the surrounding rocks, hurling boulders and seaweed through the night air.

As the waves subsided momentarily, Lilly glanced across to the cliffs of Alderney and spotted the reflection of the lighthouse beam from the top of her light staff in the Madonna Stone. Every time the beam of light hit her light staff, Lilly inched her way forward across the slippery rocks, towards where the reflected light was revealing the anticipated location of the Inca treasure. *Nearly there. A couple more rotations.*

The light swung round again .... And there they were. Three gold Inca statues, sitting like ornaments on a stone shelf, below a small window in the north west tower, secured by padlocks and galvanised steel mesh. Lilly could feel her pulse quickening with excitement as she broke away the mesh and padlocks. "I have them Annie. Three Inca statues. I have them."

"Copy that Lilly."

The platform came to a shuddering halt at the bottom of the shaft as the sound of the hydraulics faded into the distance. Lilly stepped from the platform, glancing upwards to the metal door that was now closed four metres above her. She walked through the dimly lit tunnel and entered the underground command centre to be met by Annie and a very wet Usha who was wrapped in a blanket.

"Hi girls," said Lilly. "Look what I've got." She held the three Inca statues aloft as if she'd just won a trophy at a football match. Her smile was one of satisfaction as she handed them to Annie and then threw her arms around her sister Usha. "How did you get on with that fishing boat sis'?"

"Piece of cake, ha! It was awesome out there sis'. The sea was ferocious but you should have seen Sam, she was something else. We'd have never rescued that fishing boat and the three fishermen if it hadn't have been for Sam's magical powers."

"That's good then." Lilly glanced around. "So, where is Sam?"

Annie pointed to an open doorway down one of the many corridors leading away from the main hub of of the underground centre. "In there I think Lilly."

Lilly casually wandered down the corridor closely followed by Annie and Usha. They stood in the open doorway and watched as Sam and Chloe caressed each other intimately and were kissing passionately ….

"Knock knock," Lilly said as she tapped on the door frame. "Sorry girls, didn't mean to startle you."

"Jeez, Lilly!" Sam quickly bent down to pick up her discarded blanket and quickly wrapped it around herself and Chloe to protect their modesty.

"A good result out there for all of us girls. A rough night but we all pulled through," said Lilly.

Annie clapped her hands. "Right everyone. A de-brief in an hour and then some shut eye, 'cos it's a big day tomorrow. We have two funerals to attend, okay?"

Usha nudged Annie in the ribs and whispered, "De-briefed Annie? I think the girls are one step ahead of you!"

CHAPTER 48

GAY PAREE

"It was good to see plenty of people at the church for Alex's funeral. So young eh? Why would anyone want to murder him? Nothing makes sense any more. The world has gone mad." Ben sighed. He lifted his pint glass of beer to his mouth and took a couple of gulps, before pushing his hand into a dish of peanuts and grabbing a fist full. He offered a few to Luis before tipping the rest into his mouth.

Luis shuffled himself on his bar stool as he waved Ben's offering away. "No thanks mate, I'll just get myself another drink." He raised his arm to attract the barmaid's attention from across the bar. "Hi Tessa, could you get me another pint please and whatever Ben's having. Cheers." Luis turned on the bar stool and acknowledged Beth and Frank Bean, who were sat quietly in the corner across the bar room. "Christ, they're going to miss Alex," he mumbled.

"You got that right mate," Ben replied. "And to think, they've just come into all that money."

"Yeah. Fat lot of good it'll do them now," Luis moaned as he shook his head.

The main door of the Campania public house swung open as Lucy, Annie and Bea walked in, immediately followed by Lilly, Usha, Sam and Chloe.

"I hear they had a graveside service for Mr Morgan. I bet there were plenty there," said Ben.

"Yeah, I'm sure of it," replied Luis. It'll be interesting to see who takes charge of the family, if you know what I mean."

Ben nodded in agreement.

The pub bustled with activity through the afternoon as mourners from both funerals joined in with life celebrations and memories.

"Okay girls, I'm going now," Annie announced. "I need to get home and set up the security systems for tonight. I take it you're still going to Paris tonight?"

"Yeah of course. We'll see you before we go," replied Usha.

Annie left the Campania, unaware that she was being followed.

"So whilst we're all together let's talk about Paris," said Lilly. "What intel do we have actually have?"

"Well we know the location," Sam explained. "We understand that the Inca statues are in the basement of a cafe. The Cafe Les Paris."

"Yeah. And they'll be well guarded I'm sure, by demons and the like," added Usha.

"If our sources are correct, the Inca statues are in an old bank safe, which should be of no concern to us. Easily dealt with," said Chloe. "But we believe that Roberto, one of Garcia's henchman is there as well."

"Excuse me girls." It was Bea. She'd had another ghostly 'visit', this time from Richard, to warn her that Gabriel would be in Paris. She'd waited until Annie and Lucy had left the Campania separately before approaching the girls. "I know that you're travelling to Paris tonight, so you need to be aware that the archangel Gabriel will be there."

There was an audible gasp around the table as Bea walked away from the girls and left the pub.

Lilly stood up. "Girls, we've always known that we have to battle with the archangels. We took Michael down the other night. This will be no different."

The group of friends cheered before leaving the pub to make their way to the command centre to meet up with Annie.

Annie was deep in her own thoughts as she sauntered home, preoccupied as to how they were going to fare later that night, in their planned assault on the cafe premises in Paris. *We've got to find those Inca statues. Must make sure all the equipment is set up correctly....*

"HEY YOU!!" A woman's voice. "YOU THERE!" The same voice shouted again.

Annie stopped and quickly checked her body cam was switched on. She nervously looked around as she grabbed her ear piece out of her pocket and frantically pushed it into her ear.

"HEY!"

The voice was in front of Annie. *Jeez, who is it?*

Annie could feel her heart pounding in her chest. Her hands felt hot and clammy. She felt threatened. She ducked into an open doorway and desperately tried to keep herself calm as she whispered into her headset …. *"Can anyone hear me?... Please …. Someone is after me …. Help."*

"OY! I KNOW WHERE YOU'RE HIDING." The woman's voice seemed closer.

Annie panicked and ran into the street, narrowly avoiding being hit by a truck as the driver swerved and hit a lamppost, bringing the truck to a halt. Her legs carried her to the corner and into the next street not stopping to look back. *"Help me please."*

"There's no help coming." A woman's voice again.

Annie stopped running as Carol Mollins stepped out in front of her brandishing a vicious looking hunting knife. She paced up to Annie and pinned her against the wall ….

"You didn't think you'd see me again eh?" Carol sneered. "Do you REALLY think you're goin' to win?" She ran the blade of the knife across Annie's left cheek drawing blood, before running her fingers across the red liquid and placing them in her mouth. "Hmm, lovely."

Annie winced in pain as Carol sliced open her right cheek. "You, you don't want to do this Carol," Annie stuttered.

"How would YOU know what I want to do. Ha! You've no idea what I'm capable of …. But you're about to find out." Carol raised her arm and swung the knife down, as a single gunshot from behind her echoed in the street and Carol collapsed to the ground to reveal Lucy, standing gun in hand, five metres away.

Annie sunk to her knees, shaking in relief and then realised Lilly was stood across the street, watching. Annie glanced over at Carol's bloodied body in front of her. *She's still alive, just.*

Lucy walked up to Carol's body and used a foot to push her over onto her back. Neither of them uttered a word as Lucy pulled the gun from her waist and without hesitation, fired a single shot between Carol's eyes and casually walked away.

Bloody hell! thought Annie.

Lilly crossed the street and picked Annie up with the strength of four men. "Come on, let's get you out of here."

"Did you see that Lilly? Did you see the look in her eyes?"

"Yeah. Lucy may have saved your life but she's a callous bastard. S'pose she has to be if she's a CIA agent. Have to say that Carol had it coming, but who's gonna' tell Chloe her Mum's been killed?"

Jeez, hadn't thought of that.

Lilly and Annie disappeared in a heart beat, save for the faintest flutter of wings.

Annie winced with pain as Lilly laid her down on one of the beds in front of Chloe who immediately held her pendant over her heart and chanted ... "I am Alnitak the Healer and Child of the Stars." She passed her hand over Annie's bloodied face as a bright white glow hovered over Annie until all her injuries were healed.

"Thank you Chloe." Annie sat up and swung her legs round, off the bed and onto the floor. She kissed Chloe on the cheek.

"You've been thinking about me haven't you?" Chloe asked.

"I, er."

"It's alright Annie. I know about my Mum. I knew as soon as she died, I had a feeling you know. It's all to do with this power of healing I control. The connections with the sparks of life I s'pose."

"Oh, right. It's just, you know, Lucy was so callous about it. No feelings, no remorse. Just nothing," replied Annie.

"Yeah I know. The over riding problem was my Mum's inability to deal with the booze and her addiction to drugs. Once the Mafia had tapped into her weak psyche, they brainwashed her into being their puppet basically. There was never goin' to be any redemption. She was too far gone."

"She was still your Mum though Chloe."

"Yeah I know and she had a rough time." Chloe sighed. "But life has to move on. I have to move on .... Come on, let's see if the rest of the crew are ready for tonight's shenanigans."

Annie and Chloe stepped into the main chamber of the command centre and joined Lilly, Usha and Sam who were stood around a large oval mahogany table studying the plans of the Cafe Les Paris.

"Oh hi you two. You feeling better now Annie?" asked Usha.

"Yeah, fine thanks," Annie replied. "So does everyone know what they're doing?"

"Yeah, sure. We'll have a better idea of numbers when we arrive," Lilly replied.

"Okay. Right you lot, I'll do what I can from this end. The bottom line is we need the Inca statues but more importantly, look out for each other. Check your headsets and cams'," ordered Annie. "I've nothing else to say apart from good luck everyone."

Sam held Chloe's hand and they disappeared in a magical pillar of fire followed by Lilly carrying Usha, to the faintest sound of the flutter of wings.

Lilly and Usha hid in the shadows across the road from the scruffy looking cafe, which was on the ground floor of a dilapidated four storey building, one of many in the dimly lit street. The heavy rain bounced off the rooftops as Sam and Chloe appeared in a magical pillar of fire on the roof above the cafe.

"We're all here Annie," Lilly spoke into her head mic'.

"Copy that. How many heat sources are you detecting Chloe?"

"Just one Annie, which probably means the whole building is teeming with demons."

"Yeah, sorry Chloe, it was a stupid question. I forgot that demons don't have heat signatures."

"Chloe, come over here," Sam hissed. She was looking over the crumbling parapet of the flat roof. She called again.

"What's up gal?" Chloe knelt down close to Sam and placed her hand on her shoulder.

"Look down the street babe. Tell me what d'ya see?"

Chloe strained her eyes as she peered left and right through the pouring rain. "I see nothing Sam."

Sam sighed. "Exactly, there's nothing apart from this sodding rain." She shook herself. "Chloe, there's not a light on anywhere down the street. It looks like the bastards were expecting us and they've probably cut the power to the whole street. Now we're in complete darkness ... And listen .... Not a sound."

"That's not good is it?" Chloe sat back in resignation.

"What's going off up there?" Usha's voice cut through the silence on the headphones.

"Usha. Can you see anything from down on the street? Any lights? Any sign of life?" asked Sam. *This feels like a trap.*

"That's a negative, we have nothing." Usha shook her head.

"Use your night vision goggles girls."

"And if all else fails, we can call on our light staffs," added Lilly. "Come on guys, we need to make a move. Sam, Chloe, keep to the plan. Check out each floor as you move down the block. I'll take the front door of the cafe whilst Usha keeps an eye on the street. Let's do this."

The rain had eased slightly as Lilly and Usha crossed the street to the cafe. Usha tried the door handle.

"You're kidding me right?" Lilly joked to Usha. "You're trying the door, expecting it to be unlocked?"

Usha shrugged her shoulders and smirked as the door swung open hitting a dining table that had seen better days. "Whatever!" She stepped to the side and Lilly walked confidently through the doorway into the cafe.

Usha felt nervous as she stood by herself in the street. She'd been on these sort of missions many times before, fighting demons and evil minions. *This seems different though,* she thought. *We're so close to finding the Lima Treasure and yet* .... "Who's there?" Her pulse quickened as she heard a noise to her side. A large ginger tomcat howled as it leapt down out of the darkness from a crumbling stone windowsill and ran between her legs, before scooting off across the road avoiding the puddles as it ran. "Jeez, a bloody cat." Usha sighed with relief. *Get a grip gal.* She glanced nervously up and down the

396

street to reassure herself. A cry broke from her lips as a hand clamped over her mouth then …. darkness ….

The floor creaked and groaned as Lilly stood on the rotting floorboards in the middle of what would have been the dining area of the cafe. As her eyes adjusted to using her night vision goggles she could see to her left the bar area and what appeared to be a serving hatch through to the kitchen area she surmised. She pulled out her angel blade as two shadows moved ominously across the room in front of her and disappeared through an open doorway. Broken glass crunched under Lilly's feet as she turned, giving her presence away. *Damn it.* A heavy blow with a blunt instrument from behind sent Lilly sprawling across the floor, as her angel blade spun from her hand disappearing into the darkness. Lilly dragged herself up onto her knees as a heavy steel toe capped boot swung into her midriff. She twisted across the floor as another boot connected with her head causing Lilly to wince in pain. *My head's bleeding and I've got no power. Something's wrong. Shit, and I've lost my head mic' and goggles.*

"So what's it feel like angel?" Roberto cackled as he stepped out from behind the bar and placed an old gas light, that had seen better days, on the work surface. The light revealed some sort of pattern on the ceiling, that Lilly recognised as a warding symbol to render angels harmless.

I'm really in the shit now. The flickering gas light betrayed the presence of at least twenty mean and nasty demons.

"As you can see, we're not alone angel. So how does it feel to be like a mere mortal again?"

Two demons pulled Lilly up from the floor and pulled her arms back behind her. "What have you done you bastard?" She spluttered as blood continued to run from her mouth. "USHA," she shouted.

"Don't concern yourself about your sister. Let's just say that she's currently preoccupied, ha!" hissed Roberto.

"So what d'ya want?" Lilly struggled in vain as the demons dug their talons further into her arms.

"Want? The only thing we want from you is your last breath, bitch."

"Sam, Chloe, where are you? I'm getting no response from Usha or Lilly."

"Annie," Chloe whispered. "We're both in the back room of the cafe, what used to be the kitchen I suppose. It's bloody filthy. Health and Safety would have a field day in here, ha! We've faced no resistance on the upper floors and there's no sign of Usha or Lilly."

Sam and Chloe were crouched down on the kitchen floor below the serving hatch.

Chloe lifted herself slowly to peer through the hole in the wall and quickly bobbed down next to Sam. "There's at least twenty demons in there," whispered Chloe, "and they've got hold of Lilly."

"How's that possible?" asked Sam, as she covered her mouth to keep her voice quiet.

Chloe popped her head up to the serving hatch again. Moments passed before she ducked back down. "There's some sort of large symbol on the ceiling …. Lilly's in a bad way and if we don't act soon, she'll be dead."

"The symbol will be an angel warding or rune. It prevents an angel from attacking and using any powers. It's like a magic spell and you need to break any part of the drawing to break the spell."

"Thanks for the information Annie." Sam crawled across the filthy kitchen floor and grabbed hold of an old style fireman's axe from the wall that she'd spotted earlier, hanging next to a fire extinguisher. Chloe watched open mouthed, as Sam disappeared in a magical pillar of fire.

"So angel, anything you wanna' say before I slit your throat?" Roberto flashed the huge hunting blade in front of Lilly, her eyes half open as the life slowly drained from her ….

"WHAT THE HELL!" Roberto looked up to the ceiling as plaster began to fall around him.

Chloe watched through the serving hatch. She could hear Sam on the floor above, smashing the axe into the rotten floorboards above Lilly until …. The ceiling caved in with an almighty rumble to the cafe floor. Through the overpowering clouds of dust and rubble, Lilly rose up, her mighty wings fully outstretched. Her bright white eyes pierced the gloom and a searing white laser light from her eyes destroyed the demons instantly in clouds of dust.

Chloe clambered through the rubble into the remains of the cafe as Roberto struggled to his feet still clutching his hunting knife. "YOU LUCKY BITCH ANGEL! IF I CAN'T HAVE YOU I'LL HAVE THIS WHORE." He lurched towards Chloe who instinctively recoiled backwards, gasping in astonishment as his head rolled off his shoulders and hit the floor in front of her. His body collapsing in a bloody heap.

Sam dropped the bloodied axe to the floor. "Nobody has my babe today." She smiled wryly as Chloe flung her arms around her and they kissed before both turning to hug Lilly.

"Thanks girls," said Lilly. "Still no sign of Usha?"

Sam and Chloe shook their heads.

"I've got a heat signature in the basement, but that's all I've got girls, sorry."

"That has to be Usha," replied Lilly. "C'mon girls, let's get down there." The rickety old door creaked as Lilly opened it to reveal the steep stairs down to the basement. "No lights, so be on your guard."

At the bottom of the stairs the three girls stepped into the basement and immediately the ground beneath their feet began to shudder. A huge dazzling flash of blue light lit up the basement to reveal Usha bound and gagged on the floor, on the other side of the room next to an old bank safe. A swirling cloud of smoke appeared and then dispersed as the archangel Gabriel materialised, throwing bolts of blue lightening directly at Lilly, which she deflected out of harms way with her angel blade.

Two magical fireballs from Sam found their target causing the archangel to reel back, giving Chloe the opportunity to dash across the floor to Usha and release her from her bonds.

Gabriel unleashed two bolts of blue lightening at Sam as she disappeared in a magical pillar of fire.

"Sam's drawing Gabriel's attention," Chloe muttered. "Summon your light staff Usha.

"NOW GUY'S," Lilly shouted. Her eyes emitted searing beams of white light directly at Gabriel. Sam fired two magical fireballs hitting their target, whilst lightening bolts from the light staffs of Usha and Chloe hit the archangel repeatedly, until a huge explosion of light and dust. The friends watched in awe as the archangel disintegrated into dust.

"Everyone okay?"

"All good Annie," replied Usha.

"Great to hear your voice again Usha."

Usha turned to face the safe and grabbed the handle. "Let's hope it was all worth it guys." She concentrated as her physical power built up and then …. The door of the safe flew across the basement floor as Usha ripped it from it's hinges. "I can imagine Grandad saying now, 'you were only meant to blow the bloody doors off!' Ha! Just like in the Italian Job movie." She reached in as the others watched and pulled out what looked like a bundle of rags and placed them on top of the old bank safe.

"The moment of truth eh?" said Chloe.

Usha pulled at the rags. "Ta da!" She held up the six golden Inca statues.

"Time to go guys," said Lilly. She picked Usha up with the strength of four men and disappeared with the faintest flutter of wings followed by Sam and Chloe in a magical pillar of fire, unbeknown that they'd been watched.

"We have to destroy them before they achieve invincibility," Abaddon cackled as she peered through the gloom of the basement.

"We have a plan oh master," sneered Garcia. "We will destroy them …."

CHAPTER 49

ALL RIGHT NOW

Jubilation and celebrations were in the air down in the command centre ....

"Great party Annie." Bea poured herself another shot of whiskey as Annie tapped her feet to the beat of the music. She nudged Annie with her elbow, "this track playing now...."

Annie nodded.

".... It was one of Richard's favourite tracks by Depeche Mode. Enjoy The Silence isn't it?"

"Yeah I know," replied Annie. She kissed Bea tenderly on her cheek. "I miss him too Bea."

"The girls seem to be enjoying themselves. It's great to see them being themselves, you know, teenagers."

"Totally," replied Annie. "But you must remember Bea, they may be teenagers, but in reality they've matured into responsible young adults, both intellectually and sexually."

"Oh absolutely. I entirely agree with you, but still, they are my Granddaughters. And Sam, well she's beautiful."

"Well we'll let them have their fun tonight before we tackle the archangel Abaddon and her minions tomorrow."

"So soon Annie?"

"We have to Bea. If we wait too long, we'll be giving her more time to organise her followers."

Bea nodded in agreement. *We don't even have a plan of action yet .... And we still need the last Inca gold statue!*

"Miguel?"

"I'm here master," hissed Miguel as he shuffled forward across the concrete floor and bowed his head to Abaddon, her enormous wings outstretched, blotting out what bit of moonlight there was, penetrating the old stained windows of the town church.

"And Garcia. What of him?"

The huge oak doors at the far end of the church swung open and they clattered into heaps of broken and discarded church pews, dust flying into the air. The sudden commotion caused the many assembled minions to scatter as Garcia, followed by two mean looking Muki goblins who were dragging a bloodied woman by her hair, strode in.

"Ah, Garcia. Good news I hope?" Abaddon continued to pace back and forth.

The two goblins pulled the exhausted woman onto the steps leading up to Abaddon and released their grip. They muttered and then scuttled to hide behind Garcia as Abaddon moved down the steps and lifted the woman's head as she groaned in pain.

The archangel stared down at the woman and then kicked her aside as Garcia moved closer. "So Garcia, what's this garbage you've brought me? Or is she just another one of your trollops looking for vengeance?"

"Master, this is my wife. Her name is Lucy and she's an agent with the CIA," replied Garcia.

"You, you bastard," Lucy spluttered. "How long have you known?" She spat some blood in Garcia's direction.

"Ah my dear, I've always known. After I murdered Luis' Mother, I needed a cover story and you my dear, turned up at the right time. You was the perfect opportunity for me to hide in plain sight once we were married. How d'ya think I've always been one step ahead of you?"

"This is all very touching, this, this family reunion," Abaddon sneered, "but what the hell is she doing here Garcia?"

"Er. Well master. She could be useful to us with a little more of their persuasion." Garcia pointed to the goblins. "We've already found out that the angel and her friends intend to strike as early as tomorrow."

"The fools," hissed Abaddon.

"She's also submitted evidence that we have a traitor amongst your closest allies."

"Ha! She obviously thinks that I'm totally oblivious as to who is against our cause."

"And master, she's also told us that the group don't have all of the Lima Treasure. They are missing one Inca gold statue."

"Ha! Then they are fools," growled the archangel. "Very well Garcia, keep the woman alive for now .... But kill her when she has no further use."

A column of swirling white smoke appeared in front of Abaddon which gradually dispersed to reveal the archangel Raphael, who immediately knelt in submission.

"Welcome my brother. Stand up so that I might see you in a better light." Abaddon motioned to Raphael.

"Master, I am concerned that not all is going to plan."

"Walk with me brother, that we might talk privately." Abaddon's voice softened as she placed her arm around Raphael's waist and encouraged him to slowly walk. "What concerns you brother?"

"Sister, we have lost two brothers in this campaign of yours, Michael and now Gabriel. The angel hybrid Lilly is clearly more dangerous than you thought. Don't you think it would be prudent to reassess your strategy?"

"Dear Raphael, always the worrier and never the warrior. You dare to question my strategy and ultimately my authority?"

Raphael shook his head nervously.

Abaddon stretched her wings as she lifted her brother off his feet. "I WILL rule both heaven and earth." She unsheathed a silver dagger. "But I don't need snivelling little toe rags like you." She plunged the dagger between Raphael's eyes and tossed him down below to the floor, to the hungry hordes of minions. "Goodbye brother."

Chloe gently cupped Sam's silky breasts from behind whilst Sam nestled into Chloe's midriff, as they lay in bed contented from their earlier lovemaking through the night. Sam slowly turned in her lover's arms and kissed her passionately on the lips before kneeling up in bed next to Chloe. "Morning babe."

Chloe half opened her eyes. "Uh, er morning Sam. What time is it?"

"It's time you were both up," said Annie is she tapped on the door and popped her head round, causing the two girls to cover up as they grabbed the duvet. "Ha!"

"Are Lilly and Usha here yet?"

"They're both due back here in the next ten minutes so come on girls, time to move." Annie walked down the corridor and into the main room of the command centre.

"I'm glad Lilly and Usha had time to catch up with Luis and Ben," Sam said as she fastened the zip on the back of Chloe's top.

"Yeah, I bet they had a great time," replied Chloe. She stood up and looked in the full length mirror. "Oh."

"What is it babe?"

"I can see my Dad. He's stood behind me, clear as day."

"All I can see is you babe. Looking as gorgeous as ever."

"Don't turn round Chloe." Philip placed his hand on his daughter's shoulder. "I'm very proud of you Chloe and I'm so pleased that you've found happiness with Samantha."

"It's Sam, Dad." Chloe held Sam's hand as she continued to look in the mirror.

"Today will be full of danger Chloe. More than you can possibly imagine. But whatever happens, you must follow your heart and remember, I will always be with you."

Chloe's eyes filled up with tears. "I will always love you Dad."

"I love you too Chloe. There is one last thing you need to know. You have a child …."

"WHAT? That can't be. I lost my baby, Alex's baby."

"That's what you was led to believe and needed to believe."

"Mama Killa, the Moon Goddess told me she couldn't save my baby," Chloe sobbed.

"I know Chloe. But the Gods felt it was the best way of protecting both yourself and your daughter from the Mafia and the archangel, Abaddon."

"I have a little girl?"

"Yes you do."

"I have a little girl …. And Lilly knew didn't she?"

"Yes she knows and always has. She so wanted to tell you," replied Philip.

"Your dreams will come true. That's what Lilly told me, bless her. Oh Dad."

"Stay focused Chloe and remember, I will always be with you."

Chloe moved her hand to touch Philip's hand on her shoulder as he disappeared.

"You okay babe?"

"Er, yeah. Of course I am." Chloe smiled to herself.

"That's alright then. Only you went a bit weird on me when you looked in the mirror, you know, like being in a trance babe."

"I'm fine Sam. Honestly." Chloe kissed her girlfriend on the cheek. "C'mon, let's join the others. Lilly and Usha should be here by now."

".... So is everyone clear as to what needs to be done?" Annie asked the group. "The biggest factor today is that we all have to watch each others backs."

"But you can't do any of this without the power of the Lima Treasure," Bea interrupted. "What have you done with the two gold Inca platter style dishes, the statues and the two rocks?"

"They've been taken up to Fort Tourgis and hidden, as we discussed earlier. And before you ask, they are being watched and protected by Sam's sisters, the fairies Ruby and Lola," Annie replied.

"Yeah, they've cast temporary magical spells on the Lima Treasure to hide them from demons and archangels," explained Sam.

"But you still require the last Inca statue to activate the power that comes from the Lima Treasure." Bea was getting frustrated. "And more to the point, does anyone actually know where it is?"

The group muttered amongst themselves.

"Actually, I know where it is." Usha had a smug grin on her face. "It's in the old German Second World War ammunition store below Fort Tourgis. The store's owned by Ben's Dad, Albert Allens, don't you remember Lilly? The statue is a lever that operates the trapdoor from above. We removed the statue that was used as a lever for the trapdoor from beneath, to deter any demons from entering this world from Ukhu Pacha, the world below." Usha rummaged about in her pockets and then held her arm aloft. "And I've still got a copy of the key to get in the place …. Awesome!"

Lilly smiled in admiration at her sister.

"Okay then. So Chloe, you go with Usha to get the final sta …. What's that noise?" Annie covered her ears as the entire command complex became a cacophony of noise and started to shake violently. "What have we got on the monitors from the outside cameras Bea?"

"Heads up guys." Bea motioned to the monitors. "We're in big trouble. We have incoming blue lightening bolts that can only mean one thing."

"Abaddon." Lilly glared at the monitors.

"And judging by these pictures, there must be two, maybe three hundred demons out there," Annie said.

The command centre shook violently once more.

"How long can this place hold out?" asked Sam.

"Not sure to be honest," replied Annie. "The complex has never had to withstand the power of an archangel."

"WATCH OUT GUYS," Usha shouted, as a huge crack appeared in the ceiling above Annie and Bea, causing lumps of concrete to crash to the floor.

"There's your answer," Sam said. "Not too long."

"Annie, is there another way out of here?" asked Chloe. "Annie?"

"Er, yeah," she stuttered. "It's down there." Annie pointed down the corridor. "Past the bedrooms. I'll show you." She ran down the corridor followed by Lilly, Usha, Chloe and Sam until they reached what looked like, an oval, solid steel door with a central locking wheel.

"It looks like a door you'd find in a submarine. Like a water tight hatch," Usha said.

"Exactly." Annie nodded. "It works the same way. You can only release the central locking wheel from this side, so once you go through, there's no way back. There's a tunnel on the other side which will take you to the basement of the Water Tower, you know, what was the World War 2 Luftwaffe Command Post."

"Yeah I know the one," Chloe replied, "and from the top, you can see all of Alderney in every direction."

Another huge explosion outside shook the command centre.

"You have to go girls," said Annie. "Try and keep your head sets and body cams on. Bea and I will do what we can from here." She hugged and kissed the girls in turn before grabbing the central locking wheel and spun it to release the door, which opened automatically with a loud hissing sound.

Lilly and Usha stepped through the doorway. They watched as Chloe embraced Sam ....

"If I don't survive Sam, promise me you'll find my baby daughter," whispered Chloe. She pushed her lover to the ground and stepped through the open doorway to join Lilly and Usha. "CLOSE THE DOOR ANNIE."

The door slammed shut and the wheel spun.

"Oh Sam," Chloe sobbed.

"You did the right thing gal," said Usha. "Come on, let's get out of here."

Annie offered Sam a helping hand off the floor.

"I can manage." She huffed and puffed as she got to her feet and stormed off back down the corridor, avoiding the fallen plaster and concrete as she headed to the main room, where Bea was closely watching the monitors. "How are we doing Bea?" asked Sam.

"Could be better." The building shook violently again. "How are you doing Sam? Don't answer that 'cos I can see it on your face. Believe me when I tell you that Chloe prevented you from going for a very good reason."

"And what would that be?"

Bea placed her hand on Sam's shoulder. "Chloe knows that for the girls to defeat Abaddon the archangel, she and Usha have to become angel hybrids like Lilly. Part human part angel you know. You are a fairy, which means you're part angel and part demon."

"And?"

"We're not absolutely certain, but we believe that whatever power the Lima Treasure possesses will destroy any demons," explained Bea. "The girls were not willing to put your life in danger, especially Chloe."

The ground shook again sending shock waves through the command centre. More plaster and stonework fell to the floor as Annie re-joined Bea and Sam. "You okay Sam?" asked Annie.

"I s'pose."

"Good. Let's hope the girls are okay."

The girls were at the top of the Water Tower looking out over the many buildings and landmarks.

"It's quite surreal Lilly," said Usha. We're surrounded by blue skies and yet, if you look over there," she pointed towards Annie's property, "it looks like a war zone with its dark skies, lightening bolts, fires out of control and explosions."

"We've no time to lose," Lilly said. "Chloe, you must shape-shift and take Usha to Ben's Dad's store below Fort Tourgis, to get the Inca statue and then to the white navigation marker above the fort. In the meantime, I'll try and keep Abaddon and his minions occupied. Just give me a shout when everything is set up."

"Are you sure about this?" asked Usha.

"No more arguments sis', just don't let me down." Lilly kissed Usha on the cheek and disappeared in a heartbeat save for the faintest fluttering of wings.

"We have to go Usha. Just remember to pick up my clothes. MORPH!" Chloe clapped her hands over her head and her form changed, as she shape-shifted into a huge Phoenix. Usha picked up the clothes and climbed on the bird's back and clung on as the Phoenix took flight over the town towards Fort Tourgis.

"KEEP US LOW" Usha shouted as the wind rattled in her ears and for a moment, all thoughts of demons and angels were lost as the world below flew by. *What's going on down there by the town church?* "CHLOE. CIRCLE ROUND THE CHURCH. BUT LOWER." The giant bird swooped down as it circled the church of St Annes. *Just there. It's Miguel and Diego Garcia, Luis' Dad.* Usha heard gunshots from the ground below. "GET US OUT OF HERE CHLOE."

Two minutes later and the narrow coastal lane which led to Fort Clonque about half a mile away on the other side of the bay came into view.

"TAKE US DOWN CHLOE. LAND IN THE SMALL CAR PARK IF YOU CAN."

The Phoenix landed and immediately shape-shifted back to Chloe, took her clothes from Usha and started to get dressed.

Usha spoke into her mic' on her headset. "Annie, just so you know. I've spotted Miguel and Garcia at the town church. They must have seen us 'cos we heard gunfire so I reckon they're up to no good."

"Copy that Usha."

Usha approached the tangled mess of brambles and ivy which cascaded down the western stone walls and banks of Fort Tourgis, at the rear of the parking area. She pulled at the vegetation to reveal the old wooden door of the store and inserted her duplicate key to unlock the door.

The old door creaked as Usha pushed it open into the darkness.

"Any lights gal?" Chloe asked.

Usha grabbed her pendant and the store was bathed in light as the two girls stepped into the store.

"Ha! I'd forgotten about all this dust," remarked Usha, as she carefully walked to the far end of the store.

"We need to get a move on Usha. Where's the Inca statue?"

"Here it is." Usha pulled it from the wall.

"Chloe. Usha. What are you two doing here? And how did you get in here?"

"Oh er, hi Ben, Luis," Usha stuttered. "This is awkward. Help me out here Chloe."

Chloe shrugged her shoulders.

"Chloe?"

"Come on girls, what are you doing here?" asked Luis. There was a bit more firmness in his voice. "We've come down here to pick up some tools for a job and find you two have broken in. What's it all about girls?"

Usha sighed and gave Chloe a knowing glance. "D'ya know what guys, we really don't have time for this," Usha explained. She held out her hand to show them the Inca statue. "You can disbelieve me if you want, but this gold statue will help us save the world. If we don't get this statue to it's rightful place, this world will cease as you know it."

"Usha's right guys. You have to believe her," said Chloe.

"And if we don't?" Ben asked.

"We'll take the statue anyway. We have to," replied Usha.

Ben turned to Luis. "I told you didn't I? All this time, something was goin' on. I said to you Luis, didn't I?"

"Yeah you did mate, you told me. Ha! So girls, what can we do to help? To, to save the world .... I don't believe I'm saying that!"

"Well we have to be somewhere else with this statue," said Usha, "but firstly we'll take you to the town church. Promise me you won't both freak out in the next few minutes."

"Ha, scouts honour," Ben replied as he winked at Luis.

"Right Chloe, do your stuff," ordered Usha.

"Okay guys. MORPH!" Chloe clapped her hands over her head and her form changed as she shape-shifted into a huge Phoenix. Usha picked up Chloe's clothes and climbed on the bird's back whilst the two lads stood open mouthed at what they'd witnessed.

"Guys. Come on guys, we need to go. Climb on," said Usha.

"Oh shoot, what the hell, come on Ben." Luis clambered up onto the giant bird behind Usha and pulled Ben up beside him. They all clung on as the Phoenix took flight over the town towards the church.

"Annie, if you can hear me, we have the statue and we're on our way to the church," Usha spoke into her headset.

"Copy that Usha. I'll meet you in the graveyard."

In no time at all, the Phoenix was back on the ground, inside the graveyard of the church. Chloe quickly got dressed much to the two lads amusement.

"Keep your heads down," said Usha. "Right guys, we're relying on you."

"Chloe, Usha. Can you hear me?" It was Bea in the command centre. *"Annie should be with you now. I have some intel from Lilly. She managed to capture a minion alive and it told her that Lucy was being held captive in the old church."*

"Copy that Bea," said Chloe. "How's it looking at your end?"

"The command centre is holding up pretty well. And that's down to Lilly's efforts. I'm not sure how much longer she can hold these demons and the archangel off. Gotta sign off now, I've got more incoming to deal with."

"Usha. Chloe." It was Annie. "What the hell's goin' on?" She pointed at Ben and Luis. "What are they doin' here?"

"We don't have time to explain Annie. We'll sort the lads out later," said Chloe. "Did you bring any weapons with you?"

"Yeah sure, a couple of revolvers and some hunting knives."

"Wow, look at these Luis." Ben sifted through the weapons.

"Right guys, listen up," said Usha. "There are two armed members of the Mafia in the church and they have a hostage who is badly injured. These guys are extremely dangerous. Chloe here, will get you inside the church but then you're on your own 'cos we need to be somewhere else."

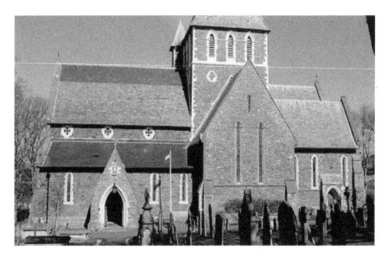

"Yeah we know," replied Ben. "Saving the world." He nudged Luis in the ribs as he grinned.

"Look," Chloe snapped. "This is serious. The hostage is Lucy, your Step Mum, Luis."

"What?"

"Lucy is an agent for the CIA and has been working this case ever since she married your Dad." Chloe prodded her finger into Luis' chest. "She needs our help okay?"

Luis nervously nodded his head.

"You of all people should know that your Dad is dangerous. In fact, he's extremely dangerous, he will kill either of you without any hesitation, so don't let your judgement be clouded. Okay?" Usha was using her serious face.

"Who's the other guy?" asked Ben.

"His name is Miguel," replied Chloe. "He's a nasty piece of work. Not to be trusted."

"Everyone ready?" asked Chloe. " MORPH!" Chloe clapped her hands over her head and her form changed as she shape-shifted into the archangel Abaddon.

"Excellent stuff Chloe. Let's just hope your form is good enough to fool them into letting us into the town church," said Usha. "Right everyone, put your hands around your backs and Chloe and I will tie your hands loosely to make out that Chloe has captured us."

The group quickly did as they were told. Chloe, disguised as Abaddon took charge ....

Chloe walked and pushed the group into the full view of Miguel who was pacing back and forth outside the main door to the church. "Move it you lot." She pushed Annie in the back who then purposely fell over. "Get up bitch," Chloe snarled.

"Master." Miguel stepped forward, gun in hand. "I wasn't expecting to see you today. Is everything going to plan?"

"So far," replied Chloe. "Where's Garcia?"

"He's in the nave trying to get more intel out of that CIA woman. Why have you brought more prisoners?"

"How dare you question my motives," Chloe snarled.

"Sorry master." Miguel bowed his head.

"Take us to Garcia, now!"

Miguel turned and as he did, Usha slipped the rope binding her hands and threw it around his neck, drawing it ever tighter and she snapped his neck in two. Without uttering a word, Annie helped Usha drag the lifeless body behind a bush, took his knife and passed it to Luis. Ben picked up the gun.

"Awesome," said Ben.

"Bloody brilliant," Luis added.

"I need to change guys," Chloe said. "I can only hold a form for so long and then I need to shape-shift back." She changed back to Chloe as she spoke and got dressed.

"I suggest we split up inside the church," said Annie. "The main focus is to get Lucy out alive."

"Leave it to me," replied Luis. "She's my Step Mum."

"Okay, but let myself and Chloe deal with Garcia," Usha snapped.

413

"NOT BEFORE ME," shouted Luis, as he ran headlong through the open church door. "MUM, WHERE ARE YOU?"

"Come on guys, he needs help." Chloe urged her friends into the church as a hail of bullets swept across the aisles forcing them to throw themselves to the floor amongst the church pews.

"IS THAT ALL YOU'VE GOT?" Garcia shouted from the nave.

"Where's Luis?" whispered Usha to Annie.

"I'm not sure."

Garcia stood up in the nave holding on to a struggling Lucy by her hair. She was bleeding heavily. "No-one move a muscle, or she gets it." He held a huge hunting knife to her throat as she screamed in terror.

The girls watched as Luis rose up from between two of the pews. He was holding what appeared to be a flick knife behind his back. "Mum, it'll be alright. I promise."

"Ha! That's rich coming from you son. Since when have you shown any attachment to Lucy?" Garcia hissed.

"You have no idea have you? You've used Lucy like a piece of meat, just like you did with Mum. You murdered her, didn't you?"

"So, it looks like you've finally grown some balls my lad." Lucy struggled in vain again as Garcia tightened his grip.

Chloe had been slowly making her way around the church pews and was now only four metres away from Garcia and Lucy. She shape-shifted into a pigeon and waited for her moment.

"You're nothing but a bully Dad, always have been. Just let Lucy go."

"Nah, don't think so. What you gonna do about it?" Garcia moved his knife across her throat as she screamed again in panic.

The pigeon took off to Garcia's right, momentarily gaining his attention as Luis threw his flick knife with unerring precision and hit Garcia between the eyes, dropping him to the floor, dead.

"Awesome," whispered Usha.

Luis ran to Lucy as the pigeon reverted to Chloe.

414

The group huddled around Lucy as Luis comforted her until Chloe appeared. "Okay guys, give me some space." She knelt besides Lucy holding her pendant over her heart and chanted … "I am Alnitak the Healer and Child of the Stars." She passed her hand around Lucy's bloodied face and body as a bright white glow hovered over her until all her injuries were healed.

"Wow," Ben said. "I never knew you could throw a knife like that Luis."

"My Dad taught me. How ironic is that?" replied Luis.

Annie took Usha and Chloe to one side as the boys spoke to Lucy. "What do we do with the boys? They've seen too much don't you think? Usha, you can erase their memories can't you?"

"I would leave it for now Annie. What d'ya think Chloe?"

"I'm not sure. Let's forget about it for now," replied Chloe. "We must get going Usha, to help Lilly. Take them to the command centre Annie."

Chloe shape-shifted into a giant Phoenix. Usha picked up Chloe's clothes and climbed onto the bird's back. She clung on as the Phoenix took off and flew in the direction of Fort Tourgis before landing by the white navigation marker.

"Did you see Lilly fighting the archangel Abaddon as we passed over the command centre?" asked Usha, as Chloe dressed herself.

"Yeah. But she can't keep it up for much longer, so we need to contact Inti, the Sun God."

The two girls placed both hands on the white masonry as the colour of their eyes changed to a dazzling ice white and they collapsed on the ground as their spirits travelled on a Shamanic journey.

Usha hugged Chloe as they both realised they were in the realm of Hanan Pacha on a Shamanic journey.

"WELCOME." A powerful voice reverberated through the two girls bodies. They stepped forward and then dropped to one knee as they saw Inti, the Sun God in front of them.

"WELCOME TO THE GATEWAY OF THE UPPER REALM OF HANAN PACHA. IT ALSO CONTAINS A MYSTICAL DOORWAY TO ONE OF THE MOST POWERFUL WEAPONS IN THE UNIVERSE, AN ANGEL BLADE THAT ONLY YOU CAN USE. YOU WILL NEED THIS WEAPON TO SUCCEED IN YOUR QUEST TO DEFEAT ABADDON THE ARCHANGEL. THERE WILL HOWEVER, BE CONSEQUENCES. IF YOU DECIDE TO ENTER THIS DOORWAY THERE IS ONLY ONE WAY TO RETURN. YOU MUST DRINK THE BLOOD OF THE GODS FROM THE CHALICE YOU WILL SEE ON THE PLINTH. YOUR POWERS WILL BECOME MUCH STRONGER AND MORE VARIED BUT YOU WILL NO LONGER BE WHOLLY HUMAN. YOU WILL BECOME A SERVANT OF GOD. SO WHAT IS YOUR DECISION?"

"We are ready to be your servant," the girls said.

A huge gold door which was covered in intricate carvings of mythological creatures and gods materialised in front of Usha and Chloe.

"ENTER." The Sun God raised his arms and the door swung open to reveal a small candlelit chamber. A bronze plinth stood in the centre of the dimly lit chamber, upon which stood two silver chalices.

The girls entered the chamber and the gold door closed behind them.

The teenagers looked at each other and stepped up to the plinth to see two silver chalices. They each picked up a silver chalice. Their eyes glanced down at the contents before lifting the chalices to their lips. They closed their eyes and started to drink the blood which was thick and warm. Usha momentarily gagged and choked as the thick blood ran down her throat. They both placed an empty silver chalice onto the plinth which in turn descended into the floor. Moments later, the plinth rose up from the floor with two silver triple edged daggers approximately sixty centimetres in length.

They each grasped a dagger as the gold door opened to release them from the chamber and as they stepped out they felt an overwhelming sense of power within their whole being.

A booming voice cut into their thoughts. It was Inti, the Sun God. "YOU ARE NOW OUR SERVANTS. YOU ARE ANGELS WITH ALMOST LIMITLESS POWERS. BOTH OF YOU AND LILLY NOW HAVE THE POWERS TO DEFEAT THE ARCHANGEL ABADDON AND USE THE POWER OF THE LIMA TREASURE TO SAVE THE WORLD FROM THE IMPENDING CATACLYSMIC EVENTS THAT COULD CHANGE THE WORLD ORDER .... USE YOUR POWERS WISELY. PROTECT YOUR LOVED ONES AND ABOVE ALL REMEMBER, YOU ARE OUR SERVANTS."

Chloe and Usha knelt on one knee and nodded. "My heart is yours."

"GO NOW FOR THERE IS MUCH TO DO."

The two girls sucked in a huge gulp of air as they relinquished their hold from the navigation aid and fell to the ground unconscious.

Chloe came too and shook Usha. "You okay gal?"

"Er yeah, I think." Usha sat up. "Don't want to be doing that again any time soon."

They both stood up, holding the angel blades up to the sky, glinting in the rays of the sun causing rainbows to dance across the sky.

"Have you seen our shadows Chloe?"

Chloe gasped at their shadows being cast over the grass bank. She could see two sets of wings, spanning four metres across. "We're angels!"

"Angel hybrids to be exact," Usha said.

"Usha, Chloe. If you can hear me, you need to set up at Fort Tourgis as soon as possible 'cos Lilly won't last much longer."

"Copy that Annie," replied Chloe. "We're on our way now."

Usha and Chloe flapped their wings and disappeared in a heartbeat. They instantly met up with the two fairies, Ruby and Lola, who'd been protecting the Lima Treasure on the roof of Fort Tourgis.

"Hi Ruby, Lola. Really good to see you." The four girls hugged and kissed as Usha told the two fairies to disguise their half demon blood with magic spells to protect themselves from the power of the Lima Treasure.

"We've no time to lose girls," said Chloe. "Lola, you take the one dish with the statues and the hexagonal rock and place it up there on the northern perimeter of the fort and just sit tight until Annie contacts you on your head set." Chloe pointed northwards as Lola vanished in a magical pillar of fire and reappeared up on the northern rampart.

"Ruby, you take the other dish up to the southern rampart and wait for instructions from Annie."

"Okay Chloe." Ruby disappeared instantly in a magical pillar of fire. Chloe spotted her as she appeared to the south.

"Ruby, Lola. You must follow my instructions precisely." The two fairies could hear Annie on their head sets. *"You both have six statues. If you look on their bases you will see an Inca symbol which you must match up with the symbols you see on the platter dish, but there's a catch. And this is important. They have to be placed in the indentations in a specific order. If you look closely at the inside of the symbols on the statues, you should be able to see a very small number from one to six. That is the order you need. Be very careful you don't make any mistakes. When Abaddon the archangel arrives and touches the ground, place the stone in the centre of the dish. Good luck girls."*

"Right Usha, you take the west and I'll take the east side. Good luck gal." The two girls hugged before disappearing with the faintest flutter of wings.

Usha could hear Lilly and Abaddon fighting in the distance and then it fell quiet ….

"INCOMING!" Lilly shouted as she appeared on the ground in the main courtyard of Fort Tourgis, bloodied and bruised.

Usha gasped when she saw the extent of Lilly's injuries but knew she had to stay focused as the archangel Abaddon appeared on the ground and immediately attacked Lilly.

"Now girls."

Ruby and Lola placed the last statues in the platter style dishes which began to vibrate as they communicated with each other. The six statues in each dish morphed into cylinders of different colours and emitted laser lights that connected each one. As the vibrations increased, the intensity of the laser lights were all powerful.

"The stones, girls. Place the stones!"

As the hexagonal rocks were placed in the centre of the platter dishes, the laser lights concentrated their power towards the rocks, which immediately turned an iridescent green and emitted powerful green laser lights hitting Chloe and Usha's pendants which completed the circuit.

Lilly glanced up and spotted the green laser lights and as she dodged another blow from Abaddon's sword, she summoned her light staff and hit the ground with all her might. She lifted herself

419

above the ground as the lasers from all four points above her, pinpointed the head of the staff creating a whirlwind of dust and light as a portal to hell opened up below her

"YOU THINK I'LL FALL INTO THAT?" Abaddon screamed as she lunged at Lilly once more.

Lilly back flipped and recoiled upwards. She hovered above the maelstrom below her as she twisted her pendant through ninety degrees in it's clasp and threw her arms out. "WE NEED MORE POWER GIRLS," Lilly screamed.

Usha & Chloe positioned themselves above Lilly about fifty metres apart emitting powerful green lasers from their eyes towards Lilly's pendant.

The green lasers from every conceivable source concentrated on Lilly's pendant, producing a huge and powerful explosion of many colours ….

It seemed forever as the clouds of dust and rock dispersed to reveal Lilly calmly standing in the middle of the main courtyard, angel blade in hand and the portal closed.

Usha, Chloe, Ruby and Lola quickly joined Lilly.

"So where's Abaddon?" asked Chloe.

"Banished to the underworld, Ukhu Pacha," Lilly replied.

"Well done everyone …. What the hell?!" A searing bright flash filled the grounds of Fort Tourgis and then subsided to reveal three biblical figures.

Lilly, Usha and Chloe immediately knelt down on one knee. "Welcome oh mighty Gods to our world," they chanted.

Illapa, the God of Thunder and Lightening spoke first. "You three angels have done well in defeating the treacherous archangel."

Mama Killa, the Moon Goddess spoke next. "We have come for what is rightfully ours, the Lima Treasure."

"Do you need all of it?" asked Usha.

"Be careful what you say angel. However, as tokens of our gratitude, you may all keep your amulets and pendants. You will need them in your future battles for good over evil. But the Lima Treasure is ours to take."

"What about my baby?" asked Chloe.

"So you know?" Mama Killa replied, as she wryly glanced at her fellow gods.

"Of course I do and I understand why you kept it a secret from me, but she is my daughter."

"Very well Chloe. If it is your wish." Mama Killa raised her arms to instantly summon an angel. "Here you are Chloe, your baby daughter. Look after her wisely as she will be capable of many great things as she grows older." The angel gently handed over the young child to Chloe.

They all gathered round as Chloe kissed her baby and stroked her blonde hair as the baby smiled contentedly.

"All your dreams will come true." Lilly kissed Chloe on the cheek.

"Thank you Lilly," Chloe whispered in her ear.

"So Chloe, what's her name?" asked Usha.

"Her name will be Alex."

The group of friends nodded in appreciation and instantly understood the meaning behind the name.

"Alex Mary," added Chloe.

"Just perfect," said Lilly. "Another Mary in the family."

Inti, the Sun God rose to his feet. "Enough of this frivolity. We thank you once again for retrieving what was rightfully ours, the Lima Treasure, and for restoring the equilibrium between good and evil. We have had our day."

"Before we leave …." Mama Killa, the Moon Goddess spoke softly, "Your journey has only just begun. As I speak, many evil atrocities continue around the world and it is up to you three, Las Tres Marias, The Three Marys, to continue your battle in whatever shape or form, for good over evil. As angel hybrids able to walk not only on this earth, but also above and below, it is and forever will be, your destiny to protect and serve. God speed Las Tres Marias."

CHAPTER 50

MEANWHILE

"The girls did it, Bea."

"They sure did Annie. I always knew they would 'cos it was Lilly's destiny."

"You don't seem to happy about it."

Bea took Annie to one side, out of earshot from the two boys and Sam and Lucy. "What happens now eh? Lilly's destiny to save the world has come to pass, but at what cost?"

"We've all lost friends and family Bea but we have to move forward you know. Be positive and all that."

"Excuse me you two." Ben and Luis interrupted Annie's conversation with Bea.

"We've been discussing the situation," said Ben, "and we want to help with your next adventure."

Annie smirked as she noticed Lucy and Sam, across the main room in the command centre, shaking their heads.

"Well we'll see lads," replied Bea. "Let's wait until the girls are back. I'm sure Lilly and Usha will be happy to talk to you." *You've got absolutely no chance lads. You'll soon forget about all this if Usha has anything to do with it.*

Meanwhile, somewhere in Peru ....

"Ha, the fools. Did they really think it was going to be easy to defeat me," hissed Lucifer as he swung round to face his army of demons. He turned to Sally and Alex stood by his side. "How many portals to hell do we have open?"

"We believe there are twelve portals around the world master." Alex bowed his head. "One portal for every Inca statue taken from our world."

Sally tossed her hair back over her shoulders. "The fools didn't realise the very real and true consequences of using the

Inca statues, to entrap Abaddon the archangel, master." Sally dragged her talons across her voluptuous breasts to draw blood and then pulled Alex closer as he dutifully licked the blood.

"ENOUGH! I didn't resurrect you two minions to play with each other."

Sally and Alex cowered into the shadows as Lucifer faced his demon army, his arms outstretched. "FIND THE PORTALS, CREATE DESTRUCTION AND MAYHEM .... ENJOY!!"

Song Title References

Wasted Years - Iron Maiden
Woman - Scorpions
Rule The World - Take That
Eternal Flame - The Bangles
The Wild, The Willing And The Innocent - UFO
Radar Love - Golden Earring
Uprising – Muse
The Zoo - Scorpions
Run - Snow Patrol
Run To The Hills - Iron Maiden
Don't Speak - No Doubt
Soon I Will Be Gone - Free
Ready For Love - Bad Company
Fanfare To The Common People - Emerson Lake & Palmer
Highway To Hell - ACDC
Walk Like An Egyptian - The Bangles
Firework - Katy Perry
Enjoy The Silence - Depeche Mode
Immigrant Song - Led Zeppelin
What Is Love - Hadaway
Stupid Girl - Garbage
Mirror Mirror - Def Leppard
There She Goes - The La's
I Could be Happy - Altered Images
Bohemian - The Dandy Warhols
You're Beautiful - James Blunt
Always Somewhere - The Scorpions
Here With Me - Dido
Zombie - The Cranberries
Sound Of Silence - Simon & Garfunkel
Death Walks Behind You - Atomic Rooster
Perfect - Ed Sheeran
The Nomad - Iron Maiden
Epitaph - King Crimson
You're In The Army Now - Status Quo
Will You? - Hazel O'Connor
Enjoy The Silence - Depeche Mode

Television/ Movie References

To Hell And Back
Chronicles Of Narnia
The Muppet Show
Die Hard
Buffy The Vampire Slayer
The Italian Job
E.T.
Alien
The Force Awakens
Where Angels Fear To Tread
Cinderella
Harry Potter
The Italian Job

Acknowledgements

Scott Gaunt - Cover Design
Richard Bowen - Photography
World Heritage Ireland - Photography
Neil Howard - Photography
Visit Alderney - Map

Don't miss any books in the Alderney series

2024 RELEASE ...

Las Tres Marias

Timeline: November 2031. Ten years had passed since the three teenage angel hybrids had battled and defeated Abaddon the archangel to restore the balance between heaven and hell. In truth though, back in 2021, Lilly, Usha and Chloe, Las Tres Marias or The Three Marys, had been led blindly into battle by a combination of Inca and family beliefs. It was their destiny they were told. They would save the world they were told.

The ten intervening years had proved to the now, three grown women, that their sacrifices had all been for nothing. A global pandemic had ripped through the world decimating the population, creating dysfunctional governments. Trade and transport was non existent as the remaining vaccinated humans struggled to survive.

The twelve portals to hell the angel hybrids had inadvertently created around the world on that fateful day, thrust the human race into a downward spiral as they battled against all the evil monstrosities that God in his wisdom, had imprisoned since the dawn of time, in particular, the feeders, as they were known to the embattled humans. The pandemic had been over for the humans for the last 3 years due to the high rates of vaccinations, but the virus had now mutated and in turn, infected the vampire population creating hybrids of unimaginable ferocity.

Footnote: Feeders are hybrid vampires that have contracted the virus. To live with the virus, these monsters must feed on healthy vaccinated humans every 24 hours.

ABOUT THE AUTHOR

Born in Bridgnorth Shropshire in 1954, Richard Bowen moved to the beautiful Channel Island of Alderney in 1998. A former editor and self publisher of an 8-bit computer magazine and a writer of blogs. He now concentrates on writing poetry and fantasy adventure novels.

CURRENT WORKS

Alderney - A Fantasy Adventure. A trilogy following the lives of three teenage girls as they discover the hidden powers of mysterious Inca treasure which could ultimately control heaven and hell. This coming of age fantasy brings into play, not only magical and mystical scenarios, but also the everyday problems of becoming responsible adults as the girls tackle love and death daily. Set amongst real life settings, the story becomes ever expansive to, not only include Alderney, but France, the Isle of Man and indeed the world, as the girls strive to keep the equilibrium between heaven and hell.
NOTE : CONTAINS ADULT CONTENT (18+)

WORKS IN PROGRESS

Las Tres Marias - Third person fantasy

Behind The Mask - Autobiography

The Chronicals of Koradane - First person fantasy series

Milton Keynes UK
Ingram Content Group UK Ltd.
UKHW051111111223
433947UK00012B/62